THE GREAT GATSBY

broadview editions
series editor: Martin R. Boyne

THE GREAT GATSBY

second edition

F. Scott Fitzgerald

edited by Michael Nowlin

broadview editions

BROADVIEW PRESS – www.broadviewpress.com
Peterborough, Ontario, Canada

Founded in 1985, Broadview Press remains a wholly independent publishing house. Broadview's focus is on academic publishing; our titles are accessible to university and college students as well as scholars and general readers. With over 800 titles in print, Broadview has become a leading international publisher in the humanities, with world-wide distribution. Broadview is committed to environmentally responsible publishing and fair business practices.

Library and Archives Canada Cataloguing in Publication

Title: The great Gatsby / F. Scott Fitzgerald ; edited by Michael Nowlin.
Names: Fitzgerald, F. Scott (Francis Scott), 1896-1940, author. | Nowlin, Michael, 1962- editor.
Series: Broadview editions.
Description: Second edition. | Series statement: Broadview editions | Includes bibliographical references.
Identifiers: Canadiana (print) 20210306882 | Canadiana (ebook) 20210306890 | ISBN 9781554814992 (softcover) | ISBN 9781770488212 (PDF) | ISBN 9781460407707 (EPUB)
Classification: LCC PS3511.I9 G7 2021 | DDC 813/.52—dc23

Broadview Editions
The Broadview Editions series is an effort to represent the ever-evolving canon of texts in the disciplines of literary studies, history, philosophy, and political theory. A distinguishing feature of the series is the inclusion of primary source documents contemporaneous with the work.

Advisory editor for this volume: Colleen Humbert

Broadview Press handles its own distribution in North America:
PO Box 1243, Peterborough, Ontario K9J 7H5, Canada
555 Riverwalk Parkway, Tonawanda, NY 14150, USA
Tel: (705) 743-8990; Fax: (705) 743-8353
email: customerservice@broadviewpress.com

For all territories outside of North America, distribution is handled by Eurospan Group.

Broadview Press acknowledges the financial support of the Government of Canada for our publishing activities.

Typesetting and assembly: True to Type Inc., Claremont, Canada
Cover Design: Lisa Brawn

PRINTED IN CANADA

Contents

Acknowledgements

For this second, expanded edition I am especially grateful for the support and encouragement of Don LePan and Marjorie Mather at Broadview Press, and especially want to acknowledge Don's suggestions for additional contextual materials and other editorial revisions. I also want to thank Colleen Humbert and Martin Boyne for their work in preparing the manuscript for publication; Tara Trueman for getting this book into the best possible form; and Joe Davies for proofreading the galleys.

Again, I thank the Social Sciences and Humanities Research Council of Canada and the University of Victoria, from which I received funding for the original edition on which this is based. I got crucial help for that edition from Professor Jennifer Douglas, who gathered and photographed most of the advertisements in Appendix C, in addition to doing some preliminary work on the notes. Thanks, too, to Madeline Walker for her help with the notes for the first edition, and Deborah Ogilvie for her help with the notes for this one.

Finally, I would like to thank the following individuals and organizations for permission to reprint the material described below.

Fitzgerald, F. Scott. Excerpt from *The Crack-Up*, copyright © 1931 by Charles Scribner's Sons. Originally published as *Echoes of the Jazz Age* by Scribner's Magazine 90 (November 1934): 460–62. Reprinted by permission of New Directions Publishing Corp. Excerpts from *Dear Scott/Dear Max*, eds. John Kuehl and Jackson R. Bryer. First published by Charles Scribner's Sons, 1971. pp. 61, 70, 75–76, 80–87, 89–90, 92–94, 100–02. Reprinted by permission of Charles Scribner III. Excerpts from *A Life in Letters*, ed. Matthew J. Broccoli. Copyright © 1994 by The Trustees under agreement dated July 3, 1975, created by Frances Scott Fitzgerald Smith. Reprinted with the permission of Scribner, a division of Simon & Schuster, Inc. All rights reserved.

Lippmann, Walter. Excerpts from Chapter I: The Problem of Unbelief, *A Preface to Morals*. Transaction Publishers, 1982. Copyright © 1982 Taylor & Francis. Reproduced by permission of Taylor and Francis Group, LLC, a division of Informa plc, conveyed through Copyright Clearance Center, Inc.

Introduction

While planning and writing the novel he finally called *The Great Gatsby*, F. Scott Fitzgerald revealed enough about the scope of his ambition to make a fool of himself if the novel proved, like its title character, an ultimate failure. He had recently suffered the embarrassment of seeing his 1923 play *The Vegetable*, which he trusted to make him a fortune on Broadway, flop during try-outs in Atlantic City. But by the late summer of 1924, he was feeling supremely confident again, or so his boast to his editor Maxwell Perkins (1884–1947) suggests: "I think my novel is about the best American novel ever written" (Kuehl and Bryer 76). The draft he was working on at that point would only get better: first, as a result of his usual intensive work revising a book before submitting it for publication, and second, as a result of extensive revisions he made to the galleys, largely in response to Perkins's gentle but pointed criticism of the submitted typescript. By the time the finished novel appeared in the spring of 1925, Fitzgerald's boast seemed all the more warranted, his faith in the work steeling him against the vulgar criticism of contemporary reviewers: "Some day they'll eat grass, by God! This thing, both the effort and the result have hardened me and I think now that I'm much better than any of the young Americans *without exception*" (Kuehl and Bryer 106).

Literary history has obviously borne Fitzgerald out. The reviewers who thought *The Great Gatsby* inconsequential or downright bad (actually a minority) now suffer the punishment of all reviewers who misjudge a future classic, which is to exemplify critical obtuseness to a more knowing posterity. *The Great Gatsby* is now widely considered one of the greatest American novels, if not *the* greatest, and a 1998 survey of the board members of Random House's Modern Library ranked *The Great Gatsby* second only to James Joyce's *Ulysses* (1922) on a list of the one hundred greatest twentieth-century novels. But there are two aspects to this fortunate issue more interesting than Fitzgerald's vindicated confidence, and more pertinent to our appreciation of his novel. The first is the barely sublimated competitive spirit animating his project, his desire to beat his peers at the writing game and have his work live on long after theirs was forgotten. This is hardly irrelevant to a novel that has both masculine competition and the transience of human experience and achievement at its thematic core. The second is the purity of purpose or intense aesthetic commitment that he brought to his work-in-progress from the moment of conception and sustained until its realization in book form. It was one thing to brag about writing the greatest American novel of his generation, another to write it.

Fitzgerald followed developments in the literary field of his day astutely enough that we can fairly ask what kind of American novel was most likely to outshine the competition in 1925, and survive as a classic for generations to come. Whatever boy-wonderish success he had enjoyed with his first two novels, *This Side of Paradise* (1920) and *The Beautiful and Damned* (1922), he sensed quickly enough that these were not likely to win him immortality. Both were loosely constructed, to put it mildly, and drew heavily on autobiographical material. Their difference from each other stems in good part from Fitzgerald's movement away from the contemporary British literary models who inspired his first novel—the novelists Compton Mackenzie (1883–1972), H.G. Wells (1866–1946), and John Galsworthy (1867–1933)— toward the newly discovered American realists and naturalists championed by the powerful critic H.L. Mencken (1880–1956) —such novelists as Theodore Dreiser (1871–1945), Frank Norris (1870–1902), and the now largely forgotten Harold Frederic (1856–98). He even worked his shifting literary orientation into the final revisions of *This Side of Paradise* by having his hero Amory Blaine discover Mencken and avidly read the recent novels he was acclaiming.

As editor of *The Smart Set*, Mencken published some of Fitzgerald's best early stories ("May Day" in 1920, "The Diamond as Big as the Ritz" in 1922) that the more commercially oriented and higher paying *Saturday Evening Post* refused, but the effect of his critical pronouncements on Fitzgerald's art was happily short-lived, extending mainly to *The Beautiful and Damned*. In a "Literary Spotlight" profile for the *Bookman* that appeared at the time of the second novel, Fitzgerald's good friend Edmund Wilson (1895–1972), another critic powerful enough to counter Mencken's influence, gently mocked Fitzgerald for the derivative, affected strain that had hitherto characterized his artistic development: "Since writing This Side of Paradise—on the inspiration of Wells and Mackenzie—Fitzgerald has become acquainted with another school of fiction: the ironical-pessimistic. In college, he had supposed that the thing to do was to write biographical novels with a burst of ideas toward the close; since his advent into the literary world, he has discovered that there is another genre in favor: the kind which makes much of the tragedy and 'the meaninglessness of life'" (Kazin 81). Though he remained on good terms with Mencken throughout his life, Fitzgerald formally repudiated Mencken's program for American literature in his most notable literary-critical pronouncement, the first half of a 1926 essay called "How to Waste Material: A Note on My Generation." There he condemned a naively objective, documentary approach to American subject matter as crude and unimaginative, describing Mencken's offspring as "a family of hammer and tongs men—insensitive, suspicious of glamour, pre-occupied with the external, the contemptible, the 'national' and the drab," as "men who manufactured enthusiasm when each new mass of raw data was dumped on the literary platform—mistaking incoherence for vitality, chaos for vitality" (Bruccoli and Baughman 106). Or to put this in the terms of *The Great Gatsby*, theirs was a "material" world "without being real." Fitzgerald's judgment of this strand of American realism with which he temporarily identified was sweeping and unequivocal: "most of it—the literary beginnings of what was to have been a golden age—is as dead as if it had never been written" (Bruccoli and Baughman 106).

Fitzgerald had essentially made this argument already, indirectly and aesthetically, through *The Great Gatsby*, the "consciously artistic achievement" he told Perkins that he was writing in the spring of 1924, a year after telling fellow writer Thomas Boyd (1898–1935) that he would "never write another document-novel" (Kuehl and Bryer 70; Bruccoli and Duggan 126). For polemical purposes he no doubt exaggerated the extent to which the data-amassing chroniclers of the contemporary American scene had reached a dead end, as well as his own disdain for them. Fitzgerald would voice nothing but admiration for Dreiser's just-published and much-acclaimed *An American Tragedy*, for example, about a Midwestern social climber whose criminal downfall is motivated (in part) by his love for an unattainable rich girl. But despite the uncanny thematic similarity between *An American Tragedy* and *The Great Gatsby*, now perhaps the two most famous American novels from 1925, they could hardly be more stylistically different, a difference apparent at a glimpse by the eight hundred or so closely printed pages of the one and the just over two hundred sparser pages of the other. They each epitomized the difference between what critics and novelists at the time would have recognized, thanks to earlier critical exchanges between H.G. Wells and Henry James (1843–1916), as novels of saturation and novels of selection

(Miller 1–16). Fitzgerald's repudiation of the former in favor of the latter comes across emphatically in his letter responding to Mencken's disappointing review of *Gatsby*: "Despite your admiration for Conrad you have lately—perhaps in reaction against the merely well-made novels of James' imitators—become used to the formless. It is in protest against my own formless two novels, and Lewis' and Dos Passos' that this was written" (Bruccoli, *F. Scott Fitzgerald: A Life in Letters* [hereafter *Life in Letters*] 111).[1]

New literary discoveries surely prompted this reaction. Modern American realism had reached a kind of apex in Lewis's hugely successful novels about middle-America, *Main Street* (1920) and *Babbitt* (1922), and Fitzgerald felt compelled to move beyond it. Between the spring of 1922, when *The Beautiful and Damned* appeared, and the summer of 1924, when he was writing *The Great Gatsby*, Fitzgerald's appreciation for Conrad's and James's artistry—particularly their rigorous handling of point of view and their unique stylistic stamps—had intensified, probably under Wilson's tutelage. He belatedly discovered Gertrude Stein's (1874–1946) prose experiment "Melanctha," the centerpiece of her narrowly circulating 1909 triptych *Three Lives*, which he recalled reading with Wilson in the summer of 1922, declaring Stein "some sort of punctuation mark in literary history" (Bruccoli and Duggan 412). By 1923 he had come to appreciate the significance for all serious literary artists of two other modernist landmarks published in 1922—James Joyce's *Ulysses* and T.S. Eliot's *The Waste Land*—and possibly three, given that translations of the first volumes of Marcel Proust's *Remembrance of Things Past* were appearing, followed by reviews underscoring their importance by Paul Rosenfeld (1890–1946) and Burton Rascoe (1892–1957), two other important critics with whom he was friendly. Despite private misgivings, he put himself on record in a 1923 *Richmond Times-Dispatch* interview as a champion of *Ulysses*, proclaiming it "the great novel of the future" (Bruccoli and Baughman 91). He sent Eliot (1888–1965) a copy of *The Great Gatsby* bearing the inscription, "Greatest of Living Poets from his entheusiastic worshipper" (Bruccoli, *Life in Letters* 128).[2] And if

---

1 Fitzgerald is referring to novelists Joseph Conrad (1857–1924), Sinclair Lewis (1885–1951), and John Dos Passos (1896–1970).

2 The spelling errors in Fitzgerald's correspondence have been retained here and in subsequent citations.

he did not actually begin avidly reading *Remembrance of Things Past* until later in the decade, he came to recognize Proust (1871–1922) as one of the greatest writers of his time.

A common thread joining these otherwise radically different works was their experimental boldness and reputation for difficulty, their authors' willingness to risk being commercially unviable (in the short run) while commanding the adulation of fellow writers and cosmopolitan literary critics. Eliot's and Joyce's titles may have prodded Fitzgerald to title his third novel *Trimalchio* or *Trimalchio in West Egg*, alluding in either case to the former slave become decadent banquet host in the first-century CE Roman writer Petronius's *Satyricon*. (Eliot used a passage from the original—in Latin and Greek—as the epigraph of his great poem; a risqué limited-edition English translation of the Roman classic was published by the New York firm Boni and Liveright in 1922.) Fitzgerald's relatively conservative publishers were no doubt happier when the obscurer title gave way to *The Great Gatsby*, with its show-biz evocations. Another commonality: behind all these writers stood the towering figure of Gustave Flaubert (1821–80), the great nineteenth-century French novelist who put the highest artistic premium on style and *le mot juste*. In his influential 1922 review of *Ulysses*, Wilson described its pages as "probably the most 'written' ... to be seen in any novel since Flaubert" (164). The ideal evoked here, so manifest as well in Stein's "Melanctha," seems to be what Fitzgerald had in mind when he wrote Perkins in July 1922, "I want to write something new— something extraordinary and beautiful and simple + intricately patterned" (Bruccoli and Duggan 112). Such elevated literary aims did not inhibit him from churning out stories for the *Saturday Evening Post* or penning the ludicrous comedy meant for Broadway; on the contrary, he justified these as means to a higher end, ways of bankrolling the freedom he needed to devote himself to purer literary art. He ultimately sought to make the most of that freedom in France, where he sailed in the spring of 1924, where he joined other expatriates, and where he carefully composed, from an estranged vantage point, as it were, the "intricately patterned" novel about contemporary America that would cast so much American realism in its shadow.

In a novel as meticulously "written" as *The Great Gatsby*, it makes sense that George Wilson's garage sits "on the edge of the waste land, a sort of compact Main Street ministering to it, and contiguous to absolutely nothing" (p. 71). George and Myrtle Wilson—a plodding, inarticulate husband barely able to make a living, a vivacious wife dying from cultural and sexual starvation—seem transplanted from Lewis's middle-American villages to a symbolic desert populated by ashen men and overseen by an ominous billboard optometrist named Dr. T.J. Eckleburg. Fitzgerald's symbolic use of the landscape accords with his repudiation in particular of a certain regionalist strain within modern American realism that pretended to find authenticity in the lives of rural Americans. His hero Jay Gatsby's parents, notably, are "shiftless and unsuccessful farm people" (p. 124) and Gatsby's early upbringing is provincial. But that part of his life is of little intrinsic interest and is thus recalled in the most cursory manner. Jay Gatsby is of interest—and his story of a potentially mythical cast—because of his in some ways typically modern, in some ways typically American transformation from rural "rough-neck" to glamorous and fabulously wealthy host of parties on Long Island, the ostentatious suburban enclave of the nation's cosmopolitan center, New York City. Fitzgerald was adept enough at depicting place, as he demonstrated in writing about Princeton in *This Side of Paradise* and about New York City in "May Day" and *The Beautiful and Damned*. But more so than in his second novel, the carefully registered locale of *The Great Gatsby* is an explicitly modernist terrain, a site of regionally dislocated people, distorted perceptions, and experimental mores. Gatsby unabashedly claims to be from the "Middle West" city of San Francisco (p. 100). Nick Carraway feels his "Middle West" roots most profoundly when recalling the "thrilling" returning train rides back from Eastern prep schools and colleges through Illinois, Wisconsin, and Minnesota, distinguishing *his* "Middle West" of festive social rituals from "the wheat or the prairies or the lost Swede towns" (p. 179) that evoke the novels of Willa Cather (1876–1947), the elder American realist about whose influence Fitzgerald seems to have felt some anxiety. In *The Great Gatsby*, the particularities of place matter less than what might be rendered through what Fitzgerald called "the sustained imagination of a sincere and radiant world" (Kuehl and Bryer 70). Thus Fitzgerald poetically transforms the two actual (and physically dissimilar) peninsulas of Great Neck and Manhasset Neck into "a pair of enormous eggs, identical in contour," West Egg and East Egg respectively, so as to underscore the incongruity between the very real social distinctions they represent and the inability to see these from the transcendental perspective of the seagulls overhead (p. 58). The artist who can hold such incongruities in his own mind recognizes the need for and, to a limited but important extent, the authority of personal vision—vision that finds the terrain from Long Island to New York composed of a false pastoral suburb linked by ash-heaps to a corrupting "city" that nonetheless appears before initiates "in white heaps and sugar lumps all built with a wish out of non-olfactory money" (p. 103).

Fitzgerald's newfound appreciation for the centrality of form to art not only brought him beyond the putative formlessness, the verbal crudity, and the situational clichés of American realism (his own instances included) but also granted him greater distance from the autobiographical material he had exploited for his first two novels. As he wrote Perkins in 1924, "I don't know anyone who has used up so much personal experience as I have at 27" (Kuehl and Bryer 76). Not that *The Great Gatsby* left auto-biographical content behind. On the contrary, it drew more honestly than Fitzgerald had before on his most intimate, emotionally charged experience: his rejection at the hands of Ginevra King years earlier and his wife Zelda's infidelity in the summer of 1924 with French aviator Edouard Jozan; his anxiety about his own facile celebrity and the expensive and often wasteful, alcoholic life in which he indulged for a year and a half on Long Island; his deep-rooted ambivalence (not untainted by resentment) toward wealth and privilege. His aim of achieving formal perfection—structural concision, stylistic precision, deft character and scene development, careful use of leitmotifs, rigorous modulation of tone throughout—gave him emotional control over his material without sacrificing the passionate insight garnered from experience. Fitzgerald undoubtedly identified with his romantic, upstart hero; indeed, he might have echoed Flaubert's alleged proclamation about his Emma Bovary and declared of Jay Gatsby: "c'est moi!" But he cast his novel so that Gatsby might be seen as he really is, conveyed by a lucid, objectifying imagination at once aware of his crass ambition and attuned to his uncanny purity of purpose. Gatsby needed to be seen by a controlling intelligence that could grasp his emblematic significance for an aimless generation; for the over-confident, materialistic democracy whose seemingly boundless economic opportunities harbored fateful catastrophes; and for the whole modern West irrevocably unmoored from compelling traditions or religious beliefs.

Fitzgerald surely felt delight when reviewer William Curtis wrote of *The Great Gatsby* that, precisely because of its technical accomplishment, "it can be put on the same book shelf with the best of London, Vienna, Paris, or Rome" (Appendix B4, p. 213).

Before his thirtieth birthday, Fitzgerald had reached what in hindsight he recognized as the high point of his artistic career. Near the end of his relatively short life he wrote to his daughter Scottie, "I wish now I'd *never* relaxed or looked back—but said at the end of *The Great Gatsby*: 'I've found my line—from now on this comes first. This is my immediate duty—without this I am nothing'" (Bruccoli, *Life in Letters* 451). What followed *The Great Gatsby* can hardly be called an unproductive career, but in obvious respects it fell short of the promise opened up by his triumph in 1925. His subsequent artistic struggles were exacerbated by nearly insurmountable personal woes, so from the vantage point of his death in 1940, his claim to have written "about the best American novel ever" seems an act of hubris that set the stage for the romantic tragedy that Fitzgerald's life became.

F. Scott Fitzgerald: Life, Works, and Critical Reputation

Late in his life, Fitzgerald described himself as a perennial outsider, marked by the experience of having been "a poor boy in a rich town; a poor boy in a rich boy's school; a poor boy in a rich man's club at Princeton" (Bruccoli, *Life in Letters* 352). As the antithetical phrasing betrays, his poverty was relative. Born in St. Paul, Minnesota, on 24 September 1896, he enjoyed an only moderately unstable middle-class upbringing and, christened Francis Scott Key after the remote cousin (1779–1843) who wrote the American national anthem, was encouraged to cultivate upper-middle-class social aspirations.

His namesake belonged to the paternal branch of the family, which traced its roots back to colonial Maryland and fought on the Confederate side during the Civil War. His father, Edward Fitzgerald (1853–1931), showed some of the traces of his Southern pedigree in his fine manners and taste for romantic legend, particularly tales of Confederate war heroes and the novels of Sir Walter Scott (1771–1832). Fortunately, the family was not wholly dependent on him as breadwinner. His furniture manufacturing business failed soon after Scott was born. He then took a job as a wholesale grocery salesman with Proctor & Gamble, which took the family to Buffalo and Syracuse. He was fired in 1908, when Scott was twelve, and as his son later recollected, he never quite recovered from that blow. The real money propping up the Fitzgerald household came from his mother's side of the family. Mollie McQuillan (1859–1936) was the daughter of an

Irish immigrant who had come to America in the 1850s and built up a successful wholesale grocery business. When the Fitzgeralds returned to St. Paul in 1908, Scott's father worked for the McQuillans; and it was McQuillan money that paid for Scott's elite education at Newman preparatory school and Princeton University.

The Fitzgeralds never owned their own home, but after returning to St. Paul they rented decent housing in the respectable Summit Avenue neighborhood. The teenage Fitzgerald and his younger sister, Annabel, grew up among wealthy and socially prominent families, not far from the imposing mansion of financier and railroad tycoon James J. Hill. His parents enrolled him in the private St. Paul Academy, his mother sent him to a dance school to mingle with the right social set, and he tried unsuccessfully to shine as an athlete. By most accounts something of a show-off, Fitzgerald discovered early a talent for writing amusing stories and plays in which he could star for the city's amateur Elizabethan Dramatic Club. He carried this talent first to Newman School and then to Princeton, where he made many discoveries, including models of intellectual seriousness—first in Father Sigourney Fay, the eventual headmaster who served as a crucial mentor until his untimely death in 1919, then in contemporaries like Edmund Wilson, the poet John Peale Bishop (1892–1944), and the politically rebellious Henry Strater (1896–1987), who led a failed revolt against the exclusive eating clubs at Princeton. These would leave their mark on his emerging literary aspirations, insofar as they encouraged him to gauge success by a higher measure than popularity.

Probably the most formative experience of his youth was his romance with Ginevra King (1898–1980), the daughter of a Chicago stockbroker with a home in the affluent suburb of Lake Forest. The eighteen-year-old Fitzgerald met her in St. Paul in January 1915 while home for Christmas during his sophomore year at Princeton. She was sixteen and home from Westover, an exclusive finishing school in Connecticut. She was beautiful, popular, and immensely rich, and Fitzgerald fell in love with her—or, so it might seem in hindsight, with the idea of her—almost immediately. His talent for writing held him in good stead as he carried on an intense epistolary relationship with her, punctuated by visits to Westover and Lake Forest, prom and football dates, and the odd trip to New York. Though Scott undoubtedly charmed her for a while, Ginevra could have her pick of wealthy suitors and inevitably recognized the social obstacles that stood in the way of any serious future with him. Fitzgerald was made to recognize them too. After an unsatisfying visit to Lake Forest in August 1916, he entered into his ledger the quoted statement, "Poor boys shouldn't think of marrying rich girls" (West 62). Ginevra King's rejection of Fitzgerald—or Fitzgerald's pursuit of a woman who for social reasons was bound to reject him—ended up facilitating his writing career and indirectly affected his relationship with his future wife, Zelda Sayre (1900–48). Before Ginevra formally broke with him in January 1917, Fitzgerald had written a piece about her for Princeton's *Nassau Literary Magazine* called "The Débutante," which would eventually find its way into his first novel. And she provided the model for several of his heroines thereafter, including Daisy Buchanan.

America's entry into World War I in April 1917 gave him an escape route from his sorrows and from his academic difficulties at Princeton (he never graduated). He received a commission as second lieutenant in the infantry, and while stationed at Fort Leavenworth in the fall began the novel that would soon make him famous. He finished what he first fittingly called "The Romantic Egotist" in March of 1918, while at Princeton on a furlough. He had the author Shane Leslie (1885–1971) recommend it to his publisher, the respectable and conservative firm of Charles Scribner's Sons, which rejected it twice in that year. In the meantime he met Zelda while stationed from June to November at Camp Sheridan outside Montgomery, Alabama. She was the daughter of a justice of the Alabama Supreme Court, and a flamboyant, mischievous Southern belle who, like Ginevra, thrived on the attention of many men. Fitzgerald fell in love with her in September (notably, the month Ginevra married William Mitchell). He acquired pride of place in Zelda's affections, but again he held it precariously. Though the Sayres were not rich, they had social standing, and Zelda would have looked to make an economically sensible match. After being discharged from the army (the war ended just before Fitzgerald was sent overseas), Fitzgerald continued to court Zelda from New York, both by letter and by making trips south that he could barely afford. By July 1919, she broke off their unofficial engagement. Fitzgerald's efforts to make it as a writer in New York were going nowhere, and despite Zelda's romantic temperament, she realistically balked at the idea of marrying a struggling writer.

But Fitzgerald's life took the kind of dramatic turn for the better that would contribute to his most memorable characters' sense that, as he wrote in a late retrospective essay, "life is a romantic matter" (Fitzgerald, *The Crack-Up* 89). Zelda's rejection spurred him to return home to St. Paul to revise his novel and send it to Scribner's one more time. Now called *This Side of Paradise*, it drew the favorable attention of Perkins, the firm's most forward-looking editor, and was finally accepted. Fitzgerald also had the good luck to place his stories in the high-paying and widely circulating *Saturday Evening Post*, as well as low-paying but more prestigious venues like Mencken and George Jean Nathan's *The Smart Set*. Fitzgerald had become "a professional," as he wrote in "Early Success" (Fitzgerald, *The Crack-Up* 89). He convinced Zelda to marry him at the outset of 1920, when a promising career seemed to be unfolding before him. She left Montgomery for New York in April 1920; they married on 3 April, a week after *This Side of Paradise* was published.

Based on his life at Princeton, *This Side of Paradise* struck a chord with a generation of readers and gave Fitzgerald a notoriety to capitalize upon as a spokesperson for rebellious and disenchanted youth. Very tame by today's standards, it was mildly shocking for its revelations about the sexual escapades and drinking sprees of the young and privileged. And it sold well for a first novel, abetted by the generally comic stories about leisure-class youth that Fitzgerald was writing for magazines. Both Fitzgeralds were quick to encourage publicity that depicted them as a glamorously wild, sexy, and carefree couple, epitomizing the spirit of the new post-war era that Fitzgerald would dub "the jazz age." But privately the marriage was showing ominous strains. Zelda could behave impetuously to get the attention Scott could not always give her while meeting his commitments as a writer. Scott was becoming an alcoholic. And they enjoyed living beyond their means, a bad habit that Fitzgerald had established early in his writing career. He drew advances from his publisher and his agent on the strength of future book sales and his ability to write magazine stories with apparent ease.

The Fitzgeralds returned from their first trip to Europe in 1921 to St. Paul, where their daughter, "Scottie" (Frances Scott, 1921–86), was born and where Scott oversaw the publication (first in serial, then in book form) of his second novel, *The Beautiful and Damned*. It drew heavily on the first year of their marriage, which had been spent in New York and in a rented house in Westport, Connecticut, prophetically following its young couple to a sordid end, in keeping with the naturalistic emphasis on "character in decay" championed by Mencken (41). Though generally regarded as Fitzgerald's most flawed novel, it sold better than any of his other novels.

Having outlined the idea for his third novel as early as the summer of 1922, he worked mainly on his play after moving in the fall to Great Neck on Long Island, a community boasting a good share of showbusiness people and journalists, and well supplied with illegal liquor. At a quick glance, *The Vegetable, or From President to Postman*, with its stock figure of the hen-pecked husband, its topical jokes about Prohibition and contemporary American politics, and its extravagant fantasy sequences, seems incongruous alongside the carefully measured, verbally and morally nuanced masterpiece he wrote shortly after it. It reminds us, though, of the prominent satirical strain in Fitzgerald's writing (let alone the extravagant imagination that in 1922 gave us "The Diamond as Big as the Ritz" and "The Curious Case of Benjamin Button"). Like *The Beautiful and Damned*, it betrays a certain snobbery about which he would be more guardedly ironic and even critical in his better work. For although he is a far cry from Jay Gatsby, the play's "hero," Jerry Frost, is another social striver, who in this case (with a little help from illegal booze) finds himself president of the United States before realizing his more banal ambition of becoming a postman. It is not surprising that *The Great Gatsby* was read primarily as social satire by many of its first readers (and thus not so strange that Fitzgerald should have considered first serializing it in the magazine *College Humor* before thinking better of the idea).

However wasteful his ceaseless partying in Great Neck may have seemed to him in the short run, he soon immortalized it in *The Great Gatsby*. There he made good friends with journalist and humorist Ring Lardner (1885–1933), who had covered the 1919 World Series and the ensuing "Black Sox" scandal; followed the trials of Edward Fuller and William McGee, a pair of stockbrokers charged (and ultimately convicted) for misusing clients' funds; and met models for his most memorable hero, Jay Gatsby. The most notable of these was Max Gerlach, a sophisticated dealer in used cars and an alleged bootlegger—and perhaps most pertinently, a German immigrant given to colorful fabrications of his biography. The adventures of Robert C. Kerr Jr. also provided Fitzgerald with some details for Gatsby's story.[1] As surely as the Great Neck period provided Fitzgerald with crucial material for

---

1 See the indispensable "Backgrounds" chapter in Bruccoli, *F. Scott Fitzgerald's "The Great Gatsby,"* especially 12–45. For the most authoritative account of Gerlach as a model for Gatsby, see Kruse 4–73.

The Great Gatsby, so did his move to France in April 1924 provide him with the atmosphere, time, and distance needed to turn that material into literature.

Fitzgerald's second trip to Europe lasted nearly three years and helped transform a still somewhat provincial writer into a world-class author. He first settled in St. Raphael on the Riviera, where he became good friends with the charming expatriate couple Gerald (1888–1964) and Sara (1883–1975) Murphy, who drew on family wealth to establish a villa in Cap d'Antibes (as well as a residence in Paris) dedicated to a high aesthetic pleasure: the cultivation of rare company; the enjoyment of the good food and wine and of the geography and culture of southern France; and the making and appreciation of modern art. They were especially hospitable to artists and attuned to the latest continental developments in painting and music; they counted among their friends and guests American writers John Dos Passos and Archibald MacLeish (1892–1982), the popular composer Cole Porter (1891–1964), European painters Fernand Léger (1881–1955) and Pablo Picasso (1881–1973), and soon after Fitzgerald befriended him in Paris in May 1925, Ernest Hemingway (1899–1961). When Fitzgerald later settled in Paris, he became acquainted with such key figures in the development of international literary modernism as Gertrude Stein, Sylvia Beach (1887–1962), Robert McAlmon (1895–1956), and even James Joyce (1882–1941). (This despite his telling decision to live on the more conservative and commercially oriented Right Bank of Paris.) Fitzgerald wrote the bulk of *The Great Gatsby* on the Riviera in the summer of 1924. His work on the novel may have been critically disrupted by Zelda's brief affair that summer with Edouard Jozan, but her affair also deepened the novel's increasingly fundamental theme of disillusionment. "[T]hat's the whole burden of this novel," he wrote his friend Ludlow Fowler in August, "the loss of those illusions that give such color to the world, so that you don't care whether things are true or false as long as they partake of the magical glory" (Bruccoli and Duggan 145). He revised it for publication while traveling in Italy in the winter of 1925, and *The Great Gatsby* appeared to mixed reviews in April 1925.

After the publication of *The Great Gatsby*, the story of Fitzgerald's embattled and dissipated life tends to overshadow his work. He lived nearly sixteen more years but finished just one more novel, left substantial fragments and notes toward another, and published numerous short stories and essays. Buoyed especially by the kind of response he was getting from his fellow writers about *Gatsby*, he proclaimed to Perkins in May 1925 that his new novel was "something really NEW in form, idea, structure—the model for the age that Joyce and Stien are searching for, that Conrad didn't find" (Bruccoli, *Life in Letters* 108). The novel that finally appeared in 1934 as *Tender Is the Night* is by most estimates an important one, but it can hardly be characterized as the epoch-defining artistic wonder-work Fitzgerald projected while feeling at the peak of his powers.

A number of factors contributed to Fitzgerald's slide, though his alcoholism surely ranks among the foremost. He had also grown used to lavish living, such that he had continually to set aside the novel-in-progress to write short stories and potentially lucrative scenarios for the movies. By 1929 he was one of the highest-paid contributors of magazine fiction in the United States (the *Saturday Evening Post* was paying him $4,000 per story), but financial exigencies continued to press upon him. Drinking and spending habits as well as sexual jealousy were a constant source of friction in the Fitzgeralds' marriage, which was exacerbated further when Zelda passionately took up ballet dancing under the tutelage of the Russian émigré Lubov Egorova (1880–1972). Finally, in hindsight it seems that Fitzgerald had chosen intractable material for his fourth novel. His projected plot about a young Hollywood technician who murders his mother on the Riviera generated some fine writing that he would later transpose to good effect, but he kept coming to a dead end with it. Meanwhile he watched Hemingway, the writer whose career he had helped launch, surpass him as the decade's most acclaimed American novelist and become a condescending friend.

Taking a rather austere view of things, one could say that public and personal catastrophe rescued Fitzgerald. The stock market crash of October 1929 and Zelda's coincidental mental breakdown six months later came brimming with dramatic meaning for an author in search of material, as his superb story "Babylon Revisited" (published in February 1931) attested. As he finished his years in Europe overseeing Zelda's treatment in a high-priced Swiss psychiatric clinic and witnessing the onset of what would prove to be one of the worst economic depressions in modern history, Fitzgerald began working out a complex historical perspective and a hard-earned moral vision of the American experience of the 1920s, though these had arguably been implicit in the best of his earlier work. Upon returning to the United

States in the fall of 1931, he conveyed these in his great essay "Echoes of the Jazz Age" (see Appendix D1). By the end of 1932, living outside Baltimore, and after a bitter struggle with Zelda over her own novel about their experience, *Save Me the Waltz* (1932), he found the plot of his fourth novel in the demise of a promising psychiatrist after his marriage to a wealthy patient and cultivation of the kind of rarefied life of leisure modeled in real life by the Murphys. Fitzgerald's long-awaited novel *Tender Is the Night* appeared in 1934. Though it sold reasonably well under depression conditions and, contrary to common assumption, received some favorable reviews, Fitzgerald's financial and critical hopes for the novel were disappointed.

Fitzgerald reached the sorriest stage of his life in the three years following the publication of *Tender Is the Night*. His heart was no longer into writing the kind of magazine fiction desired by the *Saturday Evening Post*, and prices were in any case dropping. An ill-conceived project about a medieval French count was soon aborted. Relations with Zelda, who would remain in and out of costly mental institutions for the rest of her life, were as fraught as ever. Living in North Carolina for health reasons, he carried on at least one extramarital affair and continued to drink heavily. At the outset of 1936 he published in *Esquire* a three-part confessional essay called "The Crack-Up," which was regarded by peers as maudlin and self-indulgent. (The essay has been more kindly judged by posterity.) A suicide attempt followed an unflattering *New York Post* profile written on the occasion of his fortieth birthday. Fitzgerald found his reprieve from this hellish existence when he was offered a generous six-month contract as a screenwriter with Metro-Goldwyn-Mayer. Overwhelmingly in debt, he could hardly refuse.

When Fitzgerald moved to Los Angeles in the summer of 1937, he was making his third attempt as a Hollywood screenwriter (he had gone there in 1927 and 1931 for specific assignments that were not adopted). This time, as things turned out, he was going for good, and he went open to the possibility of establishing a second career in the movie industry (though his disdain for it never ceased to surface). His life was enriched there by the relationship he soon began with gossip-columnist Sheilah Graham (1904–88). He gained screen credit for his work on the film *Three Comrades* (1938), had his contract renewed for a year, and managed (temporarily) to pay off his debts. His contract was not renewed at the outset of 1939, however, and he would struggle as a freelancer from this point forward. Cautiously confident that in the long run his importance as an American novelist would not be forgotten, Fitzgerald worked during his final years both to consolidate and to renew his reputation, even as he courageously came to grips with what he took to be a very different set of historical circumstances from the ones that had allowed for his quick rise to literary stardom at the outset of the 1920s. He tapped into his gift for satire and wrote a series of sketch-length stories for *Esquire* about a hack screenwriter named Pat Hobby; although low paying, they became something of a literary lifeline thanks to editor Arnold Gingrich's (1903–76) faith in him. He became more politically astute, supporting President Franklin D. Roosevelt's New Deal policies at home while following the developments that were leading the world to what might prove to be an apocalyptic war abroad. He tried with some success to quit drinking. He admonished his daughter to take full advantage of the education at Vassar College that he was paying for and created a liberal-arts curriculum for his companion Graham. And perhaps most importantly, he outlined and began writing a new novel about Hollywood known as *The Last Tycoon*, basing his hero on the late Irving Thalberg (1899–1936), M-G-M's visionary production chief. It was still in progress when Fitzgerald died of a heart attack in Graham's apartment on 21 December 1940.

By the measure of his early success, Fitzgerald died a failure: his books were hard to come by, he tried to no avail to get Scribner's to issue an omnibus edition of his novels, and he could not get a magazine interested in serializing his new novel. Editorials following on the heels of his obituaries pegged him as a passé product of the 1920s. But Fitzgerald's resurrection was not slow in coming. In 1941, the *New Republic* published a series of appreciations by noteworthy writers and critics. This preceded by six months the publication of *The Last Tycoon*, the unfinished novel introduced and edited by Edmund Wilson, in a volume that also contained *The Great Gatsby* and some of his best stories. Wilson did more for his friend's reputation when in 1945 he published *The Crack-Up* with New Directions, a collection of Fitzgerald's essays and notebook entries, along with the *New Republic* tributes and other testimonials to his importance. In the same year, Viking published the two major novels and other writings in *The Portable F. Scott Fitzgerald*, and thus a Fitzgerald revival was well under way. It was bolstered by Arthur Mizener's popular scholarly biography *The Far Side of Paradise* (1951) and Alfred Kazin's collection of the better essays on Fitzgerald to date, *F. Scott Fitzgerald: The Man and His Work* (1951).

By the 1960s, largely on the strength of *The Great Gatsby* and *Tender Is the Night*, F. Scott Fitzgerald held the secure place that he enjoys today among critics and common readers as one of the major twentieth-century American novelists. Editions of his novels and stories became widely available, as they are to this day, and academic criticism on every facet of his work began appearing with the steadiness with which American literary scholars have become accustomed. Fitzgerald facilitated his posthumous canonization by leaving much organized information about himself—his ledger, manuscripts, notebooks, and correspondence. No one worked so tirelessly with this material as the late Matthew J. Bruccoli (1931–2008) to establish the soundest possible foundation for studying Fitzgerald's writing, though this same foundation may account for the relatively conservative and repetitive character of much Fitzgerald scholarship. To the extent that there are any divisive controversies, they have been over textual matters and, since Nancy Milford's 1970 biography *Zelda*, the place of Zelda in Scott's life and art. Bruccoli's textual scholarship proved especially influential in displacing the problematic editions of *The Last Tycoon* and *Tender Is the Night* put forth, respectively, by Wilson in 1941 and Malcolm Cowley in 1951, and in launching the *Cambridge Edition of the Works of F. Scott Fitzgerald*, a multivolume, uniform, authoritative critical edition of all of Fitzgerald's writings, which was soon taken over and finally brought to completion in 2019 by James L. W. West III. Bruccoli's biographical work also went some lengths to challenge superficial and overly romantic assumptions about Fitzgerald. But such assumptions have inevitably and perhaps intractably gathered around a figure who, with Zelda, circulates among the iconography of American popular culture as the handsome, muse-bidden, fast-living, tragic representative of the jazz age.

The Great Gatsby: Composition and Critical Reception

Though Fitzgerald was envisioning his third novel as early as mid-1922, he did not really devote himself to writing it until he went to France in April 1924.

Fitzgerald's tendency to disparage his short stories as "trash" obscures the extent to which they often served as more than an economic foundation for his "art." Short fiction served as the medium through which he tried out thematic material and verbal passages for his novels. He later described the story "Winter Dreams," for example, published in *Metropolitan Magazine* in

December 1922, as "A sort of 1st draft of the Gatsby idea" (Bruccoli, *Life in Letters* 108). "Winter Dreams" dealt with a young Midwesterner rejected by the wealthier girl of his dreams only to hear later in life, after he has achieved success, that time and experience have not been kind to Judy Jones. The story is less about the lost girl than about the loss of the dream she embodies, a theme that clearly anticipates the romantic disillusionment of Jay Gatsby. His second most important proto-Gatsby story was "Absolution," written in the summer of 1923 and published a year later in Mencken's *American Mercury*. Sometimes referred to as the "Ur-Gatsby," it may be closer to what Fitzgerald had in mind when he wrote Perkins in 1922 that his next novel would be set in "the middle west and New York" and "have a catholic element" (see Appendix A1, p. 185). Young Rudolph Miller, in conflict with his religious, immigrant father and baffled by a priest unhinged by his attraction to the world, can be recognized as an early avatar of Gatsby; Fitzgerald later said this story was "intended to be a picture of [Gatsby's] early life, but that [he] cut it ... to preserve the sense of mystery" (Turnbull 509). Finally, in late 1923 he wrote "The Sensible Thing" (published in *Liberty*, July 1924), a story that recalled his painful experience of being rejected by Zelda because of insufficient prospects. Like Fitzgerald did, its protagonist opportunely makes his fortune and returns to recapture his beloved's hand, but without seeking, as Gatsby will, to restore the former magic of their relationship.

With such stories and his Great Neck experience behind him, Fitzgerald wrote *The Great Gatsby* in about eight months, finishing his working draft by September 1924 and revising in the early fall. Perkins received his finished typescript in November 1924 and, while acknowledging its brilliance, offered what turned out to be very valuable criticism. Perkins got Fitzgerald to see two fundamental flaws in the book. The first was that the title character was inadequately developed. Granting that Gatsby was supposed to be shrouded in mystery, Perkins thought the reader still needed to have a better physical picture of him, recognize him through a few more telling characteristics, and gain a surer sense of how he made his money. Second, he thought that by having Gatsby tell the bulk of his story in the first person late in the novel, Fitzgerald violated his own narrative method of sticking to Nick Carraway's impressionistic recollection of events (see Appendix A6). The upshot of this criticism was that, while traveling in Italy, Fitzgerald substantially revised his novel after it had already been set in galleys to meet the scheduled April publication date. Alongside some extensive rewriting of passages and scenes (especially in Chapters III, VI, and VII) that alters our impressions of characters and their motives, Fitzgerald broke up the account of Gatsby's real history in Chapter VIII and transposed part of it to the beginning of Chapter VI, even though he had done more to hint at the nature of Gatsby's character throughout the course of the novel. He also made Nick's splendid, lyrical description of Gatsby and Daisy's first kiss the climax of Chapter VI, rather than burying it early in Chapter VII. And he took most of Gatsby's story out of Gatsby's own mouth for the sake of the more aesthetically effective order with which Nick could recount it. Most readers agree with Fitzgerald that Perkins's criticism helped him bring the novel closer to perfection.

Fitzgerald was destined to have his high commercial expectations for the novel disappointed: the novel sold reasonably well but was no bestseller, and he made more money from selling the dramatization rights than he did from sales of the book itself.[1] He characteristically gnawed over the matter, blaming low sales on the fact that it did not appeal enough to women readers. On the other hand, he should have been more pleased than he was with the critical response. There were some daft, dismissive reviews, as the early one appearing in the *New York World* with the title "F. Scott Fitzgerald's Latest a Dud"; and even an admiring critic like Isabel Paterson in the *New York Herald Tribune* deemed it "a book of the season only" (see Appendix B1, p. 205). But most reviewers, whether they read the novel as satiric or as tragic, acknowledged it to be the best work yet of a noteworthy young writer. Critics were compelled to recognize the force of Fitzgerald's style and the novel's formal ingenuity. They may have been divided as to whether *The Great Gatsby* fulfilled the promise suggested by Fitzgerald's earlier novels, or was itself the surer promise of greater work to come; for some, his subject matter would simply never rank as important enough. But a characteristic refrain in the early criticism was that *The Great Gatsby* signaled a new maturity in Fitzgerald, not merely on account of its craftsmanship but because it showed him taking a more objective look at the rebellious cultural milieu and some of

---

1 Owen Davis's dramatic treatment was produced on Broadway in 1926; in the same year, the novel was made into a silent film that has not survived.

the attitudes with which he had become identified. Most flatter-
ing of all for Fitzgerald—on top of Perkins's praise and the
laudatory reviews in high places (see Appendix B)—must have
been the private congratulations of important writers whom he
esteemed, most notably John Peale Bishop, Edith Wharton
(1862–1937), Gertrude Stein, and T.S. Eliot, who deemed it
"the first step that American fiction has taken since Henry
James" (Fitzgerald, *The Crack-Up* 310).

In hindsight, it is hard to appreciate the extent to which *The
Great Gatsby* was nearly forgotten by the time of Fitzgerald's
death in 1940. (A planned 1934 Modern Library edition for
which Fitzgerald had already written an introduction was
scrapped for economic reasons.) Fitzgerald would have felt as
vindicated by the fact that the judgment of its earliest "highbrow"
admirers has been generally endorsed as he would have been
delighted by the fact that it became one of the twentieth century's
most popular classics, whether in new Scribner's editions or in
pulpy paperbacks. Its central love story and evocation of an historical moment both glamorous and decadent have made it ideal
fodder for movies: after the lost silent version of 1926, there has
been a 1949 "gangster" version starring Alan Ladd, the Robert
Redford/Mia Farrow adaptation of 1975, and, most recently, Baz
Luhrmann's 2013 3D extravaganza with Leonardo DiCaprio in
the title role. It has inspired a Black film version entitled *G*
(2002). It has also been adapted into a ballet (1996), an opera
(1999), and a seven-and-a-half-hour experimental play called
Gatz (2010), in which the novel is read in its entirety. At the same
time, its less alienable literary virtues have long made it a staple
of undergraduate and even high-school English curricula
throughout North America and abroad.

Reading *The Great Gatsby*

The Great Gatsby's earliest admirers recognized that Fitzgerald's
new level of technical accomplishment and ability to penetrate
beneath the surface details of and maintain a more coherent relation to his material stemmed from his narrative method. "You
adopted exactly the right method of telling it," Perkins told him,
"that of employing a narrator who is more of a spectator than an
actor: this puts the reader upon a point of observation on a higher
level than that on which the characters stand and at a distance
that gives perspective. In no other way could your irony have
been so immensely effective" (Kuehl and Bryer 82). One could

go so far as to claim that Nick Carraway makes the novel the "beautiful and simple + intricately patterned" work Fitzgerald projected in the summer of 1922 (see Appendix A2, p. 185). And yet by the same token, one need look no further than Nick to find a flaw in the design. His status poses perennial interpretive problems; at the very least it demands of us a certain suspension of disbelief. For as narrator Nick is at once a relatively objective witness of events, an interested participant who acts in ways that drive the events, and, as the last section of Chapter III suggests, the author-surrogate, that is, the writer of the very book we are reading, with a capacity for brilliant flights of lyricism, inimitable deadpan satire, elaborate symbolic organization, and tragic insight that one would hardly expect from a bond salesman, even one who "was rather literary in college"—but that we can readily attribute to F. Scott Fitzgerald. This last aspect is what sets him apart from Joseph Conrad's Marlow—an obvious influence—and from the witness-narrators Henry James was using in several of his middle-period tales. Marlow relays his "yarns" about the story-worthy characters he's encountered—Kurtz, Lord Jim— orally, with interlocutors present.[1] A more underappreciated analogue might be the narrator of Cather's 1918 novel *My Ántonia*: the nostalgic Jim Burden supposedly writes a manuscript for the frame narrator/author, who in turn presents it to us, and in anticipation of *Gatsby* his story is ostensibly about a more vital, inspiring American than himself, the hardy immigrant Ántonia—but is about himself as well. As arguably *The Great Gatsby*'s most complex character, Nick, like Jim in Cather's novel, has a specific social background and hinted-at psychological conflicts that presumably compromise the accuracy and determine the economy of his point-of-view. But if we are tempted to read Nick as an unreliable narrator, as many critics have, we must face the problem of how to interpret his self-exposure as an unreliable narrator in the novel that he appears to have written.

Most critics have followed Perkins in granting Nick Carraway a special authority to tell Gatsby's story because of qualities of perception and judgment that set him apart from the other characters in the novel, and Fitzgerald never gainsaid Perkins's conservative interpretation. Such qualities would have to be grounded in the succinct but revealing information about himself

---

1 Conrad's Marlow appears most influentially as the narrator of the novella *Heart of Darkness* (1899) and the novel *Lord Jim* (1900).

that Nick gives us in the novel's opening pages and at key junctures throughout the novel (most notably in Chapters III and IX). Nick begins by recalling the advice of an apparently honored father, and his sense of himself is inseparable from his sense of the respectable, solidly bourgeois, Midwestern, three-generation American "clan" to which he belongs. Nick refers ironically enough to his family's aristocratic pretensions, but this kind of self-deprecation in no way undermines his social and economic security. Despite the metaphor of pioneering that he attaches to his journey eastward at the outset of the novel, he is in fact an Ivy League graduate (from the Princetonian Fitzgerald's rival school, Yale) backed by his family for a career on Wall Street. And though he rents a modest home at West Egg, his kinship with Daisy Buchanan aligns him to some degree with the "old money" class across the bay from him at East Egg, which Daisy's husband Tom also thinks of as the pinnacle of the white race.

But what has happened to draw Nick to a man like Jay Gatsby—someone, he tells us at the outset, "who represented everything for which I have an unaffected scorn"—and repudiate with damning, epigrammatic finality those "careless people" the Buchanans? (p. 181) And why has Gatsby's story left him so profoundly disillusioned? These are the enigmas that Nick's narrative purports to answer. Crucial to our understanding of this narrative is its retrospective and melancholic quality. The man who set out to make a respectable living on Wall Street in the summer of 1922 has returned west to his family home to tell the story of Gatsby, which becomes the story of an ever-elusive, because forever lost, American dream of regeneration.

As several of its initial reviewers noted, *The Great Gatsby* departs from Fitzgerald's earlier novels in no longer concerning itself with young people. Nick turns thirty midway through the novel; Gatsby is described as looking just over thirty; Daisy is in her early twenties, but married and a mother; Tom is Nick's contemporary. These are grown-ups, in Fitzgerald's terms, who have lived past the moment of youth when the horizon lay open for glorious deeds and erotic bliss, the moment the incorrigibly romantic Fitzgerald took to be the high point of life. Gatsby from the outset epitomizes the spirit of youth, with his "extraordinary gift for hope" and "romantic readiness" that Nick feels sure he will never meet with again (p. 56). It might seem odd that Nick, a veteran of some nasty campaigns during World War I, had any illusions intact, or was receptive to the illusions of others, when he ventured east in 1922. But we must accept what Fitzgerald, who did not see combat, shows us: the experiences of that summer doing for Nick what the war somehow did not manage to do.

The war that left Nick as restless as so many others of his generation presumably made him more receptive to the modern, sensually alluring, morally emancipated, mildly anarchic terrain of jazz-age America he encounters on Long Island and in New York. But he inhabits this world still psychologically bound to the moral sureties of his father's house, so to speak, "within and without" the scenes he describes, "simultaneously enchanted and repelled by the inexhaustible variety of life" (p. 79). It is precisely his deep-seated ambivalence toward the cultural shift epitomized by Gatsby's spectacular parties that makes him an ideal witness to Gatsby's romantic project of winning back his lost love Daisy. Before he learns of Gatsby's plan, he becomes privy to Tom's adultery with Myrtle Wilson, indulges in a sordid afternoon party, has one brief affair before taking up with the incorrigibly dishonest Jordan Baker, lunches with one Meyer Wolfshiem, the gangster responsible for fixing the 1919 World Series, and at one of Gatsby's parties experiences what we might call the restorative power of alcoholic vision: "I had taken two finger-bowls of champagne, and the scene had changed before my eyes into something significant, elemental, and profound" (p. 87). Soon after he learns of Gatsby's plan, he helps him realize it by arranging the tryst with Daisy that re-kindles their romance. By this time, even as we see Nick incrementally compromising his provincial, bourgeois code of conduct, we acquire a fuller picture of who the mysterious Gatsby is and what he is all about—though we will not get a complete picture until the end. Nick artfully reveals Gatsby to us as Gatsby was revealed to him (he does not appear until a quarter of the way into the book), withholding crucial information about him that he gathered later and adumbrating his deeper significance as it occurred to him.

Nick's artfulness is essential to the novel's power, and we diminish that power if we reduce artfulness here to a strategy for exonerating himself for his role in the catastrophe that unfolds. In a novel as time-haunted as *The Great Gatsby*, which above all things is about a man striving to recapture an ideal moment in his past, a poetic reconstruction of the potentially forgettable summer of 1922 seems all the more imperative. Nick does not simply narrate events but, to the extent that we are invited to regard him as the author of what we are reading, imposes an "intricate pattern" on them, to recall Fitzgerald's terms for what he aspired to do. *The Great Gatsby* shares with other noteworthy modernist prose works the quality Joseph Frank some time ago described as "spatial form," the quality by which, as he says with reference to Djuna Barnes's *Nightwood* (1936), a novel is held together "by the continual reference and cross reference of images and symbols that must be referred to each other spatially throughout the time-act of reading" (Frank 32).

There are plenty of these images, symbols, and even leitmotifs (to draw on a term from the temporal art of music) to which we can attend in *The Great Gatsby*, beginning with Nick's acknowledgment of his father's saying—in a novel about a man who disowns his father—and culminating in Nick's vision of the original Dutch sailors spellbound before the "fresh, green breast of the new world" (p. 182). That return to the origins of America, and to the possibilities inherent in "the new world" figured as a natural, erotic object, becomes the prototype, once we get to the end of the novel, of Gatsby's desire to return to the moment in time before he "took" Daisy. That "green breast" invites comparison at once with "the green light at the end of Daisy's dock" (p. 183) and the green cards Daisy gives out at Gatsby's party. It also recalls the more prosaic breast of Myrtle Wilson, the other female character named after something natural rather than, like Jordan, something mechanical (a car), despite being married to a garage keeper and living in an anti-pastoral waste land. The Dutch sailors traveling westward remind us of the westward and eastward movement and the East/West binary pervading the novel, both laden with meanings accrued from American history and mythography. And the Dutch sailors' vision brings to a climax the recurring trope of blindness and vision introduced in Chapter II through the reference to T.J. Eckleburg's billboard. One could go on citing such details as evidence for Fitzgerald's careful composition.

Such artful patterning tends, as much modernist art does, toward abstraction, and it reflects in Nick's case the rage for moral order he expresses after the unsettling journey east. But it is kept from becoming overly abstract by the messy historical particulars for which Fitzgerald had such a good eye and ear, and through which Gatsby's peculiar vitality makes itself felt. The dominant trope for the novel's concrete, historical circumstances seems to be, paradoxically, music—specifically, the musical sound of Daisy Buchanan's seductive voice, the sound of the world's (feminine) body alluring masculine fortune seekers with what Nick hears as "an arrangement of notes that will never be played again" (p. 61). There is something inherently deadly in this appeal. To Gatsby's crassly materialistic ears, as we discover, Daisy's voice "is full of money" (p. 139); and those with too much money, so Nick judges, are part of the "foul dust" floating in the wake of Gatsby's dreams (p. 56). But Gatsby intuitively knows that whatever ideal self he envisions must be embodied according to the possibilities offered by modern America's "vast, vulgar, and meretricious beauty" (p. 124). Ambivalent toward it though he is, Nick deftly captures the numerous forms this beauty takes, beginning with the vernacular someone like Myrtle Wilson retains even after her transformation from garage keeper's wife to high-born lady ("The only *crazy* I was was when I married him," p. 79). Myrtle's transformation is buttressed, of course, by consumer products: cosmetics, a puppy, a new dress, an apartment with furniture upholstered in images of Versailles. The small party that she hosts anticipates Gatsby's parties, which manifest conspicuous consumption and oddly assorted company on a far grander scale.

The sensually entrancing and thoroughly alcoholic character of Gatsby's parties barely veils the social leveling that they facilitate, paid for as they are by money furnished by Prohibition and a bullish stock market, and gravitating as they do around a new celebrity class created by Broadway and the movie industry. In the "amusement park" atmosphere of Gatsby's newly acquired mansion, characters dance promiscuously to the music that gave the era its name, and as Fitzgerald well knew, "jazz"—like so much of the nation's modern popular culture—was largely created by African Americans and Jewish American immigrants. Gatsby gets associated throughout the novel with these "alien" or abject Americans, newcomers or perennial outsiders laying their claim to America's promise in fancy suits and shiny automobiles. Though Nick underscores the association in places, his narrative on the whole works to redeem Gatsby from its more sordid implications, to purify his ambition so that we recognize in Gatsby something more than a tasteless, social-climbing, racially suspect, criminally opportunistic poor boy trying to win the hand of a rich, white Southern belle. In purifying Gatsby's designs, Nick sacrifices his cousin Daisy, her Siren-like voice included, as (like Jordan presumably, and perhaps even Myrtle) too shallow and unworthy a vessel.

The surer vessel for embodying Gatsby's extraordinary romantic idealism—his belief in the green light, his project of self-regeneration—is the book we are reading. For against the story's thematic admonitions about the folly of trying to repeat the past, its intricate formal pattern compels us instead to re-read. In Gatsby's desire to recapture everything signified by Daisy, Nick recognizes a "purposeless splendor" such as we attribute to the boldest artistic endeavors, and which, in writing the otherwise forgettable Gatsby's story, he appropriates as his own. Re-reading Nick's artful rendering of that story brings us again and again to that "transitory enchanted moment" when universal "man" is imagined to be staring breathless before an unsullied America, "compelled into an aesthetic contemplation he neither understood nor desired, face to face for the last time in history with something commensurate to his capacity for wonder" (pp. 182–83). This great passage figures forth the ideal reader response to the wonder work of American literature that it concludes. *The Great Gatsby* stands in as best it can for a sublime aesthetic experience forever irrecoverable, and yet forever bound to the irreversible, corruptive, materialistic course of American history to which its most representative men fall prey.

The Great Gatsby in Cultural Context: The Appendices

Though *The Great Gatsby* should be enjoyed as the beautifully intricate novel Fitzgerald conceived it to be, like all great works of literature it was a product of its time and place and spoke to that time and place before managing to speak beyond them. If this introduction has suggested ways in which the novel resonates with Fitzgerald's biography, the five appendices that follow the text should encourage readers to think about ways in which it resonated with the cultural context that Fitzgerald observed acutely without being able to dissociate himself from it.

Appendices A and B—selections from Fitzgerald's correspondence and contemporary reviews—reveal something of the literary field in which Fitzgerald was working. As the correspondence shows, his aesthetic goals were bound up with more ordinary commercial interests and domestic concerns, and his artistic success depended on professional savvy, a sympathetic and intelligent editor, and, when it was demanded, self-discipline and a practiced understanding of his craft. The reviews by some of the leading critics of the day give us a good sense of what we might call contemporary scales of literary expectation by which the measure of an original work like *The Great Gatsby* could be taken. The first reviewers inevitably read the novel against the backdrop of Fitzgerald's still burgeoning reputation and inevitably judged it not merely for its intrinsic qualities or deficiencies but for how it could be related positively or negatively to his other works and to a familiar range of other authors, novels, and literary trends.

Appendix C, "Class, Consumption, and Economy," offers select texts from the 1920s, including a selection of advertisements from 1922, that shed light on the socio-economic landscape of *The Great Gatsby*. The famed economic boom of the 1920s (made famous, in part, by the spectacular 1929 stock market crash that issued in the Great Depression) did not spread affluence equally—despite the best-laid plans of business leader John J. Raskob (1879–1950) to make "everybody" rich—nor did it do away with pre-war, even nineteenth-century notions of social class. Indeed, historians and social critics alarmed by growing economic inequality in our own time tend to look back to the 1920s for parallel developments, noting as one of the decade's more salient economic facts for Americans the growing share of the national income being amassed by its top "one percent." Timothy Noah has recently written that "to embrace the fantasy of a poverty-free America," as he accuses popular historian Frederick Lewis Allen (1890–1954) of having influentially done in his 1931 book *Only Yesterday*, "one had to be unaware that during the 1920s the bottom 95 percent saw its proportion of the nation's income drop from 72 percent to 64 percent" (15). For Fitzgerald looking back on the decade in "Echoes of the Jazz Age," the party was reserved for the affluent, "the whole upper tenth of a nation living with the insouciance of grand ducs and the casualness of chorus girls" (Fitzgerald, *The Crack-Up* 21). Fitzgerald was able to join the party thanks to the considerable income he was making from his stories, which made him and Zelda, as he half-humorously puts it in his essay "How to Live on $36,000 a Year" (Appendix C3)—the equivalent of roughly half a million today—members of the *nouveau riche*. Most *Saturday Evening Post* readers were no doubt meant to be bemused by the story of the Fitzgeralds' inability to live within a budget that they could only imagine. Fitzgerald's literary earnings, as well as money from screen rights, allowed him to rent something more than Nick's bungalow on Long Island but nothing like Gatsby's mansion; yet even that mansion, as the novel shows, would never be enough for Gatsby to win Daisy for good. Despite Gatsby's fantastic rise from rags to riches—which as more than one critic has suggested recalls the popular, quasi-mythical Horatio Alger stories[1] from the late nineteenth century while getting vaguely attributed in the novel to rum running and crooked stock market machinations—he will always be *nouveau riche,* and gaudily so. The more ostentatiously he tries to achieve status, the more he confirms the rule that one cannot buy "class." That rule accords with a certain economic and moral realism fundamental to Fitzgerald's literary vision at its best that the promise of America as a land of opportunity and self-invention could never dispel: the facts remain, in Fitzgerald's fiction, that poor boys shouldn't think of marrying rich girls, and pseudo-aristocratic plutocrats like the Buchanans can do pretty much whatever they want to do, destroying pathetic strivers along the way.

Such a vision accounts for *The Great Gatsby*'s kinship with Edith Wharton's novels *The House of Mirth* (1905) and *The Custom of the Country* (1913; though there the more ruthless class interloper triumphs): their common literary ancestor is Honoré de Balzac (1799–1850), who left the fictional templates for the modern novel of manners in a society in flux. Edmund Wilson thought of Fitzgerald when reflecting on one of the bestselling books of the decade, first published in 1922—Emily Post's *Etiquette* (Appendix C1): after looking through it, Fitzgerald was "inspired with the idea of a play in which all the motivations should consist of trying to do the right thing" (Wilson, *Classics* 374). "What Is Best Society?," Post's book begins by asking, and what follows for hundreds of pages is a guide to meeting the standards of a once-exclusive conception of society supposedly democratized. However democratic the thrust of Post's book was in spirit, it assumes that class—or more damningly, vulgarity—tells. Gatsby unknowingly exposes himself before the well-mannered Nick by the way he talks, and probably by the way he dresses too, though only the ill-mannered Tom is boorish enough to say so out loud. Advertisements, of course, made more ubiquitous by more mass media in the 1920s, were also democratic in spirit while appealing to the citizen-consumer's sense of "class" in a world where money could be imagined to buy anything. The novel's numerous references to commodities, to sporadic buying, to large-scale waste, and especially to the extravagant tokens of

---

1 Horatio Alger Jr. (1832–99) became famous for his novels for young boys, such as *Ragged Dick* (1868), in which through virtuous behavior and a stroke or two of good fortune a poor young man becomes comfortably middle class.

Gatsby's *nouveau riche* pretensions (a "real" library, multi-colored shirts from London, an aquaplane) suggest that Fitzgerald was attending to the fracturing and diminishment of selfhood or "character" being wrought by a consumerist economy orienting human desires not merely toward things but toward cheapened forms of culture and distinction. The most disturbing symptom of this in the novel is not so much the demise of America's much-touted Protestant work ethic (an ethic the stock market champion Raskob derided, *pace* Ben Franklin, as *not* "the way to wealth"; Appendix C4), but rather the epistemological and aesthetic difficulty of distinguishing the real from the fake. Paradoxically enough, Gatsby's endearing genuineness, for Nick, inheres in his transparent fraudulence; listening to his story "was like skimming hastily through a dozen magazines" (p. 101).

Appendix D, "The Irreverent Spirit of the Jazz Age," contextualizes the satirical aspect of Fitzgerald's novel while also suggesting something of the lost certainties and moral aimlessness that for Fitzgerald marked his generation. *This Side of Paradise* ended somewhat pretentiously with the young Amory Blaine identifying himself with a generation "grown up to find all Gods dead, all wars fought, all faiths in man shaken" (Fitzgerald, *This Side of Paradise* 260). But such portentousness seems at odds with Gatsby's nearly non-stop summer party of 1922, where most people seem to be having tremendous fun. The "jazz" on trial in Duncan Poole's 1922 *Vanity Fair* satire (Appendix D2) refers most generally to the mocking, anti-authoritarian, experimental ethos the music expressed, and that made it anathema to the Reformers and guardians of Public Morality whom Mencken ritualistically ridiculed. These killjoys were behind Prohibition, which went into effect at the beginning of 1920 and whose main effect was to make illegal, excessive alcohol consumption a sign of cultural rebellion, even as its normalized prevalence made bootlegging a highly lucrative business. (They were also the ones who tried but failed to stop the flow of more sexually frank literature that Fitzgerald approvingly catalogues in "Echoes of the Jazz Age," Appendix D1.)

But laughable, moralistic elders are absent from the world of *The Great Gatsby* (in contrast to *The Beautiful and Damned*). Tom Buchanan pretends to be one when he dissociates himself from "the modern world," but he's speaking pure cant (p. 146). By 1923, as Fitzgerald retrospectively tells it, the elders had taken over the "children's party" (Appendix D1, p. 253). The ambivalent, on-the-cusp-of-30 Nick will have to stand in for the old-fashioned, and he comes close to sounding like a prig at the outset of the novel when he declares that "[c]onduct may be founded on the hard rock or the wet marshes, but after a certain point I don't care what it's founded on" (p. 55). But he can also be very funny, as in his survey of Gatsby's guests at the outset of Chapter IV, where we hear of "the Willie Voltaires," one "James B. ('Rot-Gut') Ferrett," and "a prince of something, whom we called Duke" (pp. 98–99). Nick's irony, though, seems more clearly directed at the decadence of the post-war rebellion than the pre-war cultural order it displaced. Nick wants to found conduct on something more solid than his father's word, but he knows irreparably, as the simpler George Wilson does not, that there is no God watching and judging "careless people," that the symbol he conjures up in Dr. T.J. Eckleburg's billboard is just an advertisement (p. 167). *The Great Gatsby* leaves behind the relatively innocent phase of cultural rebellion before the more widespread hedonism that displaced it (and that Fitzgerald would recapture in his Basil Duke Lee stories at the end of the decade). It thus finds a wistful counterpart in Zelda's tribute to the "flapper" from the same year (Appendix D5).[1] It also finds a judicious sequel in the post-Crash "Echoes of the Jazz Age," in which "a whole race going hedonistic, deciding on pleasure" met its secular form of divine judgment, though without expunging good memories. The section concludes with public intellectual Walter Lippmann's somber assessment at decade's end of the peculiar disillusionment afflicting Fitzgerald's generation: "that they should rebel sadly and without faith in their own rebellion, that they should distrust the new freedom no less than the old certainties—that is something of a novelty" (Appendix D6, p. 273).

The materials gathered in Appendix E, "Race, Immigration, and the National Culture, 1920–25," are meant to enrich and complicate our understanding of Fitzgerald's picture of the national culture in *The Great Gatsby*, which acquires its "decadent" connotations in the novel largely from the point of view of

---

1 "Flappers" were the rebellious, carefree, supposedly sexually licentious young women notable for their bobbed hairstyles, slim physiques, clothing styles that downplayed maternal-feminine attributes such as large breasts and broad hips, and open indulgence of traditionally masculine vices like smoking and drinking. The name probably derived from the fashion of wearing unbuttoned, flapping galoshes as well as hats with flapping ear muffs, though it was also associated with the term "fledgling," as in a young bird learning to flap its wings.

a small group of multi-generation white Americans—"Nordics," as Tom Buchanan would have it (p. 64)—whose orbit Jay Gatsby, né James Gatz, enters and unsettles. The theme of American decline, harnessed to the grander narrative of civilization "going to pieces," was not lightly introduced into this carefully patterned novel, even if its initial mouthpiece is the novel's dull-witted, super-rich bully; and it cannot be disentangled from the ascension or upward-mobility narrative conjured by the title of the fictional book by which Tom has been alarmed, "The Rise of the Colored Empires." At first glance, Fitzgerald is in his satiric mode here, and Nick quickly distances himself from Tom's "stale ideas" (p. 69). But Greil Marcus has recently reminded us that Nick may be protesting too much: "Tom's ideas weren't remotely stale in 1922," they have undergirded horrific violence throughout the twentieth century, and they have enjoyed a less respectable but powerful resurgence at our own moment nearly a century later (Marcus 65–67). Books like Madison Grant's *The Passing of the Great Race* (1916) and Lothrop Stoddard's *The Rising Tide of Color against White World-Supremacy* (Appendix E1), the one that Fitzgerald parodically evokes, were published by Scribner's. They contributed influentially to the racially charged discourse about American identity that culminated in the passage of restrictive immigration laws in 1921 and 1924 while federal anti-lynching legislation was blocked (Perrett 82–83, 183–84, 245). The immigration laws were aimed in particular at curtailing the influx of supposedly darker southern and eastern European immigrants (such as the "scrawny Italian child" setting up firecrackers for the Fourth of July in Chapter II, or the southeastern European mourners Nick and Gatsby cross on the Queensboro Bridge in Chapter IV). They were also aimed at curtailing Jewish immigrants. And the failure to get federal anti-lynching legislation was due to the usual disproportionate political power of the Jim Crow South, which Black Americans had been fleeing since the war years in what we know as the Great Migration northward, and, for the most part, toward the promise of the great metropolitan centers. Gatsby is first and foremost a class interloper, whose rise from rags to riches is in the American grain. But the novel tends to racialize class distinctions by associating Gatsby with immigrants, with Jewish Americans, and with Black Americans.

None of the materials in Appendix E need be used to support dubious arguments that Gatsby *is* Jewish or Black, though the case for an immigrant background is easier to make in light of some characteristics of the late-appearing Mr. Gatz, the novel's relation to the story "Absolution," and Fitzgerald's partial use of Max Gerlach as a model. Gatsby's name change is suggestive, and young Jimmy Gatz seems to have Americanized himself in classic fashion through a Ben Franklinesque schedule and list of resolves and immersion in the mythology of the West via popular books like *Hopalong Cassidy*.[1] His real "Western" tutelage under Dan Cody will be rather sordid, but that counts for little in the face of his adoption, so to speak, by a more sinister paternal figure, the urban gangster Meyer Wolfshiem. Wolfshiem is at once a memorable character who delivers some choice lines in a colorful vernacular and a problematic reminder of the pervasive, reflexive anti-Semitism current throughout the 1920s, which could readily find its way into serious fiction (fellow novelist Wharton complimented Fitzgerald on his *"perfect* Jew" [Fitzgerald, *The Crack-Up* 309]). There was, of course, a far more vicious, obsessive anti-Semitism, epitomized in the United States by Henry Ford's widely circulating 1921 volume on *Jewish Influences in American Life* (Appendix E2). Notable there is the spotlight shone on Wolfshiem's model Arnold Rothstein (1882–1928), the gangster and gambler allegedly behind the World Series scandal of 1919. Even more notable in Ford's screed is the association of Rothstein with "Broadway" and the outraged recognition that "Jewish Jazz" has become the national music. Whether or not Fitzgerald read Ford, these cultural "givens" are evident in *The Great Gatsby* and inflect our understanding of its hero. Gatsby's association with Jews was more emphatic in the surviving manuscript, where the "Jazz History of the World" composer is Leo Epstien, not Vladimir Tostoff; where Gatsby sings a Tin Pan Alley-style song of his own composition; and where Tom compares the "theatrical people" populating West Egg to Jews: "One Jew is all right but when you get a crowd of them—" (Fitzgerald, *The Great Gatsby: An Edition of the Manuscript* 29, 92, 98). It is evoked more suggestively when Nick tells us he "would have accepted without question the information that Gatsby sprang from the swamps of Louisiana or from the lower East Side of New York" (p. 89). The latter neighborhood was the launching point for ambitious Jewish American immigrants, such as the

---

1   On Benjamin Franklin and *Hopalong Cassidy*, see p. 177, notes 1 and 2.

heroes of Abraham Cahan's 1917 novel *The Rise of David Levinsky* or Anzia Yezierska's *Bread Givers* (Appendix E4), published in the same year as *Gatsby*. The other possibility—that Gatsby "sprang from the swamps of Louisiana"—is more ambiguous, aligning him with Southern "white trash" but also perhaps more consistently with a migrating African American who has managed to "pass." I say more consistently because of the way in which Gatsby is pointedly associated with Black American arrivistes when he and Nick are passed by "a limousine" over Blackwell's Island, "driven by a white chauffeur, in which sat three modish negroes, two bucks and a girl." "'Anything can happen now,'" thinks Nick to himself, "Even Gatsby could happen, without any particular wonder" (p. 103).

The contextual materials in Appendix E should collectively suggest that Fitzgerald could not write his great American novel about American aspiration in the 1920s, and signal his artistic affiliations with an American modernism, without imaginatively confronting the contradiction between the nation's longstanding "Anglo-saxonist" or "Nordicist" or simply white-supremacist idea of itself and the fact of its being a multiracial nation of immigrants whose defining Black presence must complicate the idea of American exceptionalism evoked in its glorious final paragraphs. Ben Railton recently suggested, in a piece called "Considering History: *The Great Gatsby*, Multicultural New York, and America in 1925," that *Gatsby* would gain from our reading it alongside two other "New York" books from 1925, Yezierska's novel *Bread Givers* and Alain Locke's landmark anthology *The New Negro*. Thanks to his reflections, the original "Appendix E," which mainly pitted the racist visions of Stoddard and Ford against Frederick Howe's 1921 essay on "The Alien," has been expanded to include a chapter from *Bread Givers*, about a real "lower East side" striver entering the world in which most Fitzgerald characters are more at home via "College" (Appendix E4), and two excerpts from *The New Negro* (Appendix E5) that might shed more light on the significance of that stylish Black trio being driven into Manhattan (and presumably Harlem). Joel Rogers's essay (Appendix E6) will certainly shed more light on the Black American contribution to the national music, which Fitzgerald thought was culturally transformative enough to give its name to his era without adequately appreciating it. (W.C. Handy's "Beale Street Blues" serves as the soundtrack to Daisy's social resurgence after missing Gatsby, but it gets reduced to a "hopeless comment" [p. 161].)

The Great Gatsby's greatness has much to do with the compellingly poetic vision that Nick offers of an ever elusive, because always already lost, American dream of finding some sublime object commensurate with the Self's desire. Through Nick's "single window" (p. 57), it betrays prejudices and anxieties about the erosion or passing of white cultural authority, placing "the last and greatest of all human dreams" squarely in the past. But an unequivocal judgment also issues from Nick's standpoint against the "foul dust" that carelessly makes a scapegoat of Gatsby. To the extent that *The Great Gatsby* anticipates the popular historian James Truslow Adams's definition of the "American dream" in 1931 as "a better, richer and happier life for all our citizens" (Churchwell, *Careless People* 344–45), the Buchanans are the plutocratic nemeses of that dream. It is Gatsby who gives his name to this book: the yearning, dreaming American outsider's story was ultimately more commensurate with Fitzgerald's literary ambition and imaginative sympathies than noxious ideas about the displacement of "*real* Americans" circulating either then or now.

F. Scott Fitzgerald:
A Brief Chronology

1896	24 September: Francis Scott Key Fitzgerald born, St. Paul, Minnesota.
1898–1908	The Fitzgerald family moves to upstate New York following the failure of Edward Fitzgerald's business.
1908–11	The Fitzgeralds return to St. Paul when Fitzgerald's father loses his job. Fitzgerald enters St. Paul Academy in the fall of 1908; he begins publishing stories in the school newspaper as early as 1909, and writes and acts in plays for the Elizabethan Dramatic Club.
1911–13	Attends Newman School, a preparatory boarding school in Hackensack, New Jersey.
1913–17	Enters Princeton University in the fall of 1913. Due to poor grades, withdraws from Princeton in the fall of 1915. During the Christmas holiday of 1914–15, he meets and falls in love with Ginevra King.
1917	January: Ginevra formally breaks with him. Enlists following America's entry into World War I. Begins writing his first novel.
1918	Finishes "The Romantic Egotist" in March. While at Camp Sheridan outside Montgomery, Alabama in June, meets Zelda Sayre at a country-club dance. Scribner's rejects "The Romantic Egotist." Sent to Camp Mills, New York, for deployment overseas just before the war ends.
1919	Moves to New York City after being discharged from the army; works for the Barron Collier advertising company and tries with little success to make it as a writer. Zelda breaks off their unofficial engagement in July. *This Side of Paradise* accepted by Scribner's in September.

	Begins placing several stories in noteworthy periodicals like *The Smart Set, Scribner's Magazine,* and the *Saturday Evening Post.*
	Hires Harold Ober as his agent.
1920	Fitzgerald and Zelda renew their engagement.
	March: *This Side of Paradise* is published.
	3 April: Marries Zelda.
	September: *Flappers and Philosophers,* his first collection of stories, is published.
1921	May–July: With Zelda pregnant, the Fitzgeralds visit England, France, and Italy.
	They return to St. Paul, where Scott finishes his second novel and begins a play.
	September–December: *The Beautiful and Damned* runs serially in *Metropolitan.*
	26 October: Daughter Frances Scott (Scottie) Fitzgerald born.
1922	March: *The Beautiful and Damned* published.
	September: *Tales of the Jazz Age,* his second collection of stories, published.
	The Fitzgeralds return east and settle for almost a year and a half in Great Neck, on Long Island in New York.
	December: "Winter Dreams" appears in *Metropolitan.*
1923	Fitzgerald's play, *The Vegetable,* published in April, bombs in production at Atlantic City in November.
1924	April: Sails for France and begins a nearly three-year sojourn abroad.
	June: "Absolution" appears in *American Mercury.*
	Works on *The Great Gatsby.*
1925	April: *The Great Gatsby* published.
1926	February: *All the Sad Young Men,* his third collection of stories, published; includes "The Rich Boy," published in January and February issues of *Redbook.*
	December: Returns with family to the US.
1927	January–February: First trip to Hollywood to work (unsuccessfully) on "Lipstick," a flapper vehicle for Constance Talmadge.
	March: Rents Ellerslie, a mansion outside Wilmington, Delaware.

1928	Returns to Paris in the spring. Writes Basil Duke Lee stories for the *Saturday Evening Post*. Zelda studies ballet under the Russian émigré Lubov Egorova. Returns to Ellerslie in the fall.
1929	April: Returns to France.
1930	Zelda's first serious mental breakdown: she enters Malmaison clinic outside Paris in April and spends summer in Dr. Oscar Forel's Les Rives de Prangins clinic on Lake Geneva. Writes several high priced stories for the *Post*, including "Babylon Revisited" (published December) and the Josephine Perry stories.
1931	January: Fitzgerald's father dies, and he returns to the US alone for funeral.
	June: Zelda discharged from Prangins.
	September: Fitzgeralds return to the US for good, stopping at Montgomery.
	November: "Echoes of the Jazz Age" published in *Scribner's Magazine*; brief trip to Hollywood to work on Jean Harlow vehicle.
1932	February: Zelda enters Phipps Clinic in Baltimore and works on novel she began in late 1931.
	October: Zelda's novel, *Save Me the Waltz*, published by Scribner's.
1933	Works intensely on re-conceived fourth novel.
1934	*Tender Is the Night* serialized in *Scribner's Magazine* January through April; book published in April. Zelda returns to Phipps Clinic in February, ends up in Sheppard and Enoch Pratt Hospital in May. Fitzgerald begins "Philippe, Count of Darkness" series, soon aborted.
1935	March: *Taps at Reveille*, his fourth collection of stories, published.
1936	February–April: The three autobiographical "Crack-Up" essays appear in *Esquire*.
	April: Zelda transferred to Highlands Hospital in Asheville.
	August: Fitzgerald's mother dies.
1937	July: Goes to Hollywood on a six-month contract with Metro-Goldwyn-Mayer.
	July: Meets gossip columnist Sheilah Graham.
	Works on and gets only screen credit for adaptation of Erich Maria Remarque's *Three Comrades*.

1938	M-G-M renews Fitzgerald's contract for the year. Works on "Infidelity," a Joan Crawford vehicle; an adaptation of Claire Booth Luce's "The Women"; and "Madame Curie," a Greta Garbo vehicle. Daughter Scottie enters Vassar College in Poughkeepsie, New York.
1939	M-G-M does not renew contract; Fitzgerald goes freelance. Works briefly on "Gone with the Wind" script. With Budd Schulberg, takes trip to Dartmouth College to work on the movie "Winter Carnival"; ends up fired and hospitalized for alcoholism. October: Begins novel about Hollywood.
1940	Pat Hobby stories appear regularly in *Esquire*. 21 December: Dies of a heart attack in Graham's apartment. Buried in Rockville Union Cemetery.
1941	*The Last Tycoon* appears in its unfinished form with *The Great Gatsby*, edited by Edmund Wilson.
1975	Re-buried in St. Mary's alongside Zelda, who died in a fire at Highlands Hospital in 1948.

A Note on the Text

The copy-text for this edition of *The Great Gatsby* is the 1925 first edition, published by Charles Scribner's Sons in April 1925. Amendments to the copy-text are as follows.

Six changes (revisions or corrections) were introduced into subsequent imprints of the text in accordance with Fitzgerald's directions, and are included here:

1) Chapter 3, page 89, line 30: "echolalia" replaced "chatter";
2) Chapter 6, page 125, line 16: "northern" was corrected to "southern";
3) Chapter 7, page 152, line 9: "it's" was corrected to "its";
4) Chapter 7, page 152, line 19: period was put in after "away";
5) Chapter 9, page 175, line 18: "sickantired" replaced "sick and tired";
6) Chapter 9, page 179, line 6: "Union Street station" was corrected to "Union Station" (Bruccoli, *F. Scott Fitzgerald: A Descriptive Bibliography* 67).

This edition restores three words from the existent holograph manuscript that underwent corruption in the course of being typed and set in galleys:

1) Chapter 1, page 66, line 12: "startlingly" replaces "startingly";
2) Chapter 2, page 73, line 41: "was" replaces "saw" (a change further authorized by Fitzgerald's marked personal copy);
3) Chapter 3, page 90, line 20: "with" replaces "for."

Despite the dubious authority of the holograph manuscript in the case of *The Great Gatsby* (since the intervening and undoubtedly revised typescript from which the galleys were set has been lost), the restored words here either accord with usage or make better sense.

This edition also restores two space-breaks indicated by Fitzgerald in his revisions to the galleys, the space-breaks marking either a change of scene or the passage of time:

1) Chapter 6, page 128, after line 41 (end of page);
2) Chapter 6, page 132, after line 28.

This Broadview Edition furthermore incorporates most of the roughly forty holograph revisions Fitzgerald made in his personal copy of the first edition now housed at the Firestone Library at Princeton University (Rare Books and Manuscripts, C0187, Box 5b). These have been documented by Jennifer E. Atkinson (28–33) and by Matthew J. Bruccoli (*Apparatus* 61–64.) In practically every instance, these changes improve upon the printed version, by excising redundant words or phrases, making descriptions more precise, or correcting details. My own examination of Fitzgerald's marked copy leads me to depart from Atkinson's and Bruccoli's description in only one instance:

Chapter 4, page 107, line 3: "on" replaces "with."

I have not incorporated any of the changes beside which Fitzgerald put a question mark, for the obvious reason that he himself was not sure whether he should or would make it. In the one instance where Fitzgerald suggested alternative changes—inserting "sub-or suppressed" before the word "journalism" in Chapter 6, page 125, line 31—I have chosen the former as better conveying what I take to be his intended meaning. Finally, I have adopted the change from "children" to "little girls" in Chapter 4, page 110, lines 20–21, on the assumption that it is authorized in Fitzgerald's handwriting.

Fitzgerald was a notoriously bad speller, and I have corrected four obvious errors that withstood his (and Scribner's copy editors') scrutiny. I have corrected "Vladmir" to Vladimir" (twice in Chapter 3: page 89, line 33 and page 90, line 4); "Jaqueline" to "Jacqueline" (in Chapter 4, page 98, line 30); "self-absorbtion" to "self-absorption" (in Chapter 6, page 125, line 3); and "rythmic" to "rhythmic" (in Chapter 6, page 132, line 3). In Chapter 9, I have corrected one instance of "Wolfsheim" to Fitzgerald's usual spelling of "Wolfshiem" (page 173, line 23), resisting the temptation to follow Edmund Wilson and make "Wolfsheim" the proper spelling throughout. (Fitzgerald almost invariably misspelled "ei" as "ie," and "Wolfs-heim" would carry the presumably intended suggestive meaning "wolf's home" [Crunden 437n48].)

I have made two substantive corrections to diction or phrasing errors that have withstood editorial scrutiny:

1) "urbane" for "urban" (Chapter 3, page 89, line 27), which more precisely conveys Fitzgerald's meaning;
2) "in" for "on" (Chapter 5, page 122, line 36), which conforms with usage and Fitzgerald's use of the phrase "in the air" elsewhere in the novel.

I have also silently corrected a few accidental errors: commas instead of periods, a period missing after "Mr," and three ellipses points where there should be four. I have changed "33d" to "33rd" and capitalized "village" after "West Egg" in Chapter 1, page 57, line 12, and Chapter 9, page 170, line 13 (as it's capitalized elsewhere in the novel).

Finally, I have allowed errors of fact (e.g., chronological, geographical, physical) to stand, noting some of these if they might prove disconcerting. I have also allowed Scribner's house style to stand (notably in the matters of punctuation and the use of quotation marks around titles) on the ground that there is little to no evidence that Fitzgerald was ever troubled by it. He did, however, pointedly request that "some one" be printed as one word. I have accordingly made this change, and by analogy made single words of "any one" and "every one."

The Great Gatsby

Then wear the gold hat, if that will move her;
If you can bounce high, bounce for her too,
Till she cry "Lover, gold-hatted, high-bouncing lover,
I must have you!"
—THOMAS PARKE D'INVILLIERS.[1]

---

1 D'Invilliers is a fictional character from Fitzgerald's first novel, *This Side of Paradise*, modeled on Princeton classmate and fellow writer John Peale Bishop (1892–1944).

ONCE AGAIN
TO
ZELDA

Chapter I

In my younger and more vulnerable years my father gave me some advice that I've been turning over in my mind ever since.

"Whenever you feel like criticising anyone," he told me, "just remember that all the people in this world haven't had the advantages that you've had."

He didn't say any more, but we've always been unusually communicative in a reserved way, and I understood that he meant a great deal more than that. In consequence, I'm inclined to reserve all judgments, a habit that has opened up many curious natures to me and also made me the victim of not a few veteran bores. The abnormal mind is quick to detect and attach itself to this quality when it appears in a normal person, and so it came about that in college I was unjustly accused of being a politician, because I was privy to the secret griefs of wild, unknown men. Most of the confidences were unsought—frequently I have feigned sleep, preoccupation, or a hostile levity when I realized by some unmistakable sign that an intimate revelation was quivering on the horizon; for the intimate revelations of young men, or at least the terms in which they express them, are usually plagiaristic and marred by obvious suppressions. Reserving judgments is a matter of infinite hope. I am still a little afraid of missing something if I forget that, as my father snobbishly suggested, and I snobbishly repeat, a sense of the fundamental decencies is parcelled out unequally at birth.

And, after boasting this way of my tolerance, I come to the admission that it has a limit. Conduct may be founded on the hard rock or the wet marshes, but after a certain point I don't care what it's founded on. When I came back from the East last autumn I felt that I wanted the world to be in uniform and at a sort of moral attention forever; I wanted no more riotous excursions with privileged glimpses into the human heart. Only Gatsby, the man who gives his name to this book, was exempt from my reaction—Gatsby, who represented everything for which I have an unaffected scorn. If personality is an unbroken series of successful gestures, then there was something gorgeous about him, some heightened sensitivity to the promises of life, as if he were related to one of those intricate machines that register earthquakes ten thousand miles away. This responsiveness had nothing to do with that flabby impressionability which is dignified under the name of the "creative temperament"—it was an extraordinary gift for hope, a romantic readiness such as I have never found in any other person and which it is not likely I shall ever find again. No—Gatsby turned out all right at the end; it is what preyed on Gatsby, what foul dust floated in the wake of his dreams that temporarily closed out my interest in the abortive sorrows and short-winded elations of men.

My family have been prominent, well-to-do people in this Middle Western city for three generations. The Carraways are something of a clan, and we have a tradition that we're descended from the Dukes of Buccleuch,[1] but the actual founder of my line was my grandfather's brother, who came here in fifty-one, sent a substitute to the Civil War,[2] and started the wholesale hardware business that my father carries on to-day.

I never saw this great-uncle, but I'm supposed to look like him—with special reference to the rather hard-boiled painting that hangs in father's office. I graduated from New Haven[3] in 1915, just a quarter of a century after my father, and a little later I participated in that delayed Teutonic migration known as the Great War.[4] I enjoyed the counter-raid so thoroughly that I came back restless. Instead of being the warm centre of the world, the Middle West now seemed like the ragged edge of the universe— so I decided to go East and learn the bond business. Everybody I knew was in the bond business, so I supposed it could support one more single man. All my aunts and uncles talked it over as if they were choosing a prep school[5] for me, and finally said, "Why—ye-es," with very grave, hesitant faces. Father agreed to finance me for a year, and after various delays I came East, permanently, I thought, in the spring of twenty-two.

The practical thing was to find rooms in the city, but it was a warm season, and I had just left a country of wide lawns and

---

1 A Scottish ducal house going back to the fifteenth century, commemorated among other places in Sir Walter Scott's romantic poem *The Lay of the Last Minstrel* (1805).

2 Paid the $300 required by the Conscription Act of March 1863 to have someone else take his place on the battlefield.

3 A city in southern Connecticut, home to Yale University.

4 I.e., World War I, specifically Germany's invasion of Belgium and France.

5 Preparatory school, usually a private school preparing in-residence students for elite colleges and universities.

friendly trees, so when a young man at the office suggested that we take a house together in a commuting town, it sounded like a great idea. He found the house, a weather-beaten cardboard bungalow at eighty a month, but at the last minute the firm ordered him to Washington, and I went out to the country alone. I had a dog—at least I had him for a few days until he ran away—and an old Dodge and a Finnish woman, who made my bed and cooked breakfast and muttered Finnish wisdom to herself over the electric stove.

It was lonely for a day or so until one morning some man, more recently arrived than I, stopped me on the road.

"How do you get to West Egg Village?" he asked helplessly.

I told him. And as I walked on I was lonely no longer. I was a guide, a pathfinder, an original settler. He had casually conferred on me the freedom of the neighborhood.

And so with the sunshine and the great bursts of leaves growing on the trees, just as things grow in fast movies, I had that familiar conviction that life was beginning over again with the summer.

There was so much to read, for one thing, and so much fine health to be pulled down out of the young breath-giving air. I bought a dozen volumes on banking and credit and investment securities, and they stood on my shelf in red and gold like new money from the mint, promising to unfold the shining secrets that only Midas and Morgan and Maecenas knew.[1] And I had the high intention of reading many other books besides. I was rather literary in college—one year I wrote a series of very solemn and obvious editorials for the Yale News—and now I was going to bring back all such things into my life and become again that most limited of all specialists, the "well-rounded man." This isn't just an epigram—life is much more successfully looked at from a single window, after all.

It was a matter of chance that I should have rented a house in one of the strangest communities in North America. It was on that slender riotous island which extends itself due east of New York—

---

1   In classical mythology, King Midas had the power to turn anything he touched into gold; John Pierpont Morgan (1837–1913) was an American financier, founder of the powerful banking firm J.P. Morgan and Company in 1895, and one of the wealthiest and (reputedly) most powerful men in the world when he died; Maecenas (70–8 BCE) was a close adviser to Caesar Augustus and patron of the Roman poets Virgil and Horace; the name now connotes a wealthy patron of the arts.

and where there are, among other natural curiosities, two unusual formations of land. Twenty miles from the city a pair of enormous eggs, identical in contour and separated only by a courtesy bay, jut out into the most domesticated body of salt water in the Western hemisphere, the great wet barnyard of Long Island Sound. They are not perfect ovals—like the egg in the Columbus story, they are both crushed flat at the contact end—but their physical resemblance must be a source of perpetual confusion to the gulls that fly overhead. To the wingless a more arresting phenomenon is their dissimilarity in every particular except shape and size.[1]

I lived at West Egg, the—well, the less fashionable of the two, though this is a most superficial tag to express the bizarre and not a little sinister contrast between them. My house was at the very tip of the egg, only fifty yards from the Sound, and squeezed between two huge places that rented for twelve or fifteen thousand a season. The one on my right was a colossal affair by any standard—it was a factual imitation of some Hôtel de Ville in Normandy,[2] with a tower on one side, spanking new under a thin beard of raw ivy, and a marble swimming pool, and more than forty acres of lawn and garden. It was Gatsby's mansion. Or, rather, as I didn't know Mr. Gatsby, it was a mansion inhabited by a gentleman of that name. My own house was an eyesore, but it was a small eyesore, and it had been overlooked, so I had a view of the water, a partial view of my neighbor's lawn, and the consoling proximity of millionaires—all for eighty dollars a month.

Across the courtesy bay the white palaces of fashionable East Egg glittered along the water, and the history of the summer really begins on the evening I drove over there to have dinner with the Tom Buchanans. Daisy was my second cousin once removed, and I'd known Tom in college. And just after the war I spent two days with them in Chicago.

Her husband, among various physical accomplishments, had been one of the most powerful ends that ever played football at

---

1 Fitzgerald's Long Island setting is imaginatively based on the peninsulas known as Great Neck and Manhasset Neck (West Egg and East Egg, respectively). They are not in fact as geographically identical as Nick's metaphorical description suggests. "The egg in the Columbus story" recalls how Columbus reputedly bet members of the Spanish nobility that he could make an egg stand on end, which he won by crushing the end of the egg; the legend originates in Girolamo Benzini's *Historia del Mondo Nuovo* (1565).

2 A city hall in Normandy, a northwest coastal region of France.

New Haven—a national figure in a way, one of those men who reach such an acute limited excellence at twenty-one that everything afterward savors of anti-climax. His family were enormously wealthy—even in college his freedom with money was a matter for reproach—but now he'd left Chicago and come East in a fashion that rather took your breath away: for instance, he'd brought down a string of polo ponies from Lake Forest.[1] It was hard to realize that a man in my own generation was wealthy enough to do that.

Why they came East I don't know. They had spent a year in France for no particular reason, and then drifted here and there unrestfully wherever people played polo and were rich together. This was a permanent move, said Daisy over the telephone, but I didn't believe it—I had no sight into Daisy's heart, but I felt that Tom would drift on forever seeking, a little wistfully, for the dramatic turbulence of some irrecoverable football game.

And so it happened that on a warm windy evening I drove over to East Egg to see two old friends whom I scarcely knew at all. Their house was even more elaborate than I expected, a cheerful red-and-white Georgian Colonial mansion,[2] overlooking the bay. The lawn started at the beach and ran toward the front door for a quarter of a mile, jumping over sun-dials and brick walks and burning gardens—finally when it reached the house drifting up the side in bright vines as though from the momentum of its run. The front was broken by a line of French windows, glowing now with reflected gold and wide open to the warm windy afternoon, and Tom Buchanan in riding clothes was standing with his legs apart on the front porch.

He had changed since his New Haven years. Now he was a sturdy straw-haired man of thirty with a rather hard mouth and a supercilious manner. Two shining arrogant eyes had established dominance over his face and gave him the appearance of always leaning aggressively forward. Not even the effeminate swank of his riding clothes could hide the enormous power of that body—he seemed to fill those glistening boots until he strained the top

---

1 Affluent suburb of Chicago on the southwest shore of Lake Michigan.
2 Style of architecture most prevalent in the eighteenth century, during the reigns of kings George I (1714–27), II (1727–60), and III (1760–1820). Homes in this style were symmetrical and elegant, featuring flattened columns on either side of the front door, windows across the façade, and twinned chimneys. They were especially prominent in New England and the American South.

lacing, and you could see a great pack of muscle shifting when his shoulder moved under his thin coat. It was a body capable of enormous leverage—a cruel body.

His speaking voice, a gruff husky tenor, added to the impression of fractiousness he conveyed. There was a touch of paternal contempt in it, even toward people he liked—and there were men at New Haven who had hated his guts.

"Now, don't think my opinion on these matters is final," he seemed to say, "just because I'm stronger and more of a man than you are." We were in the same senior society, and while we were never intimate I always had the impression that he approved of me and wanted me to like him with some harsh, defiant wistfulness of his own.

We talked for a few minutes on the sunny porch.

"I've got a nice place here," he said, his eyes flashing about restlessly.

Turning me around by one arm, he moved a broad flat hand along the front vista, including in its sweep a sunken Italian garden, a half acre of deep, pungent roses, and a snub-nosed motor-boat that bumped the tide offshore.

"It belonged to Demaine, the oil man." He turned me around again, politely and abruptly. "We'll go inside."

We walked through a high hallway into a bright rosy-colored space, fragilely bound into the house by French windows at either end. The windows were ajar and gleaming white against the fresh grass outside that seemed to grow a little way into the house. A breeze blew through the room, blew curtains in at one end and out the other like pale flags, twisting them up toward the frosted wedding-cake of the ceiling, and then rippled over the wine-colored rug, making a shadow on it as wind does on the sea.

The only completely stationary object in the room was an enormous couch on which two young women were buoyed up as though upon an anchored balloon. They were both in white, and their dresses were rippling and fluttering as if they had just been blown back in after a short flight around the house. I must have stood for a few moments listening to the whip and snap of the curtains and the groan of a picture on the wall. Then there was a boom as Tom Buchanan shut the rear windows and the caught wind died out about the room, and the curtains and the rugs and the two young women ballooned slowly to the floor.

The younger of the two was a stranger to me. She was extended full length at her end of the divan, completely motionless, and with her chin raised a little, as if she were balancing something on it which was quite likely to fall. If she saw me out of the corner of her eyes she gave no hint of it—indeed, I was almost surprised into murmuring an apology for having disturbed her by coming in.

The other girl, Daisy, made an attempt to rise—she leaned slightly forward with a conscientious expression—then she laughed, an absurd, charming little laugh, and I laughed too and came forward into the room.

"I'm p-paralyzed with happiness."

She laughed again, as if she said something very witty, and held my hand for a moment, looking up into my face, promising that there was no one in the world she so much wanted to see. That was a way she had. She hinted in a murmur that the surname of the balancing girl was Baker. (I've heard it said that Daisy's murmur was only to make people lean toward her; an irrelevant criticism that made it no less charming.)

At any rate, Miss Baker's lips fluttered, she nodded at me almost imperceptibly, and then quickly tipped her head back again—the object she was balancing had obviously tottered a little and given her something of a fright. Again a sort of apology arose to my lips. Almost any exhibition of complete self-sufficiency draws a stunned tribute from me.

I looked back at my cousin, who began to ask me questions in her low, thrilling voice. It was the kind of voice that the ear follows up and down, as if each speech is an arrangement of notes that will never be played again. Her face was sad and lovely with bright things in it, bright eyes and a bright passionate mouth, but there was an excitement in her voice that men who had cared for her found difficult to forget: a singing compulsion, a whispered "Listen," a promise that she had done gay, exciting things just a while since and that there were gay, exciting things hovering in the next hour.

I told her how I had stopped off in Chicago for a day on my way East, and how a dozen people had sent their love through me.

"Do they miss me?" she cried ecstatically.

"The whole town is desolate. All the cars have the left rear wheel painted black as a mourning wreath, and there's a persistent wail all night along the north shore."

"How gorgeous! Let's go back, Tom. To-morrow!" Then she added irrelevantly: "You ought to see the baby."

"I'd like to."

"She's asleep. She's three years old.[1] Haven't you ever seen her?"

"Never."

"Well, you ought to see her. She's——"

Tom Buchanan, who had been hovering restlessly about the room, stopped and rested his hand on my shoulder.

"What you doing, Nick?"

"I'm a bond man."

"Who with?"

I told him.

"Never heard of them," he remarked decisively.

This annoyed me.

"You will," I answered shortly. "You will if you stay in the East."

"Oh, I'll stay in the East, don't you worry," he said, glancing at Daisy and then back at me, as if he were alert for something more. "I'd be a God damned fool to live anywhere else."

At this point Miss Baker said: "Absolutely!" with such suddenness that I started—it was the first word she had uttered since I came into the room. Evidently it surprised her as much as it did me, for she yawned and with a series of rapid, deft movements stood up into the room.

"I'm stiff," she complained, "I've been lying on that sofa for as long as I can remember."

"Don't look at me," Daisy retorted, "I've been trying to get you to New York all afternoon."

"No, thanks," said Miss Baker to the four cocktails just in from the pantry, "I'm absolutely in training."

Her host looked at her incredulously.

"You are!" He took down his drink as if it were a drop in the bottom of a glass. "How you ever get anything done is beyond me."

I looked at Miss Baker, wondering what it was she "got done." I enjoyed looking at her. She was a slender, small-breasted girl, with an erect carriage, which she accentuated by throwing her body backward at the shoulders like a young cadet. Her gray sun-strained eyes looked back at me with polite reciprocal curiosity out of a wan, charming, discontented face. It occurred to me now that I had seen her, or a picture of her, somewhere before.

---

1 According to the account of their engagement and marriage in Chapter IV, Daisy and Tom's daughter would be two years old.

"You live in West Egg," she remarked contemptuously. "I know somebody there."

"I don't know a single——"

"You must know Gatsby."

"Gatsby?" demanded Daisy. "What Gatsby?"

Before I could reply that he was my neighbor dinner was announced; wedging his tense arm imperatively under mine, Tom Buchanan compelled me from the room as though he were moving a checker to another square.

Slenderly, languidly, their hands set lightly on their hips, the two young women preceded us out onto a rosy-colored porch, open toward the sunset, where four candles flickered on the table in the diminished wind.

"Why *candles*?" objected Daisy, frowning. She snapped them out with her fingers. "In two weeks it'll be the longest day in the year." She looked at us all radiantly. "Do you always watch for the longest day of the year and then miss it? I always watch for the longest day in the year and then miss it."

"We ought to plan something," yawned Miss Baker, sitting down at the table as if she were getting into bed.

"All right," said Daisy. "What'll we plan?" She turned to me helplessly: "What do people plan?"

Before I could answer her eyes fastened with an awed expression on her little finger.

"Look!" she complained; "I hurt it."

We all looked—the knuckle was black and blue.

"You did it, Tom," she said accusingly. "I know you didn't mean to, but you *did* do it. That's what I get for marrying a brute of a man, a great, big, hulking physical specimen of a—"

"I hate that word hulking," objected Tom crossly, "even in kidding."

"Hulking," insisted Daisy.

Sometimes she and Miss Baker talked at once, unobtrusively and with a bantering inconsequence that was never quite chatter, that was as cool as their white dresses and their impersonal eyes in the absence of all desire. They were here, and they accepted Tom and me, making only a polite pleasant effort to entertain or to be entertained. They knew that presently dinner would be over and a little later the evening too would be over and casually put away. It was sharply different from the West, where an evening was hurried from phase to phase toward its close, in a continually disappointed anticipation or else in sheer nervous dread of the moment itself.

"You make me feel uncivilized, Daisy," I confessed on my second glass of corky but rather impressive claret. "Can't you talk about crops or something?"

I meant nothing in particular by this remark, but it was taken up in an unexpected way.

"Civilization's going to pieces," broke out Tom violently. "I've gotten to be a terrible pessimist about things. Have you read 'The Rise of the Colored Empires' by this man Goddard?"[1]

"Why, no," I answered, rather surprised by his tone.

"Well, it's a fine book, and everybody ought to read it. The idea is if we don't look out the white race will be—will be utterly submerged. It's all scientific stuff; it's been proved."

"Tom's getting very profound," said Daisy, with an expression of unthoughtful sadness. "He reads deep books with long words in them. What was that word we——"

"Well, these books are all scientific," insisted Tom, glancing at her impatiently. "This fellow has worked out the whole thing. It's up to us, who are the dominant race, to watch out or these other races will have control of things."

"We've got to beat them down," whispered Daisy, winking ferociously toward the fervent sun.

"You ought to live in California—" began Miss Baker, but Tom interrupted her by shifting heavily in his chair.

"This idea is that we're Nordics. I am, and you are, and you are, and—" After an infinitesimal hesitation he included Daisy with a slight nod, and she winked at me again. "—And we've produced all the things that go to make civilization—oh, science and art, and all that. Do you see?"

There was something pathetic in his concentration, as if his complacency, more acute than of old, was not enough to him any more. When, almost immediately, the telephone rang inside and the butler left the porch Daisy seized upon the momentary interruption and leaned toward me.

"I'll tell you a family secret," she whispered enthusiastically. "It's about the butler's nose. Do you want to hear about the butler's nose?"

"That's why I came over to-night."

"Well, he wasn't always a butler; he used to be the silver polisher for some people in New York that had a silver service for two

---

1 *The Rising Tide of Color Against White World-Supremacy* by Lothrop Stoddard was published by Charles Scribner's Sons in 1920 (see Appendix E1).

hundred people. He had to polish it from morning till night, until finally it began to affect his nose——"

"Things went from bad to worse," suggested Miss Baker.

"Yes. Things went from bad to worse, until finally he had to give up his position."

For a moment the last sunshine fell with romantic affection upon her glowing face; her voice compelled me forward breathlessly as I listened—then the glow faded, each light deserting her with lingering regret, like children leaving a pleasant street at dusk.

The butler came back and murmured something close to Tom's ear, whereupon Tom frowned, pushed back his chair, and without a word went inside. As if his absence quickened something within her, Daisy leaned forward again, her voice glowing and singing.

"I love to see you at my table, Nick. You remind me of a—of a rose, an absolute rose. Doesn't he?" She turned to Miss Baker for confirmation: "An absolute rose?"

This was untrue. I am not even faintly like a rose. She was only extemporizing, but a stirring warmth flowed from her, as if her heart was trying to come out to you concealed in one of those breathless, thrilling words. Then suddenly she threw her napkin on the table and excused herself and went into the house.

Miss Baker and I exchanged a short glance consciously devoid of meaning. I was about to speak when she sat up alertly and said "Sh!" in a warning voice. A subdued impassioned murmur was audible in the room beyond, and Miss Baker leaned forward unashamed, trying to hear. The murmur trembled on the verge of coherence, sank down, mounted excitedly, and then ceased altogether.

"This Mr. Gatsby you spoke of is my neighbor—" I said.

"Don't talk. I want to hear what happens."

"Is something happening?" I inquired innocently.

"You mean to say you don't know?" said Miss Baker, honestly surprised. "I thought everybody knew."

"I don't."

"Why—" she said hesitantly, "Tom's got some woman in New York."

"Got some woman?" I repeated blankly.

Miss Baker nodded.

"She might have the decency not to telephone him at dinner time. Don't you think?"

Almost before I had grasped her meaning there was the flutter of a dress and the crunch of leather boots, and Tom and Daisy were back at the table.

"It couldn't be helped!" cried Daisy with tense gayety.

She sat down, glanced searchingly at Miss Baker and then at me, and continued: "I looked outdoors for a minute, and it's very romantic outdoors. There's a bird on the lawn that I think must be a nightingale come over on the Cunard or White Star Line.[1] He's singing away"—Her voice sang: "It's romantic, isn't it, Tom?"

"Very romantic," he said, and then miserably to me: "If it's light enough after dinner, I want to take you down to the stables."

The telephone rang inside, startlingly, and as Daisy shook her head decisively at Tom the subject of the stables, in fact all subjects, vanished into air. Among the broken fragments of the last five minutes at table I remember the candles being lit again, pointlessly, and I was conscious of wanting to look squarely at everyone, and yet to avoid all eyes. I couldn't guess what Daisy and Tom were thinking, but I doubt if even Miss Baker, who seemed to have mastered a certain hardy scepticism, was able utterly to put this fifth guest's shrill metallic urgency out of mind. To a certain temperament the situation might have seemed intriguing—my own instinct was to telephone immediately for the police.

The horses, needless to say, were not mentioned again. Tom and Miss Baker, with several feet of twilight between them, strolled back into the library, as if to a vigil beside a perfectly tangible body, while, trying to look pleasantly interested and a little deaf, I followed Daisy around a chain of connecting verandas to the porch in front. In its deep gloom we sat down side by side on a wicker settee.

Daisy took her face in her hands as if feeling its lovely shape, and her eyes moved gradually out into the velvet dusk. I saw that turbulent emotions possessed her, so I asked what I thought would be some sedative questions about her little girl.

"We don't know each other very well, Nick," she said suddenly. "Even if we are cousins. You didn't come to my wedding."

"I wasn't back from the war."

"That's true." She hesitated. "Well, I've had a very bad time, Nick, and I'm pretty cynical about everything."

---

1 The two largest transatlantic steamship companies, they merged in 1934 to become Cunard-White Star Limited.

Evidently she had reason to be. I waited but she didn't say any more, and after a moment I returned rather feebly to the subject of her daughter.

"I suppose she talks, and—eats, and everything."

"Oh, yes." She looked at me absently. "Listen, Nick; let me tell you what I said when she was born. Would you like to hear?"

"Very much."

"It'll show you how I've gotten to feel about—things. Well, she was less than an hour old and Tom was God knows where. I woke up out of the ether with an utterly abandoned feeling, and asked the nurse right away if it was a boy or a girl. She told me it was a girl, and so I turned my head away and wept. 'All right,' I said, 'I'm glad it's a girl. And I hope she'll be a fool—that's the best thing a girl can be in this world, a beautiful little fool.'

"You see I think everything's terrible anyhow," she went on in a convinced way. "Everybody thinks so—the most advanced people. And I *know*. I've been everywhere and seen everything and done everything." Her eyes flashed around her in a defiant way, rather like Tom's, and she laughed with thrilling scorn. "Sophisticated—God, I'm sophisticated!"

The instant her voice broke off, ceasing to compel my attention, my belief, I felt the basic insincerity of what she had said. It made me uneasy, as though the whole evening had been a trick of some sort to exact a contributory emotion from me. I waited, and sure enough, in a moment she looked at me with an absolute smirk on her lovely face, as if she had asserted her membership in a rather distinguished secret society to which she and Tom belonged.

Inside, the crimson room bloomed with light. Tom and Miss Baker sat at either end of the long couch and she read aloud to him from the Saturday Evening Post[1]—the words, murmurous and uninflected, running together in a soothing tune. The lamplight, bright on his boots and dull on the autumn-leaf yellow of her hair, glinted along the paper as she turned a page with a flutter of slender muscles in her arms.

When we came in she held us silent for a moment with a lifted hand.

---

1 At the time, America's most popular and commercially successful weekly periodical.

"To be continued," she said, tossing the magazine on the table, "in our very next issue."

Her body asserted itself with a restless movement of her knee, and she stood up.

"Ten o'clock," she remarked, apparently finding the time on the ceiling. "Time for this good girl to go to bed."

"Jordan's going to play in the tournament to-morrow," explained Daisy, "over at Westchester."[1]

"Oh—you're *Jor*dan Baker."

I knew now why her face was familiar—its pleasing contemptuous expression had looked out at me from many rotogravure pictures[2] of the sporting life at Asheville and Hot Springs and Palm Beach.[3] I had heard some story of her too, a critical, unpleasant story, but what it was I had forgotten long ago.

"Good night," she said softly. "Wake me at eight, won't you."

"If you'll get up."

"I will. Good night, Mr. Carraway. See you anon."

"Of course you will," confirmed Daisy. "In fact I think I'll arrange a marriage. Come over often, Nick, and I'll sort of—oh—fling you together. You know—lock you up accidentally in linen closets and push you out to sea in a boat, and all that sort of thing——"

"Good night," called Miss Baker from the stairs. "I haven't heard a word."

"She's a nice girl," said Tom after a moment. "They oughtn't to let her run around the country this way."

"Who oughtn't to?" inquired Daisy coldly.

"Her family."

"Her family is one aunt about a thousand years old. Besides, Nick's going to look after her, aren't you, Nick? She's going to spend lots of week-ends out here this summer. I think the home influence will be very good for her."

Daisy and Tom looked at each other for a moment in silence.

"Is she from New York?" I asked quickly.

---

1 Westchester County is the New York suburb on the other side of Long Island Sound from Great Neck and Manhasset Neck.

2 Magazine or newspaper photographs.

3 Asheville, Hot Springs, and Palm Beach were all affluent southern resort towns popular with the northeastern sporting set, located in North Carolina, Arkansas, and Florida, respectively.

"From Louisville. Our white girlhood was passed together there. Our beautiful white——"[1]

"Did you give Nick a little heart to heart talk on the veranda?" demanded Tom suddenly.

"Did I?" She looked at me. "I can't seem to remember, but I think we talked about the Nordic race. Yes, I'm sure we did. It sort of crept up on us and first thing you know——"

"Don't believe everything you hear, Nick," he advised me.

I said lightly that I had heard nothing at all, and a few minutes later I got up to go home. They came to the door with me and stood side by side in a cheerful square of light. As I started my motor Daisy peremptorily called: "Wait!

"I forgot to ask you something, and it's important. We heard you were engaged to a girl out West."

"That's right," corroborated Tom kindly. "We heard that you were engaged."

"It's a libel. I'm too poor."

"But we heard it," insisted Daisy, surprising me by opening up again in a flower-like way. "We heard it from three people, so it must be true."

Of course I knew what they were referring to, but I wasn't even vaguely engaged. The fact that gossip had published the banns was one of the reasons I had come East. You can't stop going with an old friend on account of rumors, and on the other hand I had no intention of being rumored into marriage.

Their interest rather touched me and made them less remotely rich—nevertheless, I was confused and a little disgusted as I drove away. It seemed to me that the thing for Daisy to do was to rush out of the house, child in arms—but apparently there were no such intentions in her head. As for Tom, the fact that he "had some woman in New York" was really less surprising than that he had been depressed by a book. Something was making him nibble at the edge of stale ideas as if his sturdy physical egotism no longer nourished his peremptory heart.

Already it was deep summer on roadhouse roofs and in front of wayside garages, where new red gas-pumps sat out in pools of light, and when I reached my estate at West Egg I ran the car under its shed and sat for a while on an abandoned grass roller in the yard. The wind had blown off, leaving a loud, bright night, with wings beating in the trees and a persistent organ sound as

---

1 Innocent and pure; possibly racially inflected.

the full bellows of the earth blew the frogs full of life. The silhouette of a moving cat wavered across the moonlight, and
turning my head to watch it, I saw that I was not alone—fifty feet
away a figure had emerged from the shadow of my neighbor's
mansion and was standing with his hands in his pockets regarding the silver pepper of the stars. Something in his leisurely movements and the secure position of his feet upon the lawn suggested
that it was Mr. Gatsby himself, come out to determine what share
was his of our local heavens.

I decided to call to him. Miss Baker had mentioned him at
dinner, and that would do for an introduction. But I didn't call to
him, for he gave a sudden intimation that he was content to be
alone—he stretched out his arms toward the dark water in a
curious way, and, far as I was from him, I could have sworn he was
trembling. Involuntarily I glanced seaward—and distinguished
nothing except a single green light, minute and far away, that might
have been the end of a dock. When I looked once more for Gatsby
he had vanished, and I was alone again in the unquiet darkness.

Chapter II

About half way between West Egg and New York the motor road
hastily joins the railroad and runs beside it for a quarter of a mile,
so as to shrink away from a certain desolate area of land. This is
a valley of ashes—a fantastic farm where ashes grow like wheat
into ridges and hills and grotesque gardens; where ashes take the
forms of houses and chimneys and rising smoke and, finally, with
a transcendent effort, of men, who move dimly and already
crumbling through the powdery air. Occasionally a line of gray
cars crawls along an invisible track, gives out a ghastly creak, and
comes to rest, and immediately the ash-gray men swarm up with
leaden spades and stir up an impenetrable cloud, which screens
their obscure operations from your sight.[1]

But above the gray land and the spasms of bleak dust which
drift endlessly over it, you perceive, after a moment, the eyes of
Doctor T.J. Eckleburg. The eyes of Doctor T.J. Eckleburg are blue
and gigantic—their retinas[2] are one yard high. They look out of

---

1 A possible reference to the Corona dumps (now Flushing Meadows-
   Corona Park) on the border of Flushing in the borough of Queens.

2 Matthew J. Bruccoli has pointed out that the retina is invisible and that
   Fitzgerald probably means irises or pupils here (*Apparatus* 33).

no face, but, instead, from a pair of enormous yellow spectacles which pass over a non-existent nose. Evidently some wild wag of an oculist set them there to fatten his practice in the borough of Queens, and then sank down himself into eternal blindness, or forgot them and moved away. But his eyes, dimmed a little by many paintless days under sun and rain, brood on over the solemn dumping ground.

The valley of ashes is bounded on one side by a small foul river, and, when the drawbridge is up to let barges through, the passengers on waiting trains can stare at the dismal scene for as long as half an hour. There is always a halt there of at least a minute, and it was because of this that I first met Tom Buchanan's mistress.

The fact that he had one was insisted upon wherever he was known. His acquaintances resented the fact that he turned up in popular restaurants with her and, leaving her at a table, sauntered about, chatting with whomsoever he knew. Though I was curious to see her, I had no desire to meet her—but I did. I went up to New York with Tom on the train one afternoon, and when we stopped by the ashheaps he jumped to his feet and, taking hold of my elbow, literally forced me from the car.

"We're getting off," he insisted. "I want you to meet my girl."

I think he'd tanked up a good deal at luncheon, and his determination to have my company bordered on violence. The supercilious assumption was that on Sunday afternoon I had nothing better to do.

I followed him over a low whitewashed railroad fence, and we walked back a hundred yards along the road under Doctor Eckleburg's persistent stare. The only building in sight was a small block of yellow brick sitting on the edge of the waste land, a sort of compact Main Street ministering to it, and contiguous to absolutely nothing. One of the three shops it contained was for rent and another was an all-night restaurant, approached by a trail of ashes; the third was a garage—*Repairs*. GEORGE B. WILSON. *Cars bought and sold.*—and I followed Tom inside.

The interior was unprosperous and bare; the only car visible was the dust-covered wreck of a Ford which crouched in a dim corner. It had occurred to me that this shadow of a garage must be a blind, and that sumptuous and romantic apartments were concealed overhead, when the proprietor himself appeared in the door of an office, wiping his hands on a piece of waste. He was a blond, spiritless man, anæmic, and faintly handsome. When he saw us a damp gleam of hope sprang into his light blue eyes.

"Hello, Wilson, old man," said Tom, slapping him jovially on the shoulder. "How's business?"

"I can't complain," answered Wilson unconvincingly. "When are you going to sell me that car?"

"Next week; I've got my man working on it now."

"Works pretty slow, don't he?"

"No, he doesn't," said Tom coldly. "And if you feel that way about it, maybe I'd better sell it somewhere else after all."

"I don't mean that," explained Wilson quickly. "I just meant ____"

His voice faded off and Tom glanced impatiently around the garage. Then I heard footsteps on a stairs, and in a moment the thickish figure of a woman blocked out the light from the office door. She was in the middle thirties, and faintly stout, but she carried her surplus flesh sensuously as some women can. Her face, above a spotted dress of dark blue crêpe-de-chine, contained no facet or gleam of beauty, but there was an immediately perceptible vitality about her as if the nerves of her body were continually smouldering. She smiled slowly and, walking through her husband as if he were a ghost, shook hands with Tom, looking him flush in the eye. Then she wet her lips, and without turning around spoke to her husband in a soft, coarse voice:

"Get some chairs, why don't you, so somebody can sit down."

"Oh, sure," agreed Wilson hurriedly, and went toward the little office, mingling immediately with the cement color of the walls. A white ashen dust veiled his dark suit and his pale hair as it veiled everything in the vicinity—except his wife, who moved close to Tom.

"I want to see you," said Tom intently. "Get on the next train."

"All right."

"I'll meet you by the news-stand on the lower level."

She nodded and moved away from him just as George Wilson emerged with two chairs from his office door.

We waited for her down the road and out of sight. It was a few days before the Fourth of July, and a gray, scrawny Italian child was setting torpedoes in a row along the railroad track.

"Terrible place, isn't it," said Tom, exchanging a frown with Doctor Eckleburg.

"Awful."

"It does her good to get away."

"Doesn't her husband object?"

"Wilson? He thinks she goes to see her sister in New York. He's so dumb he doesn't know he's alive."

So Tom Buchanan and his girl and I went up together to New York—or not quite together, for Mrs. Wilson sat discreetly in another car. Tom deferred that much to the sensibilities of those East Eggers who might be on the train.

She had changed her dress to a brown figured muslin, which stretched tight over her rather wide hips as Tom helped her to the platform in New York. At the news-stand she bought a copy of Town Tattle[1] and a moving-picture magazine, and in the station drug-store some cold cream and a small flask of perfume. Upstairs, in the solemn echoing drive she let four taxicabs drive away before she selected a new one, lavender-colored with gray upholstery, and in this we slid out from the mass of the station into the glowing sunshine. But immediately she turned sharply from the window and, leaning forward, tapped on the front glass.

"I want to get one of those dogs," she said earnestly. "I want to get one for the apartment. They're nice to have—a dog."

We backed up to a gray old man who bore an absurd resemblance to John D. Rockefeller.[2] In a basket swung from his neck cowered a dozen very recent puppies of an indeterminate breed.

"What kind are they?" asked Mrs. Wilson eagerly, as he came to the taxi-window.

"All kinds. What kind do you want, lady?"

"I'd like to get one of those police dogs; I don't suppose you got that kind?"

The man peered doubtfully into the basket, plunged in his hand and drew one up, wriggling, by the back of the neck.

"That's no police dog," said Tom.

"No, it's not exactly a police dog," said the man with disappointment in his voice. "It's more of an Airedale." He passed his hand over the brown wash-rag of a back. "Look at that coat. Some coat. That's a dog that'll never bother you with catching cold."

"I think it's cute," said Mrs. Wilson enthusiastically. "How much is it?"

"That dog?" He looked at it admiringly. "That dog will cost you ten dollars."

---

1 Fictional periodical probably based on the gossip magazine *Town Topics*, which, like moving-picture magazines, provided titillating glimpses into the lives of the wealthy and famous.

2 John D. Rockefeller (1839–1937), wealthy oil-industry leader and philanthropist, founder of Standard Oil.

The Airedale—undoubtedly there was an Airedale concerned in it somewhere, though its feet were startlingly white—changed hands and settled down into Mrs. Wilson's lap, where she fondled the weatherproof coat with rapture.

"Is it a boy or a girl?" she asked delicately.

"That dog? That dog's a boy."

"It's a bitch," said Tom decisively. "Here's your money. Go and buy ten more dogs with it."

We drove over to Fifth Avenue, so warm and soft, almost pastoral, on the summer Sunday afternoon that I wouldn't have been surprised to see a great flock of white sheep turn the corner.

"Hold on," I said, "I have to leave you here."

"No, you don't," interposed Tom quickly. "Myrtle'll be hurt if you don't come up to the apartment. Won't you, Myrtle?"

"Come on," she urged. "I'll telephone my sister Catherine. She's said to be very beautiful by people who ought to know."

"Well, I'd like to, but——"

We went on, cutting back again over the Park toward the West Hundreds. At 158th Street the cab stopped at one slice in a long white cake of apartment-houses. Throwing a regal homecoming glance around the neighborhood, Mrs. Wilson gathered up her dog and her other purchases, and went haughtily in.

"I'm going to have the McKees come up," she announced as we rose in the elevator. "And, of course, I got to call up my sister, too."

The apartment was on the top floor—a small living-room, a small dining-room, a small bedroom, and a bath. The living-room was crowded to the doors with a set of tapestried furniture entirely too large for it, so that to move about was to stumble continually over scenes of ladies swinging in the gardens of Versailles.[1] The only picture was an over-enlarged photograph, apparently a hen sitting on a blurred rock. Looked at from a distance, however, the hen resolved itself into a bonnet, and the countenance of a stout old lady beamed down into the room. Several old copies of Town Tattle lay on the table together with a copy of "Simon Called Peter,"[2] and some of the small scandal magazines of Broadway. Mrs. Wilson was first concerned with the dog. A reluctant elevator-boy went for a box full of straw and

---

1 The gardens attached to the Palace of Versailles, the principal royal residence of France from 1682 until the French Revolution.

2 Risqué British novel by Robert Keable (1887–1927), published in 1921.

some milk, to which he added on his own initiative a tin of large, hard dog-biscuits—one of which decomposed apathetically in the saucer of milk all afternoon. Meanwhile Tom brought out a bottle of whiskey from a locked bureau door.

I have been drunk just twice in my life, and the second time was that afternoon; so everything that happened has a dim, hazy cast over it, although until after eight o'clock the apartment was full of cheerful sun. Sitting on Tom's lap Mrs. Wilson called up several people on the telephone; then there were no cigarettes, and I went out to buy some at the drug-store on the corner. When I came back they had disappeared, so I sat down discreetly in the living-room and read a chapter of "Simon Called Peter"—either it was terrible stuff or the whiskey distorted things, because it didn't make any sense to me.

Just as Tom and Myrtle (after the first drink Mrs. Wilson and I called each other by our first names) reappeared, company commenced to arrive at the apartment-door.

The sister, Catherine, was a slender, worldly girl of about thirty, with a solid, sticky bob of red hair, and a complexion powdered milky white. Her eyebrows had been plucked and then drawn on again at a more rakish angle, but the efforts of nature toward the restoration of the old alignment gave a blurred air to her face. When she moved about there was an incessant clicking as innumerable pottery bracelets jingled up and down upon her arms. She came in with such a proprietary haste, and looked around so possessively at the furniture that I wondered if she lived here. But when I asked her she laughed immoderately, repeated my question aloud, and told me she lived with a girl friend at a hotel.

Mr. McKee was a pale, feminine man from the flat below. He had just shaved, for there was a white spot of lather on his cheekbone, and he was most respectful in his greeting to everyone in the room. He informed me that he was in the "artistic game," and I gathered later that he was a photographer and had made the dim enlargement of Mrs. Wilson's mother which hovered like an ectoplasm[1] on the wall. His wife was shrill, languid, handsome, and horrible. She told me with pride that her husband had photographed her a hundred and twenty-seven times since they had been married.

---

1 A term used by spiritualists for the materialized form taken by ghosts or mediums.

Mrs. Wilson had changed her costume some time before, and was now attired in an elaborate afternoon dress of cream-colored chiffon, which gave out a continual rustle as she swept about the room. With the influence of the dress her personality had also undergone a change. The intense vitality that had been so remarkable in the garage was converted into impressive hauteur. Her laughter, her gestures, her assertions became more violently affected moment by moment, and as she expanded the room grew smaller around her, until she seemed to be revolving on a noisy, creaking pivot through the smoky air.

"My dear," she told her sister in a high, mincing shout, "most of these fellas will cheat you every time. All they think of is money. I had a woman up here last week to look at my feet, and when she gave me the bill you'd of thought she had my appendicitus out."

"What was the name of the woman?" asked Mrs. McKee.

"Mrs. Eberhardt. She goes around looking at people's feet in their own homes."

"I like your dress," remarked Mrs. McKee, "I think it's adorable."

Mrs. Wilson rejected the compliment by raising her eyebrow in disdain.

"It's just a crazy old thing," she said. "I just slip it on sometimes when I don't care what I look like."

"But it looks wonderful on you, if you know what I mean," pursued Mrs. McKee. "If Chester could only get you in that pose I think he could make something of it."

We all looked in silence at Mrs. Wilson, who removed a strand of hair from over her eyes and looked back at us with a brilliant smile. Mr. McKee regarded her intently with his head on one side, and then moved his hand back and forth slowly in front of his face.

"I should change the light," he said after a moment. "I'd like to bring out the modelling of the features. And I'd try to get hold of all the back hair."

"I wouldn't think of changing the light," cried Mrs. McKee. "I think it's——"

Her husband said "*Sh!*" and we all looked at the subject again, whereupon Tom Buchanan yawned audibly and got to his feet.

"You McKees have something to drink," he said. "Get some more ice and mineral water, Myrtle, before everybody goes to sleep."

"I told that boy about the ice." Myrtle raised her eyebrows in despair at the shiftlessness of the lower orders. "These people! You have to keep after them all the time."

She looked at me and laughed pointlessly. Then she flounced over to the dog, kissed it with ecstasy, and swept into the kitchen, implying that a dozen chefs awaited her orders there.

"I've done some nice things out on Long Island," asserted Mr. McKee.

Tom looked at him blankly.

"Two of them we have framed down-stairs."

"Two what?" demanded Tom.

"Two studies. One of them I call 'Montauk Point—The Gulls,' and the other I call 'Montauk Point—The Sea.'"

The sister Catherine sat down beside me on the couch.

"Do you live down on Long Island, too?" she inquired.

"I live at West Egg."

"Really? I was down there at a party about a month ago. At a man named Gatsby's. Do you know him?"

"I live next door to him."

"Well, they say he's a nephew or a cousin of Kaiser Wilhelm's.[1] That's where all his money comes from."

"Really?"

She nodded.

"I'm scared of him. I'd hate to have him get anything on me."

This absorbing information about my neighbor was interrupted by Mrs. McKee's pointing suddenly at Catherine:

"Chester, I think you could do something with *her*," she broke out, but Mr. McKee only nodded in a bored way, and turned his attention to Tom.

"I'd like to do more work on Long Island, if I could get the entry. All I ask is that they should give me a start."

"Ask Myrtle," said Tom, breaking into a short shout of laughter as Mrs. Wilson entered with a tray. "She'll give you a letter of introduction, won't you, Myrtle?"

"Do what?" she asked, startled.

"You'll give McKee a letter of introduction to your husband, so he can do some studies of him." His lips moved silently for a moment as he invented. "'George B. Wilson at the Gasoline Pump,' or something like that."

Catherine leaned close to me and whispered in my ear:

"Neither of them can stand the person they're married to."

---

1 Kaiser Wilhelm II of Germany (1859–1941, r. 1888–1918).

"Can't they?"

"Can't *stand* them." She looked at Myrtle and then at Tom. "What I say is, why go on living with them if they can't stand them? If I was them I'd get a divorce and get married to each other right away."

"Doesn't she like Wilson either?"

The answer to this was unexpected. It came from Myrtle, who had overheard the question, and it was violent and obscene.

"You see," cried Catherine triumphantly. She lowered her voice again. "It's really his wife that's keeping them apart. She's a Catholic, and they don't believe in divorce."

Daisy was not a Catholic, and I was a little shocked at the elaborateness of the lie.

"When they do get married," continued Catherine, "they're going West to live for a while until it blows over."

"It'd be more discreet to go to Europe."

"Oh, do you like Europe?" she exclaimed surprisingly. "I just got back from Monte Carlo."[1]

"Really."

"Just last year. I went over there with another girl."

"Stay long?"

"No, we just went to Monte Carlo and back. We went by way of Marseilles.[2] We had over twelve hundred dollars when we started, but we got gyped[3] out of it all in two days in the private rooms. We had an awful time getting back, I can tell you. God, how I hated that town!"

The late afternoon sky bloomed in the window for a moment like the blue honey of the Mediterranean—then the shrill voice of Mrs. McKee called me back into the room.

"I almost made a mistake, too," she declared vigorously. "I almost married a little kyke[4] who'd been after me for years. I knew he was below me. Everybody kept saying to me: Lucille, that man's 'way below you!' But if I hadn't met Chester, he'd of got me sure."

---

1 Gambling resort in the principality of Monaco, in southeastern France.

2 The major seaport in southeastern France.

3 Usually "gypped." American slang for being cheated, derived from racist conceptions of the Roma, an itinerant, persecuted people originally from the north of India, mistakenly assumed to be from Egypt (hence "gypsies") by the Europeans amongst whom they settled.

4 Derogatory term for a Jew, usually spelled "kike."

"Yes, but listen," said Myrtle Wilson, nodding her head up and down, "at least you didn't marry him."

"I know I didn't."

"Well, I married him," said Myrtle, ambiguously. "And that's the difference between your case and mine."

"Why did you, Myrtle?" demanded Catherine. "Nobody forced you to."

Myrtle considered.

"I married him because I thought he was a gentleman," she said finally. "I thought he knew something about breeding, but he wasn't fit to lick my shoe."

"You were crazy about him for a while," said Catherine.

"Crazy about him!" cried Myrtle incredulously. "Who said I was crazy about him? I never was any more crazy about him than I was about that man there."

She pointed suddenly at me, and everyone looked at me accusingly. I tried to show by my expression that I had played no part in her past.

"The only *crazy* I was was when I married him. I knew right away I made a mistake. He borrowed somebody's best suit to get married in, and never even told me about it, and the man came after it one day when he was out." She looked around to see who was listening: "'Oh, is that your suit?' I said. 'This is the first I ever heard about it.' But I gave it to him and then I lay down and cried to beat the band all afternoon."

"She really ought to get away from him," resumed Catherine to me. "They've been living over that garage for eleven years. And Tom's the first sweetie she ever had."

The bottle of whiskey—a second one—was now in constant demand by all present, excepting Catherine, who "felt just as good on nothing at all." Tom rang for the janitor and sent him for some celebrated sandwiches, which were a complete supper in themselves. I wanted to get out and walk eastward toward the park through the soft twilight, but each time I tried to go I became entangled in some wild, strident argument which pulled me back, as if with ropes, into my chair. Yet high over the city our line of yellow windows must have contributed their share of human secrecy to the casual watcher in the darkening streets, and I was him too, looking up and wondering. I was within and without, simultaneously enchanted and repelled by the inexhaustible variety of life.

Myrtle pulled her chair close to mine, and suddenly her warm breath poured over me the story of her first meeting with Tom.

"It was on the two little seats facing each other that are always the last ones left on the train. I was going up to New York to see my sister and spend the night. He had on a dress suit and patent leather shoes, and I couldn't keep my eyes off him, but every time he looked at me I had to pretend to be looking at the advertisement over his head. When we came into the station he was next to me, and his white shirt-front pressed against my arm, and so I told him I'd have to call a policeman, but he knew I lied. I was so excited that when I got into a taxi with him I didn't hardly know I wasn't getting into a subway train. All I kept thinking about, over and over, was 'You can't live forever; you can't live forever.'"

She turned to Mrs. McKee and the room rang full of her artificial laughter.

"My dear," she cried, "I'm going to give you this dress as soon as I'm through with it. I've got to get another one to-morrow. I'm going to make a list of all the things I've got to get. A massage and a wave,[1] and a collar for the dog, and one of those cute little ashtrays where you touch a spring, and a wreath with a black silk bow for mother's grave that'll last all summer. I got to write down a list so I won't forget all the things I got to do."

It was nine o'clock—almost immediately afterward I looked at my watch and found it was ten. Mr. McKee was asleep on a chair with his fists clenched in his lap, like a photograph of a man of action. Taking out my handkerchief I wiped from his cheek the spot of dried lather that had worried me all the afternoon.

The little dog was sitting on the table looking with blind eyes through the smoke, and from time to time groaning faintly. People disappeared, reappeared, made plans to go somewhere, and then lost each other, searched for each other, found each other a few feet away. Some time toward midnight Tom Buchanan and Mrs. Wilson stood face to face discussing, in impassioned voices, whether Mrs. Wilson had any right to mention Daisy's name.

"Daisy! Daisy! Daisy!" shouted Mrs. Wilson. "I'll say it whenever I want to! Daisy! Dai——"

Making a short deft movement, Tom Buchanan broke her nose with his open hand.

Then there were bloody towels upon the bathroom floor, and women's voices scolding, and high over the confusion a long broken wail of pain. Mr. McKee awoke from his doze and started

---

1 A marcel wave, a fashionable hairstyle done with hot curling irons.

in a daze toward the door. When he had gone half way he turned around and stared at the scene—his wife and Catherine scolding and consoling as they stumbled here and there among the crowded furniture with articles of aid, and the despairing figure on the couch, bleeding fluently, and trying to spread a copy of Town Tattle over the tapestry scenes of Versailles. Then Mr. McKee turned and continued on out the door. Taking my hat from the chandelier, I followed.

"Come to lunch some day," he suggested, as we groaned down in the elevator.

"Where?"

"Anywhere."

"Keep your hands off the lever," snapped the elevator boy.

"I beg your pardon," said Mr. McKee with dignity, "I didn't know I was touching it."

"All right," I agreed, "I'll be glad to."

... I was standing beside his bed and he was sitting up between the sheets, clad in his underwear, with a great portfolio in his hands.

"Beauty and the Beast ... Loneliness ... Old Grocery Horse ... Brook'n Bridge ..."

Then I was lying half asleep in the cold lower level of the Pennsylvania Station,[1] staring at the morning Tribune,[2] and waiting for the four o'clock train.

Chapter III

There was music from my neighbor's house through the summer nights. In his blue gardens men and girls came and went like moths among the whisperings and the champagne and the stars. At high tide in the afternoon I watched his guests diving from the tower of his raft, or taking the sun on the hot sand of his beach while his two motor-boats slit the waters of the Sound, drawing aquaplanes over cataracts of foam. On week-ends his Rolls-Royce[3] became an omnibus, bearing parties to and from the city

---

1 New York City's second major railroad station spanning from 33rd to 31st Streets between 7th and 8th Avenues, completed in 1911, terminal of the commuter-carrying Long Island Railroad.

2 New York daily newspaper of a conservative turn; it merged with the *Herald* to become the *New York Herald Tribune* in 1924.

3 Top-quality British car.

between nine in the morning and long past midnight, while his station wagon scampered like a brisk yellow bug to meet all trains. And on Mondays eight servants, including an extra gardener, toiled all day with mops and scrubbing-brushes and hammers and garden-shears, repairing the ravages of the night before.

Every Friday five crates of oranges and lemons arrived from a fruiterer in New York—every Monday these same oranges and lemons left his back door in a pyramid of pulpless halves. There was a machine in the kitchen which could extract the juice of two hundred oranges in half an hour if a little button was pressed two hundred times by a butler's thumb.

At least once a fortnight a corps of caterers came down with several hundred feet of canvas and enough colored lights to make a Christmas tree of Gatsby's enormous garden. On buffet tables, garnished with glistening hors-d'oeuvre, spiced baked hams crowded against salads of harlequin designs and pastry pigs and turkeys bewitched to a dark gold. In the main hall a bar with a real brass rail was set up, and stocked with gins and liquors and with cordials so long forgotten that most of his female guests were too young to know one from another.

By seven o'clock the orchestra has arrived, no thin five-piece affair, but a whole pitful of oboes and trombones and saxophones and viols and cornets and piccolos, and low and high drums. The last swimmers have come in from the beach now and are dressing up-stairs; the cars from New York are parked five deep in the drive, and already the halls and salons and verandas are gaudy with primary colors, and hair shorn in strange new ways, and shawls beyond the dreams of Castile.[1] The bar is in full swing, and floating rounds of cocktails permeate the garden outside, until the air is alive with chatter and laughter, and casual innuendo and introductions forgotten on the spot, and enthusiastic meetings between women who never knew each other's names.

The lights grow brighter as the earth lurches away from the sun, and now the orchestra is playing yellow cocktail music, and the opera of voices pitches a key higher. Laughter is easier minute by minute, spilled with prodigality, tipped out at a cheerful word. The groups change more swiftly, swell with new arrivals, dissolve and form in the same breath; already there are wanderers, confi-

---

1 Region in northern Spain, known for the ornate and colorfully embroidered traditional women's shawls.

dent girls who weave here and there among the stouter and more stable, become for a sharp, joyous moment the centre of a group, and then, excited with triumph, glide on through the sea-change of faces and voices and color under the constantly changing light.

Suddenly one of these gypsies,[1] in trembling opal, seizes a cocktail out of the air, dumps it down for courage and, moving her hands like Frisco,[2] dances out alone on the canvas platform. A momentary hush; the orchestra leader varies his rhythm obligingly for her, and there is a burst of chatter as the erroneous news goes around that she is Gilda Gray's[3] understudy from the Follies.[4] The party has begun.

I believe that on the first night I went to Gatsby's house I was one of the few guests who had actually been invited. People were not invited—they went there. They got into automobiles which bore them out to Long Island, and somehow they ended up at Gatsby's door. Once there they were introduced by somebody who knew Gatsby, and after that they conducted themselves according to the rules of behavior associated with amusement parks. Sometimes they came and went without having met Gatsby at all, came for the party with a simplicity of heart that was its own ticket of admission.

I had been actually invited. A chauffeur in a uniform of robin's-egg blue crossed my lawn early that Saturday morning with a surprisingly formal note from his employer: the honor would be entirely Gatsby's, it said, if I would attend his "little party" that night. He had seen me several times, and had intended to call on me long before, but a peculiar combination of circumstances had prevented it—signed Jay Gatsby, in a majestic hand.

Dressed up in white flannels I went over to his lawn a little after seven, and wandered around rather ill at ease among swirls and eddies of people I didn't know—though here and there was a face I had noticed on the commuting train. I was immediately

---

1 Common, derogatory term for the Roma, denoting rootless, constantly moving people.

2 Joe Frisco (1889–1958), stage name of Louis Wilson Joseph, famous jazz dancer from the period known for his rendition of the "Black Bottom."

3 Gilda Gray (1901–59), stage name of Polish-born dancer and actress Marianna Michalski, famous for her rendition of the provocative dance called the "shimmy."

4 The Ziegfeld Follies, a song-and-dance revue.

struck by the number of young Englishmen dotted about; all well dressed, all looking a little hungry, and all talking in low, earnest voices to solid and prosperous Americans. I was sure that they were selling something: bonds or insurance or automobiles. They were at least agonizingly aware of the easy money in the vicinity and convinced that it was theirs for a few words in the right key.

As soon as I arrived I made an attempt to find my host, but the two or three people of whom I asked his whereabouts stared at me in such an amazed way, and denied so vehemently any knowledge of his movements, that I slunk off in the direction of the cocktail table—the only place in the garden where a single man could linger without looking purposeless and alone.

I was on my way to get roaring drunk from sheer embarrassment when Jordan Baker came out of the house and stood at the head of the marble steps, leaning a little backward and looking with contemptuous interest down into the garden.

Welcome or not, I found it necessary to attach myself to someone before I should begin to address cordial remarks to the passers-by.

"Hello!" I roared, advancing toward her. My voice seemed unnaturally loud across the garden.

"I thought you might be here," she responded absently as I came up. "I remembered you lived next door to——"

She held my hand impersonally, as a promise that she'd take care of me in a minute, and gave ear to two girls in twin yellow dresses, who stopped at the foot of the steps.

"Hello!" they cried together. "Sorry you didn't win."

That was for the golf tournament. She had lost in the finals the week before.

"You don't know who we are," said one of the girls in yellow, "but we met you here about a month ago."

"You've dyed your hair since then," remarked Jordan, and I started, but the girls had moved casually on and her remark was addressed to the premature moon, produced like the supper, no doubt, out of a caterer's basket. With Jordan's slender golden arm resting in mine, we descended the steps and sauntered about the garden. A tray of cocktails floated at us through the twilight, and we sat down at a table with the two girls in yellow and three men, each one introduced to us as Mr. Mumble.

"Do you come to these parties often?" inquired Jordan of the girl beside her.

"The last one was the one I met you at," answered the girl, in an alert confident voice. She turned to her companion: "Wasn't it for you, Lucille?"

It was for Lucille, too.

"I like to come," Lucille said. "I never care what I do, so I always have a good time. When I was here last I tore my gown on a chair, and he asked me my name and address—inside of a week I got a package from Croirier's[1] with a new evening gown in it."

"Did you keep it?" asked Jordan.

"Sure I did. I was going to wear it to-night, but it was too big in the bust and had to be altered. It was gas blue with lavender beads. Two hundred and sixty-five dollars."

"There's something funny about a fellow that'll do a thing like that," said the other girl eagerly. "He doesn't want any trouble with *any*body."

"Who doesn't?" I inquired.

"Gatsby. Somebody told me——"

The two girls and Jordan leaned together confidentially.

"Somebody told me they thought he killed a man once."

A thrill passed over all of us. The three Mr. Mumbles bent forward and listened eagerly.

"I don't think it's so much *that*," argued Lucille sceptically; "it's more that he was a German spy during the war."

One of the men nodded in confirmation.

"I heard that from a man who knew all about him, grew up with him in Germany," he assured us positively.

"Oh, no," said the first girl, "it couldn't be that, because he was in the American army during the war." As our credulity switched back to her she leaned forward with enthusiasm. "You look at him sometimes when he thinks nobody's looking at him. I'll bet he killed a man."

She narrowed her eyes and shivered. Lucille shivered. We all turned and looked around for Gatsby. It was testimony to the romantic speculation he inspired that there were whispers about him from those who had found little that it was necessary to whisper about in this world.

The first supper—there would be another one after midnight—was now being served, and Jordan invited me to join her own party, who were spread around a table on the other side of the garden. There were three married couples and Jordan's escort, a persistent undergraduate given to violent innuendo, and

---

1 Fictional fashion house.

obviously under the impression that sooner or later Jordan was going to yield him up her person to a greater or lesser degree. Instead of rambling this party had preserved a dignified homogeneity, and assumed to itself the function of representing the staid nobility of the country-side—East Egg condescending to West Egg, and carefully on guard against its spectroscopic gayety.

"Let's get out," whispered Jordan, after a somehow wasteful and inappropriate half-hour; "this is much too polite for me."

We got up, and she explained that we were going to find the host: I had never met him, she said, and it was making me uneasy. The undergraduate nodded in a cynical, melancholy way.

The bar, where we glanced first, was crowded, but Gatsby was not there. She couldn't find him from the top of the steps, and he wasn't on the veranda. On a chance we tried an important-looking door, and walked into a high Gothic[1] library, panelled with carved English oak, and probably transported complete from some ruin overseas.

A stout, middle-aged man, with enormous owl-eyed spectacles, was sitting somewhat drunk on the edge of a great table, staring with unsteady concentration at the shelves of books. As we entered he wheeled excitedly around and examined Jordan from head to foot.

"What do you think?" he demanded impetuously.

"About what?"

He waved his hand toward the book-shelves.

"About that. As a matter of fact you needn't bother to ascertain. I ascertained. They're real."

"The books?"

He nodded.

"Absolutely real—have pages and everything. I thought they'd be a nice durable cardboard. Matter of fact, they're absolutely real. Pages and—Here! Lemme show you."

Taking our scepticism for granted, he rushed to the bookcases and returned with Volume One of the "Stoddard Lectures."[2]

"See!" he cried triumphantly. "It's a bona-fide piece of printed matter. It fooled me. This fella's a regular Belasco.[3] It's a

---

1 The style of architecture prominent in Europe during the High and Late Middle Ages.

2 A ten-volume set of illustrated travel books by John Stoddard (1850–1931), first issued in 1897–98.

3 David Belasco (1853–1931), playwright and New York theater producer known for theatrical realism.

triumph. What thoroughness! What realism! Knew when to stop, too—didn't cut the pages. But what do you want? What do you expect?"

He snatched the book from me and replaced it hastily on its shelf, muttering that if one brick was removed the whole library was liable to collapse.

"Who brought you?" he demanded. "Or did you just come? I was brought. Most people were brought."

Jordan looked at him alertly, cheerfully, without answering.

"I was brought by a woman named Roosevelt," he continued. "Mrs. Claud Roosevelt. Do you know her? I met her somewhere last night. I've been drunk for about a week now, and I thought it might sober me up to sit in a library."

"Has it?"

"A little bit, I think. I can't tell yet. I've only been here an hour. Did I tell you about the books? They're real. They're——"

"You told us."

We shook hands with him gravely and went back outdoors.

There was dancing now on the canvas in the garden; old men pushing young girls backward in eternal graceless circles, superior couples holding each other tortuously, fashionably, and keeping in the corners—and a great number of single girls dancing individualistically or relieving the orchestra for a moment of the burden of the banjo or the traps. By midnight the hilarity had increased. A celebrated tenor had sung in Italian, and a notorious contralto had sung in jazz, and between the numbers people were doing "stunts" all over the garden, while happy, vacuous bursts of laughter rose toward the summer sky. A pair of stage twins, who turned out to be the girls in yellow, did a baby act in costume, and champagne was served in glasses bigger than finger-bowls. The moon had risen higher, and floating in the Sound was a triangle of silver scales, trembling a little to the stiff, tinny drip of the banjoes on the lawn.

I was still with Jordan Baker. We were sitting at a table with a man of about my age and a rowdy little girl, who gave way upon the slightest provocation to uncontrollable laughter. I was enjoying myself now. I had taken two finger-bowls of champagne, and the scene had changed before my eyes into something significant, elemental, and profound.

At a lull in the entertainment the man looked at me and smiled.

"Your face is familiar," he said, politely. "Weren't you in the Third Division during the war?"

"Why, yes. I was in the Ninth Machine-Gun Battalion."

"I was in the Seventh Infantry until June nineteen-eighteen. I knew I'd seen you somewhere before."

We talked for a moment about some wet, gray little villages in France. Evidently he lived in this vicinity, for he told me that he had just bought a hydroplane,[1] and was going to try it out in the morning.

"Want to go with me, old sport? Just near the shore along the Sound."

"What time?"

"Any time that suits you best."

It was on the tip of my tongue to ask his name when Jordan looked around and smiled.

"Having a gay time now?" she inquired.

"Much better." I turned again to my new acquaintance. "This is an unusual party for me. I haven't even seen the host. I live over there—" I waved my hand at the invisible hedge in the distance, "and this man Gatsby sent over his chauffeur with an invitation."

For a moment he looked at me as if he failed to understand.

"I'm Gatsby," he said suddenly.

"What!" I exclaimed. "Oh, I beg your pardon."

"I thought you knew, old sport. I'm afraid I'm not a very good host."

He smiled understandingly—much more than understandingly. It was one of those rare smiles with a quality of eternal reassurance in it, that you may come across four or five times in life. It faced—or seemed to face—the whole external world for an instant, and then concentrated on *you* with an irresistible prejudice in your favor. It understood you just so far as you wanted to be understood, believed in you as you would like to believe in yourself, and assured you that it had precisely the impression of you that, at your best, you hoped to convey. Precisely at that point it vanished—and I was looking at an elegant young rough-neck, a year or two over thirty, whose elaborate formality of speech just missed being absurd. Some time before he introduced himself I'd got a strong impression that he was picking his words with care.[2]

Almost at the moment when Mr. Gatsby identified himself a butler hurried toward him with the information that Chicago was

---

1 A seaplane.

2 See Appendix C1 on the importance of cultivating "an agreeable speech."

calling him on the wire. He excused himself with a small bow that included each of us in turn.

"If you want anything just ask for it, old sport," he urged me. "Excuse me. I will rejoin you later."

When he was gone I turned immediately to Jordan—constrained to assure her of my surprise. I had expected that Mr. Gatsby would be a florid and corpulent person in his middle years.

"Who is he?" I demanded. "Do you know?"

"He's just a man named Gatsby."

"Where is he from, I mean? And what does he do?"

"Now *you*'re started on the subject," she answered with a wan smile. "Well, he told me once he was an Oxford man."[1]

A dim background started to take shape behind him, but at her next remark it faded away. "However, I don't believe it."

"Why not?"

"I don't know," she insisted, "I just don't think he went there."

Something in her tone reminded me of the other girl's "I think he killed a man," and had the effect of stimulating my curiosity. I would have accepted without question the information that Gatsby sprang from the swamps of Louisiana or from the lower East Side of New York.[2] That was comprehensible. But young men didn't—at least in my provincial inexperience I believed they didn't—drift coolly out of nowhere and buy a palace on Long Island Sound.

"Anyhow, he gives large parties," said Jordan, changing the subject with an urbane distaste for the concrete. "And I like large parties. They're so intimate. At small parties there isn't any privacy."

There was the boom of a bass drum, and the voice of the orchestra leader rang out suddenly above the echolalia[3] of the garden.

"Ladies and gentlemen," he cried. "At the request of Mr. Gatsby we are going to play for you Mr. Vladimir Tostoff 's latest work, which attracted so much attention at Carnegie Hall[4] last

---

1 A graduate of one of the colleges of Oxford University.

2 See Introduction (pp. 40–41).

3 Pathological condition wherein one compulsively repeats others' words or phrases, or, more generally, the subordination of sense to sound. Fitzgerald chose this word at the last minute to replace "chatter" (too late for the first imprint of the first edition).

4 Concert hall on 7th Avenue and 57th Street in Manhattan.

May. If you read the papers you know there was a big sensation." He smiled with jovial condescension, and added: "Some sensation!" Whereupon everybody laughed.

"The piece is known," he concluded lustily, "as 'Vladimir Tostoff's Jazz History of the World.'"[1]

The nature of Mr. Tostoff's composition eluded me, because just as it began my eyes fell on Gatsby, standing alone on the marble steps and looking from one group to another with approving eyes. His tanned skin was drawn attractively tight on his face and his short hair looked as though it were trimmed every day. I could see nothing sinister about him. I wondered if the fact that he was not drinking helped to set him off from his guests, for it seemed to me that he grew more correct as the fraternal hilarity increased. When the "Jazz History of the World" was over, girls were putting their heads on men's shoulders in a puppyish, convivial way, girls were swooning backward playfully into men's arms, even into groups, knowing that someone would arrest their falls—but no one swooned backward on Gatsby, and no French bob touched Gatsby's shoulder, and no singing quartets were formed with Gatsby's head for one link.

"I beg your pardon."

Gatsby's butler was suddenly standing beside us.

"Miss Baker?" he inquired. "I beg your pardon, but Mr. Gatsby would like to speak to you alone."

"With me?" she exclaimed in surprise.

"Yes, madame."

She got up slowly, raising her eyebrows at me in astonishment, and followed the butler toward the house. I noticed that she wore her evening-dress, all her dresses, like sports clothes—there was a jauntiness about her movements as if she had first learned to walk upon golf courses on clean, crisp mornings.

I was alone and it was almost two. For some time confused and intriguing sounds had issued from a long, many-windowed room which overhung the terrace. Eluding Jordan's undergraduate, who was now engaged in an obstetrical conversation with two chorus girls, and who implored me to join him, I went inside.

The large room was full of people. One of the girls in yellow was playing the piano, and beside her stood a tall, red-haired young lady from a famous chorus, engaged in song. She had

---

1 A fictional piece. For commentary, see Breitwieser, "*The Great Gatsby*" and "Jazz Fractures."

drunk a quantity of champagne, and during the course of her song she had decided, ineptly, that everything was very, very sad—she was not only singing, she was weeping too. Whenever there was a pause in the song she filled it with gasping, broken sobs, and then took up the lyric again in a quavering soprano. The tears coursed down her cheeks—not freely, however, for when they came into contact with her heavily beaded eyelashes they assumed an inky color, and pursued the rest of their way in slow black rivulets. A humorous suggestion was made that she sing the notes on her face, whereupon she threw up her hands, sank into a chair, and went off into a deep vinous sleep.

"She had a fight with a man who says he's her husband," explained a girl at my elbow.

I looked around. Most of the remaining women were now having fights with men said to be their husbands. Even Jordan's party, the quartet from East Egg, were rent asunder by dissension. One of the men was talking with curious intensity to a young actress, and his wife, after attempting to laugh at the situation in a dignified and indifferent way, broke down entirely and resorted to flank attacks—at intervals she appeared suddenly at his side like an angry diamond, and hissed: "You promised!" into his ear.

The reluctance to go home was not confined to wayward men. The hall was at present occupied by two deplorably sober men and their highly indignant wives. The wives were sympathizing with each other in slightly raised voices.

"Whenever he sees I'm having a good time he wants to go home."

"Never heard anything so selfish in my life."

"We're always the first ones to leave."

"So are we."

"Well, we're almost the last to-night," said one of the men sheepishly. "The orchestra left half an hour ago."

In spite of the wives' agreement that such malevolence was beyond credibility, the dispute ended in a short struggle, and both wives were lifted, kicking, into the night.

As I waited for my hat in the hall the door of the library opened and Jordan Baker and Gatsby came out together. He was saying some last word to her, but the eagerness in his manner tightened abruptly into formality as several people approached him to say good-by.

Jordan's party were calling impatiently to her from the porch, but she lingered for a moment to shake hands.

"I've just heard the most amazing thing," she whispered. "How long were we in there?"

"Why, about an hour."

"It was ... simply amazing," she repeated abstractedly. "But I swore I wouldn't tell it and here I am tantalizing you." She yawned gracefully in my face. "Please come and see me.... Phone book.... Under the name of Mrs. Sigourney Howard.... My aunt...." She was hurrying off as she talked—her brown hand waved a jaunty salute as she melted into her party at the door.

Rather ashamed that on my first appearance I had stayed so late, I joined the last of Gatsby's guests, who were clustered around him. I wanted to explain that I'd hunted for him early in the evening and to apologize for not having known him in the garden.

"Don't mention it," he enjoined me eagerly. "Don't give it another thought, old sport." The familiar expression held no more familiarity than the hand which reassuringly brushed my shoulder. "And don't forget we're going up in the hydroplane to-morrow morning, at nine o'clock."

Then the butler, behind his shoulder:

"Philadelphia wants you on the 'phone, sir."

"All right, in a minute. Tell them I'll be right there.... Good night."

"Good night."

"Good night." He smiled—and suddenly there seemed to be a pleasant significance in having been among the last to go, as if he had desired it all the time. "Good night, old sport.... Good night."

But as I walked down the steps I saw that the evening was not quite over. Fifty feet from the door a dozen headlights illuminated a bizarre and tumultuous scene. In the ditch beside the road, right side up, but violently shorn of one wheel, rested a new coupé[1] which had left Gatsby's drive not two minutes before. The sharp jut of a wall accounted for the detachment of the wheel, which was now getting considerable attention from half a dozen curious chauffeurs. However, as they had left their cars blocking the road, a harsh, discordant din from those in the rear had been audible for some time, and added to the already violent confusion of the scene.

---

1 Closed, two-door car.

A man in a long duster[1] had dismounted from the wreck and now stood in the middle of the road, looking from the car to the tire and from the tire to the observers in a pleasant, puzzled way.

"See!" he explained. "It went in the ditch."

The fact was infinitely astonishing to him, and I recognized first the unusual quality of wonder, and then the man—it was the late patron of Gatsby's library.

"How'd it happen?"

He shrugged his shoulders.

"I know nothing whatever about mechanics," he said decisively.

"But how did it happen? Did you run into the wall?"

"Don't ask me," said Owl Eyes, washing his hands of the whole matter. "I know very little about driving—next to nothing. It happened, and that's all I know."

"Well, if you're a poor driver you oughtn't to try driving at night."

"But I wasn't even trying," he explained indignantly, "I wasn't even trying."

An awed hush fell upon the bystanders.

"Do you want to commit suicide?"

"You're lucky it was just a wheel! A bad driver and not even *try*ing!"

"You don't understand," explained the criminal. "I wasn't driving. There's another man in the car."

The shock that followed this declaration found voice in a sustained "Ah-h-h!" as the door of the coupé swung slowly open. The crowd—it was now a crowd—stepped back involuntarily, and when the door had opened wide there was a ghostly pause. Then, very gradually, part by part, a pale, dangling individual stepped out of the wreck, pawing tentatively at the ground with a large uncertain dancing shoe.

Blinded by the glare of the headlights and confused by the incessant groaning of the horns, the apparition stood swaying for a moment before he perceived the man in the duster.

"Wha's matter?" he inquired calmly. "Did we run outa gas?"

"Look!"

Half a dozen fingers pointed at the amputated wheel—he

---

1   A long light overcoat worn in the early days of the automobile to protect oneself from dust.

stared at it for a moment, and then looked upward as though he suspected that it had dropped from the sky.

"It came off," someone explained.

He nodded.

"At first I din' notice we'd stopped."

A pause. Then, taking a long breath and straightening his shoulders, he remarked in a determined voice:

"Wonder'ff tell me where there's a gas'line station?"

At least a dozen men, some of them a little better off than he was, explained to him that wheel and car were no longer joined by any physical bond.

"Back out," he suggested after a moment. "Put her in reverse."

"But the *wheel's* off!"

He hesitated.

"No harm in trying," he said.

The caterwauling horns had reached a crescendo and I turned away and cut across the lawn toward home. I glanced back once. A wafer of a moon was shining over Gatsby's house, making the night fine as before, and surviving the laughter and the sound of his still glowing garden. A sudden emptiness seemed to flow now from the windows and the great doors, endowing with complete isolation the figure of the host, who stood on the porch, his hand up in a formal gesture of farewell.

Reading over what I have written so far, I see I have given the impression that the events of three nights several weeks apart were all that absorbed me. On the contrary, they were merely casual events in a crowded summer, and, until much later, they absorbed me infinitely less than my personal affairs.

Most of the time I worked. In the early morning the sun threw my shadow westward as I hurried down the white chasms of lower New York to the Probity Trust. I knew the other clerks and young bond-salesmen by their first names, and lunched with them in dark, crowded restaurants on little pig sausages and mashed potatoes and coffee. I even had a short affair with a girl who lived in Jersey City[1] and worked in the accounting department, but her brother began throwing mean looks in my direction, so when she went on her vacation in July I let it blow quietly away.

---

1   New Jersey port city across the Hudson River from Manhattan.

I took dinner usually at the Yale Club[1]—for some reason it was the gloomiest event of my day—and then I went up-stairs to the library and studied investments and securities for a conscientious hour. There were generally a few rioters around, but they never came into the library, so it was a good place to work. After that, if the night was mellow, I strolled down Madison Avenue past the old Murray Hill Hotel, and over 33rd Street to the Pennsylvania Station.

I began to like New York, the racy, adventurous feel of it at night, and the satisfaction that the constant flicker of men and women and machines gives to the restless eye. I liked to walk up Fifth Avenue and pick out romantic women from the crowd and imagine that in a few minutes I was going to enter into their lives, and no one would ever know or disapprove. Sometimes, in my mind, I followed them to their apartments on the corners of hidden streets, and they turned and smiled back at me before they faded through a door into warm darkness. At the enchanted metropolitan twilight I felt a haunting loneliness sometimes, and felt it in others—poor young clerks who loitered in front of windows waiting until it was time for a solitary restaurant dinner—young clerks in the dusk, wasting the most poignant moments of night and life.

Again at eight o'clock, when the dark lanes of the Forties[2] were five deep with throbbing taxi-cabs, bound for the theatre district, I felt a sinking in my heart. Forms leaned together in the taxis as they waited, and voices sang, and there was laughter from unheard jokes, and lighted cigarettes outlined unintelligible gestures inside. Imagining that I, too, was hurrying toward gayety and sharing their intimate excitement, I wished them well.

For a while I lost sight of Jordan Baker, and then in midsummer I found her again. At first I was flattered to go places with her, because she was a golf champion, and everyone knew her name. Then it was something more. I wasn't actually in love, but I felt a sort of tender curiosity. The bored haughty face that she turned to the world concealed something—most affectations conceal something eventually, even though they don't in the beginning—and one day I found what it was. When we were on a house-party together up in Warwick,[3] she left a borrowed car out

---

1 Private club at Vanderbilt Avenue and 44th Street founded by Yale University's alumni association in 1897.

2 Mid-town Manhattan.

3 Rural getaway 50 miles north of New York City.

in the rain with the top down, and then lied about it—and suddenly I remembered the story about her that had eluded me that night at Daisy's. At her first big golf tournament there was a row that nearly reached the newspapers—a suggestion that she had moved her ball from a bad lie in the semi-final round. The thing approached the proportions of a scandal—then died away. A caddy retracted his statement, and the only other witness admitted that he might have been mistaken. The incident and the name had remained together in my mind.

Jordan Baker instinctively avoided clever, shrewd men, and now I saw that this was because she felt safer on a plane where any divergence from a code would be thought impossible. She was incurably dishonest. She wasn't able to endure being at a disadvantage and, given this unwillingness, I suppose she had begun dealing in subterfuges when she was very young in order to keep that cool, insolent smile turned to the world and yet satisfy the demands of her hard, jaunty body.

It made no difference to me. Dishonesty in a woman is a thing you never blame deeply—I was casually sorry, and then I forgot. It was on that same house party that we had a curious conversation about driving a car. It started because she passed so close to some workmen that our fender flicked a button on one man's coat.

"You're a rotten driver," I protested. "Either you ought to be more careful, or you oughtn't to drive at all."

"I am careful."

"No, you're not."

"Well, other people are," she said lightly.

"What's that got to do with it?"

"They'll keep out of my way," she insisted. "It takes two to make an accident."

"Suppose you met somebody just as careless as yourself."

"I hope I never will," she answered. "I hate careless people. That's why I like you."

Her gray, sun-strained eyes stared straight ahead, but she had deliberately shifted our relations, and for a moment I thought I loved her. But I am slow-thinking and full of interior rules that act as brakes on my desires, and I knew that first I had to get myself definitely out of that tangle back home. I'd been writing letters once a week and signing them: "Love, Nick," and all I could think of was how, when that certain girl played tennis, a faint mustache of perspiration appeared on her upper lip. Nevertheless there was a vague understanding that had to be tactfully broken off before I was free.

Everyone suspects himself of at least one of the cardinal virtues, and this is mine: I am one of the few honest people that I have ever known.

Chapter IV

On Sunday morning while church bells rang in the villages alongshore, the world and its mistress returned to Gatsby's house and twinkled hilariously on his lawn.

"He's a bootlegger," said the young ladies, moving somewhere between his cocktails and his flowers. "One time he killed a man who had found out that he was nephew to Von Hindenburg[1] and second cousin to the devil. Reach me a rose, honey, and pour me a last drop into that there crystal glass."

Once I wrote down on the empty spaces of a time-table the names of those who came to Gatsby's house that summer. It is an old time-table now, disintegrating at its folds, and headed "This schedule in effect July 5th, 1922." But I can still read the gray names, and they will give you a better impression than my generalities of those who accepted Gatsby's hospitality and paid him the subtle tribute of knowing nothing whatever about him.

From East Egg, then, came the Chester Beckers and the Leeches, and a man named Bunsen, whom I knew at Yale, and Doctor Webster Civet, who was drowned last summer up in Maine. And the Hornbeams and the Willie Voltaires, and a whole clan named Blackbuck, who always gathered in a corner and flipped up their noses like goats at whosoever came near. And the Ismays and the Chrysties (or rather Hubert Auerbach and Mr. Chrystie's wife), and Edgar Beaver, whose hair, they say, turned cotton-white one winter afternoon for no good reason at all.

Clarence Endive was from East Egg, as I remember. He came only once, in white knickerbockers, and had a fight with a bum named Etty in the garden. From farther out on the Island came the Cheadles and the O.R.P. Schraeders, and the Stonewall Jackson Abrams of Georgia, and the Fishguards and the Ripley Snells. Snell was there three days before he went to the penitentiary, so

---

1 Paul Von Hindenburg (1847–1934), commander-in-chief of the German army during the last half of World War I, and German president from 1925 to 1934.

drunk out on the gravel drive that Mrs. Ulysses Swett's automobile ran over his right hand. The Dancies came, too, and S.B. Whitebait, who was well over sixty, and Maurice A. Flink, and the Hammerheads, and Beluga the tobacco importer, and Beluga's girls.

From West Egg came the Poles and the Mulreadys and Cecil Roebuck and Cecil Schoen and Gulick the State senator and Newton Orchid, who controlled Films Par Excellence, and Eckhaust and Clyde Cohen and Don S. Schwartze (the son) and Arthur McCarty, all connected with the movies in one way or another. And the Catlips and the Bembergs and G. Earl Muldoon, brother to that Muldoon who afterward strangled his wife. Da Fontano the promoter came there, and Ed Legros and James B. ("Rot-Gut") Ferret and the De Jongs and Ernest Lilly— they came to gamble, and when Ferret wandered into the garden it meant he was cleaned out and Associated Traction would have to fluctuate profitably next day.

A man named Klipspringer was there so often and so long that he became known as "the boarder"—I doubt if he had any other home. Of theatrical people there were Gus Waize and Horace O'Donavan and Lester Myer and George Duckweed and Francis Bull. Also from New York were the Chromes and the Backhyssons and the Dennickers and Russel Betty and the Corrigans and the Kellehers and the Dewars and the Scullys and S.W. Belcher and the Smirkes and the young Quinns, divorced now, and Henry L. Palmetto, who killed himself by jumping in front of a subway train in Times Square.

Benny McClenahan arrived always with four girls. They were never quite the same ones in physical person, but they were so identical one with another that it inevitably seemed they had been there before. I have forgotten their names—Jacqueline, I think, or else Consuela, or Gloria or Judy or June, and their last names were either the melodious names of flowers and months or the sterner ones of the great American capitalists whose cousins, if pressed, they would confess themselves to be.

In addition to all these I can remember that Faustina O'Brien came there at least once and the Baedeker girls and young Brewer, who had his nose shot off in the war, and Mr. Albrucksburger and Miss Haag, his fiancée, and Ardita Fitz-Peters and Mr. P. Jewett, once head of the American Legion,[1] and Miss Claudia Hip, with a man reputed to be her chauffeur, and a

---

1 Veterans' organization formed in 1919.

prince of something, whom we called Duke, and whose name, if I ever knew it, I have forgotten.

All these people came to Gatsby's house in the summer.

At nine o'clock, one morning late in July, Gatsby's gorgeous car lurched up the rocky drive to my door and gave out a burst of melody from its three-noted horn. It was the first time he had called on me, though I had gone to two of his parties, mounted in his hydroplane, and, at his urgent invitation, made frequent use of his beach.

"Good morning, old sport. You're having lunch with me to-day and I thought we'd ride up together."

He was balancing himself on the dashboard of his car with that resourcefulness of movement that is so peculiarly American—that comes, I suppose, with the absence of lifting work or rigid sitting in youth and, even more, with the formless grace of our nervous, sporadic games. This quality was continually breaking through his punctilious manner in the shape of restlessness. He was never quite still; there was always a tapping foot somewhere or the impatient opening and closing of a hand.

He saw me looking with admiration at his car.

"It's pretty, isn't it, old sport?" He jumped off to give me a better view. "Haven't you ever seen it before?"

I'd seen it. Everybody had seen it. It was a rich cream color, bright with nickel, swollen here and there in its monstrous length with triumphant hat-boxes and supper-boxes and tool-boxes, and terraced with a labyrinth of wind-shields that mirrored a dozen suns. Sitting down behind many layers of glass in a sort of green leather conservatory, we started to town.

I had talked with him perhaps half a dozen times in the past month and found, to my disappointment, that he had little to say. So my first impression, that he was a person of some undefined consequence, had gradually faded and he had become simply the proprietor of an elaborate road-house next door.

And then came that disconcerting ride. We hadn't reached West Egg Village before Gatsby began leaving his elegant sentences unfinished and slapping himself indecisively on the knee of his caramel-colored suit.

"Look here, old sport," he broke out surprisingly, "what's your opinion of me, anyhow?"

A little overwhelmed, I began the generalized evasions which that question deserves.

"Well, I'm going to tell you something about my life," he interrupted. "I don't want you to get a wrong idea of me from all these stories you hear."

So he was aware of the bizarre accusations that flavored conversation in his halls.

"I'll tell you God's truth." His right hand suddenly ordered divine retribution to stand by. "I am the son of some wealthy people in the Middle West—all dead now. I was brought up in America but educated at Oxford, because all my ancestors have been educated there for many years. It is a family tradition."

He looked at me sideways—and I knew why Jordan Baker had believed he was lying. He hurried the phrase "educated at Oxford," or swallowed it, or choked on it, as though it had bothered him before. And with this doubt, his whole statement fell to pieces, and I wondered if there wasn't something a little sinister about him, after all.

"What part of the Middle West?" I inquired casually.

"San Francisco."

"I see."

"My family all died and I came into a good deal of money."

His voice was solemn, as if the memory of that sudden extinction of a clan still haunted him. For a moment I suspected that he was pulling my leg, but a glance at him convinced me otherwise.

"After that I lived like a young rajah in all the capitals of Europe—Paris, Venice, Rome—collecting jewels, chiefly rubies, hunting big game, painting a little, things for myself only, and trying to forget something very sad that had happened to me long ago."

With an effort I managed to restrain my incredulous laughter. The very phrases were worn so threadbare that they evoked no image except that of a turbaned "character" leaking sawdust at every pore as he pursued a tiger through the Bois de Boulogne.[1]

"Then came the war, old sport. It was a great relief, and I tried very hard to die, but I seemed to bear an enchanted life. I accepted a commission as first lieutenant when it began. In the Argonne Forest[2] I took two machine-gun detachments so far forward that there was a half mile gap on either side of us where

---

1 Park on the western edge of Paris.
2 Reference to the American-led offensive battles that began on 26 September 1918.

the infantry couldn't advance. We stayed there two days and two nights, a hundred and thirty men with sixteen Lewis guns,[1] and when the infantry came up at last they found the insignia of three German divisions among the piles of dead. I was promoted to be a major, and every Allied government gave me a decoration—even Montenegro,[2] little Montenegro down on the Adriatic Sea!"

Little Montenegro! He lifted up the words and nodded at them—with his smile. The smile comprehended Montenegro's troubled history and sympathized with the brave struggles of the Montenegrin people. It appreciated fully the chain of national circumstances which had elicited this tribute from Montenegro's warm little heart. My incredulity was submerged in fascination now; it was like skimming hastily through a dozen magazines.

He reached in his pocket, and a piece of metal, slung on a ribbon, fell into my palm.

"That's the one from Montenegro."

To my astonishment, the thing had an authentic look. "Orderi di Danilo," ran the circular legend, "Montenegro, Nicolas Rex."

"Turn it."

"Major Jay Gatsby," I read, "For Valour Extraordinary."

"Here's another thing I always carry. A souvenir of Oxford days. It was taken in Trinity Quad[3]—the man on my left is now the Earl of Doncaster."

It was a photograph of half a dozen young men in blazers loafing in an archway through which were visible a host of spires. There was Gatsby, looking a little, not much, younger—with a cricket bat in his hand.

Then it was all true. I saw the skins of tigers flaming in his palace on the Grand Canal;[4] I saw him opening a chest of rubies

---

1 Machine-guns invented by American Colonel Isaac Newton Lewis (1858–1931) in 1911 and used by the Belgians and British before being belatedly adopted by the American forces in 1917.

2 A then-independent kingdom on the Adriatic coastline in the southern part of the Balkan peninsula. It fought on the side of the allies during World War I. Despite popular resistance and the principles laid out at the Treaty of Versailles by American president Woodrow Wilson (1856–1924), it was annexed by Serbia and eventually became part of Yugoslavia after the war. It regained its independence after the breakup of Yugoslavia.

3 Quadrangle, or courtyard, of Trinity College at Oxford.

4 Largest waterway in Venice, Italy.

to ease, with their crimson-lighted depths, the gnawings of his broken heart.

"I'm going to make a big request of you to-day," he said, pocketing his souvenirs with satisfaction, "so I thought you ought to know something about me. I didn't want you to think I was just some nobody. You see, I usually find myself among strangers because I drift here and there trying to forget the sad thing that happened to me." He hesitated. "You'll hear about it this afternoon."

"At lunch?"

"No, this afternoon. I happened to find out that you're taking Miss Baker to tea."

"Do you mean you're in love with Miss Baker?"

"No, old sport, I'm not. But Miss Baker has kindly consented to speak to you about this matter."

I hadn't the faintest idea what "this matter" was, but I was more annoyed than interested. I hadn't asked Jordan to tea in order to discuss Mr. Jay Gatsby. I was sure the request would be something utterly fantastic, and for a moment I was sorry I'd ever set foot upon his overpopulated lawn.

He wouldn't say another word. His correctness grew on him as we neared the city. We passed Port Roosevelt,[1] where there was a glimpse of red-belted ocean-going ships, and sped along a cobbled slum lined with the dark, undeserted saloons of the faded-gilt nineteen-hundreds. Then the valley of ashes opened out on both sides of us, and I had a glimpse of Mrs. Wilson straining at the garage pump with panting vitality as we went by.

With fenders spread like wings we scattered light through half Astoria[2]—only half, for as we twisted among the pillars of the elevated I heard the familiar "jug-jug-*spat!*" of a motorcycle, and a frantic policeman rode alongside.

"All right, old sport," called Gatsby. We slowed down. Taking a white card from his wallet, he waved it before the man's eyes.

"Right you are," agreed the policeman, tipping his cap. "Know you next time, Mr. Gatsby. Excuse *me!*"

"What was that?" I inquired. "The picture of Oxford?"

"I was able to do the commissioner a favor once, and he sends me a Christmas card every year."

---

1 Fictional port.
2 Fitzgerald meant Long Island City, which has an elevated train and is connected to Manhattan by the Queensboro Bridge.

Over the great bridge, with the sunlight through the girders making a constant flicker upon the moving cars, with the city rising up across the river in white heaps and sugar lumps all built with a wish out of non-olfactory money. The city seen from the Queensboro Bridge is always the city seen for the first time, in its first wild promise of all the mystery and the beauty in the world.

A dead man passed us in a hearse heaped with blooms, followed by two carriages with drawn blinds, and by more cheerful carriages for friends. The friends looked out at us with the tragic eyes and short upper lips of southeastern Europe, and I was glad that the sight of Gatsby's splendid car was included in their sombre holiday. As we crossed Blackwell's Island[1] a limousine passed us, driven by a white chauffeur, in which sat three modish negroes, two bucks[2] and a girl. I laughed aloud as the yolks of their eyeballs rolled toward us in haughty rivalry.

"Anything can happen now that we've slid over this bridge," I thought; "anything at all...."

Even Gatsby could happen, without any particular wonder.

Roaring noon. In a well-fanned Forty-second Street cellar I met Gatsby for lunch. Blinking away the brightness of the street outside, my eyes picked him out obscurely in the anteroom, talking to another man.

"Mr. Carraway, this is my friend Mr. Wolfshiem."

A small, flat-nosed Jew[3] raised his large head and regarded me with two fine growths of hair which luxuriated in either nostril. After a moment I discovered his tiny eyes in the half-darkness.

"—So I took one look at him," said Mr. Wolfshiem, shaking my hand earnestly, "and what do you think I did?"

"What?" I inquired politely.

But evidently he was not addressing me, for he dropped my hand and covered Gatsby with his expressive nose.

"I handed the money to Katspaugh and I sid: 'All right,

---

1 Island in the East River between Manhattan and Queens, notorious for its prison, almshouse, workhouse, and insane asylum. It was renamed Welfare Island in 1921.

2 Racist term for young Black men. See the Introduction (p. 41) and Appendices E5–7 for commentary on and further context for this Black presence in the novel.

3 See the Introduction (p. 40) for a discussion of the context for Fitzgerald's use of anti-Semitic descriptors in the novel.

Katspaugh, don't pay him a penny till he shuts his mouth.' He shut it then and there."

Gatsby took an arm of each of us and moved forward into the restaurant, whereupon Mr. Wolfshiem swallowed a new sentence he was starting and lapsed into a somnambulatory abstraction.

"Highballs?" asked the head waiter.

"This is a nice restaurant here," said Mr. Wolfshiem, looking at the Presbyterian nymphs on the ceiling. "But I like across the street better!"

"Yes, highballs," agreed Gatsby, and then to Mr. Wolfshiem: "It's too hot over there."

"Hot and small—yes," said Mr. Wolfshiem, "but full of memories."

"What place is that?" I asked.

"The old Metropole."[1]

"The old Metropole," brooded Mr. Wolfshiem gloomily. "Filled with faces dead and gone. Filled with friends gone now forever. I can't forget so long as I live the night they shot Rosy Rosenthal there. It was six of us at the table, and Rosy had eat and drunk a lot all evening. When it was almost morning the waiter came up to him with a funny look and says somebody wants to speak to him outside. 'All right,' says Rosy, and begins to get up, and I pulled him down in his chair.

"'Let the bastards come in here if they want you, Rosy, but don't you, so help me, move outside this room.'

"It was four o'clock in the morning then, and if we'd of raised the blinds we'd of seen daylight."

"Did he go?" I asked innocently.

"Sure he went." Mr. Wolfshiem's nose flashed at me indignantly. "He turned around in the door and says: 'Don't let that waiter take away my coffee!' Then he went out on the sidewalk, and they shot him three times in his full belly and drove away."

"Four of them were electrocuted," I said, remembering.

"Five, with Becker."[2] His nostrils turned to me in an in-

---

1 Popular hotel restaurant and bar at Broadway and 42nd Street, patronized by showbusiness celebrities and underworld figures.

2 Charles Becker (1869–1915), a New York City police lieutenant who ordered mobsters to gun down gambler Herman "Beansy" Rosenthal (1874–1912) as Rosenthal was in the process of exposing Becker for corruption. Becker was soon implicated in the murder, tried, and executed in 1915.

terested way. "I understand you're looking for a business gonnegtion."

The juxtaposition of these two remarks was startling. Gatsby answered for me:

"Oh, no," he exclaimed, "this isn't the man."

"No?" Mr. Wolfshiem seemed disappointed.

"This is just a friend. I told you we'd talk about that some other time."

"I beg your pardon," said Mr. Wolfshiem, "I had a wrong man."

A succulent hash arrived, and Mr. Wolfshiem, forgetting the more sentimental atmosphere of the old Metropole, began to eat with ferocious delicacy. His eyes, meanwhile, roved very slowly all around the room—he completed the arc by turning to inspect the people directly behind. I think that, except for my presence, he would have taken one short glance beneath our own table.

"Look here, old sport," said Gatsby, leaning toward me, "I'm afraid I made you a little angry this morning in the car."

There was the smile again, but this time I held out against it. "I don't like mysteries," I answered, "and I don't understand why you won't come out frankly and tell me what you want. Why has it all got to come through Miss Baker?"

"Oh, it's nothing underhand," he assured me. "Miss Baker's a great sportswoman, you know, and she'd never do anything that wasn't all right."

Suddenly he looked at his watch, jumped up, and hurried from the room, leaving me with Mr. Wolfshiem at the table.

"He has to telephone," said Mr. Wolfshiem, following him with his eyes. "Fine fellow, isn't he? Handsome to look at and a perfect gentleman."

"Yes."

"He's an Oggsford man."

"Oh!"

"He went to Oggsford College in England. You know Oggsford College?"

"I've heard of it."

"It's one of the most famous colleges in the world."

"Have you known Gatsby for a long time?" I inquired.

"Several years," he answered in a gratified way. "I made the pleasure of his acquaintance just after the war. But I knew I had discovered a man of fine breeding after I talked with him an hour. I said to myself: 'There's the kind of man you'd like to take home and introduce to your mother and sister.'" He paused. "I see you're looking at my cuff buttons."

I hadn't been looking at them, but I did now. They were composed of oddly familiar pieces of ivory.

"Finest specimens of human molars," he informed me.

"Well!" I inspected them. "That's a very interesting idea."

"Yeah." He flipped his sleeves up under his coat. "Yeah, Gatsby's very careful about women. He would never so much as look at a friend's wife."

When the subject of this instinctive trust returned to the table and sat down Mr. Wolfshiem drank his coffee with a jerk and got to his feet.

"I have enjoyed my lunch," he said, "and I'm going to run off from you two young men before I outstay my welcome."

"Don't hurry, Meyer," said Gatsby, without enthusiasm. Mr. Wolfshiem raised his hand in a sort of benediction.

"You're very polite, but I belong to another generation," he announced solemnly. "You sit here and discuss your sports and your young ladies and your—" He supplied an imaginary noun with another wave of his hand. "As for me, I am fifty years old, and I won't impose myself on you any longer."

As he shook hands and turned away his tragic nose was trembling. I wondered if I had said anything to offend him.

"He becomes very sentimental sometimes," explained Gatsby. "This is one of his sentimental days. He's quite a character around New York—a denizen of Broadway."

"Who is he, anyhow, an actor?"

"No."

"A dentist?"

"Meyer Wolfshiem? No, he's a gambler." Gatsby hesitated, then added coolly: "He's the man who fixed the World's Series back in 1919."[1]

"Fixed the World's Series?" I repeated.

The idea staggered me. I remembered, of course, that the World's Series had been fixed in 1919, but if I had thought of it

---

1 Eight members of the heavily favored Chicago White Sox were paid by gamblers to lose the baseball championship series to the Cincinnati Reds. Arnold Rothstein (1882–1928), a businessman and gambler tied to organized crime, was reputed to be the mastermind behind the scheme but was never indicted. See Appendix E2. "World's Series" was the original term for what has since been called the "World Series."

at all I would have thought of it as a thing that merely *happened*, the end of some inevitable chain. It never occurred to me that one man could start to play on the faith of fifty million people— with the single-mindedness of a burglar blowing a safe.

"How did he happen to do that?" I asked after a minute.

"He just saw the opportunity."

"Why isn't he in jail?"

"They can't get him, old sport. He's a smart man."

I insisted on paying the check. As the waiter brought my change I caught sight of Tom Buchanan across the crowded room.

"Come along with me for a minute," I said; "I've got to say hello to someone."

When he saw us Tom jumped up and took half a dozen steps in our direction.

"Where've you been?" he demanded eagerly. "Daisy's furious because you haven't called up."

"This is Mr. Gatsby, Mr. Buchanan."

They shook hands briefly, and a strained, unfamiliar look of embarrassment came over Gatsby's face.

"How've you been, anyhow?" demanded Tom of me. "How'd you happen to come up this far to eat?"

"I've been having lunch with Mr. Gatsby."

I turned toward Mr. Gatsby, but he was no longer there.

One October day in nineteen-seventeen——

(said Jordan Baker that afternoon, sitting up very straight on a straight chair in the tea-garden at the Plaza Hotel)[1]

—I was walking along from one place to another, half on the sidewalks and half on the lawns. I was happier on the lawns because I had on shoes from England with rubber nobs on the soles that bit into the soft ground. I had on a new plaid skirt also that blew a little in the wind, and whenever this happened the red, white, and blue banners in front of all the houses stretched out stiff and said *tut-tut-tut-tut*, in a disapproving way.

The largest of the banners and the largest of the lawns belonged to Daisy Fay's house. She was just eighteen, two years older than me, and by far the most popular of all the young girls in Louisville. She dressed in white, and had a little white

---

1 Luxurious hotel overlooking Central Park on 59th Street.

roadster,[1] and all day long the telephone rang in her house and excited young officers from Camp Taylor demanded the privilege of monopolizing her that night. "Anyways, for an hour!"

When I came opposite her house that morning her white roadster was beside the curb, and she was sitting in it with a lieutenant I had never seen before. They were so engrossed in each other that she didn't see me until I was five feet away.

"Hello, Jordan," she called unexpectedly. "Please come here."

I was flattered that she wanted to speak to me, because of all the older girls I admired her most. She asked me if I was going to the Red Cross and make bandages. I was. Well, then, would I tell them that she couldn't come that day? The officer looked at Daisy while she was speaking, in a way that every young girl wants to be looked at sometime, and because it seemed romantic to me I have remembered the incident ever since. His name was Jay Gatsby, and I didn't lay eyes on him again for over four years—even after I'd met him on Long Island I didn't realize it was the same man.

That was nineteen-seventeen. By the next year I had a few beaux myself, and I began to play in tournaments, so I didn't see Daisy very often. She went with a slightly older crowd—when she went with anyone at all. Wild rumors were circulating about her—how her mother had found her packing her bag one winter night to go to New York and say good-by to a soldier who was going overseas. She was effectually prevented, but she wasn't on speaking terms with her family for several weeks. After that she didn't play around with the soldiers any more, but only with a few flat-footed, short-sighted young men in town, who couldn't get into the army at all.

By the next autumn she was gay again, gay as ever. She had a début after the armistice, and in February she was presumably engaged to a man from New Orleans. In June she married Tom Buchanan of Chicago, with more pomp and circumstance than Louisville ever knew before. He came down with a hundred people in four private cars, and hired a whole floor of the Sealbach Hotel, and the day before the wedding he gave her a string of pearls valued at three hundred and fifty thousand dollars.

I was a bridesmaid. I came into her room half an hour before the bridal dinner, and found her lying on her bed as lovely as the June night in her flowered dress—and as drunk as a monkey. She had a bottle of Sauterne in one hand and a letter in the other.

---

1 Sporty two-seat convertible.

"'Gratulate me," she muttered. "Never had a drink before, but oh how I do enjoy it."

"What's the matter, Daisy?"

I was scared, I can tell you; I'd never seen a girl like that before.

"Here, deares'." She groped around in a waste-basket she had with her on the bed and pulled out the string of pearls. "Take 'em down-stairs and give 'em back to whoever they belong to. Tell 'em all Daisy's change' her mine. Say: 'Daisy's change' her mine!'"

She began to cry—she cried and cried. I rushed out and found her mother's maid, and we locked the door and got her into a cold bath. She wouldn't let go of the letter. She took it into the tub with her and squeezed it up into a wet ball, and only let me leave it in the soap-dish when she saw that it was coming to pieces like snow.

But she didn't say another word. We gave her spirits of ammonia and put ice on her forehead and hooked her back into her dress, and half an hour later, when we walked out of the room, the pearls were around her neck and the incident was over. Next day at five o'clock she married Tom Buchanan without so much as a shiver, and started off on a three months' trip to the South Seas.

I saw them in Santa Barbara when they came back, and I thought I'd never seen a girl so mad about her husband. If he left the room for a minute she'd look around uneasily, and say: "Where's Tom gone?" and wear the most abstracted expression until she saw him coming in the door. She used to sit on the sand with his head in her lap by the hour, rubbing her fingers over his eyes and looking at him with unfathomable delight. It was touching to see them together—it made you laugh in a hushed, fascinated way. That was in August. A week after I left Santa Barbara Tom ran into a wagon on the Ventura road[1] one night, and ripped a front wheel off his car. The girl who was with him got into the papers, too, because her arm was broken—she was one of the chambermaids in the Santa Barbara Hotel.

The next April Daisy had her little girl, and they went to France for a year. I saw them one spring in Cannes, and later in Deauville, and then they came back to Chicago to settle down. Daisy was popular in Chicago, as you know. They moved with a

---

1   California highway connecting the coastal city of Santa Barbara to Los Angeles to the south.

fast crowd, all of them young and rich and wild, but she came out with an absolutely perfect reputation. Perhaps because she doesn't drink. It's a great advantage not to drink among hard-drinking people. You can hold your tongue, and, moreover, you can time any little irregularity of your own so that everybody else is so blind that they don't see or care. Perhaps Daisy never went in for amour at all—and yet there's something in that voice of hers....

Well, about six weeks ago, she heard the name Gatsby for the first time in years. It was when I asked you—do you remember?—if you knew Gatsby in West Egg. After you had gone home she came into my room and woke me up, and said: "What Gatsby?" and when I described him—I was half asleep—she said in the strangest voice that it must be the man she used to know. It wasn't until then that I connected this Gatsby with the officer in her white car.

When Jordan Baker had finished telling all this we had left the Plaza for half an hour and were driving in a victoria[1] through Central Park. The sun had gone down behind the tall apartments of the movie stars in the West Fifties, and the clear voices of little girls, already gathered like crickets on the grass, rose through the hot twilight:

"I'm the Sheik of Araby. Your love belongs to me.
At night when you're asleep
Into your tent I'll creep——"[2]

"It was a strange coincidence," I said.
"But it wasn't a coincidence at all."
"Why not?"
"Gatsby bought that house so that Daisy would be just across the bay."

Then it had not been merely the stars to which he had aspired on that June night. He came alive to me, delivered suddenly from the womb of his purposeless splendor.

---

1 Horse-drawn four-wheeled carriage for two with raised seat for the driver.
2 From the popular 1921 song "The Sheik of Araby," music by Ted Snyder, lyrics by Harry B. Smith and Francis Wheeler, inspired by the hit 1921 movie *The Sheik*, starring Rudolph Valentino and Agnes Ayres.

"He wants to know," continued Jordan, "if you'll invite Daisy to your house some afternoon and then let him come over."

The modesty of the demand shook me. He had waited five years and bought a mansion where he dispensed starlight to casual moths—so that he could "come over" some afternoon to a stranger's garden.

"Did I have to know all this before he could ask such a little thing?"

"He's afraid, he's waited so long. He thought you might be offended. You see, he's a regular tough underneath it all."

Something worried me.

"Why didn't he ask you to arrange a meeting?"

"He wants her to see his house," she explained. "And your house is right next door."

"Oh!"

"I think he half expected her to wander into one of his parties, some night," went on Jordan, "but she never did. Then he began asking people casually if they knew her, and I was the first one he found. It was that night he sent for me at his dance, and you should have heard the elaborate way he worked up to it. Of course, I immediately suggested a luncheon in New York—and I thought he'd go mad:

"'I don't want to do anything out of the way!' he kept saying. 'I want to see her right next door.'

"When I said you were a particular friend of Tom's, he started to abandon the whole idea. He doesn't know very much about Tom, though he says he's read a Chicago paper for years just on the chance of catching a glimpse of Daisy's name."

It was dark now, and as we dipped under a little bridge I put my arm around Jordan's golden shoulder and drew her toward me and asked her to dinner. Suddenly I wasn't thinking of Daisy and Gatsby any more, but of this clean, hard, limited person, who dealt in universal scepticism, and who leaned back jauntily just within the circle of my arm. A phrase began to beat in my ears with a sort of heady excitement: "There are only the pursued, the pursuing, the busy and the tired."

"And Daisy ought to have something in her life," murmured Jordan to me.

"Does she want to see Gatsby?"

"She's not to know about it. Gatsby doesn't want her to know. You're just supposed to invite her to tea."

We passed a barrier of dark trees, and then the façade of Fifty-ninth Street, a block of delicate pale light, beamed down into the park. Unlike Gatsby and Tom Buchanan, I had no girl whose disembodied face floated along the dark cornices and blinding signs, and so I drew up the girl beside me, tightening my arms. Her wan, scornful mouth smiled, and so I drew her up again closer, this time to my face.

Chapter V

When I came home to West Egg that night I was afraid for a moment that my house was on fire. Two o'clock and the whole corner of the peninsula was blazing with light, which fell unreal on the shrubbery and made thin elongating glints upon the roadside wires. Turning a corner, I saw that it was Gatsby's house, lit from tower to cellar.

At first I thought it was another party, a wild rout that had resolved itself into "hide-and-go-seek" or "sardines-in-the-box" with all the house thrown open to the game. But there wasn't a sound. Only wind in the trees, which blew the wires and made the lights go off and on again as if the house had winked into the darkness. As my taxi groaned away I saw Gatsby walking toward me across his lawn.

"Your place looks like the World's Fair," I said.

"Does it?" He turned his eyes toward it absently. "I have been glancing into some of the rooms. Let's go to Coney Island,[1] old sport. In my car."

"It's too late."

"Well, suppose we take a plunge in the swimming-pool? I haven't made use of it all summer."

"I've got to go to bed."

"All right."

He waited, looking at me with suppressed eagerness.

"I talked with Miss Baker," I said after a moment. "I'm going to call up Daisy to-morrow and invite her over here to tea."

"Oh, that's all right," he said carelessly. "I don't want to put you to any trouble."

"What day would suit you?"

"What day would suit *you?*" he corrected me quickly. "I don't want to put you to any trouble, you see."

---

1 Neighborhood of Brooklyn famous by the 1920s for its gaudy, state-of-the-art amusement park.

"How about the day after to-morrow?"

He considered for a moment. Then, with reluctance:

"I want to get the grass cut," he said.

We both looked at the grass—there was a sharp line where my ragged lawn ended and the darker, well-kept expanse of his began. I suspected that he meant my grass.

"There's another little thing," he said uncertainly, and hesitated.

"Would you rather put it off for a few days?" I asked.

"Oh, it isn't about that. At least—" He fumbled with a series of beginnings. "Why, I thought—why, look here, old sport, you don't make much money, do you?"

"Not very much."

This seemed to reassure him and he continued more confidently.

"I thought you didn't, if you'll pardon my—you see, I carry on a little business on the side, a sort of side line, you understand. And I thought that if you don't make very much—You're selling bonds, aren't you, old sport?"

"Trying to."

"Well, this would interest you. It wouldn't take up much of your time and you might pick up a nice bit of money. It happens to be a rather confidential sort of thing."

I realize now that under different circumstances that conversation might have been one of the crises of my life. But, because the offer was obviously and tactlessly for a service to be rendered, I had no choice except to cut him off there.

"I've got my hands full," I said. "I'm much obliged but I couldn't take on any more work."

"You wouldn't have to do any business with Wolfshiem." Evidently he thought that I was shying away from the "gonnegtion" mentioned at lunch, but I assured him he was wrong. He waited a moment longer, hoping I'd begin a conversation, but I was too absorbed to be responsive, so he went unwillingly home.

The evening had made me light-headed and happy; I think I walked into a deep sleep as I entered my front door. So I don't know whether or not Gatsby went to Coney Island, or for how many hours he "glanced into rooms" while his house blazed gaudily on. I called up Daisy from the office next morning, and invited her to come to tea.

"Don't bring Tom," I warned her.

"What?"

"Don't bring Tom."

"Who is 'Tom'?" she asked innocently.

The day agreed upon was pouring rain. At eleven o'clock a man in a raincoat, dragging a lawn-mower, tapped at my front door and said that Mr. Gatsby had sent him over to cut my grass. This reminded me that I had forgotten to tell my Finn to come back, so I drove into West Egg Village to search for her among soggy whitewashed alleys and to buy some cups and lemons and flowers.

The flowers were unnecessary, for at two o'clock a greenhouse arrived from Gatsby's, with innumerable receptacles to contain it. An hour later the front door opened nervously, and Gatsby, in a white flannel suit, silver shirt, and gold-colored tie, hurried in. He was pale, and there were dark signs of sleeplessness beneath his eyes.

"Is everything all right?" he asked immediately.

"The grass looks fine, if that's what you mean."

"What grass?" he inquired blankly. "Oh, the grass in the yard."

He looked out the window at it, but, judging from his expression, I don't believe he saw a thing.

"Looks very good," he remarked vaguely. "One of the papers said they thought the rain would stop about four. I think it was The Journal. Have you got everything you need in the shape of—of tea?"

I took him into the pantry, where he looked a little reproachfully at the Finn. Together we scrutinized the twelve lemon cakes from the delicatessen shop.

"Will they do?" I asked.

"Of course, of course! They're fine!" and he added hollowly, "... old sport."

The rain cooled about half-past three to a damp mist, through which occasional thin drops swam like dew. Gatsby looked with vacant eyes through a copy of Clay's "Economics,"[1] starting at the Finnish tread that shook the kitchen floor, and peering toward the bleared windows from time to time as if a series of invisible but alarming happenings were taking place outside. Finally he got up and informed me, in an uncertain voice, that he was going home.

"Why's that?"

"Nobody's coming to tea. It's too late!" He looked at his watch

---

1 British economist Henry Clay's *Economics: An Introduction for the General Reader*, first published in England in 1916, in the United States in 1918.

as if there was some pressing demand on his time elsewhere. "I can't wait all day."

"Don't be silly; it's just two minutes to four."

He sat down miserably, as if I had pushed him, and simultaneously there was the sound of a motor turning into my lane. We both jumped up, and, a little harrowed myself, I went out into the yard.

Under the dripping bare lilac-trees a large open car was coming up the drive. It stopped. Daisy's face, tipped sideways beneath a three-cornered lavender hat, looked out at me with a bright ecstatic smile.

"Is this absolutely where you live, my dearest one?"

The exhilarating ripple of her voice was a wild tonic in the rain. I had to follow the sound of it for a moment, up and down, with my ear alone, before any words came through. A damp streak of hair lay like a dash of blue paint across her cheek, and her hand was wet with glistening drops as I took it to help her from the car.

"Are you in love with me," she said low in my ear, "or why did I have to come alone?"

"That's the secret of Castle Rackrent.[1] Tell your chauffeur to go far away and spend an hour."

"Come back in an hour, Ferdie." Then in a grave murmur: "His name is Ferdie."

"Does the gasoline affect his nose?"

"I don't think so," she said innocently. "Why?"

We went in. To my overwhelming surprise the living-room was deserted.

"Well, that's funny," I exclaimed.

"What's funny?"

She turned her head as there was a light dignified knocking at the front door. I went out and opened it. Gatsby, pale as death, with his hands plunged like weights in his coat pockets, was standing in a puddle of water glaring tragically into my eyes.

With his hands still in his coat pockets he stalked by me into the hall, turned sharply as if he were on a wire, and disappeared into the living-room. It wasn't a bit funny. Aware of the loud beating of my own heart I pulled the door to against the increasing rain.

---

1 Estate of a family of Anglo-Irish landlords in the novel *Castle Rackrent* (1800) by Maria Edgeworth (1767–1849).

For half a minute there wasn't a sound. Then from the living-room I heard a sort of choking murmur and part of a laugh, followed by Daisy's voice on a clear artificial note:

"I certainly am awfully glad to see you again."

A pause; it endured horribly. I had nothing to do in the hall, so I went into the room.

Gatsby, his hands still in his pockets, was reclining against the mantelpiece in a strained counterfeit of perfect ease, even of boredom. His head leaned back so far that it rested against the face of a defunct mantelpiece clock, and from this position his distraught eyes stared down at Daisy, who was sitting, frightened but graceful, on the edge of a stiff chair.

"We've met before," muttered Gatsby. His eyes glanced momentarily at me, and his lips parted with an abortive attempt at a laugh. Luckily the clock took this moment to tilt dangerously at the pressure of his head, whereupon he turned and caught it with trembling fingers, and set it back in place. Then he sat down, rigidly, his elbow on the arm of the sofa and his chin in his hand.

"I'm sorry about the clock," he said.

My own face had now assumed a deep tropical burn. I couldn't muster up a single commonplace out of the thousand in my head.

"It's an old clock," I told them idiotically.

I think we all believed for a moment that it had smashed in pieces on the floor.

"We haven't met for many years," said Daisy, her voice as matter-of-fact as it could ever be.

"Five years next November."

The automatic quality of Gatsby's answer set us all back at least another minute. I had them both on their feet with the desperate suggestion that they help me make tea in the kitchen when the demoniac Finn brought it in on a tray.

Amid the welcome confusion of cups and cakes a certain physical decency established itself. Gatsby got himself into a shadow and, while Daisy and I talked, looked conscientiously from one to the other of us with tense, unhappy eyes. However, as calmness wasn't an end in itself, I made an excuse at the first possible moment, and got to my feet.

"Where are you going?" demanded Gatsby in immediate alarm.

"I'll be back."

"I've got to speak to you about something before you go."

He followed me wildly into the kitchen, closed the door, and whispered: "Oh, God!" in a miserable way.

"What's the matter?"

"This is a terrible mistake," he said, shaking his head from side to side, "a terrible, terrible mistake."

"You're just embarrassed, that's all," and luckily I added: "Daisy's embarrassed too."

"She's embarrassed?" he repeated incredulously.

"Just as much as you are."

"Don't talk so loud."

"You're acting like a little boy," I broke out impatiently. "Not only that, but you're rude. Daisy's sitting in there all alone."

He raised his hand to stop my words, looked at me with unforgettable reproach, and, opening the door cautiously, went back into the other room.

I walked out the back way—just as Gatsby had when he had made his nervous circuit of the house half an hour before—and ran for a huge black knotted tree, whose massed leaves made a fabric against the rain. Once more it was pouring, and my irregular lawn, well-shaved by Gatsby's gardener, abounded in small muddy swamps and prehistoric marshes. There was nothing to look at from under the tree except Gatsby's enormous house, so I stared at it, like Kant at his church steeple,[1] for half an hour. A brewer had built it early in the "period" craze, a decade before, and there was a story that he'd agreed to pay five years' taxes on all the neighboring cottages if the owners would have their roofs thatched with straw. Perhaps their refusal took the heart out of his plan to Found a Family—he went into an immediate decline. His children sold his house with the black wreath still on the door. Americans, while occasionally willing to be serfs, have always been obstinate about being peasantry.

After half an hour, the sun shone again, and the grocer's automobile rounded Gatsby's drive with the raw material for his servants' dinner—I felt sure he wouldn't eat a spoonful. A maid began opening the upper windows of his house, appeared momentarily in each, and, leaning from a large central bay, spat meditatively into the garden. It was time I went back. While the

---

1 German philosopher Immanuel Kant (1724–1804) of Königsberg reputedly had the habit of staring while deep in thought at the church steeple in view of his study window.

rain continued it had seemed like the murmur of their voices, rising and swelling a little now and then with gusts of emotion. But in the new silence I felt that silence had fallen within the house too.

I went in—after making every possible noise in the kitchen, short of pushing over the stove—but I don't believe they heard a sound. They were sitting at either end of the couch, looking at each other as if some question had been asked, or was in the air, and every vestige of embarrassment was gone. Daisy's face was smeared with tears, and when I came in she jumped up and began wiping at it with her handkerchief before a mirror. But there was a change in Gatsby that was simply confounding. He literally glowed; without a word or a gesture of exultation a new well-being radiated from him and filled the little room.

"Oh, hello, old sport," he said, as if he hadn't seen me for years. I thought for a moment he was going to shake hands.

"It's stopped raining."

"Has it?" When he realized what I was talking about, that there were twinkle-bells of sunshine in the room, he smiled like a weather man, like an ecstatic patron of recurrent light, and repeated the news to Daisy. "What do you think of that? It's stopped raining."

"I'm glad, Jay." Her throat, full of aching, grieving beauty, told only of her unexpected joy.

"I want you and Daisy to come over to my house," he said, "I'd like to show her around."

"You're sure you want me to come?"

"Absolutely, old sport."

Daisy went up-stairs to wash her face—too late I thought with humiliation of my towels—while Gatsby and I waited on the lawn.

"My house looks well, doesn't it?" he demanded. "See how the whole front of it catches the light."

I agreed that it was splendid.

"Yes." His eyes went over it, every arched door and square tower. "It took me just three years to earn the money that bought it."

"I thought you inherited your money."

"I did, old sport," he said automatically, "but I lost most of it in the big panic—the panic of the war."

I think he hardly knew what he was saying, for when I asked him what business he was in he answered: "That's my affair," before he realized that it wasn't an appropriate reply.

"Oh, I've been in several things," he corrected himself. "I was in the drug business and then I was in the oil business. But I'm not in either one now." He looked at me with more attention. "Do you mean you've been thinking over what I proposed the other night?"

Before I could answer, Daisy came out of the house and two rows of brass buttons on her dress gleamed in the sunlight.

"That huge place *there?*" she cried pointing.

"Do you like it?"

"I love it, but I don't see how you live there all alone."

"I keep it always full of interesting people, night and day. People who do interesting things. Celebrated people."

Instead of taking the short cut along the Sound we went down to the road and entered by the big postern. With enchanting murmurs Daisy admired this aspect or that of the feudal silhouette against the sky, admired the gardens, the sparkling odor of jonquils and the frothy odor of hawthorn and plum blossoms and the pale gold odor of kiss-me-at-the-gate. It was strange to reach the marble steps and find no stir of bright dresses in and out the door, and hear no sound but bird voices in the trees.

And inside, as we wandered through Marie Antoinette music-rooms and Restoration Salons,[1] I felt that there were guests concealed behind every couch and table, under orders to be breathlessly silent until we had passed through. As Gatsby closed the door of "the Merton College Library"[2] I could have sworn I heard the owl-eyed man break into ghostly laughter.

We went up-stairs, through period bedrooms swathed in rose and lavender silk and vivid with new flowers, through dressing-rooms and poolrooms, and bathrooms with sunken baths—intruding into one chamber where a dishevelled man in pajamas was doing liver exercises on the floor. It was Mr. Klipspringer, the "boarder." I had seen him wandering hungrily about the beach that morning. Finally we came to Gatsby's own apartment, a bedroom and a bath, and an Adam's study,[3] where we sat down and drank a glass of some Chartreuse he took from a cupboard in the wall.

He hadn't once ceased looking at Daisy, and I think he revalued everything in his house according to the measure of response

---

1   Rooms decorated in period styles.

2   Merton College Library at Oxford University, founded in 1373.

3   Referring to the neo-classical style of Scottish architects, interior decorators, and furniture designers Robert and James Adams (1728–92 and 1730–94, respectively).

it drew from her well-loved eyes. Sometimes, too, he stared around at his possessions in a dazed way, as though in her actual and astounding presence none of it was any longer real. Once he nearly toppled down a flight of stairs.

His bedroom was the simplest room of all—except where the dresser was garnished with a toilet set[1] of pure dull gold. Daisy took the brush with delight, and smoothed her hair, whereupon Gatsby sat down and shaded his eyes and began to laugh.

"It's the funniest thing, old sport," he said hilariously. "I can't—When I try to——"

He had passed visibly through two states and was entering upon a third. After his embarrassment and his unreasoning joy he was consumed with wonder at her presence. He had been full of the idea so long, dreamed it right through to the end, waited with his teeth set, so to speak, at an inconceivable pitch of intensity. Now, in the reaction, he was running down like an overwound clock.

Recovering himself in a minute he opened for us two hulking patent cabinets which held his massed suits and dressing-gowns and ties, and his shirts, piled like bricks in stacks a dozen high.

"I've got a man in England who buys me clothes. He sends over a selection of things at the beginning of each season, spring and fall."

He took out a pile of shirts and began throwing them, one by one, before us, shirts of sheer linen and thick silk and fine flannel, which lost their folds as they fell and covered the table in many colored disarray. While we admired he brought more and the soft rich heap mounted higher—shirts with stripes and scrolls and plaids in coral and apple-green and lavender and faint orange, with monograms of Indian blue. Suddenly, with a strained sound, Daisy bent her head into the shirts and began to cry stormily.

"They're such beautiful shirts," she sobbed, her voice muffled in the thick folds. "It makes me sad because I've never seen such—such beautiful shirts before."

After the house, we were to see the grounds and the swimming-pool, and the hydroplane and the midsummer flowers—but outside Gatsby's window it began to rain again, so we stood in a row looking at the corrugated surface of the Sound.

---

1   A set of grooming tools.

"If it wasn't for the mist we could see your home across the bay," said Gatsby. "You always have a green light that burns all night at the end of your dock."

Daisy put her arm through his abruptly, but he seemed absorbed in what he had just said. Possibly it had occurred to him that the colossal significance of that light had now vanished forever. Compared to the great distance that had separated him from Daisy it had seemed very near to her, almost touching her. It had seemed as close as a star to the moon. Now it was again a green light on a dock. His count of enchanted objects had diminished by one.

I began to walk about the room, examining various indefinite objects in the half darkness. A large photograph of an elderly man in yachting costume attracted me, hung on the wall over his desk.

"Who's this?"

"That? That's Mr. Dan Cody, old sport."

The name sounded faintly familiar.

"He's dead now. He used to be my best friend years ago."

There was a small picture of Gatsby, also in yachting costume, on the bureau—Gatsby with his head thrown back defiantly—taken apparently when he was about eighteen.

"I adore it," exclaimed Daisy. "The pompadour![1] You never told me you had a pompadour—or a yacht."

"Look at this," said Gatsby quickly. "Here's a lot of clippings—about you."

They stood side by side examining it. I was going to ask to see the rubies when the phone rang, and Gatsby took up the receiver.

"Yes.... Well, I can't talk now.... I can't talk now, old sport.... I said a *small* town.... He must know what a small town is.... Well, he's no use to us if Detroit is his idea of a small town...."

He rang off.

"Come here *quick!*" cried Daisy at the window.

The rain was still falling, but the darkness had parted in the west, and there was a pink and golden billow of foamy clouds above the sea.

"Look at that," she whispered, and then after a moment: "I'd like to just get one of those pink clouds and put you in it and push you around."

I tried to go then, but they wouldn't hear of it; perhaps my presence made them feel more satisfactorily alone.

---

1   Hairstyle in which hair is combed high in the front.

"I know what we'll do," said Gatsby, "we'll have Klipspringer play the piano."

He went out of the room calling "Ewing!" and returned in a few minutes accompanied by an embarrassed, slightly worn young man, with shell-rimmed glasses and scanty blond hair. He was now decently clothed in a "sport shirt," open at the neck, sneakers, and duck[1] trousers of a nebulous hue.

"Did we interrupt your exercises?" inquired Daisy politely.

"I was asleep," cried Mr. Klipspringer, in a spasm of embarrassment. "That is, I'd *been* asleep. Then I got up ..."

"Klipspringer plays the piano," said Gatsby, cutting him off. "Don't you, Ewing, old sport?"

"I don't play well. I don't—I hardly play at all. I'm all out of prac——"

"We'll go down-stairs," interrupted Gatsby. He flipped a switch. The gray windows disappeared as the house glowed full of light.

In the music-room Gatsby turned on a solitary lamp beside the piano. He lit Daisy's cigarette from a trembling match, and sat down with her on a couch far across the room, where there was no light save what the gleaming floor bounced in from the hall.

When Klipspringer had played "The Love Nest"[2] he turned around on the bench and searched unhappily for Gatsby in the gloom.

"I'm all out of practice, you see. I told you I couldn't play. I'm all out of prac——"

"Don't talk so much, old sport," commanded Gatsby. "Play!"

> "In the morning,
>   In the evening,
>   Ain't we got fun——"

Outside the wind was loud and there was a faint flow of thunder along the Sound. All the lights were going on in West Egg now; the electric trains, men-carrying, were plunging home through the rain from New York. It was the hour of a profound human change, and excitement was generating in the air.

---

1 Light durable cotton.

2 Popular 1920 song, music by Louis A. Hirsch, lyrics by Otto Harbach, from the musical comedy *Mary*.

"One thing's sure and nothing's surer
The rich get richer and the poor get—children.
   In the meantime,
   In between time——"[1]

As I went over to say good-by I saw that the expression of bewilderment had come back into Gatsby's face, as though a faint doubt had occurred to him as to the quality of his present happiness. Almost five years! There must have been moments even that afternoon when Daisy tumbled short of his dreams— not through her own fault, but because of the colossal vitality of his illusion. It had gone beyond her, beyond everything. He had thrown himself into it with a creative passion, adding to it all the time, decking it out with every bright feather that drifted his way. No amount of fire or freshness can challenge what a man will store up in his ghostly heart.

As I watched him he adjusted himself a little, visibly. His hand took hold of hers, and as she said something low in his ear he turned toward her with a rush of emotion. I think that voice held him most, with its fluctuating, feverish warmth, because it couldn't be over-dreamed—that voice was a deathless song.

They had forgotten me, but Daisy glanced up and held out her hand; Gatsby didn't know me now at all. I looked once more at them and they looked back at me, remotely, possessed by intense life. Then I went out of the room and down the marble steps into the rain, leaving them there together.

Chapter VI

About this time an ambitious young reporter from New York arrived one morning at Gatsby's door and asked him if he had anything to say.

"Anything to say about what?" inquired Gatsby politely.

"Why—any statement to give out."

It transpired after a confused five minutes that the man had heard Gatsby's name around his office in a connection which he either wouldn't reveal or didn't fully understand. This was his day off and with laudable initiative he had hurried out "to see."

---

1 From the popular 1921 song "Ain't We Got Fun," music and lyrics by Richard A. Whiting.

It was a random shot, and yet the reporter's instinct was right. Gatsby's notoriety, spread about by the hundreds who had accepted his hospitality and so become authorities upon his past, had increased all summer until he fell just short of being news. Contemporary legends such as the "underground pipe-line to Canada"[1] attached themselves to him, and there was one persistent story that he didn't live in a house at all, but in a boat that looked like a house and was moved secretly up and down the Long Island shore. Just why these inventions were a source of satisfaction to James Gatz of North Dakota, isn't easy to say.

James Gatz—that was really, or at least legally, his name. He had changed it at the age of seventeen and at the specific moment that witnessed the beginning of his career—when he saw Dan Cody's yacht drop anchor over the most insidious flat on Lake Superior. It was James Gatz who had been loafing along the beach that afternoon in a torn green jersey and a pair of canvas pants, but it was already Jay Gatsby who borrowed a rowboat, pulled out to the *Tuolomee*, and informed Cody that a wind might catch him and break him up in half an hour.

I suppose he'd had the name ready for a long time, even then. His parents were shiftless and unsuccessful farm people—his imagination had never really accepted them as his parents at all. The truth was that Jay Gatsby of West Egg, Long Island, sprang from his Platonic[2] conception of himself. He was a son of God—a phrase which, if it means anything, means just that—and he must be about His Father's business,[3] the service of a vast, vulgar, and meretricious beauty. So he invented just the sort of Jay Gatsby that a seventeen year-old boy would be likely to invent, and to this conception he was faithful to the end.

For over a year he had been beating his way along the south shore of Lake Superior as a clam-digger and a salmon-fisher or in any other capacity that brought him food and bed. His brown, hardening body lived naturally through the half-fierce, half-lazy work of the bracing days. He knew women early, and since they

---

1 Canada was a primary source of bootleg liquor, both by land and by sea.

2 Ideal.

3 Refers to Luke 2:41–52. Searching anxiously for their missing son, Joseph and Mary find the twelve-year-old Jesus discoursing with his teachers in the temple and admonish him. Luke 2:49: And he said to them: How is it that you sought me? did you not know, that I must be about my Father's business?

spoiled him he became contemptuous of them, of young virgins because they were ignorant, of the others because they were hysterical about things which in his overwhelming self-absorption he took for granted.

But his heart was in a constant, turbulent riot. The most grotesque and fantastic conceits haunted him in his bed at night. A universe of ineffable gaudiness spun itself out in his brain while the clock ticked on the wash-stand and the moon soaked with wet light his tangled clothes upon the floor. Each night he added to the pattern of his fancies until drowsiness closed down upon some vivid scene with an oblivious embrace. For a while these reveries provided an outlet for his imagination; they were a satisfactory hint of the unreality of reality, a promise that the rock of the world was founded securely on a fairy's wing.

An instinct toward his future glory had led him, some months before, to the small Lutheran College of St. Olaf's in southern Minnesota.[1] He stayed there two weeks, dismayed at its ferocious indifference to the drums of his destiny, to destiny itself, and despising the janitor's work with which he was to pay his way through. Then he drifted back to Lake Superior, and he was still searching for something to do on the day that Dan Cody's yacht dropped anchor in the shallows alongshore.

Cody was fifty years old then, a product of the Nevada silver fields, of the Yukon, of every rush for metal since seventy-five. The transactions in Montana copper that made him many times a millionaire found him physically robust but on the verge of soft-mindedness, and, suspecting this, an infinite number of women tried to separate him from his money. The none too savory ramifications by which Ella Kaye, the newspaper woman, played Madame de Maintenon[2] to his weakness and sent him to sea in a yacht, were common knowledge to the turgid sub-journalism of 1902. He had been coasting along all too hospitable shores for five years when he turned up as James Gatz's destiny in Little Girl Bay.

To young Gatz, resting on his oars and looking up at the railed deck, that yacht represented all the beauty and glamour in the world. I suppose he smiled at Cody—he had probably discovered that people liked him when he smiled. At any rate Cody asked

---

1   Located in Northfield, south of Minneapolis-St. Paul.

2   Françoise d'Aubigné, Marquise de Maintenon (1636–1719), influential second wife of France's King Louis XIV (r. 1643–1715).

him a few questions (one of them elicited the brand new name) and found that he was quick and extravagantly ambitious. A few days later he took him to Duluth[1] and bought him a blue coat, six pair of white duck trousers, and a yachting cap. And when the *Tuolomee* left for the West Indies and the Barbary Coast[2] Gatsby left too.

He was employed in a vague personal capacity—while he remained with Cody he was in turn steward, mate, skipper, secretary, and even jailor, for Dan Cody sober knew what lavish doings Dan Cody drunk might soon be about, and he provided for such contingencies by reposing more and more trust in Gatsby. The arrangement lasted five years, during which the boat went three times around the Continent. It might have lasted indefinitely except for the fact that Ella Kaye came on board one night in Boston and a week later Dan Cody inhospitably died.

I remember the portrait of him up in Gatsby's bedroom, a gray, florid man with a hard, empty face—the pioneer debauchee, who during one phase of American life brought back to the Eastern seaboard the savage violence of the frontier brothel and saloon. It was indirectly due to Cody that Gatsby drank so little. Sometimes in the course of gay parties women used to rub champagne into his hair; for himself he formed the habit of letting liquor alone.

And it was from Cody that he inherited money—a legacy of twenty-five thousand dollars. He didn't get it. He never understood the legal device that was used against him, but what remained of the millions went intact to Ella Kaye. He was left with his singularly appropriate education; the vague contour of Jay Gatsby had filled out to the substantiality of a man.

He told me all this very much later, but I've put it down here with the idea of exploding those first wild rumors about his antecedents, which weren't even faintly true. Moreover he told it to me at a time of confusion, when I had reached the point of believing everything and nothing about him. So I take advantage of this short halt, while Gatsby, so to speak, caught his breath, to clear this set of misconceptions away.

---

1 Port city on Lake Superior in northeast Minnesota.
2 Probably the saloon and brothel district in old San Francisco, as the yacht travels "around the Continent."

It was a halt, too, in my association with his affairs. For several weeks I didn't see him or hear his voice on the phone—mostly I was in New York, trotting around with Jordan and trying to ingratiate myself with her senile aunt—but finally I went over to his house one Sunday afternoon. I hadn't been there two minutes when somebody brought Tom Buchanan in for a drink. I was startled, naturally, but the really surprising thing was that it hadn't happened before.

They were a party of three on horseback—Tom and a man named Sloane and a pretty woman in a brown riding-habit, who had been there previously.

"I'm delighted to see you," said Gatsby, standing on his porch. "I'm delighted that you dropped in."

As though they cared!

"Sit right down. Have a cigarette or a cigar." He walked around the room quickly, ringing bells. "I'll have something to drink for you in just a minute."

He was profoundly affected by the fact that Tom was there. But he would be uneasy anyhow until he had given them something, realizing in a vague way that that was all they came for. Mr. Sloane wanted nothing. A lemonade? No, thanks. A little champagne? Nothing at all, thanks.... I'm sorry——

"Did you have a nice ride?"

"Very good roads around here."

"I suppose the automobiles——"

"Yeah."

Moved by an irresistible impulse, Gatsby turned to Tom, who had accepted the introduction as a stranger.

"I believe we've met somewhere before, Mr. Buchanan."

"Oh, yes," said Tom, gruffly polite, but obviously not remembering. "So we did. I remember very well."

"About two weeks ago."

"That's right. You were with Nick here."

"I know your wife," continued Gatsby, almost aggressively.

"That so?"

Tom turned to me.

"You live near here, Nick?"

"Next door."

"That so?"

Mr. Sloane didn't enter into the conversation, but lounged back haughtily in his chair; the woman said nothing either—until unexpectedly, after two highballs, she became cordial.

"We'll all come over to your next party, Mr. Gatsby," she suggested. "What do you say?"

"Certainly; I'd be delighted to have you."

"Be ver' nice," said Mr. Sloane, without gratitude. "Well—think ought to be starting home."

"Please don't hurry," Gatsby urged them. He had control of himself now, and he wanted to see more of Tom. "Why don't you—why don't you stay for supper? I wouldn't be surprised if some other people dropped in from New York."

"You come to supper with *me*," said the lady enthusiastically. "Both of you."

This included me. Mr. Sloane got to his feet.

"Come along," he said—but to her only.

"I mean it," she insisted. "I'd love to have you. Lots of room."

Gatsby looked at me questioningly. He wanted to go, and he didn't see that Mr. Sloane had determined he shouldn't.

"I'm afraid I won't be able to," I said.

"Well, you come," she urged, concentrating on Gatsby.

Mr. Sloane murmured something close to her ear.

"We won't be late if we start now," she insisted aloud.

"I haven't got a horse," said Gatsby. "I used to ride in the army, but I've never bought a horse. I'll have to follow you in my car. Excuse me for just a minute."

The rest of us walked out on the porch, where Sloane and the lady began an impassioned conversation aside.

"My God, I believe the man's coming," said Tom. "Doesn't he know she doesn't want him?"

"She says she does want him."

"She has a big dinner party and he won't know a soul there." He frowned. "I wonder where in the devil he met Daisy. By God, I may be old-fashioned in my ideas, but women run around too much these days to suit me. They meet all kinds of crazy fish."

Suddenly Mr. Sloane and the lady walked down the steps and mounted their horses.

"Come on," said Mr. Sloane to Tom, "we're late. We've got to go." And then to me: "Tell him we couldn't wait, will you?"

Tom and I shook hands, the rest of us exchanged a cool nod, and they trotted quickly down the drive, disappearing under the August foliage just as Gatsby, with hat and light overcoat in hand, came out the front door.

Tom was evidently perturbed at Daisy's running around alone, for on the following Saturday night he came with her to Gatsby's party. Perhaps his presence gave the evening its peculiar quality of oppressiveness—it stands out in my memory from Gatsby's other parties that summer. There were the same people, or at least the same sort of people, the same profusion of champagne, the same many-colored, many-keyed commotion, but I felt an unpleasantness in the air, a pervading harshness that hadn't been there before. Or perhaps I had merely grown used to it, grown to accept West Egg as a world complete in itself, with its own standards and its own great figures, second to nothing because it had no consciousness of being so, and now I was looking at it again, through Daisy's eyes. It is invariably saddening to look through new eyes at things upon which you have expended your own powers of adjustment.

They arrived at twilight, and, as we strolled out among the sparkling hundreds, Daisy's voice was playing murmurous tricks in her throat.

"These things excite me *so*," she whispered. "If you want to kiss me any time during the evening, Nick, just let me know and I'll be glad to arrange it for you. Just mention my name. Or present a green card. I'm giving out green——"

"Look around," suggested Gatsby.

"I'm looking around. I'm having a marvellous——"

"You must see the faces of many people you've heard about."

Tom's arrogant eyes roamed the crowd.

"We don't go around very much," he said; "in fact, I was just thinking I don't know a soul here."

"Perhaps you know that lady." Gatsby indicated a gorgeous, scarcely human orchid of a woman who sat in state under a white-plum tree. Tom and Daisy stared, with that peculiarly unreal feeling that accompanies the recognition of a hitherto ghostly celebrity of the movies.

"She's lovely," said Daisy.

"The man bending over her is her director."

He took them ceremoniously from group to group:

"Mrs. Buchanan ... and Mr. Buchanan——" After an instant's hesitation he added: "the polo player."

"Oh no," objected Tom quickly, "not me."

But evidently the sound of it pleased Gatsby for Tom remained "the polo player" for the rest of the evening.

"I've never met so many celebrities," Daisy exclaimed, "I liked that man—what was his name?—with the sort of blue nose."

Gatsby identified him, adding that he was a small producer.

"Well, I liked him anyhow."

"I'd a little rather not be the polo player," said Tom pleasantly, "I'd rather look at all these famous people in—in oblivion."

Daisy and Gatsby danced. I remember being surprised by his graceful, conservative fox-trot—I had never seen him dance before. Then they sauntered over to my house and sat on the steps for half an hour, while at her request I remained watchfully in the garden. "In case there's a fire or a flood," she explained, "or any act of God."

Tom appeared from his oblivion as we were sitting down to supper together. "Do you mind if I eat with some people over here?" he said. "A fellow's getting off some funny stuff."

"Go ahead," answered Daisy genially, "and if you want to take down any addresses here's my little gold pencil...." She looked around after a moment and told me the girl was "common but pretty," and I knew that except for the half-hour she'd been alone with Gatsby she wasn't having a good time.

We were at a particularly tipsy table. That was my fault— Gatsby had been called to the phone, and I'd enjoyed these same people only two weeks before. But what had amused me then turned septic on the air now.

"How do you feel, Miss Baedeker?"

The girl addressed was trying, unsuccessfully, to slump against my shoulder. At this inquiry she sat up and opened her eyes.

"Wha'?"

A massive and lethargic woman, who had been urging Daisy to play golf with her at the local club to-morrow, spoke in Miss Baedeker's defence:

"Oh, she's all right now. When she's had five or six cocktails she always starts screaming like that. I tell her she ought to leave it alone."

"I do leave it alone," affirmed the accused hollowly.

"We heard you yelling, so I said to Doc Civet here: 'There's somebody that needs your help, Doc.'"

"She's much obliged, I'm sure," said another friend, without gratitude, "but you got her dress all wet when you stuck her head in the pool."

"Anything I hate is to get my head stuck in a pool," mumbled Miss Baedeker. "They almost drowned me once over in New Jersey."

"Then you ought to leave it alone," countered Doctor Civet.

"Speak for yourself!" cried Miss Baedeker violently. "Your hand shakes. I wouldn't let you operate on me!"

It was like that. Almost the last thing I remember was standing with Daisy and watching the moving-picture director and his Star. They were still under the white-plum tree and their faces were touching except for a pale, thin ray of moonlight between. It occurred to me that he had been very slowly bending toward her all evening to attain this proximity, and even while I watched I saw him stoop one ultimate degree and kiss at her cheek.

"I like her," said Daisy, "I think she's lovely."

But the rest offended her—and inarguably, because it wasn't a gesture but an emotion. She was appalled by West Egg, this unprecedented "place" that Broadway had begotten upon a Long Island fishing village—appalled by its raw vigor that chafed under the old euphemisms and by the too obtrusive fate that herded its inhabitants along a short-cut from nothing to nothing. She saw something awful in the very simplicity she failed to understand.

I sat on the front steps with them while they waited for their car. It was dark here in front; only the bright door sent ten square feet of light volleying out into the soft black morning. Sometimes a shadow moved against a dressing-room blind above, gave way to another shadow, an indefinite procession of shadows, who rouged and powdered in an invisible glass.

"Who is this Gatsby anyhow?" demanded Tom suddenly. "Some big bootlegger?"[1]

"Where'd you hear that?" I inquired.

"I didn't hear it. I imagined it. A lot of these newly rich people are just big bootleggers you know."

"Not Gatsby," I said shortly.

He was silent for a moment. The pebbles of the drive crunched under his feet.

"Well, he certainly must have strained himself to get this menagerie together."

A breeze stirred the gray haze of Daisy's fur collar.

"At least they're more interesting than the people we know," she said with an effort.

"You didn't look so interested."

"Well, I was."

Tom laughed and turned to me.

---

1 Seller of illegal alcohol; see Appendix D3 for a satiric contemporary account of the wealth and respectability to be gained through this trade.

"Did you notice Daisy's face when that girl asked her to put her under a cold shower?"

Daisy began to sing with the music in a husky, rhythmic whisper, bringing out a meaning in each word that it had never had before and would never have again. When the melody rose her voice broke up sweetly, following it, in a way contralto voices have, and each change tipped out a little of her warm human magic upon the air.

"Lots of people come who haven't been invited," she said suddenly. "That girl hadn't been invited. They simply force their way in and he's too polite to object."

"I'd like to know who he is and what he does," insisted Tom. "And I think I'll make a point of finding out."

"I can tell you right now," she answered. "He owned some drug-stores, a lot of drug-stores. He built them up himself."

The dilatory limousine came rolling up the drive. "Good night, Nick," said Daisy.

Her glance left me and sought the lighted top of the steps, where "Three o'Clock in the Morning," a neat, sad little waltz of that year,[1] was drifting out the open door. After all, in the very casualness of Gatsby's party there were romantic possibilities totally absent from her world. What was it up there in the song that seemed to be calling her back inside? What would happen now in the dim, incalculable hours? Perhaps some unbelievable guest would arrive, a person infinitely rare and to be marvelled at, some authentically radiant young girl who with one fresh glance at Gatsby, one moment of magical encounter, would blot out those five years of unwavering devotion.

I stayed late that night, Gatsby asked me to wait until he was free, and I lingered in the garden until the inevitable swimming party had run up, chilled and exalted, from the black beach, until the lights were extinguished in the guest-rooms overhead. When he came down the steps at last the tanned skin was drawn unusually tight on his face, and his eyes were bright and tired.

"She didn't like it," he said immediately.

"Of course she did."

"She didn't like it," he insisted. "She didn't have a good time."

---

1 Actually published in 1919, the song was popular in 1921; music by Julián Robledo, lyrics by Dorothy Terriss.

He was silent, and I guessed at his unutterable depression.

"I feel far away from her," he said. "It's hard to make her understand."

"You mean about the dance?"

"The dance?" He dismissed all the dances he had given with a snap of his fingers. "Old sport, the dance is unimportant."

He wanted nothing less of Daisy than that she should go to Tom and say: "I never loved you." After she had obliterated four years with that sentence they could decide upon the more practical measures to be taken. One of them was that, after she was free, they were to go back to Louisville and be married from her house—just as if it were five years ago.

"And she doesn't understand," he said. "She used to be able to understand. We'd sit for hours——"

He broke off and began to walk up and down a desolate path of fruit rinds and discarded favors and crushed flowers.

"I wouldn't ask too much of her," I ventured. "You can't repeat the past."

"Can't repeat the past?" he cried incredulously. "Why of course you can!"

He looked around him wildly, as if the past were lurking here in the shadow of his house, just out of reach of his hand.

"I'm going to fix everything just the way it was before," he said, nodding determinedly. "She'll see."

He talked a lot about the past, and I gathered that he wanted to recover something, some idea of himself perhaps, that had gone into loving Daisy. His life had been confused and disordered since then, but if he could once return to a certain starting place and go over it all slowly, he could find out what that thing was....

... One autumn night, five years before, they had been walking down the street when the leaves were falling, and they came to a place where there were no trees and the sidewalk was white with moonlight. They stopped here and turned toward each other. Now it was a cool night with that mysterious excitement in it which comes at the two changes of the year. The quiet lights in the houses were humming out into the darkness and there was a stir and bustle among the stars. Out of the corner of his eye Gatsby saw that the blocks of the sidewalks really formed a ladder and mounted to a secret place above the trees—he could climb to it, if he climbed alone, and once there he could suck on the pap of life, gulp down the incomparable milk of wonder.

His heart beat faster and faster as Daisy's white face came up to his own. He knew that when he kissed this girl, and forever wed his unutterable visions to her perishable breath, his mind would never romp again like the mind of God. So he waited, listening for a moment longer to the tuning-fork that had been struck upon a star. Then he kissed her. At his lips' touch she blossomed for him like a flower and the incarnation was complete.

Through all he said, even through his appalling sentimentality, I was reminded of something—an elusive rhythm, a fragment of lost words, that I had heard somewhere a long time ago. For a moment a phrase tried to take shape in my mouth and my lips parted like a dumb man's, as though there was more struggling upon them than a wisp of startled air. But they made no sound, and what I had almost remembered was uncommunicable forever.

Chapter VII

It was when curiosity about Gatsby was at its highest that the lights in his house failed to go on one Saturday night—and, as obscurely as it had begun, his career as Trimalchio[1] was over. Only gradually did I become aware that the automobiles which turned expectantly into his drive stayed for just a minute and then drove sulkily away. Wondering if he were sick I went over to find out—an unfamiliar butler with a villainous face squinted at me suspiciously from the door.

"Is Mr. Gatsby sick?"

"Nope." After a pause he added "sir" in a dilatory, grudging way.

"I hadn't seen him around, and I was rather worried. Tell him Mr. Carraway came over."

"Who?" he demanded rudely.

"Carraway."

"Carraway. All right, I'll tell him."

Abruptly he slammed the door.

My Finn informed me that Gatsby had dismissed every servant in his house a week ago and replaced them with half a dozen others, who never went into West Egg Village to be bribed

---

1 A wealthy ex-slave who gives a lavish, alcoholic banquet in the *Satyricon*, a satiric treatment of a decadent Roman Empire by Petronius (c. 27–66 CE). See Introduction (p. 13) for *The Great Gatsby*'s indebtedness to the *Satyricon*.

by the tradesmen, but ordered moderate supplies over the telephone. The grocery boy reported that the kitchen looked like a pigsty, and the general opinion in the village was that the new people weren't servants at all.

Next day Gatsby called me on the phone.

"Going away?" I inquired.

"No, old sport."

"I hear you fired all your servants."

"I wanted somebody who wouldn't gossip. Daisy comes over quite often—in the afternoons."

So the whole caravansary[1] had fallen in like a card house at the disapproval in her eyes.

"They're some people Wolfshiem wanted to do something for. They're all brothers and sisters. They used to run a small hotel."

"I see."

He was calling up at Daisy's request—would I come to lunch at her house to-morrow? Miss Baker would be there. Half an hour later Daisy herself telephoned and seemed relieved to find that I was coming. Something was up. And yet I couldn't believe that they would choose this occasion for a scene—especially for the rather harrowing scene that Gatsby had outlined in the garden.

The next day was broiling, almost the last, certainly the warmest, of the summer. As my train emerged from the tunnel into sunlight, only the hot whistles of the National Biscuit Company broke the simmering hush at noon. The straw seats of the car hovered on the edge of combustion; the woman next to me perspired delicately for a while into her white shirtwaist,[2] and then, as her newspaper dampened under her fingers, lapsed despairingly into deep heat with a desolate cry. Her pocket-book slapped to the floor.

"Oh, my!" she gasped.

I picked it up with a weary bend and handed it back to her, holding it at arm's length and by the extreme tip of the corners to indicate that I had no designs upon it—but everyone near by, including the woman, suspected me just the same.

"Hot!" said the conductor to familiar faces. "Some weather! ... Hot! ... Hot! ... Hot! ... Is it hot enough for you? Is it hot? Is it ... ?"

---

1 An inn with a courtyard for caravans.
2 Tailored shirt or blouse.

My commutation ticket came back to me with a dark stain from his hand. That anyone should care in this heat whose flushed lips he kissed, whose head made damp the pajama pocket over his heart!

...Through the hall of the Buchanans' house blew a faint wind, carrying the sound of the telephone bell out to Gatsby and me as we waited at the door.

"The master's body!" roared the butler into the mouthpiece. "I'm sorry, madame, but we can't furnish it—it's far too hot to touch this noon!"

What he really said was: "Yes ...Yes ... I'll see."

He set down the receiver and came toward us, glistening slightly, to take our stiff straw hats. "Madame expects you in the salon!" he cried, needlessly indicating the direction. In this heat every extra gesture was an affront to the common store of life.

The room, shadowed well with awnings, was dark and cool. Daisy and Jordan lay upon an enormous couch, like silver idols weighing down their own white dresses against the singing breeze of the fans.

"We can't move," they said together.

Jordan's fingers, powdered white over their tan, rested for a moment in mine.

"And Mr. Thomas Buchanan, the athlete?" I inquired.

Simultaneously I heard his voice, gruff, muffled, husky, at the hall telephone.

Gatsby stood in the centre of the crimson carpet and gazed around with fascinated eyes. Daisy watched him and laughed, her sweet, exciting laugh; a tiny gust of powder rose from her bosom into the air.

"The rumor is," whispered Jordan, "that that's Tom's girl on the telephone."

We were silent. The voice in the hall rose high with annoyance: "Very well, then, I won't sell you the car at all.... I'm under no obligations to you at all.... And as for your bothering me about it at lunch time, I won't stand that at all!"

"Holding down the receiver," said Daisy cynically.

"No, he's not," I assured her. "It's a bona-fide deal. I happen to know about it."

Tom flung open the door, blocked out its space for a moment with his thick body, and hurried into the room.

"Mr. Gatsby!" He put out his broad, flat hand with well-concealed dislike. "I'm glad to see you, sir.... Nick...."

"Make us a cold drink," cried Daisy.

As he left the room again she got up and went over to Gatsby and pulled his face down, kissing him on the mouth.

"You know I love you," she murmured.

"You forget there's a lady present," said Jordan. Daisy looked around doubtfully.

"You kiss Nick too."

"What a low, vulgar girl!"

"I don't care!" cried Daisy, and began to clog[1] on the brick fireplace. Then she remembered the heat and sat down guiltily on the couch just as a freshly laundered nurse leading a little girl came into the room.

"Bles-sed pre-cious," she crooned, holding out her arms. "Come to your own mother that loves you."

The child, relinquished by the nurse, rushed across the room and rooted shyly into her mother's dress.

"The bles-sed pre-cious! Did mother get powder on your old yellowy hair? Stand up now, and say—How-de-do."

Gatsby and I in turn leaned down and took the small reluctant hand. Afterward he kept looking at the child with surprise. I don't think he had ever really believed in its existence before.

"I got dressed before luncheon," said the child, turning eagerly to Daisy.

"That's because your mother wanted to show you off." Her face bent into the single wrinkle of the small white neck. "You dream, you. You absolute little dream."

"Yes," admitted the child calmly. "Aunt Jordan's got on a white dress too."

"How do you like mother's friends?" Daisy turned her around so that she faced Gatsby. "Do you think they're pretty?"

"Where's Daddy?"

"She doesn't look like her father," explained Daisy. "She looks like me. She's got my hair and shape of the face."

Daisy sat back upon the couch. The nurse took a step forward and held out her hand.

"Come, Pammy."

"Good-by, sweetheart!"

With a reluctant backward glance the well-disciplined child held to her nurse's hand and was pulled out the door, just as Tom came back, preceding four gin rickeys that clicked full of ice.

Gatsby took up his drink.

---

1 Beat out a clattering rhythm. From the folk "clog dance."

"They certainly look cool," he said, with visible tension.

We drank in long, greedy swallows.

"I read somewhere that the sun's getting hotter every year," said Tom genially. "It seems that pretty soon the earth's going to fall into the sun—or wait a minute—it's just the opposite—the sun's getting colder every year.

"Come outside," he suggested to Gatsby, "I'd like you to have a look at the place."

I went with them out to the veranda. On the green Sound, stagnant in the heat, one small sail crawled slowly toward the fresher sea. Gatsby's eyes followed it momentarily; he raised his hand and pointed across the bay.

"I'm right across from you."

"So you are."

Our eyes lifted over the rose-beds and the hot lawn and the weedy refuse of the dog-days alongshore. Slowly the white wings of the boat moved against the blue cool limit of the sky. Ahead lay the scalloped ocean and the abounding blessed isles.

"There's sport for you," said Tom, nodding. "I'd like to be out there with him for about an hour."

We had luncheon in the dining-room, darkened too against the heat, and drank down nervous gayety with the cold ale.

"What'll we do with ourselves this afternoon?" cried Daisy, "and the day after that, and the next thirty years?"

"Don't be morbid," Jordan said. "Life starts all over again when it gets crisp in the fall."

"But it's so hot," insisted Daisy, on the verge of tears, "and everything's so confused. Let's all go to town!"

Her voice struggled on through the heat, beating against it, molding its senselessness into forms.

"I've heard of making a garage out of a stable," Tom was saying to Gatsby, "but I'm the first man who ever made a stable out of a garage."

"Who wants to go to town?" demanded Daisy insistently. Gatsby's eyes floated toward her. "Ah," she cried, "you look so cool." Their eyes met, and they stared together at each other, alone in space. With an effort she glanced down at the table.

"You always look so cool," she repeated.

She had told him that she loved him, and Tom Buchanan saw. He was astounded. His mouth opened a little, and he looked at Gatsby, and then back at Daisy as if he had just recognized her as someone he knew a long time ago.

"You resemble the advertisement of the man," she went on innocently. "You know the advertisement of the man——"

"All right," broke in Tom quickly, "I'm perfectly willing to go to town. Come on—we're all going to town."

He got up, his eyes still flashing between Gatsby and his wife. No one moved.

"Come on!" His temper cracked a little. "What's the matter, anyhow? If we're going to town, let's start."

His hand, trembling with his effort at self-control, bore to his lips the last of his glass of ale. Daisy's voice got us to our feet and out on to the blazing gravel drive.

"Are we just going to go?" she objected. "Like this? Aren't we going to let anyone smoke a cigarette first?"

"Everybody smoked all through lunch."

"Oh, let's have fun," she begged him. "It's too hot to fuss."

He didn't answer.

"Have it your own way," she said. "Come on, Jordan."

They went up-stairs to get ready while we three men stood there shuffling the hot pebbles with our feet. A silver curve of the moon hovered already in the western sky. Gatsby started to speak, changed his mind, but not before Tom wheeled and faced him expectantly.

"Have you got your stables here?" asked Gatsby with an effort.

"About a quarter of a mile down the road."

"Oh."

A pause.

"I don't see the idea of going to town," broke out Tom savagely. "Women get these notions in their heads——"

"Shall we take anything to drink?" called Daisy from an upper window.

"I'll get some whiskey," answered Tom. He went inside.

Gatsby turned to me rigidly:

"I can't say anything in his house, old sport."

"She's got an indiscreet voice," I remarked. "It's full of—" I hesitated.

"Her voice is full of money," he said suddenly.

That was it. I'd never understood before. It was full of money—that was the inexhaustible charm that rose and fell in it, the jingle of it, the cymbals' song of it.... High in a white palace the king's daughter, the golden girl....

Tom came out of the house wrapping a quart bottle in a towel, followed by Daisy and Jordan wearing small tight hats of metallic cloth and carrying light capes over their arms.

"Shall we all go in my car?" suggested Gatsby. He felt the hot, green leather of the seat. "I ought to have left it in the shade."

"Is it standard shift?" demanded Tom.

"Yes."

"Well, you take my coupé and let me drive your car to town."

The suggestion was distasteful to Gatsby.

"I don't think there's much gas," he objected.

"Plenty of gas," said Tom boisterously. He looked at the gauge.

"And if it runs out I can stop at a drug-store. You can buy anything at a drug-store nowadays."

A pause followed this apparently pointless remark. Daisy looked at Tom frowning, and an indefinable expression, at once definitely unfamiliar and vaguely recognizable, as if I had only heard it described in words, passed over Gatsby's face.

"Come on, Daisy," said Tom, pressing her with his hand toward Gatsby's car. "I'll take you in this circus wagon."

He opened the door, but she moved out from the circle of his arm.

"You take Nick and Jordan. We'll follow you in the coupé."

She walked close to Gatsby, touching his coat with her hand. Jordan and Tom and I got into the front seat of Gatsby's car, Tom pushed the unfamiliar gears tentatively, and we shot off into the oppressive heat, leaving them out of sight behind.

"Did you see that?" demanded Tom.

"See what?"

He looked at me keenly, realizing that Jordan and I must have known all along.

"You think I'm pretty dumb, don't you?" he suggested. "Perhaps I am, but I have a—almost a second sight, sometimes, that tells me what to do. Maybe you don't believe that, but science——"

He paused. The immediate contingency overtook him, pulled him back from the edge of the theoretical abyss.

"I've made a small investigation of this fellow," he continued. "I could have gone deeper if I'd known——"

"Do you mean you've been to a medium?"[1] inquired Jordan humorously.

"What?" Confused, he stared at us as we laughed. "A medium?"

"About Gatsby."

---

1 A spiritualist capable of divining hidden truths.

"About Gatsby! No, I haven't. I said I'd been making a small investigation of his past."

"And you found he was an Oxford man," said Jordan helpfully.

"An Oxford man!" He was incredulous. "Like hell he is! He wears a pink suit."[1]

"Nevertheless he's an Oxford man."

"Oxford, New Mexico," snorted Tom contemptuously, "or something like that."

"Listen, Tom. If you're such a snob, why did you invite him to lunch?" demanded Jordan crossly.

"Daisy invited him; she knew him before we were married— God knows where!"

We were all irritable now with the fading ale, and aware of it we drove for a while in silence. Then as Doctor T.J. Eckleburg's faded eyes came into sight down the road, I remembered Gatsby's caution about gasoline.

"We've got enough to get us to town," said Tom.

"But there's a garage right here," objected Jordan. "I don't want to get stalled in this baking heat."

Tom threw on both brakes impatiently, and we slid to an abrupt dusty spot under Wilson's sign. After a moment the proprietor emerged from the interior of his establishment and gazed hollow-eyed at the car.

"Let's have some gas!" cried Tom roughly. "What do you think we stopped for—to admire the view?"

"I'm sick," said Wilson without moving. "Been sick all day."

"What's the matter?"

"I'm all run down."

"Well, shall I help myself?" Tom demanded. "You sounded well enough on the phone."

With an effort Wilson left the shade and support of the doorway and, breathing hard, unscrewed the cap of the tank. In the sunlight his face was green.

"I didn't mean to interrupt your lunch," he said. "But I need money pretty bad, and I was wondering what you were going to do with your old car."

"How do you like this one?" inquired Tom. "I bought it last week."

"It's a nice yellow one," said Wilson, as he strained at the handle.

---

1 On the significance of dress, see Appendix C1.

"Like to buy it?"

"Big chance," Wilson smiled faintly. "No, but I could make some money on the other."

"What do you want money for, all of a sudden?"

"I've been here too long. I want to get away. My wife and I want to go West."

"Your wife does," exclaimed Tom, startled.

"She's been talking about it for ten years." He rested for a moment against the pump, shading his eyes. "And now she's going whether she wants to or not. I'm going to get her away."

The coupé flashed by us with a flurry of dust and the flash of a waving hand.

"What do I owe you?" demanded Tom harshly.

"I just got wised up to something funny the last two days," remarked Wilson. "That's why I want to get away. That's why I been bothering you about the car."

"What do I owe you?"

"Dollar twenty."

The relentless beating heat was beginning to confuse me and I had a bad moment there before I realized that so far his suspicions hadn't alighted on Tom. He had discovered that Myrtle had some sort of life apart from him in another world, and the shock had made him physically sick. I stared at him and then at Tom, who had made a parallel discovery less than an hour before—and it occurred to me that there was no difference between men, in intelligence or race, so profound as the difference between the sick and the well. Wilson was so sick that he looked guilty, unforgivably guilty—as if he had just got some poor girl with child.

"I'll let you have that car," said Tom. "I'll send it over tomorrow afternoon."

That locality was always vaguely disquieting, even in the broad glare of afternoon, and now I turned my head as though I had been warned of something behind. Over the ashheaps the giant eyes of Doctor T.J. Eckleburg kept their vigil, but I perceived, after a moment, that other eyes were regarding us with peculiar intensity from less than twenty feet away.

In one of the windows over the garage the curtains had been moved aside a little, and Myrtle Wilson was peering down at the car. So engrossed was she that she had no consciousness of being observed, and one emotion after another crept into her face like objects into a slowly developing picture. Her expression was curiously familiar—it was an expression I had often seen on women's faces, but on Myrtle Wilson's face it seemed purposeless and inexplicable until I realized that her eyes, wide with jealous terror, were fixed not on Tom, but on Jordan Baker, whom she took to be his wife.

There is no confusion like the confusion of a simple mind, and as we drove away Tom was feeling the hot whips of panic. His wife and his mistress, until an hour ago secure and inviolate, were slipping precipitately from his control. Instinct made him step on the accelerator with the double purpose of overtaking Daisy and leaving Wilson behind, and we sped along toward Astoria at fifty miles an hour, until, among the spidery girders of the elevated, we came in sight of the easy-going blue coupé.

"Those big movies around Fiftieth Street are cool," suggested Jordan. "I love New York on summer afternoons when everyone's away. There's something very sensuous about it—overripe, as if all sorts of funny fruits were going to fall into your hands."

The word "sensuous" had the effect of further disquieting Tom, but before he could invent a protest the coupé came to a stop, and Daisy signalled us to draw up alongside.

"Where are we going?" she cried.

"How about the movies?"

"It's so hot," she complained. "You go. We'll ride around and meet you after." With an effort her wit rose faintly, "We'll meet you on some corner. I'll be the man smoking two cigarettes."

"We can't argue about it here," Tom said impatiently, as a truck gave out a cursing whistle behind us. "You follow me to the south side of Central Park, in front of the Plaza."

Several times he turned his head and looked back for their car, and if the traffic delayed them he slowed up until they came into sight. I think he was afraid they would dart down a side street and out of his life forever.

But they didn't. And we all took the less explicable step of engaging the parlor of a suite in the Plaza Hotel.

The prolonged and tumultuous argument that ended by herding us into that room eludes me, though I have a sharp physical memory that, in the course of it, my underwear kept climbing like a damp snake around my legs and intermittent beads of sweat raced cool across my back. The notion originated with Daisy's suggestion that we hire five bathrooms and take cold baths, and then assumed more tangible form as "a place to have a mint julep." Each of us said over and over that it was a "crazy idea"—we all talked at once to a baffled clerk and thought, or pretended to think, that we were being very funny....

The room was large and stifling, and, though it was already four o'clock, opening the windows admitted only a gust of hot shrubbery from the Park. Daisy went to the mirror and stood with her back to us, fixing her hair.

"It's a swell suite," whispered Jordan respectfully, and everyone laughed.

"Open another window," commanded Daisy, without turning around.

"There aren't any more."

"Well, we'd better telephone for an axe——"

"The thing to do is to forget about the heat," said Tom impatiently. "You make it ten times worse by crabbing about it."

He unrolled the bottle of whiskey from the towel and put it on the table.

"Why not let her alone, old sport?" remarked Gatsby. "You're the one that wanted to come to town."

There was a moment of silence. The telephone book slipped from its nail and splashed to the floor, whereupon Jordan whispered, "Excuse me"—but this time no one laughed.

"I'll pick it up," I offered.

"I've got it." Gatsby examined the parted string, muttered "Hum!" in an interested way, and tossed the book on a chair.

"That's a great expression of yours, isn't it?" said Tom sharply.

"What is?"

"All this 'old sport' business. Where'd you pick that up?"

"Now see here, Tom," said Daisy, turning around from the mirror, "if you're going to make personal remarks I won't stay here a minute. Call up and order some ice for the mint julep."

As Tom took up the receiver the compressed heat exploded into sound and we were listening to the portentous chords of Mendelssohn's Wedding March[1] from the ballroom below.

"Imagine marrying anybody in this heat!" cried Jordan dismally.

"Still—I was married in the middle of June," Daisy remembered, "Louisville in June! Somebody fainted. Who was it fainted, Tom?"

"Biloxi," he answered shortly.

---

1 The traditional "Wedding March," originally from *A Midsummer Night's Dream* (1842) by Felix Mendelssohn (1809–47).

"A man named Biloxi. 'Blocks' Biloxi, and he made boxes—that's a fact—and he was from Biloxi, Tennessee."[1]

"They carried him into my house," appended Jordan, "because we lived just two doors from the church. And he stayed three weeks, until Daddy told him he had to get out. The day after he left Daddy died." After a moment she added, as if she might have sounded irreverent, "There wasn't any connection."

"I used to know a Bill Biloxi from Memphis," I remarked.

"That was his cousin. I knew his whole family history before he left. He gave me an aluminum putter that I use to-day."

The music had died down as the ceremony began and now a long cheer floated in at the window, followed by intermittent cries of "Yea—ea—ea!" and finally by a burst of jazz as the dancing began.

"We're getting old," said Daisy. "If we were young we'd rise and dance."

"Remember Biloxi," Jordan warned her. "Where'd you know him, Tom?"

"Biloxi?" He concentrated with an effort. "I didn't know him. He was a friend of Daisy's."

"He was not," she denied. "I'd never seen him before. He came down in the private car."

"Well, he said he knew you. He said he was raised in Louisville. Asa Bird brought him around at the last minute and asked if we had room for him."

Jordan smiled.

"He was probably bumming his way home. He told me he was president of your class at Yale."

Tom and I looked at each other blankly.

"Biloxi?"

"First place, we didn't have any president——"

Gatsby's foot beat a short, restless tattoo[2] and Tom eyed him suddenly.

"By the way, Mr. Gatsby, I understand you're an Oxford man."

"Not exactly."

"Oh, yes, I understand you went to Oxford."

"Yes—I went there."

---

1 The city of Biloxi is in Mississippi, not Tennessee.
2 A rhythmic tapping.

A pause. Then Tom's voice, incredulous and insulting:

"You must have gone there about the time Biloxi went to New Haven."

Another pause. A waiter knocked and came in with crushed mint and ice but the silence was unbroken by his "thank you" and the soft closing of the door. This tremendous detail was to be cleared up at last.

"I told you I went there," said Gatsby.

"I heard you, but I'd like to know when."

"It was in nineteen-nineteen, I only stayed five months. That's why I can't really call myself an Oxford man."

Tom glanced around to see if we mirrored his unbelief. But we were all looking at Gatsby.

"It was an opportunity they gave to some of the officers after the armistice," he continued. "We could go to any of the universities in England or France."

I wanted to get up and slap him on the back. I had one of those renewals of complete faith in him that I'd experienced before.

Daisy rose, smiling faintly, and went to the table.

"Open the whiskey, Tom," she ordered, "and I'll make you a mint julep. Then you won't seem so stupid to yourself.... Look at the mint!"

"Wait a minute," snapped Tom, "I want to ask Mr. Gatsby one more question."

"Go on," Gatsby said politely.

"What kind of a row are you trying to cause in my house anyhow?"

They were out in the open at last and Gatsby was content.

"He isn't causing a row." Daisy looked desperately from one to the other. "You're causing a row. Please have a little self-control."

"Self-control!" repeated Tom incredulously. "I suppose the latest thing is to sit back and let Mr. Nobody from Nowhere make love to your wife. Well, if that's the idea you can count me out.... Nowadays people begin by sneering at family life and family institutions, and next they'll throw everything overboard and have intermarriage between black and white."

Flushed with his impassioned gibberish, he saw himself standing alone on the last barrier of civilization.

"We're all white here," murmured Jordan.

"I know I'm not very popular. I don't give big parties. I suppose you've got to make your house into a pigsty in order to have any friends—in the modern world."

Angry as I was, as we all were, I was tempted to laugh whenever he opened his mouth. The transition from libertine to prig was so complete.

"I've got something to tell *you*, old sport—" began Gatsby. But Daisy guessed at his intention.

"Please don't!" she interrupted helplessly. "Please let's all go home. Why don't we all go home?"

"That's a good idea." I got up. "Come on, Tom. Nobody wants a drink."

"I want to know what Mr. Gatsby has to tell me."

"Your wife doesn't love you," said Gatsby. "She's never loved you. She loves me."

"You must be crazy!" exclaimed Tom automatically.

Gatsby sprang to his feet, vivid with excitement.

"She never loved you, do you hear?" he cried. "She only married you because I was poor and she was tired of waiting for me. It was a terrible mistake, but in her heart she never loved anyone except me!"

At this point Jordan and I tried to go, but Tom and Gatsby insisted with competitive firmness that we remain—as though neither of them had anything to conceal and it would be a privilege to partake vicariously of their emotions.

"Sit down, Daisy." Tom's voice groped unsuccessfully for the paternal note. "What's been going on? I want to hear all about it."

"I told you what's been going on," said Gatsby. "Going on for five years—and you didn't know."

Tom turned to Daisy sharply.

"You've been seeing this fellow for five years?"

"Not seeing," said Gatsby. "No, we couldn't meet. But both of us loved each other all that time, old sport, and you didn't know. I used to laugh sometimes"—but there was no laughter in his eyes—"to think that you didn't know."

"Oh—that's all." Tom tapped his thick fingers together like a clergyman and leaned back in his chair.

"You're crazy!" he exploded. "I can't speak about what happened five years ago, because I didn't know Daisy then—and I'll be damned if I see how you got within a mile of her unless you brought the groceries to the back door. But all the rest of that's a God damned lie. Daisy loved me when she married me and she loves me now."

"No," said Gatsby, shaking his head.

"She does, though. The trouble is that sometimes she gets foolish ideas in her head and doesn't know what she's doing." He nodded sagely. "And what's more, I love Daisy too. Once in a while I go off on a spree and make a fool of myself, but I always come back, and in my heart I love her all the time."

"You're revolting," said Daisy. She turned to me, and her voice, dropping an octave lower, filled the room with thrilling scorn: "Do you know why we left Chicago? I'm surprised that they didn't treat you to the story of that little spree."

Gatsby walked over and stood beside her.

"Daisy, that's all over now," he said earnestly. "It doesn't matter any more. Just tell him the truth—that you never loved him—and it's all wiped out forever."

She looked at him blindly. "Why—how could I love him—possibly?"

"You never loved him."

She hesitated. Her eyes fell on Jordan and me with a sort of appeal, as though she realized at last what she was doing—and as though she had never, all along, intended doing anything at all. But it was done now. It was too late.

"I never loved him," she said, with perceptible reluctance.

"Not at Kapiolani?"[1] demanded Tom suddenly.

"No."

From the ballroom beneath, muffled and suffocating chords were drifting up on hot waves of air.

"Not that day I carried you down from the Punch Bowl[2] to keep your shoes dry?" There was a husky tenderness in his tone.... "Daisy?"

"Please don't." Her voice was cold, but the rancor was gone from it. She looked at Gatsby. "There, Jay," she said—but her hand as she tried to light a cigarette was trembling. Suddenly she threw the cigarette and the burning match on the carpet.

"Oh, you want too much!" she cried to Gatsby. "I love you now—isn't that enough? I can't help what's past." She began to sob helplessly. "I did love him once—but I loved you too."

Gatsby's eyes opened and closed.

"You loved me *too?*" he repeated.

"Even that's a lie," said Tom savagely. "She didn't know you were alive. Why—there're things between Daisy and me that you'll never know, things that neither of us can ever forget."

The words seemed to bite physically into Gatsby.

---

1 Large park bordering the Waikiki section of Honolulu, Hawaii.
2 Extinct volcanic crater overlooking Honolulu, a popular tourist site.

"I want to speak to Daisy alone," he insisted. "She's all excited now——"

"Even alone I can't say I never loved Tom," she admitted in a pitiful voice. "It wouldn't be true."

"Of course it wouldn't," agreed Tom.

She turned to her husband.

"As if it mattered to you," she said.

"Of course it matters. I'm going to take better care of you from now on."

"You don't understand," said Gatsby, with a touch of panic. "You're not going to take care of her any more."

"I'm not?" Tom opened his eyes wide and laughed. He could afford to control himself now. "Why's that?"

"Daisy's leaving you."

"Nonsense."

"I am, though," she said with a visible effort.

"She's not leaving me!" Tom's words suddenly leaned down over Gatsby. "Certainly not for a common swindler who'd have to steal the ring he put on her finger."

"I won't stand this!" cried Daisy. "Oh, please let's get out."

"Who are you, anyhow?" broke out Tom. "You're one of that bunch that hangs around with Meyer Wolfshiem—that much I happen to know. I've made a little investigation into your affairs—and I'll carry it further to-morrow."

"You can suit yourself about that, old sport," said Gatsby steadily.

"I found out what your 'drug-stores' were." He turned to us and spoke rapidly. "He and this Wolfshiem bought up a lot of side-street drug-stores here and in Chicago and sold grain alcohol over the counter. That's one of his little stunts. I picked him for a bootlegger the first time I saw him, and I wasn't far wrong."

"What about it?" said Gatsby politely. "I guess your friend Walter Chase wasn't too proud to come in on it."

"And you left him in the lurch, didn't you? You let him go to jail for a month over in New Jersey. God! You ought to hear Walter on the subject of *you*."

"He came to us dead broke. He was very glad to pick up some money, old sport."

"Don't you call me 'old sport'!" cried Tom. Gatsby said nothing. "Walter could have you up on the betting laws too, but Wolfshiem scared him into shutting his mouth."

That unfamiliar yet recognizable look was back again in Gatsby's face.

"That drug-store business was just small change," continued Tom slowly, "but you've got something on now that Walter's afraid to tell me about."

I glanced at Daisy, who was staring terrified between Gatsby and her husband, and at Jordan, who had begun to balance an invisible but absorbing object on the tip of her chin. Then I turned back to Gatsby—and was startled at his expression. He looked—and this is said in all contempt for the babbled slander of his garden—as if he had "killed a man." For a moment the set of his face could be described in just that fantastic way.

It passed, and he began to talk excitedly to Daisy, denying everything, defending his name against accusations that had not been made. But with every word she was drawing further and further into herself, so he gave that up, and only the dead dream fought on as the afternoon slipped away, trying to touch what was no longer tangible, struggling unhappily, undespairingly, toward that lost voice across the room.

The voice begged again to go.

"*Please*, Tom! I can't stand this any more."

Her frightened eyes told that whatever intentions, whatever courage she had had, were definitely gone.

"You two start on home, Daisy," said Tom. "In Mr. Gatsby's car."

She looked at Tom, alarmed now, but he insisted with magnanimous scorn.

"Go on. He won't annoy you. I think he realizes that his presumptuous little flirtation is over."

They were gone, without a word, snapped out, made accidental, isolated, like ghosts, even from our pity.

After a moment Tom got up and began wrapping the unopened bottle of whiskey in the towel. "Want any of this stuff? Jordan? ... Nick?"

I didn't answer.

"Nick?" He asked again.

"What?"

"Want any?"

"No ... I just remembered that to-day's my birthday."

I was thirty. Before me stretched the portentous, menacing road of a new decade.

It was seven o'clock when we got into the coupé with him and started for Long Island. Tom talked incessantly, exulting and laughing, but his voice was as remote from Jordan and me as the foreign clamor on the sidewalk or the tumult of the elevated overhead. Human sympathy has its limits, and we were content to let all their tragic arguments fade with the city lights behind. Thirty—the promise of a decade of loneliness, a thinning list of single men to know, a thinning brief-case of enthusiasm, thinning hair. But there was Jordan beside me, who, unlike Daisy, was too wise ever to carry well-forgotten dreams from age to age. As we passed over the dark bridge her wan face fell lazily against my coat's shoulder and the formidable stroke of thirty died away with the reassuring pressure of her hand.

So we drove on toward death through the cooling twilight.

The young Greek, Michaelis, who ran the coffee joint beside the ashheaps was the principal witness at the inquest. He had slept through the heat until after five, when he strolled over to the garage, and found George Wilson sick in his office—really sick, pale as his own pale hair and shaking all over. Michaelis advised him to go to bed, but Wilson refused, saying that he'd miss a lot of business if he did. While his neighbor was trying to persuade him a violent racket broke out overhead.

"I've got my wife locked in up there," explained Wilson calmly. "She's going to stay there till the day after to-morrow, and then we're going to move away."

Michaelis was astonished; they had been neighbors for four years, and Wilson had never seemed faintly capable of such a statement. Generally he was one of these worn-out men: when he wasn't working, he sat on a chair in the doorway and stared at the people and the cars that passed along the road. When anyone spoke to him he invariably laughed in an agreeable, colorless way. He was his wife's man and not his own.

So naturally Michaelis tried to find out what had happened, but Wilson wouldn't say a word—instead he began to throw curious, suspicious glances at his visitor and ask him what he'd been doing at certain times on certain days. Just as the latter was getting uneasy, some workmen came past the door bound for his restaurant, and Michaelis took the opportunity to get away, intending to come back later. But he didn't. He supposed he forgot to, that's all. When he came outside again, a little after seven, he was reminded of the conversation because he heard Mrs. Wilson's voice, loud and scolding, down-stairs in the garage.

"Beat me!" he heard her cry. "Throw me down and beat me, you dirty little coward!"

A moment later she rushed out into the dusk, waving her hands and shouting—before he could move from his door the business was over.

The "death car" as the newspapers called it, didn't stop; it came out of the gathering darkness, wavered tragically for a moment, and then disappeared around the next bend. Michaelis wasn't even sure of its color—he told the first policeman that it was light green. The other car, the one going toward New York, came to rest a hundred yards beyond, and its driver hurried back to where Myrtle Wilson, her life violently extinguished, knelt in the road and mingled her thick dark blood with the dust.

Michaelis and this man reached her first, but when they had torn open her shirtwaist, still damp with perspiration, they saw that her left breast was swinging loose like a flap, and there was no need to listen for the heart beneath. The mouth was wide open and ripped a little at the corners, as though she had choked a little in giving up the tremendous vitality she had stored so long.

We saw the three or four automobiles and the crowd when we were still some distance away.

"Wreck!" said Tom. "That's good. Wilson'll have a little business at last."

He slowed down, but still without any intention of stopping, until, as we came nearer, the hushed, intent faces of the people at the garage door made him automatically put on the brakes.

"We'll take a look," he said doubtfully, "just a look."

I became aware now of a hollow, wailing sound which issued incessantly from the garage, a sound which as we got out of the coupé and walked toward the door resolved itself into the words "Oh, my God!" uttered over and over in a gasping moan.

"There's some bad trouble here," said Tom excitedly.

He reached up on tiptoes and peered over a circle of heads into the garage, which was lit only by a yellow light in a swinging wire basket overhead. Then he made a harsh sound in his throat, and with a violent thrusting movement of his powerful arms pushed his way through.

The circle closed up again with a running murmur of expostulation; it was a minute before I could see anything at all. Then new arrivals deranged the line, and Jordan and I were pushed suddenly inside.

Myrtle Wilson's body, wrapped in a blanket, and then in another blanket, as though she suffered from a chill in the hot night, lay on a work-table by the wall, and Tom, with his back to us, was bending over it, motionless. Next to him stood a motorcycle policeman taking down names with much sweat and correction in a little book. At first I couldn't find the source of the high, groaning words that echoed clamorously through the bare garage—then I saw Wilson standing on the raised threshold of his office, swaying back and forth and holding to the doorposts with both hands. Some man was talking to him in a low voice and attempting, from time to time, to lay a hand on his shoulder, but Wilson neither heard nor saw. His eyes would drop slowly from the swinging light to the laden table by the wall, and then jerk back to the light again, and he gave out incessantly his high, horrible call:

"Oh, my Ga-od! Oh, my Ga-od! Oh, Ga-od! Oh, my Ga-od!"

Presently Tom lifted his head with a jerk and, after staring around the garage with glazed eyes, addressed a mumbled incoherent remark to the policeman.

"M-a-v—" the policeman was saying, "—o——"

"No, r—" corrected the man, "M-a-v-r-o——"[1]

"Listen to me!" muttered Tom fiercely.

"r—" said the policeman, "o——"

"g——"

"g—" He looked up as Tom's broad hand fell sharply on his shoulder. "What you want, fella?"

"What happened?—that's what I want to know."

"Auto hit her. Ins'antly killed."

"Instantly killed," repeated Tom, staring.

"She ran out ina road. Son-of-a-bitch didn't even stopus car."

"There was two cars," said Michaelis, "one comin', one goin', see?"

"Going where?" asked the policeman keenly.

"One goin' each way. Well, she"—his hand rose toward the blankets but stopped half way and fell to his side—"she ran out there an' the one comin' from N'York knock right into her, goin' thirty or forty miles an hour."

"What's the name of this place here?" demanded the officer.

"Hasn't got any name."

A pale well-dressed negro stepped near.

"It was a yellow car," he said, "big yellow car. New."

---

1 An editorial oversight; the character's name was changed from Mavromichaelis to Michaelis in galley revisions.

"See the accident?" asked the policeman.

"No, but the car passed me down the road, going faster'n forty. Going fifty, sixty."

"Come here and let's have your name. Look out now. I want to get his name."

Some words of this conversation must have reached Wilson, swaying in the office door, for suddenly a new theme found voice among his gasping cries:

"You don't have to tell me what kind of car it was! I know what kind of car it was!"

Watching Tom, I saw the wad of muscle back of his shoulder tighten under his coat. He walked quickly over to Wilson and, standing in front of him seized him, firmly by the upper arms.

"You've got to pull yourself together," he said with soothing gruffness.

Wilson's eyes fell upon Tom; he started up on his tiptoes and then would have collapsed to his knees had not Tom held him upright.

"Listen," said Tom, shaking him a little. "I just got here a minute ago, from New York. I was bringing you that coupé we've been talking about. That yellow car I was driving this afternoon wasn't mine—do you hear? I haven't seen it all afternoon."

Only the negro and I were near enough to hear what he said, but the policeman caught something in the tone and looked over with truculent eyes.

"What's all that?" he demanded.

"I'm a friend of his." Tom turned his head but kept his hands firm on Wilson's body. "He says he knows the car that did it.... It was a yellow car."

Some dim impulse moved the policeman to look suspiciously at Tom.

"And what color's your car?"

"It's a blue car, a coupé."

"We've come straight from New York," I said.

Someone who had been driving a little behind us confirmed this, and the policeman turned away.

"Now, if you'll let me have that name again correct——"

Picking up Wilson like a doll, Tom carried him into the office, set him down in a chair, and came back.

"If somebody'll come here and sit with him," he snapped authoritatively. He watched while the two men standing closest glanced at each other and went unwillingly into the room. Then Tom shut the door on them and came down the single step, his eyes avoiding the table. As he passed close to me he whispered: "Let's get out."

Self-consciously, with his authoritative arms breaking the way, we pushed through the still gathering crowd, passing a hurried doctor, case in hand, who had been sent for in wild hope half an hour ago.

Tom drove slowly until we were beyond the bend—then his foot came down hard, and the coupé raced along through the night. In a little while I heard a low husky sob, and saw that the tears were overflowing down his face.

"The God damned coward!" he whimpered. "He didn't even stop his car."

The Buchanans' house floated suddenly toward us through the dark rustling trees. Tom stopped beside the porch and looked up at the second floor, where two windows bloomed with light among the vines.

"Daisy's home," he said. As we got out of the car he glanced at me and frowned slightly.

"I ought to have dropped you in West Egg, Nick. There's nothing we can do to-night."

A change had come over him, and he spoke gravely, and with decision. As we walked across the moonlight gravel to the porch he disposed of the situation in a few brisk phrases.

"I'll telephone for a taxi to take you home, and while you're waiting you and Jordan better go in the kitchen and have them get you some supper—if you want any." He opened the door. "Come in."

"No, thanks. But I'd be glad if you'd order me the taxi. I'll wait outside."

Jordan put her hand on my arm. "Won't you come in, Nick?"

"No, thanks."

I was feeling a little sick and I wanted to be alone. But Jordan lingered for a moment more.

"It's only half-past nine," she said.

I'd be damned if I'd go in; I'd had enough of all of them for one day, and suddenly that included Jordan too. She must have seen something of this in my expression, for she turned abruptly away and ran up the porch steps into the house. I sat down for a few minutes with my head in my hands, until I heard the phone taken up inside and the butler's voice calling a taxi. Then I walked slowly down the drive away from the house, intending to wait by the gate.

I hadn't gone twenty yards when I heard my name and Gatsby stepped from between two bushes into the path. I must have felt pretty weird by that time, because I could think of nothing except the luminosity of his pink suit under the moon.

"What are you doing?" I inquired.

"Just standing here, old sport."

Somehow, that seemed a despicable occupation. For all I knew he was going to rob the house in a moment; I wouldn't have been surprised to see sinister faces, the faces of "Wolfshiem's people," behind him in the dark shrubbery.

"Did you see any trouble on the road?" he asked after a minute.

"Yes."

He hesitated.

"Was she killed?"

"Yes."

"I thought so; I told Daisy I thought so. It's better that the shock should all come at once. She stood it pretty well."

He spoke as if Daisy's reaction was the only thing that mattered.

"I got to West Egg by a side road," he went on, "and left the car in my garage. I don't think anybody saw us, but of course I can't be sure."

I disliked him so much by this time that I didn't find it necessary to tell him he was wrong.

"Who was the woman?" he inquired.

"Her name was Wilson. Her husband owns the garage. How the devil did it happen?"

"Well, I tried to swing the wheel—" He broke off, and suddenly I guessed at the truth.

"Was Daisy driving?"

"Yes," he said after a moment, "but of course I'll say I was. You see, when we left New York she was very nervous and she thought it would steady her to drive—and this woman rushed out at us just as we were passing a car coming the other way. It all happened in a minute, but it seemed to me that she wanted to speak to us, thought we were somebody she knew. Well, first Daisy turned away from the woman toward the other car, and then she lost her nerve and turned back. The second my hand reached the wheel I felt the shock—it must have killed her instantly."

"It ripped her open——"

"Don't tell me, old sport." He winced. "Anyhow—Daisy stepped on it. I tried to make her stop, but she couldn't, so I pulled on the emergency brake. Then she fell over into my lap and I drove on.

"She'll be all right to-morrow," he said presently. "I'm just going to wait here and see if he tries to bother her about that unpleasantness this afternoon. She's locked herself into her room, and if he tries any brutality she's going to turn the light out and on again."

"He won't touch her," I said. "He's not thinking about her."

"I don't trust him, old sport."

"How long are you going to wait?"

"All night, if necessary. Anyhow, till they all go to bed."

A new point of view occurred to me. Suppose Tom found out that Daisy had been driving. He might think he saw a connection in it—he might think anything. I looked at the house; there were two or three bright windows down-stairs and the pink glow from Daisy's room on the second floor.

"You wait here," I said. "I'll see if there's any sign of a commotion."

I walked back along the border of the lawn, traversed the gravel softly, and tiptoed up the veranda steps. The drawing-room curtains were open, and I saw that the room was empty. Crossing the porch where we had dined that June night three months before, I came to a small rectangle of light which I guessed was the pantry window. The blind was drawn, but I found a rift at the sill.

Daisy and Tom were sitting opposite each other at the kitchen table, with a plate of cold fried chicken between them, and two bottles of ale. He was talking intently across the table at her, and in his earnestness his hand had fallen upon and covered her own. Once in a while she looked up at him and nodded in agreement.

They weren't happy, and neither of them had touched the chicken or the ale—and yet they weren't unhappy either. There was an unmistakable air of natural intimacy about the picture, and anybody would have said that they were conspiring together.

As I tiptoed from the porch I heard my taxi feeling its way along the dark road toward the house. Gatsby was waiting where I had left him in the drive.

"Is it all quiet up there?" he asked anxiously.

"Yes, it's all quiet." I hesitated. "You'd better come home and get some sleep."

He shook his head.

"I want to wait here till Daisy goes to bed. Good night, old sport."

He put his hands in his coat pockets and turned back eagerly to his scrutiny of the house, as though my presence marred the sacredness of the vigil. So I walked away and left him standing there in the moonlight—watching over nothing.

Chapter VIII

I couldn't sleep all night; a fog-horn was groaning incessantly on the Sound, and I tossed half-sick between grotesque reality and savage, frightening dreams. Toward dawn I heard a taxi go up Gatsby's drive, and immediately I jumped out of bed and began to dress—I felt that I had something to tell him, something to warn him about, and morning would be too late.

Crossing his lawn, I saw that his front door was still open and he was leaning against a table in the hall, heavy with dejection or sleep.

"Nothing happened," he said wanly. "I waited, and about four o'clock she came to the window and stood there for a minute and then turned out the light."

His house had never seemed so enormous to me as it did that night when we hunted through the great rooms for cigarettes. We pushed aside curtains that were like pavilions, and felt over innumerable feet of dark wall for electric light switches—once I tumbled with a sort of splash upon the keys of a ghostly piano. There was an inexplicable amount of dust everywhere, and the rooms were musty, as though they hadn't been aired for many days. I found the humidor on an unfamiliar table, with two stale, dry cigarettes inside. Throwing open the French windows of the drawing-room, we sat smoking out into the darkness.

"You ought to go away," I said. "It's pretty certain they'll trace your car."

"Go away *now*, old sport?"

"Go to Atlantic City for a week, or up to Montreal."

He wouldn't consider it. He couldn't possibly leave Daisy until he knew what she was going to do. He was clutching at some last hope and I couldn't bear to shake him free.

It was this night that he told me the strange story of his youth with Dan Cody—told it to me because "Jay Gatsby" had broken up like glass against Tom's hard malice, and the long secret extravaganza was played out. I think that he would have acknowledged anything now, without reserve, but he wanted to talk about Daisy.

She was the first "nice" girl he had ever known. In various unrevealed capacities he had come in contact with such people, but always with indiscernible barbed wire between. He found her excitingly desirable. He went to her house, at first with other officers from Camp Taylor, then alone. It amazed him—he had never been in such a beautiful house before. But what gave it an air of breathless intensity, was that Daisy lived there—it was as casual a thing to her as his tent out at camp was to him. There was a ripe mystery about it, a hint of bedrooms up-stairs more beautiful and cool than other bedrooms, of gay and radiant activities taking place through its corridors, and of romances that were not musty and laid away already in lavender but fresh and breathing and redolent of this year's shining motor-cars and of dances whose flowers were scarcely withered. It excited him, too, that many men had already loved Daisy—it increased her value in his eyes. He felt their presence all about the house, pervading the air with the shades and echoes of still vibrant emotions.

But he knew that he was in Daisy's house by a colossal accident. However glorious might be his future as Jay Gatsby, he was at present a penniless young man without a past, and at any moment the invisible cloak of his uniform might slip from his shoulders. So he made the most of his time. He took what he could get, ravenously and unscrupulously—eventually he took Daisy one still October night, took her because he had no real right to touch her hand.

He might have despised himself, for he had certainly taken her under false pretenses. I don't mean that he had traded on his phantom millions, but he had deliberately given Daisy a sense of security; he let her believe that he was a person from much the same strata as herself—that he was fully able to take care of her. As a matter of fact, he had no such facilities—he had no comfortable family standing behind him, and he was liable at the whim of an impersonal government to be blown anywhere about the world.

But he didn't despise himself and it didn't turn out as he had imagined. He had intended, probably, to take what he could and go—but now he found that he had committed himself to the following of a grail. He knew that Daisy was extraordinary, but he didn't realize just how extraordinary a "nice" girl could be. She vanished into her rich house, into her rich, full life, leaving Gatsby—nothing. He felt married to her, that was all.

When they met again, two days later, it was Gatsby who was breathless, who was, somehow, betrayed. Her porch was bright with the bought luxury of star-shine; the wicker of the settee squeaked fashionably as she turned toward him and he kissed her curious and lovely mouth. She had caught a cold, and it made her voice huskier and more charming than ever, and Gatsby was overwhelmingly aware of the youth and mystery that wealth imprisons and preserves, of the freshness of many clothes, and of Daisy, gleaming like silver, safe and proud above the hot struggles of the poor.

"I can't describe to you how surprised I was to find out I loved her, old sport. I even hoped for a while that she'd throw me over, but she didn't, because she was in love with me too. She thought I knew a lot because I knew different things from her.... Well, there I was, 'way off my ambitions, getting deeper in love every minute, and all of a sudden I didn't care. What was the use of doing great things if I could have a better time telling her what I was going to do?"

On the last afternoon before he went abroad, he sat with Daisy in his arms for a long, silent time. It was a cold fall day, with fire in the room and her cheeks flushed. Now and then she moved and he changed his arm a little, and once he kissed her dark shining hair. The afternoon had made them tranquil for a while, as if to give them a deep memory for the long parting the next day promised. They had never been closer in their month of love, nor communicated more profoundly one with another, than when she brushed silent lips against his coat's shoulder or when he touched the end of her fingers, gently, as though she were asleep.

He did extraordinarily well in the war. He was a captain before he went to the front, and following the Argonne battles he got his majority[1] and the command of the divisional machine-guns. After the armistice he tried frantically to get home, but some complication or misunderstanding sent him to Oxford instead. He was worried now—there was a quality of nervous despair in Daisy's letters. She didn't see why he couldn't come. She was feeling the pressure of the world outside, and she wanted to see him and feel his presence beside her and be reassured that she was doing the right thing after all.

---

1 Promotion to major.

For Daisy was young and her artificial world was redolent of orchids and pleasant, cheerful snobbery and orchestras which set the rhythm of the year, summing up the sadness and suggestiveness of life in new tunes. All night the saxophones wailed the hopeless comment of the "Beale Street Blues"[1] while a hundred pairs of golden and silver slippers shuffled the shining dust. At the gray tea hour there were always rooms that throbbed incessantly with this low, sweet fever, while fresh faces drifted here and there like rose petals blown by the sad horns around the floor.

Through this twilight universe Daisy began to move again with the season; suddenly she was again keeping half a dozen dates a day with half a dozen men, and drowsing asleep at dawn with the beads and chiffon of an evening dress tangled among dying orchids on the floor beside her bed. And all the time something within her was crying for a decision. She wanted her life shaped now, immediately—and the decision must be made by some force—of love, of money, of unquestionable practicality—that was close at hand.

That force took shape in the middle of spring with the arrival of Tom Buchanan. There was a wholesome bulkiness about his person and his position, and Daisy was flattered. Doubtless there was a certain struggle and a certain relief. The letter reached Gatsby while he was still at Oxford.

It was dawn now on Long Island and we went about opening the rest of the windows down-stairs, filling the house with gray-turning, gold-turning light. The shadow of a tree fell abruptly across the dew and ghostly birds began to sing among the blue leaves. There was a slow, pleasant movement in the air, scarcely a wind, promising a cool, lovely day.

"I don't think she ever loved him." Gatsby turned around from a window and looked at me challengingly. "You must remember, old sport, she was very excited this afternoon. He told her those things in a way that frightened her—that made it look as if I was some kind of cheap sharper. And the result was she hardly knew what she was saying."

He sat down gloomily.

"Of course she might have loved him just for a minute, when they were first married—and loved me more even then, do you see?"

---

1 Popular blues song of 1919 by W.C. Handy (1873–1958).

Suddenly he came out with a curious remark.

"In any case," he said, "it was just personal."

What could you make of that, except to suspect some intensity in his conception of the affair that couldn't be measured?

He came back from France when Tom and Daisy were still on their wedding trip, and made a miserable but irresistible journey to Louisville on the last of his army pay. He stayed there a week, walking the streets where their footsteps had clicked together through the November night and revisiting the out-of-the-way places to which they had driven in her white car. Just as Daisy's house had always seemed to him more mysterious and gay than other houses, so his idea of the city itself, even though she was gone from it, was pervaded with a melancholy beauty.

He left feeling that if he had searched harder, he might have found her—that he was leaving her behind. The day-coach—he was penniless now—was hot. He went out to the open vestibule and sat down on a folding-chair, and the station slid away and the backs of unfamiliar buildings moved by. Then out into the spring fields, where a yellow trolley raced them for a minute with people in it who might once have seen the pale magic of her face along the casual street.

The track curved and now it was going away from the sun, which, as it sank lower, seemed to spread itself in benediction over the vanishing city where she had drawn her breath. He stretched out his hand desperately as if to snatch only a wisp of air, to save a fragment of the spot that she had made lovely for him. But it was all going by too fast now for his blurred eyes and he knew that he had lost that part of it, the freshest and the best, forever.

It was nine o'clock when we finished breakfast and went out on the porch. The night had made a sharp difference in the weather and there was an autumn flavor in the air. The gardener, the last one of Gatsby's former servants, came to the foot of the steps.

"I'm going to drain the pool to-day, Mr. Gatsby. Leaves'll start falling pretty soon, and then there's always trouble with the pipes."

"Don't do it to-day," Gatsby answered. He turned to me apologetically. "You know, old sport, I've never used that pool all summer?"

I looked at my watch and stood up.

"Twelve minutes to my train."

I didn't want to go to the city. I wasn't worth a decent stroke of work, but it was more than that—I didn't want to leave Gatsby. I missed that train, and then another, before I could get myself away.

"I'll call you up," I said finally.

"Do, old sport."

"I'll call you about noon."

We walked slowly down the steps.

"I suppose Daisy'll call too." He looked at me anxiously, as if he hoped I'd corroborate this.

"I suppose so."

"Well, good-by."

We shook hands and I started away. Just before I reached the hedge I remembered something and turned around.

"They're a rotten crowd," I shouted across the lawn. "You're worth the whole damn bunch put together."

I've always been glad I said that. It was the only compliment I ever gave him, because I disapproved of him from beginning to end. First he nodded politely, and then his face broke into that radiant and understanding smile, as if we'd been in ecstatic cahoots on that fact all the time. His gorgeous pink rag of a suit made a bright spot of color against the white steps, and I thought of the night when I first came to his ancestral home, three months before. The lawn and drive had been crowded with the faces of those who guessed at his corruption—and he had stood on those steps, concealing his incorruptible dream, as he waved them good-by.

I thanked him for his hospitality. We were always thanking him for that—I and the others.

"Good-by," I called. "I enjoyed breakfast, Gatsby."

Up in the city, I tried for a while to list the quotations on an interminable amount of stock, then I fell asleep in my swivel-chair. Just before noon the phone woke me, and I started up with sweat breaking out on my forehead. It was Jordan Baker; she often called me up at this hour because the uncertainty of her own movements between hotels and clubs and private houses made her hard to find in any other way. Usually her voice came over the wire as something fresh and cool, as if a divot from a green golf-links had come sailing in at the office window, but this morning it seemed harsh and dry.

"I've left Daisy's house," she said. "I'm at Hempstead,[1] and I'm going down to Southampton[2] this afternoon."

Probably it had been tactful to leave Daisy's house, but the act annoyed me, and her next remark made me rigid.

"You weren't so nice to me last night."

"How could it have mattered then?"

Silence for a moment. Then:

"However—I want to see you."

"I want to see you, too."

"Suppose I don't go to Southampton, and come into town this afternoon?"

"No—I don't think this afternoon."

"Very well."

"It's impossible this afternoon. Various——"

We talked like that for a while, and then abruptly we weren't talking any longer. I don't know which of us hung up with a sharp click, but I know I didn't care. I couldn't have talked to her across a tea-table that day if I never talked to her again in this world.

I called Gatsby's house a few minutes later, but the line was busy. I tried four times; finally an exasperated central told me the wire was being kept open for long distance from Detroit. Taking out my time-table, I drew a small circle around the three-fifty train. Then I leaned back in my chair and tried to think. It was just noon.

When I passed the ashheaps on the train that morning I had crossed deliberately to the other side of the car. I supposed there'd be a curious crowd around there all day with little boys searching for dark spots in the dust, and some garrulous man telling over and over what had happened, until it became less and less real even to him and he could tell it no longer, and Myrtle Wilson's tragic achievement was forgotten. Now I want to go back a little and tell what happened at the garage after we left there the night before.

They had difficulty in locating the sister, Catherine. She must have broken her rule against drinking that night, for when she arrived she was stupid with liquor and unable to understand that

---

1   A town on Long Island, about 30 miles east of New York City.
2   A town on the south shore of the eastern end of Long Island, about 100 miles from the city.

the ambulance had already gone to Flushing.[1] When they convinced her of this, she immediately fainted, as if that was the intolerable part of the affair. Someone, kind or curious, took her in his car and drove her in the wake of her sister's body.

Until long after midnight a changing crowd lapped up against the front of the garage, while George Wilson rocked himself back and forth on the couch inside. For a while the door of the office was open, and everyone who came into the garage glanced irresistibly through it. Finally someone said it was a shame, and closed the door. Michaelis and several other men were with him; first, four or five men, later two or three men. Still later Michaelis had to ask the last stranger to wait there fifteen minutes longer, while he went back to his own place and made a pot of coffee. After that, he stayed there alone with Wilson until dawn.

About three o'clock the quality of Wilson's incoherent muttering changed—he grew quieter and began to talk about the yellow car. He announced that he had a way of finding out whom the yellow car belonged to, and then he blurted out that a couple of months ago his wife had come from the city with her face bruised and her nose swollen.

But when he heard himself say this, he flinched and began to cry "Oh, my God!" again in his groaning voice. Michaelis made a clumsy attempt to distract him.

"How long have you been married, George? Come on there, try and sit still a minute and answer my question. How long have you been married?"

"Twelve years."

"Ever had any children? Come on, George, sit still—I asked you a question. Did you ever have any children?"

The hard brown beetles kept thudding against the dull light, and whenever Michaelis heard a car go tearing along the road outside it sounded to him like the car that hadn't stopped a few hours before. He didn't like to go into the garage, because the work bench was stained where the body had been lying, so he moved uncomfortably around the office—he knew every object in it before morning—and from time to time sat down beside Wilson trying to keep him more quiet.

"Have you got a church you go to sometimes, George? Maybe even if you haven't been there for a long time? Maybe I could call

---

1 Eastern section of Queens on Long Island, between Manhattan and Great Neck ("West Egg").

up the church and get a priest to come over and he could talk to you, see?"

"Don't belong to any."

"You ought to have a church, George, for times like this. You must have gone to church once. Didn't you get married in a church? Listen, George, listen to me. Didn't you get married in a church?"

"That was a long time ago."

The effort of answering broke the rhythm of his rocking—for a moment he was silent. Then the same half-knowing, half-bewildered look came back into his faded eyes.

"Look in the drawer there," he said, pointing at the desk.

"Which drawer?"

"That drawer—that one."

Michaelis opened the drawer nearest his hand. There was nothing in it but a small, expensive dog-leash, made of leather and braided silver. It was apparently new.

"This?" he inquired, holding it up.

Wilson stared and nodded.

"I found it yesterday afternoon. She tried to tell me about it, but I knew it was something funny."

"You mean your wife bought it?"

"She had it wrapped in tissue paper on her bureau."

Michaelis didn't see anything odd in that, and he gave Wilson a dozen reasons why his wife might have bought the dog-leash. But conceivably Wilson had heard some of these same explanations before, from Myrtle, because he began saying "Oh, my God!" again in a whisper—his comforter left several explanations in the air.

"Then he killed her," said Wilson. His mouth dropped open suddenly.

"Who did?"

"I have a way of finding out."

"You're morbid, George," said his friend. "This has been a strain to you and you don't know what you're saying. You'd better try and sit quiet till morning."

"He murdered her."

"It was an accident, George."

Wilson shook his head. His eyes narrowed and his mouth widened slightly with the ghost of a superior "Hm!"

"I know," he said definitely, "I'm one of these trusting fellas and I don't think any harm to *no*body, but when I get to know a thing I know it. It was the man in that car. She ran out to speak to him and he wouldn't stop."

Michaelis had seen this too, but it hadn't occurred to him that there was any special significance in it. He believed that Mrs. Wilson had been running away from her husband, rather than trying to stop any particular car.

"How could she of been like that?"

"She's a deep one," said Wilson, as if that answered the question. "Ah-h-h——"

He began to rock again, and Michaelis stood twisting the leash in his hand.

"Maybe you got some friend that I could telephone for, George?"

This was a forlorn hope—he was almost sure that Wilson had no friend: there was not enough of him for his wife. He was glad a little later when he noticed a change in the room, a blue quickening by the window, and realized that dawn wasn't far off. About five o'clock it was blue enough outside to snap off the light.

Wilson's glazed eyes turned out to the ashheaps, where small gray clouds took on fantastic shapes and scurried here and there in the faint dawn wind.

"I spoke to her," he muttered, after a long silence. "I told her she might fool me but she couldn't fool God. I took her to the window"—with an effort he got up and walked to the rear window and leaned with his face pressed against it—"and I said 'God knows what you've been doing, everything you've been doing. You may fool me, but you can't fool God!'"

Standing behind him, Michaelis saw with a shock that he was looking at the eyes of Doctor T.J. Eckleburg, which had just emerged, pale and enormous, from the dissolving night.

"God sees everything," repeated Wilson.

"That's an advertisement," Michaelis assured him. Something made him turn away from the window and look back into the room. But Wilson stood there a long time, his face close to the window pane, nodding into the twilight.

By six o'clock Michaelis was worn out, and grateful for the sound of a car stopping outside. It was one of the watchers of the night before who had promised to come back, so he cooked breakfast for three, which he and the other man ate together. Wilson was quieter now, and Michaelis went home to sleep;

when he awoke four hours later and hurried back to the garage, Wilson was gone.

His movements—he was on foot all the time—were afterward traced to Port Roosevelt and then to Gad's Hill,[1] where he bought a sandwich that he didn't eat, and a cup of coffee. He must have been tired and walking slowly, for he didn't reach Gad's Hill until noon. Thus far there was no difficulty in accounting for his time—there were boys who had seen a man "acting sort of crazy," and motorists at whom he stared oddly from the side of the road. Then for three hours he disappeared from view. The police, on the strength of what he said to Michaelis, that he "had a way of finding out," supposed that he spent that time going from garage to garage thereabout, inquiring for a yellow car. On the other hand, no garage man who had seen him ever came forward, and perhaps he had an easier, surer way of finding out what he wanted to know. By half-past two he was in West Egg, where he asked someone the way to Gatsby's house. So by that time he knew Gatsby's name.

At two o'clock Gatsby put on his bathing-suit and left word with the butler that if anyone phoned word was to be brought to him at the pool. He stopped at the garage for a pneumatic mattress that had amused his guests during the summer, and the chauffeur helped him pump it up. Then he gave instructions that the open car wasn't to be taken out under any circumstances—and this was strange, because the front right fender needed repair.

Gatsby shouldered the mattress and started for the pool. Once he stopped and shifted it a little, and the chauffeur asked him if he needed help, but he shook his head and in a moment disappeared among the yellowing trees.

No telephone message arrived, but the butler went without his sleep and waited for it until four o'clock—until long after there was anyone to give it to if it came. I have an idea that Gatsby himself didn't believe it would come, and perhaps he no longer cared. If that was true he must have felt that he had lost the old warm world, paid a high price for living too long with a single dream. He must have looked up at an unfamiliar sky through frightening leaves and shivered as he found what a grotesque thing a rose is and how raw the sunlight was upon the scarcely

---

1 Fictional place.

created grass. A new world, material without being real, where poor ghosts, breathing dreams like air, drifted fortuitously about ... like that ashen, fantastic figure gliding toward him through the amorphous trees.

The chauffeur—he was one of Wolfshiem's protégés—heard the shots—afterward he could only say that he hadn't thought anything much about them. I drove from the station directly to Gatsby's house and my rushing anxiously up the front steps was the first thing that alarmed anyone. But they knew then, I firmly believe. With scarcely a word said, four of us, the chauffeur, butler, gardener, and I, hurried down to the pool.

There was a faint, barely perceptible movement of the water as the fresh flow from one end urged its way toward the drain at the other. With little ripples that were hardly the shadows of waves, the laden mattress moved irregularly down the pool. A small gust of wind that scarcely corrugated the surface was enough to disturb its accidental course with its accidental burden. The touch of a cluster of leaves revolved it slowly, tracing, like the leg of transit, a thin red circle in the water.

It was after we started with Gatsby toward the house that the gardener saw Wilson's body a little way off in the grass, and the holocaust was complete.

Chapter IX

After two years I remember the rest of that day, and that night and the next day, only as an endless drill of police and photographers and newspaper men in and out of Gatsby's front door. A rope stretched across the main gate and a policeman by it kept out the curious, but little boys soon discovered that they could enter through my yard, and there were always a few of them clustered open-mouthed about the pool. Someone with a positive manner, perhaps a detective, used the expression "madman" as he bent over Wilson's body that afternoon, and the adventitious authority of his voice set the key for the newspaper reports next morning.

Most of those reports were a nightmare—grotesque, circumstantial, eager, and untrue. When Michaelis's testimony at the inquest brought to light Wilson's suspicions of his wife I thought the whole tale would shortly be served up in racy pasquinade[1]—

---

1 Lampoon or satire.

but Catherine, who might have said anything, didn't say a word. She showed a surprising amount of character about it too— looked at the coroner with determined eyes under that corrected brow of hers, and swore that her sister had never seen Gatsby, that her sister was completely happy with her husband, that her sister had been into no mischief whatever. She convinced herself of it, and cried into her handkerchief, as if the very suggestion was more than she could endure. So Wilson was reduced to a man "deranged by grief " in order that the case might remain in its simplest form. And it rested there.

But all this part of it seemed remote and unessential. I found myself on Gatsby's side, and alone. From the moment I telephoned news of the catastrophe to West Egg Village, every surmise about him, and every practical question, was referred to me. At first I was surprised and confused; then, as he lay in his house and didn't move or breathe or speak, hour upon hour, it grew upon me that I was responsible, because no one else was interested—interested, I mean, with that intense personal interest to which everyone has some vague right at the end.

I called up Daisy half an hour after we found him, called her instinctively and without hesitation. But she and Tom had gone away early that afternoon, and taken baggage with them.

"Left no address?"

"No."

"Say when they'd be back?"

"No."

"Any idea where they are? How I could reach them?"

"I don't know. Can't say."

I wanted to get somebody for him. I wanted to go into the room where he lay and reassure him: "I'll get somebody for you, Gatsby. Don't worry. Just trust me and I'll get somebody for you——"

Meyer Wolfshiem's name wasn't in the phone book. The butler gave me his office address on Broadway, and I called Information, but by the time I had the number it was long after five, and no one answered the phone.

"Will you ring again?"

"I've rung them three times."

"It's very important."

"Sorry. I'm afraid no one's there."

I went back to the drawing-room and thought for an instant that they were chance visitors, all these official people who suddenly filled it. But, as they drew back the sheet and looked at Gatsby with unmoved eyes, his protest continued in my brain:

"Look here, old sport, you've got to get somebody for me. You've got to try hard. I can't go through this alone."

Someone started to ask me questions, but I broke away and going up-stairs looked hastily through the unlocked parts of his desk—he'd never told me definitely that his parents were dead. But there was nothing—only the picture of Dan Cody, a token of forgotten violence, staring down from the wall.

Next morning I sent the butler to New York with a letter to Wolfshiem, which asked for information and urged him to come out on the next train. That request seemed superfluous when I wrote it. I was sure he'd start when he saw the newspapers, just as I was sure there'd be a wire from Daisy before noon—but neither a wire nor Mr. Wolfshiem arrived; no one arrived except more police and photographers and newspaper men. When the butler brought back Wolfshiem's answer I began to have a feeling of defiance, of scornful solidarity between Gatsby and me against them all.

> Dear Mr. Carraway. This has been one of the most terrible shocks of my life to me I hardly can believe it that it is true at all. Such a mad act as that man did should make us all think. I cannot come down now as I am tied up in some very important business and cannot get mixed up in this thing now. If there is anything I can do a little later let me know in a letter by Edgar. I hardly know where I am when I hear about a thing like this and am completely knocked down and out.
>
> Yours truly
> MEYER WOLFSHIEM

and then hasty addenda beneath:

> Let me know about the funeral etc do not know his family at all.

When the phone rang that afternoon and Long Distance said Chicago was calling I thought this would be Daisy at last. But the connection came through as a man's voice, very thin and far away.

"This is Slagle speaking ..."

"Yes?" The name was unfamiliar.

"Hell of a note, isn't it? Get my wire?"

"There haven't been any wires."

"Young Parke's in trouble," he said rapidly. "They picked him up when he handed the bonds over the counter. They got a circular from New York giving 'em the numbers just five minutes before. What d'you know about that, hey? You never can tell in these hick towns——"

"Hello!" I interrupted breathlessly. "Look here—this isn't Mr. Gatsby. Mr. Gatsby's dead."

There was a long silence on the other end of the wire, followed by an exclamation ... then a quick squawk as the connection was broken.

I think it was on the third day that a telegram signed Henry C. Gatz arrived from a town in Minnesota. It said only that the sender was leaving immediately and to postpone the funeral until he came.

It was Gatsby's father, a solemn old man, very helpless and dismayed, bundled up in a long cheap ulster[1] against the warm September day. His eyes leaked continuously with excitement, and when I took the bag and umbrella from his hands he began to pull so incessantly at his sparse gray beard that I had difficulty in getting off his coat. He was on the point of collapse, so I took him into the music room and made him sit down while I sent for something to eat. But he wouldn't eat, and the glass of milk spilled from his trembling hand.

"I saw it in the Chicago newspaper," he said. "It was all in the Chicago newspaper. I started right away."

"I didn't know how to reach you."

His eyes, seeing nothing, moved ceaselessly about the room.

"It was a madman," he said. "He must have been mad."

"Wouldn't you like some coffee?" I urged him.

"I don't want anything. I'm all right now, Mr.——"

"Carraway."

"Well, I'm all right now. Where have they got Jimmy?"

I took him into the drawing-room, where his son lay, and left him there. Some little boys had come up on the steps and were looking into the hall; when I told them who had arrived, they went reluctantly away.

---

1 Long, loose-fitting overcoat made of heavy material.

After a little while Mr. Gatz opened the door and came out, his mouth ajar, his face flushed slightly, his eyes leaking isolated and unpunctual tears. He had reached an age where death no longer has the quality of ghastly surprise, and when he looked around him now for the first time and saw the height and splendor of the hall and the great rooms opening out from it into other rooms, his grief began to be mixed with an awed pride. I helped him to a bedroom up-stairs; while he took off his coat and vest I told him that all arrangements had been deferred until he came.

"I didn't know what you'd want, Mr. Gatsby——"

"Gatz is my name."

"——Mr. Gatz. I thought you might want to take the body West."

He shook his head.

"Jimmy always liked it better down East. He rose up to his position in the East. Were you a friend of my boy's, Mr.——?"

"We were close friends."

"He had a big future before him, you know. He was only a young man, but he had a lot of brain power here."

He touched his head impressively, and I nodded.

"If he'd of lived, he'd of been a great man. A man like James J. Hill.[1] He'd of helped build up the country."

"That's true," I said, uncomfortably.

He fumbled at the embroidered coverlet, trying to take it from the bed, and lay down stiffly—was instantly asleep.

That night an obviously frightened person called up, and demanded to know who I was before he would give his name.

"This is Mr. Carraway," I said.

"Oh!" He sounded relieved. "This is Klipspringer."

I was relieved too, for that seemed to promise another friend at Gatsby's grave. I didn't want it to be in the papers and draw a sightseeing crowd, so I'd been calling up a few people myself. They were hard to find.

"The funeral's to-morrow," I said. "Three o'clock, here at the house. I wish you'd tell anybody who'd be interested."

---

1 James J. Hill (1838–1916), one of the most successful and ruthless of the late-nineteenth-century railway tycoons. A "self-made man," Hill developed the St. Paul and Pacific Railroad into the Great Northern Railway, which was instrumental in the commercial expansion and set-tlement of the West.

"Oh, I will," he broke out hastily. "Of course I'm not likely to see anybody, but if I do."

His tone made me suspicious.

"Of course you'll be there yourself."

"Well, I'll certainly try. What I called up about is——"

"Wait a minute," I interrupted. "How about saying you'll come?"

"Well, the fact is—the truth of the matter is that I'm staying with some people up here in Greenwich,[1] and they rather expect me to be with them to-morrow. In fact, there's a sort of picnic or something. Of course I'll do my very best to get away."

I ejaculated an unrestrained "Huh!" and he must have heard me, for he went on nervously:

"What I called up about was a pair of shoes I left there. I wonder if it'd be too much trouble to have the butler send them on. You see, they're tennis shoes, and I'm sort of helpless without them. My address is care of B.F.——"

I didn't hear the rest of the name, because I hung up the receiver.

After that I felt a certain shame for Gatsby—one gentleman to whom I telephoned implied that he had got what he deserved. However, that was my fault, for he was one of those who used to sneer most bitterly at Gatsby on the courage of Gatsby's liquor, and I should have known better than to call him.

The morning of the funeral I went up to New York to see Meyer Wolfshiem; I couldn't seem to reach him any other way. The door that I pushed open, on the advice of an elevator boy, was marked "The Swastika Holding Company,"[2] and at first

---

1 Town in Connecticut, to the north of Westchester County on the other side of Long Island Sound from Manhasset Neck ("East Egg").

2 The swastika (facing either leftward or rightward) was a common symbol in the early twentieth century before the Nazis adopted it in 1920 and, as Sarah Churchwell informs us (*Careless People* 155–56), was most familiarly associated in 1922 New York with the successful taxi company of Larry Fay (1888–1933), who laundered bootlegging profits through it. Still, even in the United States it was recognized as a symbol under which "Nordicist" organizations at home and abroad were gathering, and Fitzgerald, writing the novel in Europe, might have been aware of its growing anti-Semitic implications. In hindsight, Fitzgerald's irony here—if intended as such—comes across as tasteless and macabre, but like most of his contemporaries he could not have foreseen Hitler's political triumph nearly a decade later, nor its horrific consequences.

there didn't seem to be anyone inside. But when I'd shouted "hello" several times in vain, an argument broke out behind a partition, and presently a lovely Jewess appeared at an interior door and scrutinized me with black hostile eyes.

"Nobody's in," she said. "Mr. Wolfshiem's gone to Chicago."

The first part of this was obviously untrue, for someone had begun to whistle "The Rosary,"[1] tunelessly, inside.

"Please say that Mr. Carraway wants to see him."

"I can't get him back from Chicago, can I?"

At this moment a voice, unmistakably Wolfshiem's, called "Stella!" from the other side of the door.

"Leave your name on the desk," she said quickly. "I'll give it to him when he gets back."

"But I know he's there."

She took a step toward me and began to slide her hands indignantly up and down her hips.

"You young men think you can force your way in here any time," she scolded. "We're getting sickantired of it. When I say he's in Chicago, he's in Chicago."

I mentioned Gatsby.

"Oh-h!" She looked at me over again. "Will you just—What was your name?"

She vanished. In a moment Meyer Wolfshiem stood solemnly in the doorway, holding out both hands. He drew me into his office, remarking in a reverent voice that it was a sad time for all of us, and offered me a cigar.

"My memory goes back to when first I met him," he said. "A young major just out of the army and covered over with medals he got in the war. He was so hard up he had to keep on wearing his uniform because he couldn't buy some regular clothes. First time I saw him was when he come into Winebrenner's poolroom at Forty-third Street and asked for a job. He hadn't eat anything for a couple of days. 'Come on have some lunch with me,' I sid. He ate more than four dollars' worth of food in half an hour."

"Did you start him in business?" I inquired.

"Start him! I made him."

"Oh."

"I raised him up out of nothing, right out of the gutter. I saw right away he was a fine-appearing, gentlemanly young man, and

---

1   An 1898 song still popular in the 1920s, music by Ethelbert Nevin, lyrics by Robert Cameron Rogers.

when he told me he was an Oggsford I knew I could use him good. I got him to join up in the American Legion and he used to stand high there. Right off he did some work for a client of mine up to Albany.[1] We were so thick like that in everything"— he held up two bulbous fingers—"always together."

I wondered if this partnership had included the World's Series transaction in 1919.

"Now he's dead," I said after a moment. "You were his closest friend, so I know you'll want to come to his funeral this afternoon."

"I'd like to come."

"Well, come then."

The hair in his nostrils quivered slightly, and as he shook his head his eyes filled with tears.

"I can't do it—I can't get mixed up in it," he said.

"There's nothing to get mixed up in. It's all over now."

"When a man gets killed I never like to get mixed up in it in any way. I keep out. When I was a young man it was different—if a friend of mine died, no matter how, I stuck with them to the end. You may think that's sentimental, but I mean it—to the bitter end."

I saw that for some reason of his own he was determined not to come, so I stood up.

"Are you a college man?" he inquired suddenly.

For a moment I thought he was going to suggest a "gonnegtion," but he only nodded and shook my hand.

"Let us learn to show our friendship for a man when he is alive and not after he is dead," he suggested. "After that my own rule is to let everything alone."

When I left his office the sky had turned dark and I got back to West Egg in a drizzle. After changing my clothes I went next door and found Mr. Gatz walking up and down excitedly in the hall. His pride in his son and in his son's possessions was continually increasing and now he had something to show me.

"Jimmy sent me this picture." He took out his wallet with trembling fingers. "Look there."

It was a photograph of the house, cracked in the corners and dirty with many hands. He pointed out every detail to me eagerly. "Look there!" and then sought admiration from my eyes. He had shown it so often that I think it was more real to him now than the house itself.

---

1 The state capital of New York.

"Jimmy sent it to me. I think it's a very pretty picture. It shows up well."

"Very well. Had you seen him lately?"

"He come out to see me two years ago and bought me the house I live in now. Of course we was broke up when he run off from home, but I see now there was a reason for it. He knew he had a big future in front of him. And ever since he made a success he was very generous with me."

He seemed reluctant to put away the picture, held it for another minute, lingeringly, before my eyes. Then he returned the wallet and pulled from his pocket a ragged old copy of a book called "Hopalong Cassidy."[1]

"Look here, this is a book he had when he was a boy. It just shows you."

He opened it at the back cover and turned it around for me to see. On the last fly-leaf was printed the word SCHEDULE, and the date September 12, 1906. And underneath:

Rise from bed	6.00	A. M.
Dumbbell exercise and wall-scaling	6.15-6.30	"
Study electricity, etc	7.15-8.15	"
Work	8.30-4.30	P. M.
Baseball and sports	4.30-5.00	"
Practice elocution, poise and how to attain it	5.00-6.00	"
Study needed inventions	7.00-9.00	"

GENERAL RESOLVES

No wasting time at Shafters or [a name, indecipherable]
No more smokeing or chewing.
Bath every other day
Read one improving book or magazine per week
Save $5.00 [crossed out] $3.00 per week
Be better to parents[2]

"I come across this book by accident," said the old man. "It just shows you, don't it?"

---

1 First in a popular series of westerns by Clarence E. Mulford (1883–1956), first published in 1910.

2 Gatsby follows the example here of American icon Benjamin Franklin (1706–90), as established in Part Two of *The Autobiography of Benjamin Franklin* (1818; 1868).

"It just shows you."

"Jimmy was bound to get ahead. He always had some resolves like this or something. Do you notice what he's got about improving his mind? He was always great for that. He told me I et like a hog once, and I beat him for it."

He was reluctant to close the book, reading each item aloud and then looking eagerly at me. I think he rather expected me to copy down the list for my own use.

A little before three the Lutheran minister arrived from Flushing, and I began to look involuntarily out the windows for other cars. So did Gatsby's father. And as the time passed and the servants came in and stood waiting in the hall, his eyes began to blink anxiously, and he spoke of the rain in a worried, uncertain way. The minister glanced several times at his watch, so I took him aside and asked him to wait for half an hour. But it wasn't any use. Nobody came.

About five o'clock our procession of three cars reached the cemetery and stopped in a thick drizzle beside the gate—first a motor hearse, horribly black and wet, then Mr. Gatz and the minister and I in the limousine, and a little later four or five servants and the postman from West Egg, in Gatsby's station wagon, all wet to the skin. As we started through the gate into the cemetery I heard a car stop and then the sound of someone splashing after us over the soggy ground. I looked around. It was the man with owl-eyed glasses whom I had found marvelling over Gatsby's books in the library one night three months before.

I'd never seen him since then. I don't know how he knew about the funeral, or even his name. The rain poured down his thick glasses, and he took them off and wiped them to see the protecting canvas unrolled from Gatsby's grave.

I tried to think about Gatsby then for a moment, but he was already too far away, and I could only remember, without resentment, that Daisy hadn't sent a message or a flower. Dimly I heard someone murmur "Blessed are the dead that the rain falls on," and then the owl-eyed man said "Amen to that," in a brave voice.

We straggled down quickly through the rain to the cars. Owl-eyes spoke to me by the gate.

"I couldn't get to the house," he remarked.

"Neither could anybody else."

"Go on!" He started. "Why, my God! they used to go there by the hundreds."

He took off his glasses and wiped them again, outside and in. "The poor son-of-a-bitch," he said.

One of my most vivid memories is of coming back West from prep school and later from college at Christmas time. Those who went farther than Chicago would gather in the old dim Union Station at six o'clock of a December evening, with a few Chicago friends, already caught up into their own holiday gayeties, to bid them a hasty good-by. I remember the fur coats of the girls returning from Miss This-or-That's and the chatter of frozen breath and the hands waving overhead as we caught sight of old acquaintances, and the matchings of invitations: "Are you going to the Ordways'? the Herseys'? the Schultzes'?" and the long green tickets clasped tight in our gloved hands. And last the murky yellow cars of the Chicago, Milwaukee & St. Paul railroad looking cheerful as Christmas itself on the tracks beside the gate.

When we pulled out into the winter night and the real snow, our snow, began to stretch out beside us and twinkle against the windows, and the dim lights of small Wisconsin stations moved by, a sharp wild brace came suddenly into the air. We drew in deep breaths of it as we walked back from dinner through the cold vestibules, unutterably aware of our identity with this country for one strange hour, before we melted indistinguishably into it again.

That's my Middle West—not the wheat or the prairies or the lost Swede towns, but the thrilling returning trains of my youth, and the street lamps and sleigh bells in the frosty dark and the shadows of holly wreaths thrown by lighted windows on the snow. I am part of that, a little solemn with the feel of those long winters, a little complacent from growing up in the Carraway house in a city where dwellings are still called through decades by a family's name. I see now that this has been a story of the West, after all—Tom and Gatsby, Daisy and Jordan and I, were all Westerners, and perhaps we possessed some deficiency in common which made us subtly unadaptable to Eastern life.

Even when the East excited me most, even when I was most keenly aware of its superiority to the bored, sprawling, swollen towns beyond the Ohio, with their interminable inquisitions which spared only the children and the very old—even then it had always for me a quality of distortion. West Egg, especially, still figures in my more fantastic dreams. I see it as a night scene by El Greco:[1] a hundred houses, at once conventional and grotesque, crouching under a sullen, overhanging sky and a lustreless moon. In the foreground four solemn men in dress suits are walking along the sidewalk with a stretcher on which lies a drunken woman in a white evening dress. Her hand, which dangles over the side, sparkles cold with jewels. Gravely the men turn in at a house—the wrong house. But no one knows the woman's name, and no one cares.

After Gatsby's death the East was haunted for me like that, distorted beyond my eyes' power of correction. So when the blue smoke of brittle leaves was in the air and the wind blew the wet laundry stiff on the line I decided to come back home.

There was one thing to be done before I left, an awkward, unpleasant thing that perhaps had better have been let alone. But I wanted to leave things in order and not just trust that obliging and indifferent sea to sweep my refuse away. I saw Jordan Baker and talked over and around what had happened to us together, and what had happened afterward to me, and she lay perfectly still, listening, in a big chair.

She was dressed to play golf, and I remember thinking she looked like a good illustration, her chin raised a little jauntily, her hair the color of an autumn leaf, her face the same brown tint as the fingerless glove on her knee. When I had finished she told me without comment that she was engaged to another man. I doubted that, though there were several she could have married at a nod of her head, but I pretended to be surprised. For just a minute I wondered if I wasn't making a mistake, then I thought it all over again quickly and got up to say good-by.

"Nevertheless you did throw me over," said Jordan suddenly. "You threw me over on the telephone. I don't give a damn about you now, but it was a new experience for me, and I felt a little dizzy for a while."

We shook hands.

"Oh, and do you remember"—she added—"a conversation we had once about driving a car?"

"Why—not exactly."

"You said a bad driver was only safe until she met another bad driver? Well, I met another bad driver, didn't I? I mean it was careless of me to make such a wrong guess. I thought you were

---

1 El Greco (1541–1614), Greek artist who settled in Spain, admired by modernists for his mannered, strikingly intense style and mystical vision.

rather an honest, straightforward person. I thought it was your secret pride."

"I'm thirty," I said. "I'm five years too old to lie to myself and call it honor."

She didn't answer. Angry, and half in love with her, and tremendously sorry, I turned away.

One afternoon late in October I saw Tom Buchanan. He was walking ahead of me along Fifth Avenue in his alert, aggressive way, his hands out a little from his body as if to fight off interference, his head moving sharply here and there, adapting itself to his restless eyes. Just as I slowed up to avoid overtaking him he stopped and began frowning into the windows of a jewelry store. Suddenly he saw me and walked back, holding out his hand.

"What's the matter, Nick? Do you object to shaking hands with me?"

"Yes. You know what I think of you."

"You're crazy, Nick," he said quickly. "Crazy as hell. I don't know what's the matter with you."

"Tom," I inquired, "what did you say to Wilson that afternoon?"

He stared at me without a word, and I knew I had guessed right about those missing hours. I started to turn away, but he took a step after me and grabbed my arm.

"I told him the truth," he said. "He came to the door while we were getting ready to leave, and when I sent down word that we weren't in he tried to force his way up-stairs. He was crazy enough to kill me if I hadn't told him who owned the car. His hand was on a revolver in his pocket every minute he was in the house—" He broke off defiantly. "What if I did tell him? That fellow had it coming to him. He threw dust into your eyes just like he did in Daisy's, but he was a tough one. He ran over Myrtle like you'd run over a dog and never even stopped his car."

There was nothing I could say, except the one unutterable fact that it wasn't true.

"And if you think I didn't have my share of suffering—look here, when I went to give up that flat and saw that damn box of dog biscuits sitting there on the sideboard, I sat down and cried like a baby. By God it was awful——"

I couldn't forgive him or like him, but I saw that what he had done was, to him, entirely justified. It was all very careless and confused. They were careless people, Tom and Daisy—they smashed up things and creatures and then retreated back into their money or their vast carelessness, or whatever it was that kept them together, and let other people clean up the mess they had made....

I shook hands with him; it seemed silly not to, for I felt suddenly as though I were talking to a child. Then he went into the jewelry store to buy a pearl necklace—or perhaps only a pair of cuff buttons—rid of my provincial squeamishness forever.

Gatsby's house was still empty when I left—the grass on his lawn had grown as long as mine. One of the taxi drivers in the village never took a fare past the entrance gate without stopping for a minute and pointing inside; perhaps it was he who drove Daisy and Gatsby over to East Egg the night of the accident, and perhaps he had made a story about it all his own. I didn't want to hear it and I avoided him when I got off the train.

I spent my Saturday nights in New York because those gleaming, dazzling parties of his were with me so vividly that I could still hear the music and the laughter, faint and incessant, from his garden, and the cars going up and down his drive. One night I did hear a material car there, and saw its lights stop at his front steps. But I didn't investigate. Probably it was some final guest who had been away at the ends of the earth and didn't know that the party was over.

On the last night, with my trunk packed and my car sold to the grocer, I went over and looked at that huge incoherent failure of a house once more. On the white steps an obscene word, scrawled by some boy with a piece of brick, stood out clearly in the moonlight, and I erased it, drawing my shoe raspingly along the stone. Then I wandered down to the beach and sprawled out on the sand.

Most of the big shore places were closed now and there were hardly any lights except the shadowy, moving glow of a ferryboat across the Sound. And as the moon rose higher the inessential houses began to melt away until gradually I became aware of the old island here that flowered once for Dutch sailors' eyes—a fresh, green breast of the new world. Its vanished trees, the trees that had made way for Gatsby's house, had once pandered in whispers to the last and greatest of all human dreams; for a transitory enchanted moment man must have held his breath in the presence of this continent, compelled into an æsthetic contemplation he neither understood nor desired, face to face for the last time in history with something commensurate to his capacity for wonder.

And as I sat there brooding on the old, unknown world, I thought of Gatsby's wonder when he first picked out the green light at the end of Daisy's dock. He had come a long way to this blue lawn, and his dream must have seemed so close that he could hardly fail to grasp it. He did not know that it was already behind him, somewhere back in that vast obscurity beyond the city, where the dark fields of the republic rolled on under the night.

Gatsby believed in the green light, the orgastic future that year by year recedes before us. It eluded us then, but that's no matter—to-morrow we will run faster, stretch out our arms farther.... And one fine morning——

So we beat on, boats against the current, borne back ceaselessly into the past.

Appendix A: Fitzgerald's Correspondence about The Great Gatsby (1922–25)

[The selections from Fitzgerald's correspondence here— including letters from his editor Maxwell Perkins (1884–1947)—inform us about the gestation of the novel and make up the best testimony we have to the high aesthetic achievement for which its author was aiming. Most importantly, they offer Perkins's crucial response to the submitted typescript of the novel that led Fitzgerald to revise the galleys so substantially. Finally, they document Fitzgerald's worries over the critical reception and disappointing sales and acknowledgment of artistic flaws. With the exception of item 3, the selections below are either excerpts from longer letters or nearly complete letters with matter not pertaining to *The Great Gatsby* edited out. The texts of the letters are derived from the following two sources: Kuehl and Bryer, *Dear Scott/Dear Max: The Fitzgerald-Perkins Correspondence*, abbreviated below as *Dear Scott*; and Bruccoli, *F. Scott Fitzgerald: A Life in Letters*, abbreviated as *A Life*. I have followed the policy of the editors of these volumes and left spelling and punctuation errors as written. For the sake of regularity, all underlined titles and passages have been printed in italics.]

1. From F. Scott Fitzgerald to Maxwell Perkins, c. 20 June 1922 (*Dear Scott* 61)

When I send on this last bunch of stories I may start my novel and I may not. Its locale will be the middle west and New York of 1885 I think. It will concern less superlative beauties than I run to usually & will be centered on a smaller period of time. It will have a catholic element. I'm not quite sure whether I'm ready to start it quite yet or not. I'll write next week & tell you more definate plans.

2. From F. Scott Fitzgerald to Maxwell Perkins, c. 10 April 1924 (*Dear Scott* 70)

I feel I have an enormous power in me now, more than I've ever had in a way but it works so fitfully and with so many bogeys because I've *talked so much* and not lived enough within myself to develop the nessessary self reliance. Also I don't know anyone who has used up so much personal experience as I have at 27. Copperfield & Pendennis[1] were written at past forty while This Side of Paradise was three books & the B. & D. was two. So in my new novel I'm thrown directly on purely creative work—not trashy imaginings as in my stories but the sustained imagination of a sincere and yet radiant world. So I tread slowly and carefully & at times in considerable distress. This book will be a consciously artistic achievement & must depend on that as the 1st books did not.

3. From F. Scott Fitzgerald to Maxwell Perkins, c. 25 August 1924 (*Dear Scott* 75–76)

The novel will be done next week. That doesn't mean however that it'll reach America before October 1st. as Zelda and I are contemplating a careful revision after a weeks complete rest.

[...]

I think my novel is about the best American novel ever written. It is rough stuff in places, runs only to about 50,000 words & I hope you won't shy at it.

4. F. Scott Fitzgerald to Maxwell Perkins, 27 October 1924 (*Dear Scott* 80–81)

Under separate cover I'm sending you my third novel:

The Great Gatsby

---

1 *David Copperfield* (1850), autobiographical novel by Charles Dickens (1812–70); *The History of Pendennis* (1848–50), novel by William Makepeace Thackeray (1811–63).

(I think that at last I've done something really my own), but how good "my own" is remains to be seen.

I should suggest the following contract.

15% up to 50,000

20% after 50,000

The book is only a little over fifty thousand words long but I believe, as you know, that Whitney Darrow[1] has the wrong psychology about prices (and about what class constitute the book-buying public now that the lowbrows go to the movies) and I'm anxious to charge two dollars for it and have it a *full size book*.

Of course I want the binding to be absolutely uniform with my other books—the stamping too—and the jacket we discussed before. This time I don't want any signed blurbs on the jacket— not Mencken's or Lewis' or Howard's[2] or anyone's. I'm tired of being the author of *This Side of Paradise* and I want to start over.

[...]

I have an alternative title:

Gold-hatted Gatsby

After you've read the book let me know what you think about the title. Naturally I won't get a nights sleep until I hear from you but do tell me the absolute truth, *your first impression of the book* & tell me anything that bothers you in it.

5. From F. Scott Fitzgerald to Maxwell Perkins, c. 7 November 1924 (*Dear Scott* 81–82)

By now you've received the novel. There are things in it I'm not satisfied with in the middle of the book—Chapters 6 & 7. And I

---

1 Employee in charge of sales and promotion at Scribner's.
2 H.L. Mencken; Sinclair Lewis (1885–1951); and Sidney Howard (1891–1939), playwright and screenwriter, author of the 1924 play *They Knew What They Wanted*.

may write in a complete new scene in proof. I hope you got my telegram.

I have decided to stick to the title I put on the book.

Trimalchio in West Egg

The only other titles that seem to fit it are *Trimalchio* and *On the Road to West Egg*. I had two others *Gold-hatted Gatsby* and *The High-bouncing Lover* but they seemed too light.

We leave for Rome as soon as I finish the short story I'm working on.

6. From Maxwell Perkins to F. Scott Fitzgerald, 20 November 1924 (*Dear Scott* 82–84)

I think you have every kind of right to be proud of this book. It is an extraordinary book, suggestive of all sorts of thoughts and moods. You adopted exactly the right method of telling it, that of employing a narrator who is more of a spectator than an actor: this puts the reader upon a point of observation on a higher level than that on which the characters stand and at a distance that gives perspective. In no other way could your irony have been so immensely effective, nor the reader have been enabled so strongly to feel at times the strangeness of human circumstance in a vast heedless universe. In the eyes of Dr. Eckleberg various readers will see different significances; but their presence gives a superb touch to the whole thing: great unblinking eyes, expressionless, looking down upon the human scene. It's magnificent!

I could go on praising the book and speculating on its various elements and meanings, but points of criticism are more important now. I think you are right in feeling a certain slight sagging in chapters six and seven, and I don't know how to suggest a remedy. I hardly doubt that you will find one and I am only writing to say that I think it does need something to hold up here to the pace set, and ensuing. I have only two actual criticisms:—

One is that among a set of characters marvelously palpable and vital—I would know Tom Buchanan if I met him on the street and would avoid him—Gatsby is somewhat vague. The reader's eyes can never quite focus upon him, his outlines are dim. Now everything about Gatsby is more or less a mystery i.e. more or less vague, and this may be somewhat of an artistic intention, but I think it is mistaken. Couldn't *he* be physically described as distinctly as the others, and couldn't you add one or two characteristics like the use of that phrase "old sport",—not verbal, but physical ones, perhaps. I think that for some reason or other a reader—this was true of Mr. Scribner and of Louise[1]—gets an idea that Gatsby is a much older man than he is, although you have the writer say that he is little older than himself. But this would be avoided if on his first appearance he was seen as vividly as Daisy and Tom are, for instance;—and I do not think your scheme would be impaired if you made him so.

The other point is also about Gatsby: his career must remain mysterious, of course. But in the end you make it pretty clear that his wealth came through his connection with Wolfsheim. You also suggest this much earlier. Now almost all readers numerically are going to be puzzled by his having all this wealth and are going to feel entitled to an explanation. To give a distinct and definite one would be, of course, utterly absurd. It did occur to me though, that you might here and there interpolate some phrases, and possibly incidents, little touches of various kinds, that would suggest that he was in some active way mysteriously engaged. You do have him called on the telephone, but couldn't he be seen once or twice consulting at his parties with people of some sort of mysterious significance, from the political, the gambling, the sporting world, or whatever it may be. I know I am floundering, but that fact may help you to see what I mean. The total lack of an explanation through so large a part of the story does seem to me a defect;— or not of an explanation, but of the suggestion of an explanation. I wish you were here so I could talk about it to you for then I know I could at least make you understand what I mean. What Gatsby did ought never to be definitely imparted, even if it could be. Whether he was an innocent tool in the hands of somebody else, or to what degree he was this, ought not to be explained. But if some sort of business activity of his were simply adumbrated, it would lend further probability to that part of the story.

---

1 Charles Scribner II (1854–1930), head of the publishing firm Charles Scribner's Sons; Louise Perkins, Maxwell's wife.

There is one other point: in giving deliberately Gatsby's biography when he gives it to the narrator you do depart from the method of the narrative in some degree, for otherwise almost everything is told, and beautifully told, in the regular flow of it,— in the succession of events or in accompaniment with them. But you can't avoid the biography altogether. I thought you might find ways to let the truth of some of his claims like "Oxford" and his army career come out bit by bit in the course of actual narrative. I mention the point anyway for consideration in this interval before I send the proofs.

The general brilliant quality of the book makes me ashamed to make even these criticisms. The amount of meaning you get into a sentence, the dimensions and intensity of the impression you make a paragraph carry, are most extraordinary. The manuscript is full of phrases which make a scene blaze with life. If one enjoyed a rapid railroad journey I would compare the number and vividness of pictures your living words suggest, to the living scenes disclosed in that way. It seems in reading a much shorter book than it is, but it carries the mind through a series of experiences that one would think would require a book of three times its length.

The presentation of Tom, his place, Daisy and Jordan, and the unfolding of their characters is unequalled so far as I know. The description of the valley of ashes adjacent to the lovely country, the conversation and the action in Myrtle's apartment, the marvelous catalogue of those who came to Gatsby's house,—these are such things as make a man famous. And all these things, the whole pathetic episode, you have given a place in time and space, for with the help of T.J. Eckleberg and by an occasional glance at the sky, or the sea, or the city, you have imparted a sort of sense of eternity. You once told me you were not a natural writer—my God! You have plainly mastered the craft, of course; but you needed far more than craftsmanship for this.

7. From F. Scott Fitzgerald to Maxwell Perkins, c. 1 December 1924 (*Dear Scott* 85–86)

Your wire & your letters made me feel like a million dollars— I'm sorry I could make no better response than a telegram whining for money. But the long siege of the novel winded me a little & I've been slow on starting the stories on which I must live.

I think all your criticisms are true

(a) About the title. I'll try my best but I don't know what I can do. Maybe simply "Trimalchio" or "Gatsby." In the former case I don't see why the note shouldn't go on the back.

(b) Chapters VI & VII I know how to fix

(c) Gatsby's business affairs I can fix. I get your point about them.

(d) His vagueness I can repair by making more pointed—this doesn't sound good but wait and see. It'll make him clear

(e) But his long narrative in Chap VIII will be difficult to split up. Zelda also thought I was a little out of key but it is good writing and I don't think I could bear to sacrifice any of it

(f) I have 1000 minor corrections which I will make on the proof & several more large ones which you didn't mention.

Your criticisms were excellent & most helpful & you picked out all my favorite spots in the book to praise as high spots. Except you didn't mention my favorite of all—the chapter where Gatsby & Daisy meet.

[...]

Another point—in Chap. II of my book when Tom & Myrte go into the bedroom while Carraway reads Simon called Peter—is that raw? Let me know. I think its pretty nessessary.

I made the royalty smaller because I wanted to make up for all money you've advanced these two years by letting it pay a sort of interest on it. But I see by calculating I made it too small—a difference of 2000 dollars. Let us call it 15% up to 40,000 and 20% after that. That's a good fair contract all around.

[...]

Anyhow thanks & thanks & thanks for your letters. I'd rather have you & Bunny[1] like it than anyone I know. And I'd rather have you like it than Bunny. If its as good as you say, when I finish with the proof it'll be perfect.

Remember, by the way, to put by some cloth for the cover uniform with my other books.

As soon as I can think about the title I'll write or wire a decision.

8. From Maxwell Perkins to F. Scott Fitzgerald, 16 December 1924 (*Dear Scott* 86–87)

Your cable changing the title to "The Great Gatsby" has come and has been followed [...].

[...]

I hope you are thinking over "The Great Gatsby" in this interval and will add to it freely. The most important point I think, is that of how he comes by his wealth,—some sort of suggestion about it. He was supposed to be a bootlegger, wasn't he, at least in part, and I should think a little touch here and there would give the reader the suspicion that this was so and that is all that is needed.

9. F. Scott Fitzgerald to Maxwell Perkins, c. 20 December 1924 (*Dear Scott* 89–90)

With the aid you've given me I can make "Gatsby" perfect. The chapter VII (the hotel scene) will never quite be up to mark— I've worried about it too long & I can't quite place Daisy's reaction. But I can improve it a lot. It isn't imaginative energy that's lacking—its because I'm automatically prevented from thinking it out over again *because I must get all those characters to New York* in order to have the catastrophe on the road going back & I must have it pretty much that way. So there's no chance of bringing the freshness to it that a new free conception sometimes gives.

The rest is easy and I see my way so clear that I even see the mental quirks that queered it before. Strange to say my notion of

---

1 Nickname of Fitzgerald's friend Edmund Wilson (1895–1972).

Gatsby's vagueness was O.K. What you and Louise & Mr. Charles Scribner found wanting was that:

I myself didn't know what Gatsby looked like or was engaged in & you felt it. If I'd known & kept it from you you'd have been *too impressed with my knowledge to protest.* This is a complicated idea but I'm sure you'll understand. But I know now—and as a penalty for not having known first, in other words to make sure I'm going to tell more.

It seems of almost mystical significance to me that you thot he was older—the man I had in mind, half unconsciously, *was* older (a specific individual)[1] and evidently, without so much as a definate word, I conveyed the fact.—or rather, I must qualify this Shaw-Desmond-trash[2] by saying that I conveyed it without a word that I can at present and for the life of me, trace. [...]

Anyhow after careful searching of the files (of a man's mind here) for the Fuller Magee case[3] & after having had Zelda draw pictures until her fingers ache I know Gatsby better than I know my own child. My first instinct after your letter was to let him go & have Tom Buchanan dominate the book (I supposed he's the best character I've ever done [...]) but Gatsby sticks in my heart. I had him for awhile then lost him & now I know I have him

---

1 This may be a reference to Max (von) Gerlach, a Great Neck bootlegger long presumed to be the chief model for Gatsby.

2 After Shaw Desmond (1877–1960), prolific Irish man of letters interested in psychic research.

3 In the summer of 1922, the New York brokerage firm E.M. Fuller & Co. declared bankruptcy. Edward M. Fuller, head of the company and a Great Neck resident, was soon indicted along with William McGee on charges of gambling with customers' funds. A series of trials that began soon after Fitzgerald moved to Great Neck led to their conviction, as well as the exposure of a complex web of financial impropriety—including plans to sell fraudulent securities over the telephone—involving a number of socially prominent people. It also emerged that Fuller had ties to gambler Arnold Rothstein (1882–1928), the model for Wolfshiem. Fitzgerald read up on the case in his effort to adumbrate Gatsby's criminal activities and account for his wealth. This background to the novel explains Gatsby's offering bond salesman Nick the opportunity to partake in his "little business on the side" (Chapter V).

again. I'm sorry Myrtle is better than Daisy. Jordan of course was a great idea (perhaps you know its Edith Cummings)[1] but she fades out. Its Chap VII that's the trouble with Daisy & it may hurt the book's popularity that its *a man's book*.

Anyhow I think (for the first time since The Vegetable failed) that I'm a wonderful writer & its your always wonderful letters that help me to go on believing in myself.

Now some practical, very important questions. Please answer every one.

1. Montenegro has an order called The Order of Danilo. Is there any possible way you could find out for me there what it would look like—whether a courtesy decoration given to an American would bear an English inscription—or anything to give versimilitude to the medal which sounds horribly amateurish.

2. Please have *no blurbs of any kind on the jacket*!!! No Mencken or Lewis or Sid Howard or anything. I don't believe in them *one bit* any more.

3. Don't forget to change name of book in list of works

4. Please shift exclamation point from end of 3d line to end of 4th line in title page poem. *Please*! Important!

5. I thought that the whole episode (2 paragraphs) about their playing the Jazz History of the world at Gatsby's first party was rotten. Did you? Tell me frank *reaction—personal*, don't *think*![2] We can all think!

10. F. Scott Fitzgerald to Maxwell Perkins, c. 15 January 1925 (*Dear Scott* 91)

Proof hasn't arrived yet. Have been in bed for a week with grippe but I'm ready to attack it violently. Here are two important things.

---

1 Close friend (1899–1984) of Ginevra King (1898–1980), Fitzgerald's first love; winner of the 1923 US Women's Amateur Golf Championship.
2 In this sentence, Fitzgerald underlined the word "personal" three times and "think" twice.

1. In [Is?] the scene in Myrtes appartment—in the place where *Tom & Myrtle dissapear for awhile* noticeably raw. Does it stick out enough so that the censor might get it. Its the only place in the book I'm in doubt about on that score. Please let me know right away.

2. Please have *no quotations from any critics whatsoever on the jacket*—simply your own blurb on the back and don't give away too much of the idea—especially don't connect Daisy & Gatsby (I need the quality of surprise there.) Please be *very general*.

These points are both very important. Do drop me a line about them.

11. From Maxwell Perkins to F. Scott Fitzgerald, 20 January 1925 (*Dear Scott* 92)

You are beginning to get me worried about the scene in Myrtle's apartment for you have spoken of it several times. It never occurred to me to think there was any objection to it. I am sure there is none. No censor could make an issue on that,—nor I think on anything else in the book.

[...]

I certainly hope the proofs have got to you and that you have been at work on them for some time. If not you had better cable. They were sent first-class mail. The first lot on December 27th and the second lot on December 30th.

12. F. Scott Fitzgerald to Maxwell Perkins, 24 January 1925 (*Dear Scott* 92–94)

This is a most important letter so I'm having it typed. Guard it as your life.

1) Under a separate cover I'm sending the first part of the proof. While I agreed with the general suggestions in your first letters I differ with you in others. I *want* Myrtle Wilson's breast ripped off—its exactly the thing, I think, and I don't want to chop up the good scenes by too much tinkering. When Wolf-sheim says "sid" for "said", it's deliberate. "Orgastic" is the adjective from "orgasm" and it expresses exactly the intended ecstasy. It's not a bit dirty. I'm much more worried about the disappearance of Tom and Myrtle on Galley 9—I think it's all

right but I'm not sure. If it isn't please wire and I'll send correction.

2) Now about the page proof—under certain conditions never mind sending them (unless, of course, there's loads of time, which I suppose there isn't. I'm keen for late March or early April publication)

The conditions are two.

a.) That someone reads it *very carefully twice* to see that every one of my inserts are put in correctly. There are so many of them that I'm in terror of a mistake.

b.) That no changes *whatsoever* are made in it except in the case of a misprint so glaring as to be certain, and that only by you.

If there's some time left but not enough for the double mail send them to me and I'll simply wire O.K. which will save two weeks. However don't postpone for that. In any case send me the page proof as usual just to see.

[...]

4) This is very important. Be sure not to give away *any* of my plot in the blurb. Don't give away that Gatsby *dies* or is a *par venu* or a *crook* or anything. It's a part of the suspense of the book that all these things are in doubt until the end. You'll watch this won't you? And remember about having no quotations from critics on the jacket—*not even about my other books*!

[...]

P.S. I'm returning the proof of the title page ect. It's O.K. but my heart tells me I should have named it *Trimalchio*. However against all the advice I suppose it would have been stupid and stubborn of me. *Trimalchio in West Egg* was only a compromise. *Gatsby* is too much like Babbit and *The Great Gatsby* is weak because there's no emphasis even ironically on his greatness or lack of it. However let it pass.

13. From F. Scott Fitzgerald to Maxwell Perkins, c. 18 February 1925 (*Dear Scott* 94)

After six weeks of uninterrupted work the proof is finished and the last of it goes to you this afternoon. On the whole its been very successful labor

(1.) I've brought Gatsby to life

(2.) I've accounted for his money

(3.) I've fixed up the two weak chapers (VI and VIII)

(4.) I've improved his first party

(5.) I've broken up his long narrative in Chap. VIII

This morning I wired you to *hold up the galley of Chap 40.* The correction—and God! its important because in my other revision I made Gatsby look too mean—is enclosed herewith. Also some corrections for the page proof.

[...]

Do tell me if all corrections have been recieved. I'm worried.

I hope you're setting publication date at first possible moment.

14. From Maxwell Perkins to F. Scott Fitzgerald, 20 April 1925 (*Dear Scott* 100–01)

I wired you today rather discouragingly in the matter of the sales and I could send no qualifications in a cable. A great many of the trade have been very skeptical. I cannot make out just why. But one point is the small number of pages in the book,—an old stock objection which I thought we had got beyond. To attempt to explain to them that the way of writing which you have chosen and which is bound to come more and more into practice is one where a vast amount is said by implication, and that therefore the book is as full as it would have been if written to much greater length by another method, is of course utterly futile. The small number of pages, however, did in the end lead a couple of big distributors to reduce their orders immensely at the very last minute. The sale is up to the public and that has not yet had time to reveal itself fully. On the other hand, we have had a very good review, a very conspicuous one, in the Times and an excellent one also in the Tribune from Isabelle Patterson. William Rose Benet has announced preliminary to a review in the Saturday Review, that this is distinctly your best book. And the individuals whom I encounter like Gilbert Seldes (who will write also), Van Wyck Brooks, John Marquand, John Bishop, think this too.[1] Marquand and Seldes were both quite wild about it. These people understand it fully, which even the Times and Tribune reviewers did not.

I will send you anything that has much significance by cable. I know fully how this period must try you: it must be very hard to endure, because it is hard enough for me to endure. I like the book so much myself and see so much in it that its recognition and success mean more to me than anything else in sight at the present time,—I mean in any department of interest, not only that of literature. But it does seem to me from the comments of many who yet feel its enchantment, that it is over the heads of more people than you would probably suppose.

15. From F. Scott Fitzgerald to Maxwell Perkins, c. 24 April 1925 (*Dear Scott* 101–02)

Your telegram depressed me. I hope I'll find better news in Paris and am wiring you from Lyons. There's nothing to say until I hear more. If the book fails commercially it will be from one of two reasons or both.

1st The title is only fair, rather bad than good.

2nd *And most important*—the book contains no important woman character and women controll the fiction market at present. I don't think the unhappy end matters particularly.

---

1 For the *New York Herald Tribune* review by novelist and critic Isabel Paterson (1886–1961), see Appendix B1. For the reviews by poet and critic William Rose Benét (1886–1950) and pioneering popular culture critic Gilbert Seldes (1893–1970), see Appendices B3 and B7, respectively. Van Wyck Brooks (1886–1963), prominent American culture critic much admired by Fitzgerald; John P. Marquand (1893–1960), satiric novelist and contributor to the *Saturday Evening Post*.

It will have to sell 20,000 copies to wipe out my debt to you. I think it will do that all right—but my hope was it would do 75,000. This week will tell.

[...]

In all events I have a book of good stories for the fall. Now I shall write some cheap ones until I've accumulated enough for my next novel. When that is finished and published I'll wait and see. If it will support me with no more intervals of trash I'll go on as a novelist. If not I'm going to quit, come home, go to Hollywood and learn the movie business. I can't reduce our scale of living and I can't stand this financial insecurity. Anyhow there's no point in trying to be an artist if you can't do your best. I had my chance back in 1920 to start my life on a sensible scale and I lost it and so I'll have to pay the penalty. Then perhaps at 40 I can start writing again without this constant worry and interruption.

16. From F. Scott Fitzgerald to Edmund Wilson, May 1925 (*A Life* 109)

Thanks for your letter about the book. I was awfully happy that you liked it and that you approved of its design. The worst fault in it, I think is a Big Fault: I gave no account (and had no feeling about or knowledge of) the emotional relations between Gatsby and Daisy from the time of their reunion to the catastrophe. However the lack is so astutely concealed by the retrospect of Gatsby's past and by blankets of excellent prose that no one has noticed it—tho everyone has felt the lack and called it by another name. Mencken said (in a most entheusiastic letter received today) that the only fault was that the central story was trivial and a sort of anecdote (that is because he has forgotten his admiration for Conrad[1] and adjusted himself to the sprawling novel.) and I felt that what he really missed was the lack of any emotional backbone at the very height of it.

Without makeing any invidious comparisons between Class A. and Class C., if my novel is an anecdote so is *The Brothers Karamazoff*.[2] From one angle the latter could be reduced into a detec-

---

1 A reference to novelist Joseph Conrad (see Introduction, p. 29).
2 *The Brothers Karamazoff* (or *Karamazov*), 1880 masterpiece of Russian novelist Fyodor Dostoevsky (1821–81).

tive story. However the letters from you and Mencken have compensated me for the fact that of all the reviews, even the most entheusiastic, not one had the slightest idea what the book was about and for the even more depressing fact that it was, in comparison with the others, a financial failure (after I'd turned down fifteen thousand for the serial rights!).[1]

17. F. Scott Fitzgerald to H.L. Mencken, 4 May 1925 (*A Life* 110–11)

Your letter was the first outside word that reached me about my book. I was tremendously moved both by the fact that you liked it and by your kindness in writing me about it. By the next mail came a letter from Edmund Wilson and a clipping from Stallings,[2] both bulging with interest and approval, but as you know I'd rather have you like a book of mine than anyone in America.

There is a tremendous fault in the book—the lack of an emotional presentment of Daisy's attitude toward Gatsby after their reunion (and the consequent lack of logic or importance in her throwing him over). Everyone has felt this but no one has spotted it because its concealed beneath elaborate and overlapping blankets of prose. Wilson complained: "The characters are so uniformly unpleasant," Stallings: "a sheaf of gorgeous notes for a novel" and you say: "The story is fundamentally trivial." I think the smooth, almost unbroken pattern makes you feel that. Despite your admiration for Conrad you have lately—perhaps in reaction against the merely well-made novels of James' imitators—become used to the formless.[3] It is in protest against my own formless two novels, and Lewis' and Dos Passos' that this

---

1 Fitzgerald was unsuccessful at getting the $15–20,000 he wanted for serial rights to *The Great Gatsby*; two magazine editors turned him down. *College Humor* offered him $10,000, but he rejected the offer because he did not want to delay book publication and thought the venue would give a misleading impression of the novel.

2 Laurence Stallings (1894–1968), playwright and later screenwriter, author with Maxwell Anderson (1888–1959) of the controversial 1924 play *What Price Glory?* He wrote a good review of the novel for the *New York World*.

3 Reference to followers of the austere preoccupation with novelistic form (especially economy of incident and point-of-view) evident in the novels and criticism of American writer Henry James.

was written.[1] I admit that in comparison to *My Antonia* and *The Lost Lady* it is a failure in what it tries to do but I think in comparison to *Cytherea* or *Linda Condon* it is a success.[2] At any rate I have learned a lot from writing it and the influence on it has been the masculine one of *The Brothers Karamazov*, a thing of incomparable form, rather than the feminine one of *The Portrait of a Lady*.[3] If it seems trivial or "anecdotal" (sp) is because of an aesthetic fault, a failure in one very important episode and not a frailty in the theme—at least I don't think so. Did you ever know a writer to calmly take a just critisism and shut up?

18. F. Scott Fitzgerald to John Peale Bishop,[4] c. 9 August 1925 (*A Life* 125–26)

Thank you for your most pleasant, full, discerning and helpful letter about *The Great Gatsby*. It is about the only critisism that the book has had which has been intelligable, save a letter from Mrs. Wharton.[5] I shall duly ponder, or rather I have pondered, what you say about accuracy—I'm afraid I haven't quite reached the ruthless artistry which would let me cut out an exquisite bit that had no place in the context. I can cut out the almost exquisite, the adequate, even the brilliant—but a true accuracy is, as you say, still in the offing. Also you are right about Gatsby being blurred and patchy. I never at any one time saw him clear myself—for he started as one man I knew and then changed into myself—the amalgam was never complete in my mind.

---

1 Sinclair Lewis; John Dos Passos (1896–1970).

2 *My Ántonia* (1918) and *A Lost Lady* (1923), novels by Willa Cather (1873–1947); Fitzgerald wrote her out of concern that he might be misconstrued as having plagiarized some bits of characterization from the latter novel. *Cytherea* (1922) and *Linda Condon* (1919), novels by Joseph Hergesheimer (1880–1954).

3 *The Portrait of a Lady* (1880; 1908), novel by Henry James (1843–1916).

4 American poet and novelist (1892–1944) who befriended Fitzgerald at Princeton.

5 Edith Wharton (1862–1937), prolific novelist, who wrote Fitzgerald praising the novel (8 June 1925 letter reprinted in Fitzgerald, *The Crack-Up* 309).

19. F. Scott Fitzgerald to Marya Mannes,[1] 21 October 1925 (*A Life* 129)

Thank you for writing me about *Gatsby*—I especially appreciate your letter because women, and even intelligent women, haven't generally cared much for it. They do not like women to be presented as *emotionally* passive—as a matter of fact I think most women are, that their minds are taken up with a sort of second rate and inessential bookkeeping which their apologists call "practicality"—like the French they are centime-savers in the business of magic.

---

1 New York-based American journalist and novelist (1904–90).

Appendix B: Contemporary Reviews

[Fitzgerald's early complaints about the uncomprehending or negligent reviews of his novel should not overshadow the fact that they were generally positive. The novel received favorable reviews from some distinguished critics of the day, most notably his recent friend Gilbert Seldes (1893–1970), an early champion of T.S. Eliot (1888–1965) and James Joyce (1882–1941) and author of *The Seven Lively Arts*, a ground breaking 1924 collection of appreciations of American popular culture. Fitzgerald was particularly stung by his friend H.L. Mencken's (1880–1956) backhanded acknowledgment that the novel had style but little substance, and he seems to have been angered by the equivocal review of another occasional friend, literary columnist Burton Rascoe (1892–1957), which began by citing a defensive statement Fitzgerald sent him that repudiated unflattering comparisons between his own fiction and the popular novels of Robert W. Chambers (1865–1933). (That review, presumably alluded to in Fitzgerald's correspondence, has only recently resurfaced thanks to Sarah Churchwell, who located and reprinted it in "'The Balzacs of America.'") But even underwhelmed critics like Rascoe and Isabel Paterson (1886–1961) acknowledged its superiority to Fitzgerald's earlier novels. The more prescient judgments expressed below anticipated Fitzgerald's posthumous canonization as an aesthetically rigorous novelist in the tradition of Gustave Flaubert (1821–80), Joseph Conrad (1857–1924), and Henry James (1843–1916). The reviews by Paterson, Mencken, Benét, and Curtis have been slightly abridged; the latter half only of Van Vechten's review has been reprinted; Seldes's review has been reprinted in its entirety, as has the section on *The Great Gatsby* from Rascoe's monthly column for *Arts & Decoration*.]

1. From Isabel Paterson, "Up to the Minute," *New York Herald Tribune Books* (19 April 1925), 6

For a reviewer with a conscience, here is a nice problem—to give Scott Fitzgerald's new novel its just due without seeming to overpraise it, or, contrariwise, to say plainly that it is neither profound nor durable, without producing the impression that it is insignificant (which it is not).

This is like announcing a decision on points, when the public has been expecting a knock-out. The former method of winning is quite as honorable, but not so showy. "This Side of Paradise" was put over with a punch of a very special kind. But "The Great Gatsby" is the first convincing testimony that Mr. Fitzgerald is also an artist.

The reason why "This Side of Paradise" created such a furore was not its intrinsic literary worth, but its rare combination of precocity and true originality. The universal difficulty for beginning novelists is to use what they know. Fiction must be shaped to a pattern. Life appears to be formless, incoherent, fantastically irrelevant. [...]

Mr. Fitzgerald managed somehow to pour his glowing youth on the page before it could escape forever. His natural facility was so extraordinary that he could get along with a minimum of conscious technique. Even the inevitable crudities and banalities of his first novel were a part of its authenticity. They were genuine echoes of the gaucheries of his age and environment. The smart, swaggering, callow cubs of 1915 (was it?) were like that; such were their amusements, catchwords, standards and point of view.

It was really a sociological document. Not even a personal confession, in the main, but a snapshot of one aspect of the crowd mind.

So is "The Great Gatsby" in a sense. But it is first and foremost a novel, which its predecessor wasn't. It is beautifully and delicately balanced; its shapeliness is the more praiseworthy for the extreme fragility of the material. It is an almost perfectly fulfilled intention. There is not one accidental phrase in it, nor yet one obvious or blatant line.

And to work at all with such people, such types and backgrounds, is something of a feat. They are the froth of society, drifting sand, along the shore. Can one twist ropes of sand? Decidedly not; but one may take the sand and fuse it in the warmth of fancy, and with skill enough one may blow it into enchanting bubbles of iridescent glass.

"The Great Gatsby" is just such an imponderable and fascinating trifle. Gatsby himself is the archetype of the species of ephemerides[1] who occupy the whole tale. He was a man from nowhere, without roots or background, absolutely self-made in the image of an obscure and undefined ideal. You could not exactly call him an impostor; he was himself an artist of sorts, trying to remold himself. His stage was a Long Island summer colony, where he came in contact with the realities of his dream

---

1 Mayfly.

and was broken by them. That he was a bootlegger, a crook, maybe a killer (all on the grand scale) is part of the irony of things; for it wasn't his sins he paid for, but his aspirations. He was an incurable romanticist (I would draw a distinction between that and a romantic, as between sentimentality and sentiment), and his mistake was to accept life at its face value.

There, too, is the chief weakness of Mr. Fitzgerald as a novelist. In reproducing surfaces his virtuosity is amazing. He gets the exact tone, the note, the shade of the season and place he is working on; he is more contemporary than any newspaper, and yet he is (by the present token) an artist. But he has not, yet, gone below that glittering surface except by a kind of happy accident, and then he is rather bewildered by the results of his own intuition. Observe how he explains the duration and intensity of Gatsby's passion for Daisy Buchanan. He says it was because of Daisy's superior social status, because she was a daughter of wealth—Gatsby "hadn't realized how extraordinary a 'nice' girl could be"; and the revelation dazzled him, made him Daisy's slave forever. Pooh, there is no explanation for love. Daisy might have been a cash girl or mill hand, and made as deep a mark—it is Carmen and Don Jose[1] over again. There isn't any why about that sort of thing.

Again, Mr. Fitzgerald identifies the strange rout who came of Gatsby's incredible parties as "the East," in contrast to a more solid, integrated society of the Middle West. But these drunken spenders and migratory merrymakers exist proportionately everywhere; there are more of them in and around New York because there is more of New York, and they congregate chiefly where there is easy money—like midges dancing over a pool. And they come from all quarters. They are not even peculiar to this age; they made up the supper guests at Trimalchio's supper, and Lucian satirized them.[2]

But Gatsby hasn't the robust vitality of the vulgar Trimalchio. He and his group remain types. What has never been alive cannot very well go on living; so this is a book of the season only,

---

1　The "gypsy" heroine and soldier hero, respectively, of the opera *Carmen* (1875) by Georges Bizet (1838–75), based on an 1845 novella by Prosper Mérimée (1803–70).

2　The luxurious, decadent supper party given by the former slave Trimalchio makes up one of the main surviving chapters of the *Satyricon* (late first century CE) by Petronius. Lucian of Samosata (c. 120–180) was a Greek satirist.

but so peculiarly of the season, that it is in its own small way unique.

2. From H.L. Mencken, "Fitzgerald, The Stylist, Challenges Fitzgerald, The Social Historian," *Baltimore Evening Sun* (2 May 1925), 9

Scott Fitzgerald's new novel, "The Great Gatsby," is in form no more than a glorified anecdote, and not too probable at that. The scene is the Long Island that hangs precariously on the edges of the New York city ash dumps—the Long Island of gaudy villas and bawdy house parties. The theme is the old one of a romantic and preposterous love—the ancient *fidelis ad urrum* motif[1] reduced to a *macabre* humor. The principal personage is a bounder typical of those parts—a fellow who seems to know everyone and yet remains unknown to all—a young man with a great deal of mysterious money, the tastes of a movie actor and, under it all, the simple sentimentality of a somewhat sclerotic fat woman.

This clown Fitzgerald rushes to his death in nine short chapters. The other performers in the Totentanz[2] are of a like, or even worse quality. One of them is a rich man who carries on a grotesque intrigue with the wife of a garage keeper. Another is a woman golfer who wins championships by cheating. A third, a sort of chorus to the tragic farce, is a bond salesman—symbol of the New America! Fitzgerald clears them all off at last by a triple butchery. The garage keeper's wife, rushing out upon the road to escape her husband's third degree, is run down and killed by the wife of her lover. The garage keeper, misled by the lover, kills the lover of the lover's wife—the Great Gatsby himself. Another bullet, and the garage keeper is also reduced to offal. Choragus[3] fades away. The crooked lady golfer departs. The lover of the garage keeper's wife goes back to his own consort. The immense house of the Great Gatsby stands idle, its bedrooms given over to the bat and the owl, its cocktail shakers dry. The curtain lurches down.

---

1 Mencken seems to have in mind here the motif "faithful unto death," *fidelis ad uram* or *fidelis ad mortem* in Latin.
2 German: Dance of Death.
3 As used here, this Greek term refers to the leader of the chorus in classical Greek tragedy.

This story is obviously unimportant, and though, as I shall show, it has its place in the Fitzgerald canon, it is certainly not to be put on the same shelf with, say, "This Side of Paradise." What ails it, fundamentally, is the plain fact that it is simply a story—that Fitzgerald seems to be far more interested in maintaining its suspense than in getting under the skins of its people. It is not that they are false; it is that they are taken too much for granted. Only Gatsby himself genuinely lives and breathes. The rest are mere marionettes—often astonishingly lifelike, but nevertheless not quite alive.

What gives the story distinction is something quite different from the management of the action or the handling of the characters; it is the charm and beauty of the writing. In Fitzgerald's first days it seemed almost unimaginable that he would ever show such qualities. His writing, then, was extraordinarily slipshod—at times almost illiterate. He seemed to be devoid of any feeling for the color and savor of words. He could see people clearly, and he could devise capital situations, but as writer qua writer he was apparently little more than a bright college boy. The critics of the Republic[1] were not slow to discern the fact. They praised "This Side of Paradise" as a story, as a social document, but they were almost unanimous in denouncing it as a piece of writing.

It is vastly to Fitzgerald's credit that he appears to have taken their caveats seriously and pondered them to good effect. In "The Great Gatsby" the highly agreeable fruits of that pondering are visible. The story, for all its basic triviality, has a fine texture, a careful and brilliant finish. The obvious phrase is simply not in it. The sentences roll along smoothly, spark[l]ingly, variously. There is evidence in every line of hard and intelligent effort. It is a quite new Fitzgerald who emerges from this little book and the qualities that he shows are dignified and solid. "This Side of Paradise," after all, might have been merely a lucky accident. But "The Great Gatsby," a far inferior story at bottom, is plainly the product of a sound and stable talent, conjured into being by hard work.

I make much of this improvement because it is of an order not often witnessed in American writers, and seldom indeed in those who start off with a popular success. The usual progression, indeed, is in the opposite direction. Every year first books of great promise are published—and every year a great deal of stale drivel is printed by the promising authors of year before last. The

---

1 I.e., the United States.

rewards of literary success in this country are so vast that, when they come early, they are not unnaturally somewhat demoralizing. The average author yields to them readily. Having struck the bull's-eye once, he is too proud to learn new tricks. [...] He begins to imitate himself. He peters out.

There is certainly no sign of petering out in Fitzgerald. After his first experimenting he plainly sat himself down calmly to consider his deficiencies. They were many and serious. He was, first of all, too facile. He could write entertainingly without giving thought to form and organization. He was, secondly, somewhat amateurish. The materials and methods of his craft, I venture, rather puzzled him. He used them ineptly. His books showed brilliancy in conception, but they were crude and even ignorant in detail. They suggested, only too often, the improvisations of a pianist playing furiously by ear but unable to read notes.

These are the defects that he has now got rid of [...]. ["The Great Gatsby"] shows on every page the results of that laborious effort. [...] There are pages so artfully contrived that one can no more imagine improvising them than one can imagine improvising a fugue. They are full of little delicacies, charming turns of phrase, penetrating second thoughts. In other words, they are easy and excellent reading—which is what always comes out of hard writing.

Thus Fitzgerald, the stylist, arises to challenge Fitzgerald, the social historian, but I doubt that the latter ever quite succumbs to the former. The thing that chiefly interests the basic Fitzgerald is still the florid show of modern American life—and especially the devil's dance that goes on at the top. He is unconcerned about the sweatings and sufferings of the nether herd: what engrosses him is the high carnival of those who have too much money to spend and too much time for the spending of it. Their idiotic pursuit of sensation, their almost incredible stupidity and triviality, their glittering swinishness—these are the things that go into his notebook.

In "The Great Gatsby," though he does not go below the surface, he depicts this rattle and hullabaloo with great gusto and, I believe, with sharp accuracy. The Long Island he sets before us is no fanciful Alsatia:[1] it actually exists. More, it is

---

1   Area in Whitefriars, London, in which criminals and debtors found refuge.

worth any social historian's study, for its influence upon the rest of the country is immense and profound. What is vogue among the profiteers of Manhattan and their harlots today is imitated by the flappers of the Bible Belt country clubs weeks after next. The whole tone of American society, once so highly formalized and so suspicious of change, is now taken largely from frail ladies who were slinging hash a year ago.

3. From William Rose Benét, "An Admirable Novel," *Saturday Review of Literature* (9 May 1925), 739–40

"The Great Gatsby" is a disillusioned novel, and a mature novel. It is a novel with pace, from the first word to the last, and also a novel of admirable "control." Scott Fitzgerald started his literary career with enormous facility. His high spirits were infectious. The queer charm, color, wonder, and drama of a young and reckless world beat constantly upon his senses, stimulated a young and intensely romantic mind to a mixture of realism and extravaganza shaken up like a cocktail. [...] Scott Fitzgerald was born with a knack for writing. What they call "a natural gift." And another gift of the fairies at his christening was a reckless confidence in himself. And he was quite intoxicated with the joy of life and rather engagingly savage toward an elder world. He was out "to get the world by the neck" and put words on paper in the patterns his exuberant fancy suggested. He didn't worry much about what had gone before Fitzgerald in literature. He dreamed gorgeously of what there was in Fitzgerald to "tell the world."

And all these elements contributed to the amazing performance of "This Side of Paradise," amazing in its excitement and gusto, amazing in phrase and epithet, amazing no less for all sorts of thoroughly bad writing pitched in with the good, for preposterous carelessness, and amazing as well for the sheer pace of the narrative and the fresh quality of its oddly pervasive poetry. Short stories of flappers and philosophers displayed the same vitality and flourished much the same faults. "Tales of the Jazz Age" inhabited the same glamour. "The Beautiful and Damned," while still in the mirage, furnished a more valuable document concerning the younger generation of the first quarter of the Twentieth Century. But brilliant, irrefutably brilliant as were certain passages of the novels and tales of which the "boy wonder" of our time was so lavish, arresting as were certain gleams of insight, intensely promising as were certain observed facilities, there remained in general, glamour, glamour everywhere, and, after the glamour faded, little for the mind to hold except an impression of this kinetic glamour.

There ensued a play, in which the present writer found the first act (as read) excellent and the rest as satire somehow stricken with palsy, granted the cleverness of the original idea. There ensued a magazine phase in which, as was perfectly natural, most of the stories were negligible, though a few showed flashes. But one could discern the demands of the "market" blunting and dulling the blade of that bright sword wildly whirled. One began to believe that Fitzgerald was coming into line with the purveyors of the staple product. And suddenly one wanted him back in the phase when he was writing so well and, at the same time, writing so very badly. Today he was writing, for the most part, on an even level of magazine acceptability, and on an even level of what seemed perilously like absolute staleness of mind toward anything really creative.

But "The Great Gatsby" comes suddenly to knock all that surmise into a cocked hat. "The Great Gatsby" reveals thoroughly matured craftsmanship. It has structure. It has high occasions of felicitous, almost magic, phrase. And most of all, it is out of the mirage. For the first time Fitzgerald surveys the Babylonian captivity of this era unblinded by the bright lights. He gives you the bright lights in full measure, the affluence, the waste, but also the nakedness of the scaffolding that scrawls skeletons upon the sky when the gold and blue and red and green have faded, the ugly passion, the spiritual meagreness, the empty shell of luxury, the old irony of "fair-weather friends."

Gatsby remains. The mystery of Gatsby is a mystery saliently characteristic of this age in America. And Gatsby is only another modern instance of the eternal "fortunate youth." His actual age does not matter, in either sense. For all the cleverness of his hinted nefarious proceedings, he is the coney caught. For he is a man with a dream at the mercy of the foul dust that sometimes seems only to exist in order to swarm against the dream, whose midge-dance blots it from the sky. It is a strange dream, Gatsby's—but he was a man who had hope. He was a child. He believed in a childish thing.

It is because Fitzgerald makes so acid on your tongue the taste of the defeat of Gatsby's childishness that his book, in our opinion, "acquires merit." And there are parts of the book, notably the second chapter, that, in our opinion, could not have been better written. There are astonishing feats that no one but Fitzgerald could have brought off, notably the catalogue of guests in

Chapter IV. And Tom Buchanan, the "great hulking specimen," is an American university product of almost unbearable reality.

Yet one feels that, though irony has entered into Fitzgerald's soul, the sense of mere wonder is still stronger. And, of course, there is plenty of entertainment in the story. It arises in part from the almost photographic reproduction of the actions, gestures, speech of the types Fitzgerald has chosen in their moments of stress. Picayune[1] souls for the most part, and Gatsby heroic among them only because he is partly a crazy man with a dream. But what does all that matter with the actual narration so vivid and graphic? As for the drama of the accident and Gatsby's end, it is the kind of thing newspapers carry every day, except that here is a novelist who has gone behind the curt paragraphs and made the real people live and breathe in all their sordidness. They are actual, rich and poor, cultivated and uncultivated, seen for a moment or two only or followed throughout the story. They are memorable individuals of today—not types.

Perhaps you have gathered that we like the book! We do. It has some miscues, but they seem to us negligible. It is written with concision and precision and mastery of material.

4. From William Curtis, "Some Recent Books," *Town & Country* 81 (15 May 1925), 68

There has been a vast amount of fusfut over a stodgily inadequate play called "Processional,"[2] which claimed to interpret for an expectant public what some critic labeled the orgiastic danger of jazz. Beyond, however, some extraordinarily capable publicity work, this particular play failed to give local habitation to all those urges toward promiscuity, the loosening of the whole category of inhibitions, Freudian and economic, which this generation is pleased to associate with contemporary dance music. [...] The author of "Processional" is only one of a rather sizable group who have been trying to express the springtime restlessness of the human race, its half-believed disbelief in the moral conventions, which is as old as the Ohio mound dwellings and as new as Mr. Buckner's padlocks.[3] From where we sit, watching the swaying

---

1 Small, of little worth.
2 A 1925 play by John Howard Lawson (1894–1977).
3 Probably a reference to the practice of padlocking the entrances to speakeasies—illegal saloons—authorized by Emory R. Buckner (1877–1941), US District Attorney of southern New York.

throng, it seems very much as if F. Scott Fitzgerald in "The Great Gatsby" [...] had succeeded rather startlingly in doing just this thing. This we state in spite of the fact that it seems rather an obvious thing to expect from Mr. Fitzgerald: his previous novels have all revolved around this motive, have been quite successful, and have failed only to be completely so because they were molded in too unsophisticated a form. [...]

It is one of the very special qualities of Mr. Fitzgerald's "The Great Gatsby" that, while proceeding in the calm manner of sophistication and taste, with no trace of the moral reformer or apologist, he has given us a picture which is, to us at least, as terrifying as any tragedy Aristotle[1] could have wished for. "The Great Gatsby" is an attempt to show the workings of an urge towards license upon the lower middle class and upon the very rich, taking those selected cross sections of each which have succumbed most completely. The unfortunate gentleman from whom the book takes its title is the descendant of starved farmers in the wheat-growing country of the Middle West, a man who, in the renascence, would have been a successful condottiere,[2] who, in the Long Island of today, however, was a meteor in the boot-legging world. He had lost all his inhibitions in his flight save his belief in the monogamous treatment of a "nice" woman. The other half of the tragedy, for a tragedy "The Great Gatsby" unmistakably is, is the nice young woman upon whom the adventurer's desires are focussed. She had married resplendently and, in the progress of her years, since she and the adventurer had touched orbits at a training camp, had lost all of her inhibitions save those dealing with the super-sacredness of Property and an Assured Income. When they finally met she is quite willing to become his mistress—and he wants a divorce and a scandal. This is to reduce "The Great Gatsby" to a few syllables, to the bare skeleton of the story, to the framework upon which is suspended a panorama of the wining and wenching and rhythmic movement, all of which today we call jazzing. The book succeeds most definitely in giving the sense of dissatisfaction with the majority code of conduct, the conventional method of ordering one's life; the continual excitation of all the senses, the ordinary interpretation of Pater's so often quoted

---

1 Aristotle (384–322 BCE), Greek philosopher, who claimed in his *Poetics* (c. 330 BCE) that "pity and fear" were the emotions properly drawn out by tragedy.

2 A mercenary or soldier of fortune.

and so dangerous gemlike flame theory,[1] that restlessness which we would so like to believe is our own discovery, is here, for the first time in our knowledge, satisfactorily crystallized inside the covers of one thoroughly praisable book. For in "The Great Gatsby" Mr. Fitzgerald passes from the able and conscientious school into the cool cloisters of the literary elect.

Professionally to us, it has always been a regret that we have not, in this generation, had writers of whom one could be really proud in intellectual groups which knew and admired the best contemporary British and Continental literary art—somebody who did fine writing as distinguished from the "great," and dull, writing of the Victorian manner. We feel of "The Great Gatsby" that it can be put on the same book shelf with the best of London, Vienna, Paris, or Rome. And this is about as high a compliment as can be given any novel. When you get to a certain experience in reading, it is not so much what an author says as the way he says it that counts, the technic of his criticism upon his characters and, through them, upon life. Ever since Mr. Fitzgerald started in writing he has been saying practically what he has said in "The Great Gatsby." But meeting him again in this book is somewhat like realizing that a hopeful child has become adult. As an author Mr. Fitzgerald has ceased to chronicle events and has begun to marshal them in perspective and to give the comment upon them which, after all, are the only excuses for the existence of literature. Real life, raw, unassorted, kaleidoscopic, without meaning, is all about us. The justification of a novelist is to arrange these things into a pattern and to associate this pattern with the vast general background of conduct from the major stars of which we guide our existence. When somebody can do this in the manner not of a glorified newspaper reporter, nor of a pulpit orator, nor of a college professor, but of a thoroughly appreciative person of affairs, sympathetic in spite of sophistication, with the human touch in spite of technical writing ability far beyond average attainment, then the product has the claim to be called literature. There are two ways of achieving this: the patiently plodding, detail upon detail manner of Mr. Lewis,[2] the sort of

---

1 Articulated by British philosopher and art historian Walter Pater (1839–94) in the "Conclusion" to *The Renaissance* (1873), a collection of essays on Renaissance art and poetry that influenced late-Victorian and high-modernist aestheticism: "To burn always with this hard, gemlike flame, to maintain this ecstasy, is success in life" (236).

2 Sinclair Lewis (1885–1951), author of *Main Street* (1920) and *Babbitt* (1922).

thing one persists in reading through because of a shamed feeling that one should, or the flaming brilliancy of the specially gifted who, with almost flamboyant dexterity, sketch a situation in a series of singing sentences which one reads almost with a sense of elation, the elation with which one hears strongly emotional music or studies a perfectly poised painting. Whether or not "The Great Gatsby" has the popular sale of "The Beautiful and the Damned" [sic], it is a much abler, a much finer, a much more mature presentation of Mr. Fitzgerald's problem.

5. From Carl Van Vechten, "Fitzgerald on the March," *The Nation* 120 (20 May 1925), 575–76

In "The Great Gatsby" there are several of Mr. Fitzgerald's typical flappers who behave in the manner he has conceived as typical of contemporary flapperdom. There is again a gargantuan drinking-party, conceived in a rowdy, hilarious, and highly titillating spirit. There is also, in this novel, as I have indicated above, something else. There is the character of Jay Gatsby.

This character, and the theme of the book in general, would have appealed to Henry James. In fact, it did appeal to Henry James. In one way or another this motif is woven into the tapestry of a score or more of his stories. In Daisy Miller you may find it complete.[1] It is the theme of a soiled or rather cheap personality transfigured and rendered pathetically appealing through the possession of a passionate idealism. Although the comparison may be still further stressed, owing to the fact that Mr. Fitzgerald has chosen, as James so frequently chose, to see his story through the eyes of a spectator, it will be readily apparent that what he has done he has done in his own way, and that seems to me, in this instance, to be a particularly good way. The figure of Jay Gatsby, who invented an entirely fictitious career for himself out of material derived from inferior romances, emerges life-sized and lifelike. His doglike fidelity not only to his ideal but to his fictions, his incredibly cheap and curiously imitative imagination, awakens for him not only our interest and suffrage, but also a certain liking, as they awaken it in the narrator, Nick Carraway.

When I read Absolution in the American Mercury I realized that there were many potential qualities inherent in Scott Fitzger-

---

1 *Daisy Miller* (1878), Henry James's short novel about a young American woman traveling in Europe, conveyed from the point-of-view of an admiring but cautious follower, Frederick Winterbourne.

ald which hitherto had not been too apparent. "The Great Gatsby" confirms this earlier impression. What Mr. Fitzgerald may do in the future, therefore, I am convinced, depends to an embarrassing extent on the nature of his own ambitions.

6. From Burton Rascoe, "Contemporary Reminiscences," *Arts & Decoration* (June 1925), 66, 68

I have a letter from F. Scott Fitzgerald, inclosed with a copy of "The Great Gatsby" which he was gracious enough to have his publishers send me. In part it reads: "I give you my word of honor this isn't a moral tale—nor has it any more resemblance to Chambers because it deals with the rich than has 'The Twelve Little Peppers' to 'My Antonia' because it deals with the poor.[1] It happens to be extraordinarily difficult to write directly and simply about complex and indirect people. And I should prefer to fail ridiculously at the job as James often did than to succeed ignobly.... Dostoyefski [sic] said that people's motives are much simpler than we think [but] any uncorrupted motive has an average life of six hours or less."

After reading that letter I entertained a momentary wish that all novelists could thus briefly state their artistic intention to prospective reviewers. It would simplify matters a great deal. And it would prevent those horrible misapprehensions of intention on the part of reviewers which must now and then give authors hours of miserable rage. To mull and toil over a scene, to trim and revise, to plan and to prune all irrelevancies from the plan; and then to have some reviewer, hastily going through your book, finding fault with the least important aspect of your novel, or, worst of all, criticizing your book on the basis of the publishers' claims for it on the dust jacket— what a canker that must create in the soul of any conscientious artist!

1 Robert W. Chambers, prolific and popular American novelist and short-story writer, best known for romantic historical fiction and so-called "weird tales"; Fitzgerald considered his work trashy and resented comparisons between Chambers's fiction and his own. "The Twelve Little Peppers" presumably refers disparagingly to the "Five Little Peppers" series of children's books published over a thirty-year span by Margaret Sidney (1844–1924), confused perhaps with another children's book, "The Twelve Little Pilgrims Who Stayed Home" (1903) by Lucy Jameson Scott (1843–1920). Fitzgerald admired Willa Cather's *My Ántonia* (1918) immensely.

It is because Fitzgerald has chosen to write simply about complex and indirect people and has succeeded in a difficult task by a display of greater technical brilliance than even his warmest champions knew him capable of, that critics have been most enthusiastic in their praise for "The Great Gatsby." It is not only that Fitzgerald has hit the bell again as he did in his amazingly vivid and vital first novel, but that he has matured into a writer with a precise and effective technique. It seemed for a time that his inspiration would remain undisciplined; but in "The Great Gatsby" he triumphs by technique rather than by theme. For myself, I must confess to a minority opinion that the novel is not as good in substance as it is in technique. There are some superbly drawn scenes, and the tragic overtones are managed with great economy and skill; but the point of view is wavering, the characters dissolve too readily, my feeling is that it is more a comment upon a situation than a statement of it, and that the comment is not as well reasoned as it might be. But the novel shows that Fitzgerald is maturing in the right direction. It represents a phase of a growth; and that growth is toward increased literary excellence rather than the reverse.

7. Gilbert Seldes, "Spring Flight," *The Dial* 79 (August 1925), 162–64

There has never been any question of the talents of F. Scott Fitzgerald; there has been, justifiably until the publication of The Great Gatsby, a grave question as to what he was going to do with his gifts. The question has been answered in one of the finest of contemporary novels. Fitzgerald has more than matured; he has mastered his talents and gone soaring in a beautiful flight, leaving behind him everything dubious and tricky in his earlier work, and leaving even farther behind all the men of his own generation and most of his elders.

In all justice, let it be said that the talents are still his. The book is even more interesting, superficially, than his others; it has an intense life, it must be read, the first time, breathlessly; it is vivid and glittering and entertaining. Scenes of incredible difficulty are rendered with what seems an effortless precision, crowds and conversation and action and retrospects—everything comes naturally and persuasively. The minor people and events are threads of colour and strength, holding the principal things together. The technical virtuosity is extraordinary.

All this was true of Fitzgerald's first two novels, and even of those deplorable short stories which one feared were going to ruin him. The Great Gatsby adds many things, and two above all: the novel is composed as an artistic structure, and it exposes, again for the first time, an interesting temperament. "The vast juvenile intrigue" of This Side of Paradise is just as good subject-matter as the intensely private intrigue of The Great Gatsby; but Fitzgerald racing over the country, jotting down whatever was current in college circles, is not nearly as significant as Fitzgerald regarding a tiny section of life and reporting it with irony and pity and a consuming passion. The Great Gatsby is passionate as Some Do Not[1] is passionate, with such an abundance of feeling for the characters (feeling their integral reality, not hating or loving them objectively) that the most trivial of the actors in the drama are endowed with vitality. The concentration of the book is so intense that the principal characters exist almost as essences, as biting acids that find themselves in the same golden cup and have no choice but to act upon each other. And the *milieux* which are brought into such violent contact with each other are as full of character, and as immitigably compelled to struggle and to debase one another.

The book is written as a series of scenes, the method which Fitzgerald derived from Henry James through Mrs. Wharton,[2] and these scenes are reported by a narrator who was obviously intended to be much more significant than he is. The author's appetite for life is so violent that he found the personality of the narrator an obstacle, and simply ignored it once his actual people were in motion, but the narrator helps to give the feeling of an intense unit which the various characters around Gatsby form. Gatsby himself remains a mystery; you know him, but not by knowing about him, and even at the end you can guess, if you like, that he was a forger or a dealer in stolen bonds, or a rather mean type of bootlegger. He had dedicated himself to the accomplishment of a supreme object, to restore to himself an illusion he

---

1   A 1924 novel by British novelist Ford Madox Ford (1873–1939), the first of his four-volume series about the effects of World War I on the English aristocracy, known collectively as *Parade's End* (completed 1928).

2   Edith Wharton (1862–1937) was often regarded as a follower of her older friend Henry James because of her subject matter (the social world of the leisure class) and her careful management of scene, character development, and narrative point-of-view.

had lost; he set about it, in a pathetic American way, by becoming incredibly rich and spending his wealth in incredible ways, so that he might win back the girl he loved; and a "foul dust floated in the wake of his dreams." Adultery and drunkenness and thievery and murder make up this dust, but Gatsby's story remains poignant and beautiful.

This means that Fitzgerald has ceased to content himself with a satiric report on the outside of American life and has with considerable irony attacked the spirit underneath, and so has begun to report on life in its most general terms. His tactile apprehension remains so fine that his people and his settings are specifically of Long Island; but now he meditates upon their fate, and they become universal also. He has now something of extreme importance to say; and it is good fortune for us that he knows how to say it.

The scenes are austere in their composition. There is one, the tawdry afternoon of the satyr, Tom Buchanan, and his cheap and "vital" mistress, which is alive by the strength of the lapses of time; another, the meeting between Gatsby and his love, takes place literally behind closed doors, the narrator telling us only the beginning and the end. The variety of treatment, the intermingling of dialogue and narrative, the use of a snatch of significant detail instead of a big scene, make the whole a superb impressionistic painting, vivid in colour, and sparkling with meaning. And the major composition is as just as the treatment of detail. There is a brief curve before Gatsby himself enters; a longer one in which he begins his movement toward Daisy; then a succession of carefully spaced shorter and longer movements until the climax is reached. The plot works out not like a puzzle with odd bits falling into place, but like a tragedy, with every part functioning in the completed organism.

Even now, with The Great Gatsby before me, I cannot find in the earlier Fitzgerald the artistic integrity and the passionate feeling which this book possesses. And perhaps analysing the one and praising the other, both fail to convey the sense of elation which one has in reading his new novel. Would it be better to say that even The Great Gatsby is full of faults, and that that doesn't matter in the slightest degree? The cadences borrowed from Conrad, the occasional smartness, the frequently startling, but ineffective adjective— at last they do not signify. Because for the most part you know that Fitzgerald has consciously put these bad and half-bad things behind him, that he trusts them no more to make him the white-headed boy of The Saturday Evening Post, and that he has recognized both his capacities and his obligations as a novelist.

Appendix C: Class, Consumption, and Economy

["You resemble the advertisement of the man," Daisy tells Gatsby just before their fatal trip to the city in Chapter VII—an endearing observation that uncannily exposes something fundamental about his character. Gatsby is a walking advertisement for the full-blown consumer culture that became permanently established by the 1920s, for he is a model consumer, spending money to transform himself into an ideal shaped by the advertising industry. Like his counterpart Myrtle Wilson, he believes what the ads encourage him to believe—namely, that class can be bought, that through careful imitation of models one can become (paradoxically) one's "real," "classier" self. Fitzgerald filled his novel with references to commodity culture and may even be deliberately echoing the language of advertising in some of the novel's memorable passages, as when Daisy goes through Gatsby's shirts (Chapter V) or when Nick describes Gatsby's enchanting impressions of Daisy's Louisville home (Chapter VIII).

More widespread buying power at once challenged and reinforced assumptions about social class, which may account for Emily Post's (1872–1960) newly launched *Etiquette* topping the nonfiction bestseller list in 1923 and remaining perennially popular through its many editions ever since. The selections here from the first edition reveal something not only of Mrs. Post's literary wit (her tendency to allegorize, for example) but also of her guidebook's value as a blueprint for approaching *The Great Gatsby* as a contemporary American novel of manners.

The eight advertisements that follow were culled from 1922 issues of *Vanity Fair* and *Town & Country*, two magazines that epitomized urbane sophistication and moneyed leisure: an Arrow Collar ad featuring "the man" Daisy may have had in mind; a perfume ad graced with the image of the fashionable young American *femme du monde*; a Stutz car ad unabashedly promoting its product as a sign of wealth and success; a negligee ad flaunting the ever-widening array of colors to which consumers were becoming accustomed; an ad for a cosmetic treatment designed to revive one's youth; an ad for instant "culture" in the form of Harvard's President Charles Eliot's "Five-Foot Shelf of Books"; an ad for period furniture to fill American houses built in imitation of European period-architecture; and an ad for the fashionable sports car after which Fitzgerald probably named one of his characters.

Fitzgerald's humorous autobiographical essay "How to Live on $36,000 a Year" offers a detailed economic picture of his life in Great Neck on Long Island in 1923 as a self-styled member of "the newly rich class" that included fellow writers, journalists, and Broadway and early movie stars. Though $36,000 seems a relatively modest income when measured in relation to the neighboring millionaires (think of Nick's bungalow next door to Gatsby's mansion), its purchasing power would have been that of over half a million dollars today. The piece also offers some insight into Fitzgerald's literary economy: his need to write popular magazine stories on demand, his hopes for a lucrative Broadway hit, in order to free him to work on what he thought most artistically essential to his reputation, the novel that would become *The Great Gatsby*.

The slogan "everybody ought to be rich" conveys the economic ethos of the jazz age—at least in popular memory. It would attach itself with considerable irony to corporate business leader John J. Raskob (1879–1950), whose interview bearing that title appeared two months before the stock market crash in October 1929. Raskob, a self-made descendent of German and Irish immigrants, epitomized American business success after rising to the top of the Du Pont Company and helping his mentor Pierre DuPont (1870–1954) take over General Motors. From the beginning of the decade, he established the practice of financing automobile ownership and promoted stock-buying options for corporate employees; by the end of the decade he was working to make stock market investment schemes accessible and beneficial to "everybody," forgetting that $15 per month was a much bigger chunk of the average American's salary than popular images of ubiquitous wealth would suggest. Most pertinent to the economy informing Fitzgerald's fiction is Raskob's promotion of widespread consumption as the source of general wealth instead of the economy of deferred gratification based on the old-fashioned wisdom of "saving" (something a young Jimmy Gatz had trouble with, as his Ben Franklinesque list of "resolves" betrays).]

1. From Emily Post, *Etiquette in Society, in Business, in Politics and at Home* (Funk & Wagnalls, 1922), 1–3, 64, 65–66, 509, 540–41, 566–67, 617–19

Chapter 1: What Is Best Society?

"Society" is an ambiguous term; it may mean much or nothing. Every human being—unless dwelling alone in a cave—is a member of society of one sort or another, and therefore it is well to define what is to be understood by the term "Best Society" and why its authority is recognized. Best Society abroad is always the oldest aristocracy; composed not so much of persons of title, which may be new, as of those families and communities which have for the longest period of time known highest cultivation. Our own Best Society is represented by social groups which have had, since this is America, widest rather than longest association with old world cultivation. Cultivation is always the basic attribute of Best Society, much as we hear in this country of an "Aristocracy of wealth."

To the general public a long purse is synonymous with high position—a theory dear to the heart of the "yellow" press and eagerly fostered in the preposterous social functions of screen drama. It is true that Best Society is comparatively rich; it is true that the hostess of great wealth, who constantly and lavishly entertains, will shine, at least to the readers of the press, more brilliantly than her less affluent sister. Yet the latter, through her quality of birth, her poise, her inimitable distinction, is often the jewel of deeper water in the social crown of her time.

The most advertised commodity is not always intrinsically the best, but is sometimes merely the product of a company with plenty of money to spend on advertising. In the same way, money brings certain people before the public—sometimes they are persons of "quality," quite as often the so-called "society leaders" featured in the public press do not belong to good society at all, in spite of their many published photographs and the energies of their press-agents. Or possibly they do belong to "smart" society; but if too much advertised, instead of being the "queens" they seem, they might more accurately be classified as the court jesters of to-day.

The Imitation and the Genuine

New York, more than any city in the world, unless it be Paris, loves to be amused, thrilled and surprised all at the same time;

and will accept with outstretched hand any one who can perform this astounding feat. Do not underestimate the ability that can achieve it: a scintillating wit, an arresting originality, a talent for entertaining that amounts to genius, and gold poured literally like rain, are the least requirements.

Puritan America on the other hand demanding, as a ticket of admission to her Best Society, the qualifications of birth, manners and cultivation, clasps her hands tight across her slim trim waist and announces severely that New York's "Best" is, in her opinion, very "bad" indeed. But this is because Puritan America, as well as the general public, mistakes the jester for the queen.

As a matter of fact, Best Society is not at all like a court with an especial queen or king, nor is it confined to any one place or group, but might better be described as an unlimited brotherhood which spreads over the entire surface of the globe, the members of which are invariably people of cultivation and worldly knowledge, who have not only perfect manners but a perfect manner. Manners are made up of trivialities of deportment which can be easily learned if one does not happen to know them; manner is personality—the outward manifestation of one's innate character and attitude toward life. A gentleman, for instance, will never be ostentatious or overbearing any more than he will ever be servile, because these attributes never animate the impulses of a well-bred person. A man whose manners suggest the grotesque is invariably a person of imitation rather than of real position.

Etiquette must, if it is to be of more than trifling use, include ethics as well as manners. Certainly what one is, is of far greater importance than what one appears to be. A knowledge of etiquette is of course essential to one's decent behavior, just as clothing is essential to one's decent appearance; and precisely as one wears the latter without being self-conscious of having on shoes and perhaps gloves, one who has good manners is equally unself-conscious in the observance of etiquette, the precepts of which must be so thoroughly absorbed as to make their observance a matter of instinct rather than of conscious obedience.

Thus Best Society is not a fellowship of the wealthy, nor does it seek to exclude those who are not of exalted birth; but it *is* an association of gentle-folk, of which good form in speech, charm of manner, knowledge of the social amenities, and instinctive consideration for the feelings of others, are the credentials by which society the world over recognizes its chosen members.

From Chapter 8: Words, Phrases and Pronunciation

How to Cultivate an Agreeable Speech

First of all, remember that while affectation is odious, crudeness must be overcome. A low voice is always pleasing, not whispered or murmured, but low in pitch. Do not talk at the top of your head, nor at the top of your lungs. Do not slur whole sentences together; on the other hand, do not pronounce as though each syllable were a separate tongue and lip exercise.

As a nation we do not talk so much too fast, as too loud. Tens of thousands twang and slur and shout and burr! Many of us drawl and many others of us race tongues and breath at full speed, but, as already said, the speed of our speech does not matter so much. Pitch of voice matters very much and so does pronunciation—enunciation is not so essential—except to one who speaks in public.

Enunciation means the articulation of whatever you have to say distinctly and clearly. Pronunciation is the proper sounding of consonants, vowels and the accentuation of each syllable.

There is no better way to cultivate a perfect pronunciation, apart from association with cultivated people, than by getting a small pronouncing dictionary of words in ordinary use, and reading it word by word, marking and studying any that you use frequently and mispronounce. When you know them, then read any book at random slowly aloud to yourself, very carefully pronouncing each word. The consciousness of this exercise may make you stilted in conversation at first, but by and by the "sense" or "impulse" to speak correctly will come.

This is a method that has been followed by many men handicapped in youth through lack of education, who have become prominent in public life, and by many women, who likewise handicapped by circumstances, have not only made possible a creditable position for themselves, but have then given their children the inestimable advantage of learning their mother tongue correctly at their mother's knee.

From Chapter 9: One's Position in the Community

The Choice

First of all, it is necessary to decide what one's personal idea of position is, whether this word suggests merely a social one, comprising a large or an exclusive acquaintance and leadership in social gaiety, or position established upon the foundation of communal consequence, which may, or may not, include great social gaiety. In other words, you who are establishing yourself, either as a young husband or a stranger, would you, if you could have your wish granted by a genie, choose to have the populace look upon you askance and in awe, because of your wealth and elegance, or would you wish to be loved, not as a power conferring favors which belong really to the first picture, but as a fellow-being with an understanding heart? The granting of either wish is not a bit beyond the possibilities of anyone. It is merely a question of depositing securities of value in the bank of life.

The Bank of Life

Life, whether social or business, is a bank in which you deposit certain funds of character, intellect and heart; or other funds of egotism, hard-heartedness and unconcern; or deposit—nothing! And the bank honors your deposit, and no more. In other words, you can draw nothing out but what you have put in.

If your community is to give you admiration and honor, it is merely necessary to be admirable and honorable. The more you put in, the more will be paid out to you. It is too trite to put on paper! But it is astonishing, isn't it, how many people who are depositing nothing whatever, expect to be paid in admiration and respect?

A man of really high position is always a great citizen first and above all. Otherwise he is a hollow puppet whether he is a millionaire or has scarcely a dime to bless himself with. In the same way, a woman's social position that is built on sham, vanity, and selfishness, is like one of the buildings at an exposition; effective at first sight, but bound when slightly weather-beaten to show stucco and glue.

It would be very presumptuous to attempt to tell any man how to acquire the highest position in his community, especially as the answer is written in his heart, his intellect, his altruistic sympathy, and his ardent civic pride.

From Chapter 29: The Fundamentals of Good Behavior

Simplicity and Unconsciousness of Self

Unconsciousness of self is not so much unselfishness as it is the mental ability to extinguish all thought of one's self—exactly as one turns out the light.

Simplicity is like it, in that it also has a quality of self-efface-ment, but it really means a love of the essential and of directness. Simple people put no trimmings on their phrases, nor on their manners; but remember, simplicity is not crudeness nor anything like it. On the contrary, simplicity of speech and manners means language in its purest, most limpid form, and manners of such perfection that they do not suggest "manner" at all.

From Chapter 33: Dress

Clothes are to us what fur and feathers are to beasts and birds; they not only add to our appearance, but they *are* our appear-ance. How we look to others entirely depends upon what we wear and how we wear it; manners and speech are noted afterward, and character last of all.

In the community where we live, admirableness of character is the fundamental essential, and in order to achieve a position of importance, personality is also essential; but for the transient impression that we make at home, abroad, everywhere in public, two superficial attributes are alone indispensable: good manners and a pleasing appearance.

It is not merely a question of vanity and inclination. In New York, for instance, a woman must dress well, to pay her way. In Europe, where the title of Duchess serves in lieu of a court train of gold brocade; or in Bohemian circles where talent alone may count; or in small communities where people are known for what they really are, appearance is of esthetic rather than essential importance.

In the world of smart society—in America at any rate—clothes not only represent our ticket of admission, but our contribution to the effect of a party. What makes a brilliant party? Clothes. Good clothes. A frumpy party is nothing more nor less than a col-lection of badly dressed persons. People with all the brains, even all the beauty imaginable, make an assemblage of dowds, unless they are well dressed.

Not even the most beautiful ballroom in the world, decorated like the Garden of Eden, could in itself suggest a brilliant enter-tainment, if the majority of those who filled it were frumps—or worse yet, vulgarians! Rather be frumpy than vulgar! Much. Frumps are often celebrities in disguise—but a person of vulgar appearance is vulgar all through.

From Chapter 34: The Clothes of a Gentleman

The Business Suit

The business suit or three-piece sack is made or marred by its cut alone. It is supposed to be an every-day inconspicuous garment and should be. A few rules to follow are:

Don't choose striking patterns of materials; suitable woolen stuffs come in endless variety, and any which look plain at a short distance are "safe," though they may show a mixture of colors or pattern when viewed closely.

Don't get too light a blue, too bright a green [...]

Above everything, don't wear white socks, and don't cover yourself with chains, fobs, scarf pins, lodge emblems, etc., and don't wear "horsey" shirts and neckties. You will only make a bad impression on every one you meet. The clothes of a gentleman are always conservative; and it is safe to avoid everything than can possibly come under the heading of "novelty."

From Chapter 38: Growth of Good Taste in America

Good taste or bad is revealed in everything we are, do, or have. Our speech, manners, dress, and household goods—and even our friends—are evidences of the propriety of our taste, and all these have been the subject of this book. Rules of etiquette are nothing more than sign-posts by which we are guided to the goal of good taste.

Whether we Americans are drifting toward or from finer perceptions, both mental and spiritual, is too profound a subject to be taken up except on a broader scope than that of the present volume. Yet it is a commonplace remark that older people invariably feel that the younger generation is speeding swiftly on the road to perdition. But whether the present younger generation is really any nearer to that frightful end than any previous one, is a question that we, of the present older generation, are scarcely qualified to answer. To be sure, manners seem to have grown lax, and many of the amenities apparently have vanished. But do these things merely seem so to us because young men of fashion do not pay party calls nowadays and the young woman of fashion is informal? It is difficult to maintain that youth to-day is so very different from what it has been in other periods of the country's history, especially as "the capriciousness of beauty," the "heartlessness" and "carelessness" of youth, are charges of a too suspiciously bromidic[1] flavor to carry conviction.

The present generation is at least ahead of some of its "very proper" predecessors in that weddings do not have to be set for noon because a bridegroom's sobriety is not to be counted on later in the day! That young people of to-day prefer games to conversation scarcely proves degeneration. That they wear very few clothes is not a symptom of decline. There have always been recurring cycles of undress, followed by muffling from shoe-soles to chin. We have not yet reached the undress of Pauline Bonaparte,[2] so the muffling period may not be due!

However, leaving out the mooted question whether etiquette may not soon be a subject for an obituary rather than a guidebook, one thing is certain: we have advanced prodigiously in esthetic taste.

Never in the recollection of any one now living has it been so easy to surround oneself with lovely belongings. Each year's achievement seems to stride away from that of the year before in producing woodwork, ironwork, glass, stone, print, paint and textile that is lovelier and lovelier. One can not go into the shops or pass their windows on the streets without being impressed with the ever-growing taste of their display. Nor can one look into the magazines devoted to gardens and houses and house-furnishings and fail to appreciate the increasing wealth of the beautiful in environment.

That such exquisite "best" as America possessed in her Colonial houses and gardens and furnishings should ever have been discarded for the atrocities of the period after the Civil War, is comparable to nothing but Titania's Midsummer Night's Dream madness that made her believe an ass's features more beautiful than those of Apollo![3]

Happily, however, since we never do things by halves, we are studying and cultivating and buying and making, and trying to

---

1 Ordinary, dull.
2 Napoleon I's younger sister (1780–1825), who posed nude as Venus reclining on a couch (*Venus Victrix*) for the sculptor Antonio Canova (1757–1802).
3 Allusion to the scene in William Shakespeare's *A Midsummer Night's Dream* (c. 1595/96) in which Titania, Queen of the Fairies, falls in love under the influence of a potion with the lowly weaver Bottom, who has been turned into an ass.

forget and overcome that terrible marriage of our beautiful Colonial ancestress with the dark-wooded, plush-draped, jig-sawed upstart of vulgarity and ignorance. In another country her type would be lost in his, forever! But in a country that sent a million soldiers across three thousand miles of ocean, in spite of every obstacle and in the twinkling of an eye, why even comment that good taste is pouring over our land as fast as periodicals, books and manufacturers can take it. Three thousand miles east and west, two thousand miles north and south, white tiled bathrooms have sprung like mushrooms seemingly in a single night, charming houses, enchanting gardens, beautiful cities, cultivated people, created in thousands upon thousands of instances in the short span of one generation. Certain great houses abroad have consummate quality, it is true, but for every one of these, there are a thousand that are mediocre, even offensive. In our own country, beautiful houses and appointments flourish like field flowers in summer; not merely in the occasional gardens of the very rich, but everywhere.

And all this means? Merely one more incident added to the many great facts that prove us a wonderful nation. (But this is an aside merely, and not to be talked about to anyone except just ourselves!) At the same time it is no idle boast that the world is at present looking toward America; and whatever we become is bound to lower or raise the standards of life. The other countries are old, we are youth personified! We have all youth's glorious beauty and strength and vitality and courage. If we can keep these attributes and add finish and understanding and perfect taste in living and thinking, we need not dwell on the Golden Age[1] that is past, but believe in the Golden Age that is sure to be.

---

1 Mythical age originating in classical Greek mythology, here a commonplace metaphor.

2. Eight Contemporary Advertisements

"Always favored above all other [sic] by French ladies of fashion and by most Americans who visit Paris—the choice, now, of the ultra discerning in this country."

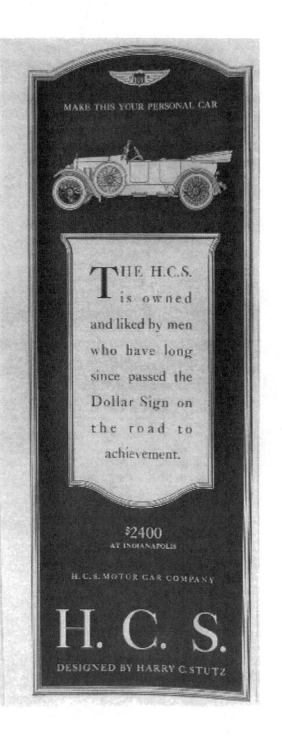

Three Maytime Creations for Madame and Mademoiselle

DREAM-LIGHT NEGLIGEES

For The Morning Hours And Intimate Tea-Time

Model 2.—TEA GOWN OF CRÊPE CHIFFON, very artistic in color effect. Three layers of chiffon one over-laying the other and each a different color; light blue, French blue, orchid, coral, black, cherry or purple predominating. Flowing sleeves. . . 39.50

Model 4.—TEA GOWN OF CRÊPE SATIN, copy of French model. Long sleeves of crêpe chiffon bound in satin. Girdle of satin roses. In fuchsia, French blue, light blue, pink or black. 27.50

Model 6.—BOUDOIR COAT OF SILK CRÊPE DE CHINE in peach, light blue, orchid, rose or turquoise. Entirely trimmed with gracious ruffles of Margot lace 18.50

NEGLIGEE SHOP—*First Floor*

Franklin Simon & Co.

Fifth Avenue, 37th and 38th Streets, New York

Like a Wizard of the Ages—

MADAME LECLAIRE

Imparts the Secrets of the Mystical Fountain of Youth

"I can make beauty blossom again.... The charm of youth is the most desired thing in the universe when one has lost it. There is an early period when we do not think of it—and then there comes a period when we never cease to think of it. The streets are full of dead faces and half dead faces.... Get back to a rebirth. Recreate the thing you sigh for. I can lead you to the Fountain of Youth."

"How can you gain, in just a few delightful minutes' reading each day, that knowledge of a few truly great books which will distinguish you always as a well-read man or woman? ... The booklet tells about it—how Dr. Eliot has put into his Five-Foot Shelf 'the books essential to the Twentieth-Century idea of a cultivated person' [...]"

Richmond
Palace

Richmond,
England

A notable example of Tudor-Gothic architecture of preNorman origin. Rebuilt by Henry VII for his occupancy about 1499

17th Century Carved Side Table

Strongly suggestive of the *rugged* tendencies of its period, with bold freedom of modeling, this *early English* sideboard truly reflected the imposing *character* of the great dining halls in which it was used. Reproductions of pieces made by *W & J Sloane* bring back through the centuries a note of precious *distinction* for the modern home.

W & J SLOANE
FIFTH AVENUE AND 47th STREET
NEW YORK
SAN FRANCISCO   WASHINGTON D.C.

THE JORDAN BLUE BOY IN BLUE DEVIL BLUE

Built for those happy people who bought a Jordan Playboy
for their honeymoon, but now want a little more room for
the friends they take for an afternoon of golf.

The wheelbase has been lengthened for lowness. Cushions
hug the floor. The top fits like a swanky sport hat—and
all is slender—'cept the tires—they are fat.

JORDAN

"Built for those happy people who bought a Jordan Playboy for their honeymoon, but now want a little more room for the friends they take for an afternoon of golf."

3. From F. Scott Fitzgerald, "How to Live on $36,000 a Year," *Saturday Evening Post* (5 April 1924), 22, 94, 97

My wife and I were married in New York in the spring of 1920, when prices were higher than they had been within the memory of man. In the light of after events it seems fitting that our career should have started at that precise point in time. I had just received a large check from the movies and I felt a little patronizing toward the millionaires riding down Fifth Avenue in their limousines—because my income had a way of doubling every month. This was actually the case. It had done so for several months—I had made only thirty-five dollars the previous August, while here in April I was making three thousand—and it seemed as if it was going to do so forever. At the end of the year it must reach half a million. Of course with such a state of affairs, economy seemed a waste of time. So we went to live at the most expensive hotel in New York, intending to wait there until enough money accumulated for a trip abroad.

To make a long story short, after we had been married for three months I found one day to my horror that I didn't have a dollar in the world, and the weekly hotel bill for two hundred dollars would be due next day.

I remembered the mixed feelings with which I issued from the bank on hearing the news.

"What's the matter?" demanded my wife anxiously, as I joined her on the sidewalk. "You look depressed."

"I'm not depressed," I answered cheerfully; "I'm just surprised. We haven't got any money."

"Haven't got any money," she repeated calmly, and we began to walk up the Avenue in a sort of trance. "Well, let's go to the movies," she suggested jovially.

It all seemed so tranquil that I was not a bit cast down. The cashier had not even scowled at me. I had walked in and said to him, "How much money have I got?" And he had looked in a big book and answered, "None."

That was all. There were no harsh words, no blows. And I knew that there was nothing to worry about. I was now a successful author, and when successful authors ran out of money all they had to do was sign checks. I wasn't poor—they couldn't fool me. Poverty meant being depressed and living in a small remote room and eating at a *rôtisserie* on the corner, while I—why, it was impossible that I should be poor! I was living in the best hotel in New York!

My first step was to try to sell my only possession—my $1000 bond. It was the first of many times I made the attempt; in all financial crises I dig it out and with it go hopefully to the bank, supposing that, as it never fails to pay the proper interest, it has at last assumed a tangible value. But as I have never been able to sell it, it has gradually acquired the sacredness of a family heirloom. It is always referred to by my wife as "your bond," and it was once turned in at the Subway offices after I left it by accident on a car seat!

This particular crisis passed next morning when the discovery that publishers sometimes advance royalties sent me hurriedly to mine. So the only lesson I learned from it was that my money usually turns up somewhere in time of need, and that at the worst you can always borrow—a lesson that would make Benjamin Franklin turn over in his grave.

For the first three years of our marriage our income averaged a little more than $20,000 a year. We indulged in such luxuries as a baby and a trip to Europe, and always money seemed to come easier and easier with less and less effort, until we felt that with just a little more margin to come and go on, we could begin to save.

We left the Middle West and moved East to a town about fifteen miles from New York, where we rented a house for $300 a month. We hired a nurse for $90 a month; a man and his wife—they acted as butler, chauffeur, yard man, cook, parlor maid and chambermaid—for $160 a month; and a laundress, who came twice a week, for $36 a month. This year of 1923, we told each other, was to be our saving year. We were going to earn $24,000, and live on $18,000, thus giving us a surplus of $6,000 with which to buy safety and security for our old age. We were going to do better at last.

Now as everyone knows, when you want to do better you first buy a book and print your name in the front of it in capital letters. So my wife bought a book, and every bill that came to the house was carefully entered in it, so that we could watch living expenses and cut them away to almost nothing—or at least to $1,500 a month.

We had, however, reckoned without our town. It is one of those little towns springing up on all sides of New York which are built especially for those who have made money suddenly but have never had money before.

My wife and I are, of course, members of this newly rich class. That is to say, five years ago we had no money at all, and what we now do away with would have seemed inestimable riches to us then. I have at times suspected that we are the only newly rich people in America, that in fact, we are the very couple at whom all the articles about the newly rich were aimed.

Now when you say "newly rich" you picture a middle-aged and corpulent man who has a tendency to remove his collar at formal dinners and is in perpetual hot water with his ambitious wife and her titled friends. As a member of the newly rich class, I assure you that this picture is entirely libelous. I myself, for example, am a mild, slightly used young man of twenty-seven, and what corpulence I may have developed is for the present a strictly confidential matter between my tailor and me. We once dined with a bona fide nobleman, but we were both far too frightened to take off our collars or even to demand corned beef and cabbage. Nevertheless we live in a town prepared for keeping money in circulation.

When we came here, a year ago, there were, all together, seven merchants engaged in the purveyance of food—three groceries, three butchers and a fisherman. But when the word went around in food-purveying circles that the town was filling up with the recently enriched as fast as houses could be built for them, the rush of butchers, grocers, fishermen and delicatessen men became enormous. Trainloads of them arrived daily with signs and scales in hand to stake out a claim and sprinkle sawdust upon it. It was like the gold rush of '49, or a big bonanza of the 70's.[1] Older and larger cities were denuded of their stores. Inside of a year eighteen food dealers had set up shop in our main street and might be seen any day waiting in their doorways with alluring and deceitful smiles.

Having long been somewhat overcharged by the seven previous food purveyors we all naturally rushed to the new men, who made it known by large numerical signs in their windows that they intended practically to give food away. But once we were snared, the prices began to rise alarmingly, until all of us scurried like frightened mice from one new man to another, seeking only justice, and seeking it in vain.

---

1 The "gold rush of '49" occurred in California after gold was discovered in the Sacramento Valley; a "big bonanza of the 70's" would have derived from investment in mining stocks after the discovery of the Comstock silver mines in Nevada.

What had happened, of course, was that there were too many food purveyors for the population. It was absolutely impossible for eighteen of them to subsist on the town and at the same time charge moderate prices. So each was waiting for some of the others to give up and move away; meanwhile the only way the rest of them could carry their loans from the bank was by selling things at two or three times the prices in the city fifteen miles away. And that is how our town became the most expensive one in the world.

Now in magazine articles people always get together and found community stores, but none of us would consider such a step. It would absolutely ruin us with our neighbors, who would suspect that we actually cared about our money. When I suggested one day to a local lady of wealth—whose husband, by the way, is reputed to have made his money by vending illicit liquids—that I start a community store known as "F. Scott Fitzgerald—Fresh Meats," she was horrified. So the idea was abandoned.

But in spite of the groceries, we began the year in high hopes. My first play was to be presented in the autumn,[1] and even if living in the East forced our expenses a little over $1,500 a month, the play would easily make up for the difference. We knew what colossal sums were earned on play royalties, and just to be sure, we asked several playwrights what was the maximum that could be earned on a year's run. I never allowed myself to be rash. I took a sum halfway between the maximum and the minimum, and put that down as what we could fairly count on its earning. I think my figures came to about $100,000.

It was a pleasant year; we always had this delightful event of the play to look forward to. When the play succeeded we could buy a house, and saving money would be so easy that we could do it blindfolded with both hands tied behind our backs.

As if in happy anticipation we had a small windfall in March from an unexpected source—a moving picture—and for almost the first time in our lives we had enough surplus to buy some bonds.

[...]

I found that from this time on I had less tendency to worry about current expenses. What if we did spend a few hundred too much now and then? What if our grocery bills did vary mysteriously

1 *The Vegetable*, Fitzgerald's first and only professional play, closed after a disastrous preview in Atlantic City (19 November 1923) and never got to Broadway.

from $85 to $165 a month, according as to how closely we watched the kitchen? Didn't I have bonds in the bank? Trying to keep under $1,500 a month the way things were going was merely niggardly. We were going to save on a scale that would make such petty economies seem like counting pennies.

The coupons on "my" bond are always sent to an office on lower Broadway. Where Liberty Bond[1] coupons are sent I never had a chance to find out, as I didn't have the pleasure of clipping any. Two of them I was unfortunately compelled to dispose of just one month after I first locked them up. I had begun a new novel, you see, and it occurred to me it would be much better business in the end to keep at the novel and live on the Liberty Bonds while I was writing it. Unfortunately the novel progressed slowly, while the Liberty Bonds went at an alarming rate of speed. The novel was interrupted whenever there was any sound above a whisper in the house, while the Liberty Bonds were never interrupted at all.

And the summer drifted too. It was an exquisite summer and it became a habit with many world-weary New Yorkers to pass their week-ends at the Fitzgerald house in the country. Along near the end of a balmy and insidious August I realized with a shock that only three chapters of my novel were done—and in the little tin safety-deposit vault, only "my" bond remained. There it lay—paying storage on itself and a few dollars more. But never mind; in a little while the box would be bursting with savings. I'd have to hire a twin box next door.

But the play was going into rehearsals in two months. To tide over the interval there were two courses open to me—I could sit down and write some short stories or I could continue to work on the novel and borrow the money to live on. Lulled into a sense of security by our sanguine anticipations I decided on the latter course, and my publishers lent me enough to pay our bills until the opening night.

So I went back to my novel, and the months and money melted away; but one morning in October I sat in the cold interior of a New York theater and heard the cast read through the first act of my play. It was magnificent; my estimate had been too low. I could almost hear the people scrambling for seats, hear the ghostly voices of the movie magnates as they bid against one another for

---

1 Liberty Bonds were sold in the United States through 1917 and 1918 to support the Allied war effort.

the picture rights. The novel was now laid aside; my days were spent at the theater and my nights in revising and improving the two or three little weak spots in what was to be the success of the year.

The time approached and life became a breathless affair. The November bills came in, were glanced at, and punched onto a bill file on the bookcase. More important questions were in the air. A disgusted letter arrived from an editor telling me I had written only two short stories during the entire year. But what did that matter? The main thing was that our second comedian got the wrong intonation in his first-act exit line.

The play opened in Atlantic City in November. It was a colossal frost. People left their seats and walked out, people rustled their programs and talked audibly in bored impatient whispers. After the second act I wanted to stop the show and say it was all a mistake but the actors struggled heroically on.

There was a fruitless week of patching and revising, and then we gave up and came home. To my profound astonishment the year, the great year, was almost over. I was $5,000 in debt, and my one idea was to get in touch with a reliable poorhouse where we could hire a room and bath for nothing a week. But one satisfaction nobody could take from us. We had spent $36,000 and purchased for one year the right to be members of the newly rich class. What more can money buy?

[...]

"I'll just have to get out of this mess the only way I know how, by making more money. Then when we've got something in the bank we can decide what we'd better do."

Over our garage is a large bare room whither I now retired with pencil, paper and the oil stove, emerging the next afternoon at five o'clock with a 7,000 word story. That was something; it would pay the rent and last month's overdue bills. It took twelve hours a day for five weeks to rise from abject poverty back into the middle class, but within that time we had paid our debts, and the cause for immediate worry was over.

But I was far from satisfied with the whole affair. A young man can work at excessive speed with no ill effects, but youth is unfortunately not a permanent condition of life.

I wanted to find out where the $36,000 had gone. Thirty-six thousand is not very wealthy—not yacht-and-Palm-Beach wealthy—but it sounds to me as though it should buy a roomy house full of furniture, a trip to Europe once a year, and a bond or two besides. But our $36,000 had bought nothing at all.

So I dug up my miscellaneous account books, and my wife dug up her complete household record for the year 1923, and we made out the monthly average. Here it is:

HOUSEHOLD EXPENSES

	Apportioned per month
Income tax	$ 198.00
Food	202.00
Rent	300.00
Coal, wood, ice, gas, light, phone and water	114.50
Servants	295.00
Golf clubs	105.50
Clothes—three people	158.00
Doctor and dentist	42.50
Drugs and cigarettes	32.50
Automobile	25.00
Books	14.50
All other household expenses	112.50
Total	$1,600.00

"Well, that's not bad," we thought when we had got thus far. "Some of the items are pretty high, especially food and servants. But there's about everything accounted for, and it's only a little more than half our income."

Then we worked out the average monthly expenditures that could be included under pleasure.

Hotel bills—this meant spending the night or charging meals in New York	$ 51.00
Trips—only two, but apportioned per month	43.00
Theater tickets	55.00
Barber and hairdresser	25.00
Charity and loans	15.00
Taxis	15.00
Gambling—this dark heading covers bridge, craps and football bets	33.00
Restaurant parties	70.00
Entertaining	70.00
Miscellaneous	23.00
Total	$400.00

Some of these items were pretty high. They will seem higher to a Westerner than to a New Yorker. Fifty-five dollars for theater tickets means between three and five shows a month, depending on the type of show and how long it's been running. Football games are also included in this, as well as ringside seats to the Dempsey-Firpo fight.[1] As for the amount marked "restaurant parties"—$70 would perhaps take three couples to a popular after-theater cabaret—but it would be a close shave.

We added the items marked "pleasure" to the items marked "household expenses," and obtained a monthly total.

"Fine," I said. "Just $3,000. Now at least we'll know where to cut down, because we know where it goes."

She frowned; then a puzzled, awed expression passed over her face.

"What's the matter?" I demanded. "Isn't it all right? Are some of the items wrong?"

"It isn't the items," she said staggeringly; "it's the total. This only adds up to $2,000 a month."

I was incredulous, but she nodded.

"But listen," I protested; "my bank statements show that we've spent $3,000 a month. You don't mean to say that every month we lose $1,000 dollars?"

"This only adds up to $2,000," she protested, "so we must have."

"Give me the pencil."

For an hour I worked over the accounts in silence, but to no avail.

"Why, this is impossible!" I insisted. "People don't lose $12,000 in a year. It's just—it's just missing."

There was a ring at the doorbell and I walked over to answer it, still dazed by these figures. It was the Banklands, our neighbors from over the way.

"Good heavens!" I announced. "We've just lost $12,000!"

Bankland stepped back alertly.

"Burglars?" he inquired.

"Ghosts," answered my wife.

Mrs. Bankland looked nervously around.

"Really?"

---

1 A 14 September 1923 fight at the Polo Grounds in New York City between heavyweight champion Jack Dempsey (1895–1983) and Argentine boxer Luis Ángel Firpo (1894–1960).

We explained the situation, the mysterious third of our incomes that had vanished into thin air.

"Well, what we do," said Mrs. Bankland, "is, we have a budget."

"We have a budget," agreed Bankland, "and we stick absolutely to it. If the skies fall we don't go over any item of that budget. That's the only way to live sensibly and save money."

"That's what we ought to do," I agreed.

Mrs. Bankland nodded enthusiastically.

"It's a wonderful scheme," she went on. "We make a certain deposit every month, and all I save on it I can have for myself to do anything I want with."

I could see that my own wife was visibly excited.

"That's what I want to do," she broke out suddenly. "Have a budget. Everybody does it that has any sense."

"I pity anyone that doesn't use that system," said Bankland solemnly. "Think of the inducement to economy—the extra money my wife'll have for clothes."

"How much have you saved so far?" my wife inquired eagerly of Mrs. Bankland.

"So far?" repeated Mrs. Bankland. "Oh, I haven't had a chance so far. You see we only began the system yesterday."

"Yesterday!" we cried.

"Just yesterday," agreed Bankland darkly. "But I wish to heaven I'd started it a year ago. I've been working over our accounts all week, and do you know, Fitzgerald, every month there's $2,000 I can't account for to save my soul."

Our financial troubles are now over. We have permanently left the newly rich class and installed the budget system. It is simple and sensible, and I can explain it to you in a few words. You consider your income an enormous pie all cut up into slices, each slice representing one class of expenses. Somebody has worked it all out; so you know just what proportion of your income you can spend on each slice. There is even a slice for founding universities, if you go in for that.

For instance, the amount you spend on the theater should be half of your drug-store bill. This will enable us to see one play every five and a half months, or two and a half plays a year. We have already picked out the first one, but if it isn't running five and a half months from now we shall be that much ahead. Our allowance for newspapers should be only a quarter of what we spend on self-improvement, so we are considering whether to get the Sunday paper once a month or to subscribe to an almanac.

According to the budget we will be allowed only three-quarters of a servant, so we are on the lookout for a one-legged cook who can come six days a week. And apparently the author of the budget book lives in a town where you can still go to the movies for a nickel and get a shave for a dime. But we are going to give up the expenditure called "Foreign missions, etc.," and apply it to the life of crime instead. Altogether, outside of the fact that there is no slice allowed for "missing" it seems to be a very complete book, and according to the testimonials in the back, if we make $36,000 again this year, the chances are that we'll save $35,000.

"But we can't get any of that first $36,000 back," I complained around the house. "If we just had something to show for it I wouldn't feel so absurd."

My wife thought a long while.

"The only thing you can do," she said finally, "is to write a magazine article and call it How to Live on $36,000 a Year."

"What a silly suggestion!" I replied coldly.

4. From Samuel Crowther, "Everybody Ought to Be Rich: An Interview with John J. Raskob," *Ladies' Home Journal* (August 1929), 9, 36

Being rich is, of course, a comparative status. A man with a million dollars used to be considered rich, but so many people have at least that much in these days, or are earning incomes in excess of a normal return from a million dollars, that a millionaire does not cause any comment.

Fixing a bulk line to define riches is a pointless performance. Let us rather say that a man is rich when he has an income from invested capital which is sufficient to support him and his family in a decent and comfortable manner—to give as much support, let us say, as has even been given by his earnings. That amount of prosperity ought to be attainable by anyone. A greater share will come to those who have greater ability.

It seems to me to be a primary duty for people to make it their business to understand how wealth is produced and not to take their ideas from writers and speakers who have the gift of words but not the gift of ordinary common sense. Wealth is not created in dens of iniquity, and it is much more to the point to understand what it is all about than to listen to the expounding of new systems which at the best can only make worse the faults of our present system.

It is quite true that wealth is not so evenly distributed as it ought to be and as it can be. And part of the reason for the unequal distribution is the lack of systematic investment and also the lack of even moderately sensible investment.

One class of investors saves money and puts it into savings banks or other mediums that pay only a fixed interest. Such funds are valuable, but they do not lead to wealth. A second class tries to get rich all at once, and buys any wildcat security that comes along with the promise of immense returns. A third class holds that the return from interest is not enough to justify savings, but at the same time has too much sense to buy fake stocks—and so saves nothing at all. Yet all the while wealth has been here for the asking.

The common stocks of this country have in the past ten years increased enormously in value because the business of the country has increased. Ten thousand dollars invested ten years ago in the common stock of General Motors would now be worth more than a million and a half dollars. And General Motors is only one of many first-class industrial corporations.

It may be said that this is a phenomenal increase and that conditions are going to be different in the next ten years. That prophecy may be true, but it is not founded on experience. In my opinion the wealth of the country is bound to increase at a very rapid rate. The rapidity of the rate will be determined by the increase in consumption, and under wise investment plans the consumption will steadily increase.

Now anyone may regret that he or she did not have ten thousand dollars ten years ago and did not put it into General Motors or some other good company—and sigh over a lost opportunity. Anyone who firmly believes that the opportunities are all closed and that from now on the country will get worse instead of better is welcome to the opinion—and to whatever increment it will bring. I think that we have scarcely started, and I have thought so for many years.

In conjunction with others I have been interested in creating and directing at least a dozen trusts for investment in equity securities. [...] Three of these trusts are now twenty years old. Fifteen dollars per month equals one hundred and eighty dollars a year. In twenty years, therefore, the total savings amounted to thirty-six hundred dollars. Each of these three trusts is now worth well in excess of eighty thousand dollars. Invested at 6 per cent interest, this eighty thousand dollars would give the trust beneficiary an annual income of four hundred dollars per month, which ordinarily would represent more than the earning power of the beneficiary, because had he been able to earn as much as four hundred dollars per month he could have saved more than fifteen dollars.

Suppose a man marries at the age of twenty-three and begins a regular savings of fifteen dollars a month—and almost anyone who is employed can do that if he tries. If he invests in good common stocks and allows the dividends and rights to accumulate, he will at the end of twenty years have at least eighty thousand and an income from investments of around four hundred dollars a month. He will be rich. And because anyone can do that I am firm in my belief that anyone not only can be rich but ought to be rich.

The obstacles to being rich are two: The trouble of saving, and the trouble of finding a medium for investment.

[...]

Everybody ought to be rich, but it is out of the question to make people rich in spite of themselves.

The millennium is not at hand. One cannot have all play and no work. But it has been sufficiently demonstrated that many of the old and supposedly conservative maxims are as untrue as the radical notions. We can only appraise things as they are.

Everyone by this time ought to know that nothing can be gained by stopping the progress of the world and dividing up everything—there would not be enough to divide, in the first place, and, in the second place, most of the world's wealth is not in such form it can be divided.

The socialistic theory of division is, however, no more irrational than some of the more hidebound theories of thrift or of getting rich by saving.

No one can become rich merely by saving. Putting aside a sum each week in a sock at no interest, or in a savings bank at ordinary interest, will not provide enough for old age unless life in the meantime be rigorously skimped down to the level of mere existence. And if everyone skimped in such fashion then the country would be so poor that living at all would hardly be worth while.

Unless we have consumption we shall not have production. Production and consumption go together and a rigid national program of saving would, if carried beyond a point, make for general poverty, for there would be no consumption to call new wealth into being.

Therefore, savings must be looked at not as a present deprivation in order to enjoy more in the future, but as a constructive method of increasing not only one's future but also one's present income.

Saving may be a virtue if undertaken as a kind of mental and moral discipline, but such a course of saving is not to be regarded as a financial plan. Constructive saving in order to increase one's income is a financial operation and to be governed by financial rules; disciplinary saving is another matter entirely. The two have been confused.

Most of the old precepts contrasting the immorality of speculation with the morality of sound investment have no basis in fact. They have just been so often repeated as true that they are taken as true.

[...]

The line between investment and speculation is a very hazy one, and a definition is not to be found in the legal form of a security or in limiting the possible return on the money. The difference is rather in the approach.

Placing a bet is very different from placing one's money with a corporation which has thoroughly demonstrated that it can normally earn profits and has a reasonable expectation of earning greater profits. That may be called speculation, but it would be more accurate to think of the operation as going into business with men who have demonstrated that they know how to do business.

The old view of debt is quite as illogical as the old view of investment. It was beyond the conception of anyone that debt could be constructive. Every old saw[1] about debt—and there must be a thousand of them—is bound up with borrowing rather than earning. We now know that borrowing may be a method of earning and beneficial to everyone concerned. Suppose a man needs a certain amount of money in order to buy a set of tools or anything else which will increase his income. He can take one of two courses. He can save the money and in the course of time buy his tools, or he can, if the proper facilities are provided, borrow the money at a reasonable rate of interest, buy the tools and immediately so increase his income that he can pay off his debt and own the tools within half the time that it would have taken him to save the money and pay cash. That loan enables him

---

1 Proverbial, conventionally wise saying.

at once to create more wealth than before and consequently makes him a more valuable citizen. By increasing his power to produce he also increases his power to consume and therefore he increases the power of others to produce in order to fill his needs and naturally increases their power to consume, and so on and on. By borrowing the money instead of saving it he increases his ability to save and steps up prosperity at once.

That is exactly what the automobile has done to the prosperity of the country through the plan of installment payments. The installment plan of paying for automobiles, when it was first launched, ran counter to the old notions of debt. It was opposed by bankers, who saw in it only an incentive for extravagance. It was opposed by manufacturers because they thought people would be led to buy automobiles instead of their products.

The results have been exactly opposite to the prediction. The ability to buy automobiles on credit gave an immediate step-up to their purchase. Manufacturing them, servicing them, building roads for them to run on, and caring for the people who used the roads have brought into existence about ten billion dollars of new wealth each year—which is roughly about the value of the new farm crops. The creation of this new wealth gave a large increase to consumption and has brought on our present very solid prosperity.

But without the facility for going into debt or the facility for the consumer's getting credit—call it what you will—this great addition to wealth might never have taken place and certainly not for many years to come. Debt may be a burden, but it is more likely to be an incentive.

The great wealth of this country has been gained by the forces of production and consumption pushing each other for supremacy. The personal fortunes of this country have been made not by saving but by producing.

Mere saving is closely akin to the socialist policy of dividing and likewise runs up against the same objection that there is not enough around to save. The savings that count cannot be static. They must be going into the production of wealth. They may go in as debt and the managers of the wealth-making enterprises take all the profit over and above the interest paid. That has been the course recommended for saving and for the reasons that have been set out—the fallacy of conservative investment which is not conservative at all.

The way to wealth is to get into the profit end of wealth production in this country.

Appendix D: The Irreverent Spirit of the Jazz Age

[Though published halfway through the decade we think of as "the Jazz Age," and set in the summer of 1922, *The Great Gatsby* already views the period retrospectively. Indeed, it anticipates Fitzgerald's more justifiably retrospective description in his 1931 essay "Echoes of the Jazz Age," where 1922 is offered as the turning point of the decade, the year in which the Jazz Age "became less and less an affair of youth," and hence decadent and potentially tragic. The selections below strike a balance between conveying the rebellious spirit of the moment—as in Duncan Poole's *Vanity Fair* satire from the summer of 1922 or H.L. Mencken's typically contemptuous attack on Prohibition—and assessing it more objectively, if still sympathetically. (Even as Mencken derides Prohibition, he recognizes the widespread alcoholism it is causing.) F.A. Austin's satiric 1922 *New York Times* piece defending Prohibition from a respectable bootlegger's point of view also lends some credibility to Jay Gatsby's quickly-made fortune. The selections are headed by a substantial excerpt from Fitzgerald's impressionistic overview of the 1920s, written after the stock market crash of 1929 and his wife's mental breakdown, and thus as pertinent to an appreciation of *Tender Is the Night* as *The Great Gatsby*. They culminate in selections from Walter Lippmann's 1929 book *A Preface to Morals*, specifically its opening chapter on "The Problem of Unbelief." Not being identified with the post-war generation, Lippmann recognized the spiritual hazards of a rebelliousness that had no positive object to it, just as Fitzgerald arguably had in his novel. Zelda Fitzgerald's 1925 essay "What Became of the Flappers?" has been included here over her 1922 "Eulogy on the Flapper" (in the June issue of *Metropolitan*) because it tallies better with the novel's depiction of Daisy Buchanan as the flapper grown older and domesticated, and it expresses in striking terms the conservative freedom claimed by the post-war emblem of sexual licentiousness.]

1. From F. Scott Fitzgerald, "Echoes of the Jazz Age," *Scribner's Magazine* 90 (November 1931), 460–62

It was an age of miracles, it was an age of art, it was an age of excess, and it was an age of satire. A Stuffed Shirt, squirming to blackmail in a lifelike way, sat upon the throne of the United States;[1] a stylish young man hurried over to represent to us the throne of England.[2] A world of girls yearned for the young Englishman; the old American groaned in his sleep as he waited to be poisoned by his wife, upon the advice of the female Rasputin who then made the ultimate decision in our national affairs.[3] But such matters apart, we had things our way at last. With Americans ordering suits by the gross in London, the Bond Street tailors perforce agreed to moderate their cut to the American long-waisted figure and loose-fitting taste, something subtle passed to America, the style of man. During the Renaissance, Francis the First[4] looked to Florence to trim his leg. Seventeenth-century England aped the court of France, and fifty years ago the German Guards officer bought his civilian clothes in London. Gentleman's clothes—symbol of "the power that man must hold and that passes from race to race."

We were the most powerful nation. Who could tell us any longer what was fashionable and what was fun? Isolated during the European War, we had begun combing the unknown South and West for folkways and pastimes and there were more ready to hand.

The first social revelation created a sensation out of all proportion to its novelty. As far back as 1915 the unchaperoned young people of the smaller cities had discovered the mobile privacy of that automobile given to young Bill at sixteen to make him "self-reliant." At first petting was a desperate adventure even under such favorable conditions, but presently confidences were exchanged and the old commandment broke down. As early as

---

1 Warren Harding (1865–1923) became president in 1921 and died in office from what was widely assumed to be food poisoning.

2 Edward, Prince of Wales (1894–1972), who became Edward VIII in 1936 before abdicating to marry his mistress Wallis Simpson (1896–1986).

3 The "female Rasputin" probably refers to Nan Britton (1896–1991), who claimed to be Harding's mistress, confidante, and mother of his illegitimate child in a 1927 tell-all memoir, *The President's Daughter*; the lingering consequences of Harding's corrupt administration helped lend popular credence to her story. Fitzgerald's allusion links her to Grigori Rasputin (1871–1916), the notorious monk who had undue influence over Tsarina Alexandra before the Romanov dynasty fell during the Russian Revolution.

4 King of France from 1515 to 1547.

1917 there were references to such sweet and casual dalliance in any number of the *Yale Record* or the *Princeton Tiger*.

But petting in its more audacious manifestations was confined to the wealthier classes—among other young people the old standards prevailed until after the War, and a kiss meant that a proposal was expected, as young officers in strange cities sometimes discovered to their dismay. Only in 1920 did the veil finally fall— the Jazz Age was in flower.

Scarcely had the staider citizens of the republic caught their breaths when the wildest of all generations, the generation which had been adolescent during the confusion of the War, brusquely shouldered my contemporaries out of the way and danced into the limelight. This was the generation whose girls dramatized themselves as flappers, the generation that corrupted its elders and eventually overreached itself less through lack of morals than through lack of taste. May one offer in exhibit the year 1922! That was the peak of the younger generation, for though the Jazz Age continued, it became less and less an affair of youth.

The sequel was like a children's party taken over by the elders, leaving the children puzzled and rather neglected and rather taken aback. By 1923 their elders, tired of watching the carnival and with ill-concealed envy, had discovered that young liquor will take the place of young blood, and with a whoop the orgy began. The younger generation was starred no longer.

A whole race going hedonistic, deciding on pleasure. The precocious intimacies of the younger generation would have come about with or without prohibition—they were implicit in the attempt to adapt English customs to American conditions. (Our South, for example, is tropical and early maturing—it has never been part of the wisdom of France and Spain to let young girls go unchaperoned at sixteen and seventeen.) But the general decision to be amused that began with the cocktail parties of 1921 had more complicated origins.

The word jazz in its progress toward respectability has meant first sex, then dancing, then music. It is associated with a state of nervous stimulation, not unlike that of big cities behind the lines of a war. To many English the War still goes on because all the forces that menace them are still active—Wherefore eat, drink and be merry, for to-morrow we die. But different causes had now brought about a corresponding state in America—though there were entire classes (people over fifty, for example) who spent a whole decade denying its existence even when its puckish face peered into the family circle. Never did they dream that they had contributed to it. The honest citizens of every class, who believed in a strict public morality and were powerful enough to enforce the necessary legislation, did not know that they would necessarily be served by criminals and quacks, and do not really believe it to-day. Rich righteousness had always been able to buy honest and intelligent servants to free the slaves or the Cubans, so when this attempt collapsed our elders stood firm with all the stubbornness of people involved in a weak case, preserving their righteousness and losing their children. Silver-haired women and men with fine old faces, people who never did a consciously dis-honest thing in their lives, still assure each other in the apartment hotels of New York and Boston and Washington that "there's a whole generation growing up that will never know the taste of liquor." Meanwhile their granddaughters pass the well-thumbed copy of "Lady Chatterley's Lover"[1] around the boarding-school and, if they get about at all, know the taste of gin and corn at sixteen. But the generation who reached maturity between 1875 and 1895 continue to believe what they want to believe.

Even the intervening generations were incredulous. In 1920 Heywood Broun[2] announced that all this hubbub was nonsense, that young men didn't kiss but told anyhow. But very shortly people over twenty-five came in for an intensive education. Let me trace some of the revelations vouchsafed them by reference to a dozen works written for various types of mentality during the decade. We begin with the suggestion that Don Juan leads an interesting life ("Jurgen," 1919); then we learn that there's a lot of sex around if we only knew it ("Winesburg, Ohio," 1920), that adolescents lead very amorous lives ("This Side of Paradise," 1920), that there are a lot of neglected Anglo-Saxon words ("Ulysses," 1922), that older people don't always resist sudden temptations ("Cytherea," 1922), that girls are sometimes seduced without being ruined ("Flaming Youth," 1922), that even rape

---

1 Notorious 1928 novel by British novelist D.H. Lawrence (1885–1930) about a wealthy Englishwoman's affair with a gamekeeper. Its explicit sexual subject matter and language kept it an underground classic until obscenity trials between 1959 and 1962 cleared the way for its publica-tion and sale in the United States, Great Britain, and Canada. Fitzger-ald's misspelling "Chatterly's" is corrected here and elsewhere in the essay.

2 Heywood Broun (1888–1939), American critic and journalist.

often turns out well ("The Sheik," 1922), that glamorous English ladies are often promiscuous ("The Green Hat," 1924), that in fact they devote most of their time to it ("The Vortex," 1926), that it's a damn good thing too ("Lady Chatterley's Lover," 1928), and finally that there are abnormal variations ("The Well of Loneliness," 1928, and "Sodome and Gomorrhe," 1929).[1]

In my opinion the erotic element in these works, even "The Sheik" written for children in the key of "Peter Rabbit,"[2] did not one particle of harm. Everything they described, and much more, was familiar in our contemporary life. The majority of the theses were honest and elucidating—their effect was to restore some dignity to the male as opposed to the he-man in American life. ("And what is a 'He-man'? demanded Gertrude Stein one day. 'Isn't it a large enough order to fill out the dimensions of all that 'a man' has meant in the past? A 'He-man'!") The married woman can now discover whether she is being cheated, or whether sex is just something to be endured, and her compensation should be to establish a tyranny of the spirit, as her mother may have hinted. Perhaps many women found that love was meant to be fun. Anyhow the objectors lost their tawdry little case, which is one reason why our literature is now the most living in the world.

Contrary to popular opinion the movies of the Jazz Age had no effect upon its morals. The social attitude of the producers was timid, behind the times and banal—for example no picture mir-

---

1 *Jurgen* (1919), by American novelist James Branch Cabell (1879–1958); *Winesburg, Ohio* (1919), interrelated short-story sequence by American writer Sherwood Anderson (1876–1941); *This Side of Paradise* (1920), Fitzgerald's own first novel; *Ulysses* (1922), by Irish novelist James Joyce; *Cytherea* (1922) by Joseph Hergesheimer; *Flaming Youth* (1923) by American writer Warner Fabian (pen name of Samuel Hopkins Adams, 1871–1958); *The Sheik* (1919 in Great Britain; 1921 in the United States), bestselling novel by British novelist E.M. Hull (pen name of Edith Maude Winstanley, 1880–1947), the basis for the popular 1921 movie starring Rudolph Valentino; *The Green Hat* (1924), by British novelist Michael Arlen (1895–1956); *The Vortex* (1925; opened 1924), play by British playwright Noel Coward (1899–1973); *The Well of Loneliness* (1928), pioneering novel about lesbianism by British writer Radclyffe Hall (1880–1943); *Sodome et Gomorrhe* (1921–22), fourth volume of French writer Marcel Proust's masterpiece *A la recherche du temps perdu* (which began appearing in C.K. Scott Moncrieff's English translation as *Remembrance of Things Past* in 1922).
2 1902 children's tale by English writer Beatrix Potter (1866–1943).

rored even faintly the younger generation until 1923, when magazines had already been started to celebrate it and it had long ceased to be news. There were a few feeble splutters and then Clara Bow in "Flaming Youth";[1] promptly the Hollywood hacks ran the theme into its cinematographic grave. Throughout the Jazz Age the movies got no farther than Mrs. Jiggs,[2] keeping up with its most blatant superficialities. This was no doubt due to the censorship as well as to innate conditions in the industry. In any case the Jazz Age now raced along under its own power, served by great filling stations full of money.

2. Duncan M. Poole, "The Great Jazz Trial: With a Few Illuminating Remarks on the Way of Reformers in General," *Vanity Fair* 18 (June 1922), 61, 108

Verily, the way of the Reformer is hard. Perhaps he likes it that way, but it has always seemed to me rather tough. It isn't as if he were always forging upstream, going contrary to the current so to speak, or always beating to windward. In both of these, some progress may be noted, some head-way made, and they are thrilling and exciting. But the Reformer's lot is much worse than that. His results appear so illusory, so evanescent. He no sooner gets some particular social evil all nice and reformed, than another breaks out to take its place. It is as though Public Morality were a large squashy hot-water bottle, partially filled. You know how the pesky things act. If you punch them in one place they bulge out in another. So it is with reforming.

Looking back over comparatively recent years, we can recall a sequence of popular vices which one by one have been attacked, suppressed and perhaps partially cured. Racing, gambling, prize-fighting, drugs, drinking and the most ancient and permanent forms of immorality have all come in for their share of attention. And the latest target for the Reformer's guns is Jazz.

Jazz is not defined in my Webster's Collegiate. It probably will be in the next edition. The nearest thing I find to it under the J's is "jig,"—a brisk dance movement in a rhythm of triplets. 2. A

---

1 Clara Bow (1906–65), one of the leading actresses of the silver screen in the 1920s. Fitzgerald's memory is at fault here: Colleen Moore (1900–88), not Clara Bow, was the star of the 1923 movie version of Warner Fabian's sensational novel.

2 Socially aspiring Irish-American wife in the syndicated comic strip *Bringing Up Father*, created in 1913 by George McManus (1884–1954).

piece of sport, a prank. 3. A kind of trolling bait. 4. An apparatus for separating impurities by agitation.

It is quite remarkable how many of these definitions fit Jazz as we know it today. It is certainly a brisk dance movement and a piece of sport or prank. "A kind of trolling bait" is not so obvious, though it might apply. Whether "an apparatus for separating impurities by agitation" applies as a description depends entirely on how you look at it. The real dyed-in-the-wool Reformer holds that Jazz, far from separating impurities brings them together, and by this same method of agitation. Its defenders say that, on the contrary, it works just exactly as Mr. Webster says, that it is a perfectly grand thing, and by its festive agitation frees all sorts of repressed emotions that would otherwise find their outlet in horrid Sunday-School and church-choir scandals. Oh, you must not suppose for an instant that this great modern dance movement is without its champions!

Let us look for a moment at the forces arrayed against each other. Let us try to stage a trial scene, and let the prisoner, Jazz, be summoned to the Bar where the witnesses, pro and con, shall be heard. As usual in such cases, we will allow the plaintiff to prefer his charges first and introduce his testimony. Jazz, whom I visualize in my poetic way, as a very attractive young lady in a sketchy evening gown, is brought before Judge Morrill by Police-Matron Grundy, a veritable wizardess in arresting, on suspicion, all doubtful characters. The charge is formidable and impressive.

"This creature," says Officer Grundy, "is one of the most dangerous criminals at large. Her character is a compound of all the vices of the age. By her example the Youth of America is becoming degenerate and debauched. She has flagrantly paraded her vicious example before the innocent people who frequent our restaurants, cabarets and theatrical performances. The purity of our New York audiences is becoming seriously undermined. We demand that she be put away for an indefinite period. We recommend a year in a Dancing Reform-School where the regulation garb is a heavy wool waist and skirt extending to the ankles. It is evident that this—"

"Kindly do not plead the case," says Judge Morrill, "call your witnesses."

The Rev. John R. Straightjacket is called and duly sworn. Dr. Straightjacket is a vice-expert, and qualifies as such by relating in great detail his past experiences in a vast number of dens, dives, and—as he adds—worse. He is very much at home in the witness chair, which seems to fit his bulging form as if made for it.

"Let us start with a basic problem," he announces in a voice which swings the court-room chandeliers with its resonance. "All pleasure is dangerous. It has a corrupting influence. Whenever pleasure steals in, the moral censor sneaks out the back door. Enjoyment encourages iniquity. This is particularly true of dancing, which is the invention of the devil. In ancient times this was not so. Dancing was an individual exercise, a spiritual expression. David danced before Solomon."[1]

"Oh, you Salome"[2] (from the rear of the court-room). Judge M.: "Order in the court. Proceed."

"But this Jazz, this wanton exhibition of lewdness which brings bodies of opposite sex into a juxtaposition which—"

Judge Morrill here requests Dr. Straightjacket to submit the rest of his testimony in the form of a brief, adding "and make it as brief as possible." The next witness is called.

This is the Rabbi Steven S. Stone of the Sho Maholem Synagogue, who repeats in substance the remarks of Dr. Straightjacket. He is, however, a much more snappy witness. His testimony is epigrammatic and pungent; he does not chin himself on his own rhetoric as does his Christian Brother. But he too is an expert. He refers to the age as "jassastrophic" and gets a good laugh from the jury. He speaks of the "mad hunger for a good time, a hunger which enables men and women to atrophy their senses through super-stimulation."

"Do you think Jazz is corrupting the stage?" he is asked.

"No. The stage is incorruptible. Most of my friends are theatrical managers and I can say——"

"You are a liar," shouts Dr. Straightjacket. "The stage is a hotbed of vice. I challenge you now to a debate on the platform of my church."

"Schlemiel!"[3] screams the Rabbi, "Meet me at the synagogue!"

---

1 The Reverend betrays his ignorance or confusion here; "David danced before the Lord," not Solomon, when the Ark of the Covenant was brought to Jerusalem (2 Samuel 6:14).

2 Prominent in art and literature for centuries, Salome was the name given to the unnamed stepdaughter of Herod who appears in Mark 6:21–26 requesting John the Baptist's head on a platter as a reward for her dancing. The figure of Salome became synonymous with the *femme fatale* of late-nineteenth-century decadent art and literature.

3 Yiddish: fool.

Both witnesses are forcibly removed and the sounds of a fierce conflict are borne in from the corridors.

Next we hear from a celebrated playwright who has written a play of which he reads the first act, showing clearly that Jazz not only destroys the home but that its horrid example is corrupting the honest labouring man of the country. It appears that the caddies at the country-club see these shocking performances going on and tell their fathers about it and thus the poison seeps into the veins of the industrial world until the first thing we know we have an enormous general strike on our hands! It is quite terrifying.

Homer Flitts, Jazz editor of the *Gotham Gazette*, says he was horrified when he saw nice people become wild and woolly under the influence of Jazz rendered by human gorillas who moaned and groaned over their musical instruments, and Professor Tasmalia, student of Infant Education paints a shocking picture of immorality in the nurseries and kindergartens introduced by Jazz records artfully included in the latest Bubble Books.[1]

Well, it looks very dark and gloomy for Jazz. She hangs her head and weeps a little. The jury is silent, impressed. But wait!

The young attorney for the defense is about to speak. He is a pleasant looking young chap and he carries a ukelele on a ribbon around his neck, upon which he occasionally plays a few chords in harmony with his musical voice.

"Your Honour," he chants, "ladies and gentlemen of the Jury, and (bowing to Jazz) Guest of Honour."

This graceful tribute brings a ripple of applause from the benches.

"Your Honour, we have listened patiently to a long line of testimony from a number of gentlemen who claim to be experts. It is customary, I believe, to be allowed to cast, if possible, some doubt on the reliability of such testimony and upon the character of such witnesses. As to its expertness, I can only point out that it is obviously true that none of these gentlemen has ever practised the vices which they so outrageously attack. They have not led the wanton and vicious life which they attribute to my client, the defendant, and they would be the first to agree with me in

---

1 Children's series of books with accompanying records published by Harper Columbia between 1917 and 1922.

this. But it is a curious fact that all Vice-Experts are invariably people who have made virtue their only pursuit. I, therefore, ask you, Your Honour, to dismiss the charges on the ground that they are supported by testimony [un?] worthy of belief, and I so move."

Judge Morrill hesitated but finally decided that it would hardly be proper not to hear a few witnesses.

"Very well then," continued the young barrister, "I will produce them and gladly. We have our experts, and real experts, too. Will Miss Zambino kindly take the stand."

An exquisite creature clad in a long cloak advanced to the rail: Standing composedly she faced the jury-box and said in a clear voice:

"Ladies and gentlemen, I have jazzed both in public and private ever since the craze started. It is now waning; other forms of dancing are taking its place, but I can assure you that I have never found in it anything but a helpful form of exercise, a physical and mental relaxation. I wish I could indicate more clearly how beneficial this may be, but without a partner ... Ah, how do you do! ... we met at Montmartre,[1] did we not?"

One of the younger jurors had leaped out of the pen. As he did so Miss Zambino dropped her long cloak disclosing the bare neck and shoulders of evening attire; an instant later, to the soft rhythm of the lawyer's ukelele they were jazzing daintily in the small inclosure before the bench.

"I object," shrieked Matron Grundy. "She is influencing the Juror."

"Objection sustained," said His Honour, with a sigh of disappointment.

The defense witnesses were called in in quick succession and an imposing array they were, a Health Commissioner, a noted Physician, a Psychologist, a Banker, one and all agreeing that Jazz was a delightful, harmless creature, and that they were united in their support of anything that made for human happiness. The jury was immensely bucked up. Even Judge Morrill looked happy when he charged them.

"Ladies and Gentlemen, you will now consider the evidence as presented to you. You have heard the charges and the evidence. It

---

1 Section of Paris popular with artists, writers, and jazz musicians, and known at the time for its bars and sexual promiscuity.

is for you to decide. You will now go out,—and don't come back."

The Jury are still out!

This is the great trial of Jazz. She is still at large, losing to be sure, a certain amount of her popularity, as is inevitable, but still found in certain localities. If she disappears entirely the Reformers will say they have killed her or driven her away.

But will they be down-hearted?

Never. For, as I said, when one reform is apparently accomplished another will surely spring up to take its place. Already we have those dreadful moving picture affairs!

But an even worse thing is going on. The young girls and children of our schools are going about with their goloshes all unbuttoned, actually flapping in the breeze![1] This is leading to all sorts of evils. The world is sure to go to hell as rapidly as progress—in goloshes—can be made.

3. F.A. Austin, "The Bootlegger Speaks," *New York Times* (16 April 1922), 53

"I fear," complained the Educated Bootlegger, with a desponding gesture which displayed the 30 carats of real diamonds adorning one hand, "that a continuance of the prevalent hue and cry for the licensing of the sale of real beer and light wines will ruin one of the few of our industries which at present is paying large dividends and shows every evidence of continuous and increasing prosperity. I refer to the industry of supplying our citizens with that remedy which is invaluable in cases of snakebite, Spanish influenza,[2] Spring fever and emaciation of the hip pocket.

"There is current a false impression that we distributors of whatever is obtainable under the general classification of 'hooch' are against the Prohibition Amendment and foes of the Volstead Enforcement act.[3] On the contrary, we are among their most ardent supporters. None would see with more genuine sorrow a return to those days of unlimited license when a man could buy a drink for 15 cents and retain his eyesight after drinking it. Superintendent Anderson and the Anti-Saloon League, the W. C.

---

1 A reference to the fashion of wearing unfastened galoshes, which may have been one source of the term "flappers."

2 Deadly pandemic that erupted in war-torn Europe in the fall of 1918 and lasted through successive waves into the spring of 1920.

3 Statute for enforcing Prohibition.

T. U.[1] and the pulpits of all denominations can count on us to fight with them to the last ditch against any restoration of the immoral privileges of open sale and purchase of malt and spirituous liquors.

"Were it not for those two beneficent and far-seeing statesmen in Washington, I should have been unable to complete at the university the education interrupted in my early youth by the necessity of working. Nor should I be able to gratify my inherent desire to acquire works of art, go to the opera, patronize the best tailors, live in a bachelor apartment, employ a valet, aid our bon-vivants in supporting such philanthropic institutions as all-night dancing clubs, and, in short, enjoy in elegant leisure all the purchasable luxuries, at the same time restricting my business dealings to transactions with our best citizens and meeting them socially on equal terms as fellow law-breakers.

"Far from using our efforts toward bringing about a modification of prohibition, the members of the Big Bootleggers' Brotherhood are bending all their energies to convincing State and national legislators that the law should remain as it is. While ours is only an infant industry in age, it has already reached a man's full stature, surpassing in size and the volume of business transacted what have heretofore been our banner industries. Like them, we realize the need of co-operation and concerted effort to prevent price-cutting, increase sales and improve morale. Our State and national lobbies, like those of the Anti-Saloon League, are constantly impressing on the lawmakers who are seeking re-election the need of maintaining the prohibition law and the national and State enforcement acts as they now stand. If they are to be tampered with at all, we favor making them even more drastic; for the harder it becomes to supply interdicted liquor, the higher the price to the consumer. We have no sympathy with those deluded legislators who put principle before profit.

"If our Congressmen and State solons[2] realized fully the benefits that the Volstead act has conferred on hundreds and thou-

---

1 William H. Anderson (1874–c. 1959) was General State Superintendent of the Prohibition-advocating lobbying group the Anti-Saloon League until he was indicted for forgery and sent to prison in 1924; W.C.T.U., the Women's Christian Temperance Union, an international temperance advocacy group founded in Cleveland in 1874.

2 Wise lawmakers, after the famed ancient Athenian statesman and law-giver Solon (c. 630–560 BCE).

sands of our citizens, directly and indirectly, they would not give a thought to suggestions for its repeal or modification. From a mere filler of beakers the bartender has jumped to a place corresponding in the social scale to that formerly occupied by the wine agent, except that he avoids the ostentation and vulgar display which were connected with that calling. Many a bartender who revealed his depravity by selling a glass of beer to a truck driver on a sizzling July day is now a trusted Government spy, drawing a salary from the income tax payers for betraying his former associates who are now violating the law and splitting with another enforcement officer the proceeds of reselling the liquor to the man from whom it was seized. The ex-bartender is responding nobly to the uplifting character of his new environment.

"I may also cite the advantages which have accrued to bellboys, chauffeurs and barbers through the workings of the Volstead act. Bellhops are no longer obliged to suffer the humiliation of depending on tips for their livelihood. They have become salesmen. Compare a $1 tip with the proceeds from a bottle of Scotch bought for $12 and sold for $25, and you get an inkling of the boon the Volstead act has conferred on the knights of the tinkling ice.

"The barber is no longer under the necessity of cutting your hair shorter on one side than on the other to insure a tip. He merely whispers 'Bay Rum' with a wink and slips a pint into your pocket while he helps you on with your coat.

"Many a poor taxi driver who struggled vainly before prohibition to amass a sum sufficient to buy a car is now his own boss, no longer a slave to pitiless taskmasters who forced him to make his taximeter show two miles for every mile traversed with a passenger. He has no need of accelerating his taximeter, he can even afford to disdain tips, for the passengers he carries in cases pay him in a day what formerly he required a week to earn.

"I wonder if Congressmen know the extent to which that monument to Federal philanthropy labeled the Eighteenth Amendment[1] is aiding our aspiring young men in gaining a college education? Working one's way through the university no longer means starvation, attic lodgings and menial tasks. Our agents among the student bodies of the various educational insti-

---

1   US constitutional amendment prohibiting "the manufacture, sale, or transportation of intoxicating liquors," ratified January 1919 (repealed December 1933).

tutions mingle with the most affluent of their fellows, able not only to vie with the sons of the wealthy in enjoying all that money will buy, but oftentimes to help the struggling parents back home.

"There can be no gainsaying that prohibition has stimulated interest in the study of handwriting and in the printing art, as is shown by the forgery of the signatures of our prohibition directors and revenue officers to bogus whisky withdrawal permits and the accuracy with which labels of brands of tried and true liquor have been reproduced for attachment to bottles containing several admissions to the pearly gates.

"Prohibition has opened the door of opportunity to the hitherto poorly paid and overworked public servants in the Internal Revenue Department. For years they have vainly pleaded for an increase in salary. Of course there are many good men among them, but those who are not good, by merely shutting their eyes and turning their backs, can now close their hands on a pay envelope which contains for the week what they have been in the habit of receiving for a year. They may gain even more by fulfilling the duty their position requires. They should, by all means, seize contraband liquor whenever they can. If they do not seize it, how can these black sheep of the Government service arrange for re-selling it at an advance of 100 per cent. in price with the proper commission for their services as middlemen?

"Before the advent of prohibition the payment of police protection money by saloonkeepers had decreased to such an extent that the grafters among our peace guardians were forced to rely almost solely on their meagre salaries. The Volstead act and supporting State and city 'dry' laws have restored protection money to circulation in even more generous amounts than of yore, and any crooked policeman may become one of the subsidiary agencies which reap a handsome profit by the transmutation of seized liquor from a frozen liability to a liquid asset.

"Our growing youth is no longer subject to the criticism once visited upon him if he was seen entering a saloon. The value of self-reliance and hip pockets is being impressed on him and the two-flask man never lacks popularity at the dance or the fraternity 'stag.' The disgraceful practice of serving punch and other intoxicants openly at such functions has been superseded by discreet and private potations in dressing rooms or hotel rooms hired for the purpose where the young of both sexes enjoy liberty unprecedented.

"By no means should the saloon be allowed again to rear its tawdry front and desecrate the architectural beauties of our street signs with its vulgar Bock Beer Goat, to the discouragement of those of our enterprising citizens who have made the mortar and pestle the symbol of safe liquor and sane irrigation for arid areas. If the truth be told, New York City's mark last year for the lowest death record would be accredited to the enormous increase in the number of our drug stores[1] and the resultant ease with which those in need of interior medication can get it without delay, oftentimes under the supervision of a policeman in full uniform.

"We bootleggers are doing more to make chemistry a popular science than all the schools, colleges and universities combined. Our efforts to make it a home study for all the family have met with enormous success, and there have been no more accidents than are to be expected when the amateur experiments with forces with which he is unfamiliar. For the housewife, the kitchen, instead of a cell of slavery, has become a source of joy. Cellars and basements, given up for years to darkness and cobwebs, now glow with light and bubble with the mirth of fermenting malt, while the glad cry of father, mother, and children, 'Is it ready yet?' sends the spiders scurrying to their lairs.

"Ours is the only infant industry which has never asked the protection of the Government from foreign competition. We can dispose of all the foreign goods sent to us without harming the protection of the native product, for the demand exceeds the supply and the capacity the obtainable filler. Ample protection is afforded us by the fact that the taxes which we would normally pay are paid for us by the general public. We pay no taxes whatever. It is eminently proper that those who were responsible for depriving the Government of the revenue it formerly enjoyed through the taxation of beer and liquor should help make up the deficit.

"Considering only the income tax factor, the bootlegging industry will always oppose with all its might any movement which would tend to reduce that proper levy on the swollen fortunes of our captains of other industries and replace it with a tax on 5 cent beer and 15 cent whisky, which would only deplete the poor man's purse through his increased consumption and force us either to go out of business or make income tax returns."

---

1 During Prohibition, drug stores were often fronts for illegal alcohol sales because they could sell legal alcohol prescribed by doctors. "You can buy anything at a drug-store nowadays," quips Tom Buchanan in Chapter VII so as to embarrass Gatsby in front of Daisy, Nick, and Jordan.

4. From H.L. Mencken, ["Five Years of Prohibition,"] *American Mercury* 3 (December 1924), 420–22

Five years of Prohibition have had, at least, this one benign effect: they have completely disposed of all the favorite arguments of the Prohibitionists. None of the great boons and usufructs that were to follow the passage of the Eighteenth Amendment has come to pass. There is not less drunkenness in the Republic, but more. There is not less crime, but more. There is not less insanity, but more. The cost of government is not smaller, but vastly greater. Respect for law has not increased, but diminished. Even the benefits that were to come from the abolition of the open saloon, long damned as a constant temptation to the young, are not visible. On the contrary, the young are now tempted as the saloon, even in its most romantic and voluptuous forms, never tempted them. We were, in 1920, a nation of mild drinkers, moving steadily and certainly toward greater and greater temperance. Business and the professions had cast off strong drink; boozy lawyers and doctors were disappearing; the very drummers were practicing their science cold sober. Few American women drank at all; among the young the vine was almost as much a stranger as the poppy. Now all those gains are lost. The absolute number of users of alcohol has at least doubled, and few of the recruits show any sign of using it with discretion. [...] One or two cocktails, in the old days of freedom, made the average American dinner party, at least outside Manhattan Island, somewhat devilish. Today the dose is as much as the liver and lights will bear.

The Methodists who gave us Prohibition hate their fellowmen, but they are not altogether asses. The facts so brilliantly displayed on all sides are not lost upon them. Hence they quietly shelve their old arguments. One no longer hears from them—save perhaps when they address remote yokels, far from all reach of sense—that Prohibition has obliterated or will presently obliterate crime, or that it is abolishing poverty and disease, or even, indeed, that it actually prohibits. What one hears is simply the doctrine that it must be enforced because it is the law.

[...]

Meanwhile, the city man himself gets used to law-breaking, and all his old instinctive antipathy to it tends to disappear. [...] It is practically impossible, in any big town, to find a man above the level of a Methodist who does not violate the Volstead Act deliberately and habitually. There may be pious minorities in back streets who obey it, but there is certainly no show of respect for it where collars are clean and there is regard for the tense of verbs.

So the matter stands after five years of relentless dragooning and blackjacking. The Bill of Rights has been suspended, the Federal courts have been reduced to impotence and absurdity, the enforcement of the ordinary laws has been impeded, the jails have been filled with men full of resentment and a bitter sense of injustice, millions and millions of the taxpayers' money has been wasted, the few remaining half-decent politicians have been converted into frauds and liars, a horde of professional thugs and blackmailers has been turned loose upon the country, and at least two-thirds of its adult citizens, not to mention millions of its younger ones, have been inoculated with the notion that breaking the law, and even violating the Constitution, is, after all, no serious thing, but simply a necessary incident of a civilized social life.

5. From Zelda Fitzgerald, "What Became of the Flappers?," *McCall's* 53 (October 1925), 12, 30, 66

Flapper wasn't a particularly fortunate cognomen. It is far too reminiscent of open galoshes and covered up ears and all other proverbial flapper paraphernalia, which might have passed unnoticed save for the name. All these things are—or were—amusing externals of a large class of females who in no way deserve the distinction of being called flappers. The flappers that I am writing this article about are a very different and intriguing lot of young people who are perhaps unstable, but who are giving us the first evidence of youth asserting itself out of the cradle. They are not originating new ideas or new customs or new moral standards. They are simply endowing the old ones that we are used to with a vitality that we are not used to. We are not accustomed to having *our* daughters think our ideas for themselves, and it is distasteful to some of us that we are no longer able to fit the younger generation into our conceptions of what the younger generation was going to be like when we watched it in the nursery. I do not think that anything my daughter could possibly do eighteen years from now would surprise me. And yet I will probably be forbidding her in frigid tones to fly more than 3,000 feet high or more than five hundred miles an hour with little Willie Jones, and bidding her never to go near that horrible Mars. I can imagine these things now, but if they should happen twenty years from now, I would certainly wonder what particular dog my child was going to....

The flapper springs full-grown, like Minerva, from the head of her once déclassé father, Jazz,[1] upon whom she lavishes affection and reverence, and deepest filial regard. She is not a "condition arisen from war unrest," as I have so often read in the shower of recent praise and protest which she has evoked, and to which I am contributing. She is a direct result of the greater appreciation of beauty, youth, gaiety and grace which is sweeping along in a carmagnole[2] (I saw one in a movie once, and I use this word advisedly) with our young anti-puritans at the head. They have placed such a premium on the flapper creed—to give and get amusement—that even the dumb-bells become Dulcies[3] and convert stupidity into charm. Dulcy is infinitely preferable to the kind of girl who, ten years ago, quoted the Rubaiyat[4] at you and told you how misunderstood she was; or the kind who straightened your tie as evidence that in her lay the spirit of the eternal mother; or the kind who spent long summer evenings telling you that it wasn't the *number* of cigarettes you smoked that she minded but just the *principle*, to show off her nobility of character. These are some of the bores of yesterday. Now even bores must be original, so the more unfortunate members of the flapper sect have each culled an individual line from their daily rounds, which amuses or not according to whether you have seen the same plays, heard the same tunes or read reviews of the same books.

The best flapper is reticent emotionally and courageous morally. You always know what she thinks, but she does all her feeling alone. These are two characteristics which will bring social intercourse to a more charming and sophisticated level. I believe in the flapper as an artist in her particular field, the art of being— being young, being lovely, being an object.

---

1 Minerva (or Athene in Greek), the Roman goddess of wisdom, was born from the head of her father Jupiter (or Greek Zeus).

2 A procession of dancers singing one of the favorite republican songs of the French Revolution.

3 Generic name for a dim-witted woman, after the heroine of Marc Connelly and George S. Kaufman's popular 1921 play *Dulcy*.

4 *The Rubáiyát of Omar Khayyám* (1859), twelfth-century Persian poem freely translated into English by Edward Fitzgerald (1809–83).

For almost the first time we are developing a class of pretty yet respectable young women, whose sole functions are to amuse and to make growing old a more enjoyable process for some men and staying young an easier one for others. Even parents have ceased to look upon their children as permanent institutions. The fashionable mother no longer keeps her children young so that she will preserve the appearance of a débutante. She helps them to mature so that she will be mistaken for a step-mother. Once her girls are old enough to be out of finishing-school a period of freedom and social activity sets in for her. The daughters are rushed home to make a chaotic début and embark upon a feverish chase for a husband. It is no longer permissible to be single at twenty-five. The flapper makes haste to marry lest she be a left-over and be forced to annex herself to the crowd just younger. She hasn't time to ascertain the degree of compatibility between herself and her fiancé before the wedding, so she ascertains that they will be separated if the compatibility should be mutually rated zero after it.

The flapper! She is growing old. She forgets her flapper creed and is conscious only of her flapper self. She is married 'mid loud acclamation on the part of relatives and friends. She has come to none of the predicted "bad ends," but has gone at last, where all good flappers go—into the young married set, into boredom and gathering conventions and the pleasure of having children, having lent a while a splendour and courageousness and brightness to life, as all good flappers should.

6. From Walter Lippmann, *A Preface to Morals* ["The Problem of Unbelief"] (Macmillan, 1929), 6, 12, 14–18

We are living in the midst of that vast dissolution of ancient habits which the emancipators believed would restore our birthright of happiness. We know now that they did not see very clearly beyond the evils against which they were rebelling. It is evident to us that their prophecies were pleasant fantasies which concealed the greater difficulties that confront men, when having won the freedom to do what they wish—that wish, as Byron said:

> which ages have not yet subdued
> In man—to have no master save his mood,[1]

---

1 From *The Island* (1823) by British Romantic poet George Gordon, Lord Byron (1788–1824).

they are full of contrary moods and do not know what they wish to do. We have come to see that Huxley[1] was right when he said that "a man's worst difficulties begin when he is able to do as he likes."

The evidences of these greater difficulties lie all about us: in the brave and brilliant atheists who have defied the Methodist God, and have become very nervous; in the women who have emancipated themselves from the tyranny of fathers, husbands, and homes, and with the intermittent but expensive help of a psychoanalyst, are now enduring liberty as interior decorators; in the young men and women who are world-weary at twenty-two; in the multitudes who drug themselves with pleasure; in the crowds enfranchised by the blood of heroes who cannot be persuaded to take an interest in their destiny; in the millions, at last free to think without fear of priest or policeman, who have made the moving pictures and the popular newspapers what they are.

These are the prisoners who have been released. They ought to be very happy. They ought to be serene and composed. They are free to make their own lives. There are no conventions, no tabus, no gods, priests, princes, fathers, or revelations which they must accept. Yet the result is not so good as they thought it would be. The prison door is wide open. They stagger out into trackless space under a blinding sun. They find it nerve-wracking.

[...]

... [T]he position of modern men who have broken with the religion of their fathers is in certain profound ways different from that of other men in other ages. This is the first age, I think, in the history of mankind when the circumstances of life have conspired with the intellectual habits of the time to render any fixed and authoritative belief incredible to large masses of men. The dissolution of the old modes of thought has gone so far, and is so cumulative in its effect, that the modern man is not able to sink back after a period of prophesying into a new but stable orthodoxy. The irreligion of the modern world is radical to a degree for which there is, I think, no counterpart. For always in the past it has been possible for new conventions to crystallize, and for men to find rest and surcease of effort in accepting them.

---

1 Thomas Henry Huxley (1825–95), British biologist and essayist.

[...]

But there is reason for thinking that a new crystallization of an enduring and popular religion is unlikely in the modern world. For analogy drawn from the experience of the past is misleading. When Luther, for example, rebelled against the authority of the Church,[1] he did not suppose the way of life for the ordinary man would be radically altered. Luther supposed that men would continue to behave much as they had learned to behave under the Catholic discipline. The individual for whom he claimed the right of private judgment was one whose prejudgments had been well fixed in a Catholic society. [...] The reformers of the Eighteenth Century made a similar assumption. They really believed in democracy for men who had an aristocratic training. Jefferson,[2] for example, had an instinctive fear of the urban rabble, that most democratic part of the population. The society of free men which he dreamed about was composed of those who had the discipline, the standards of honor and the taste, without the privileges or the corruptions, that are to be found in a society of well-bred country gentlemen.

The more recent rebels frequently betray a somewhat similar inability to imagine the consequences of their own victories. For the smashing of idols is in itself such a preoccupation that it is almost impossible for the iconoclast to look clearly into a future when there will not be many idols left to smash. Yet that future is beginning to be our present, and it might be said that men are conscious of what modernity means insofar as they realize that they are confronted not so much with the necessity of promoting rebellion as of dealing with the consequences of it. The Nineteenth Century, roughly speaking the time between Voltaire[3] and Mencken, was an age of terrific indictments and of feeble solutions. The Marxian indictment of capitalism[4] is a case in point.

---

1 Martin Luther (1483–1546), leader of the Protestant Reformation in Europe.
2 Thomas Jefferson (1743–1826), American founder, main author of "The Declaration of Independence" (1776), and third president of the United States (1801–09).
3 François-Marie Arouet de Voltaire (1694–1778), French Enlightenment philosopher renowned for his religious skepticism.
4 In the works of German political philosopher Karl Marx (1818–83), such as *The Communist Manifesto* (1848) and *Capital* (1867).

The Nietzschean transvaluation of values is another;[1] it is magnificent, but who can say, after he has shot his arrow of longing to the other shore, whether he will find Cæsar Borgia, Henry Ford, or Isadora Duncan?[2] Who knows, having read Mr. Mencken and Mr. Sinclair Lewis, what kind of world will be left when all the boobs and yokels have crawled back in their holes and have died of shame?

The rebel, while he is making his attack, is not likely to feel the need to answer such questions. For he moves in an unreal environment, one might almost say a parasitic environment. He goes forth to destroy Cæsar, Mammon, George F. Babbitt, and Mrs. Grundy.[3] As he wrestles with these demons, he leans upon them. By inversion they offer him much the same kind of support which the conformer enjoys. They provide him with an objective which enables him to know exactly what he thinks he wants to do. His energies are focussed by his indignation. He does not suffer from emptiness, doubt, and division of soul. These are the maladies which come later when the struggle is over. While the rebel is in conflict with the established nuisances he has an aim in life which absorbs all his passions. He has his own sense of righteousness and his own feeling of communion with a grand purpose. For in attacking idols there is a kind of piety, in overthrowing tyrants a kind of loyalty, in ridiculing stupidities an imitation of wisdom. In the heat of battle the rebel is exalted by a whole-hearted tension which is easily mistaken for a taste of the freedom that is to come. He is under the spell of an illusion. For what comes after the struggle is not the exaltation of freedom but a letting down of the

---

1 In the works of Friedrich Nietzsche (1844–1900), such as *Beyond Good and Evil* (1886) and *On the Genealogy of Morals* (1887).

2 Cesare Borgia (1476–1507), powerful and ruthless cardinal and statesman in northern and central Italy, the model for Machiavelli's treatise *The Prince* (1513); Henry Ford (1863–1947), pioneering American automobile manufacturer credited with creating modern assembly-line production and establishing higher wages for workers (see Appendix E2); Isadora Duncan (1878–1927), radically innovative American dancer.

3 Caesar: as used here, the personification of established political power; Mammon: the tyranny of money and the drive for material acquisition personified; George F. Babbitt: the small-city real estate salesman of Sinclair Lewis's popular 1922 novel *Babbitt*, whose name became synonymous with a small-minded, repressive, middle-Americanism; Mrs. Grundy: stock name for a conventional prude.

tension that belongs solely to the struggle itself. The happiness of the rebel is as transient as the iconoclasm which produced it. When he has slain the dragon and rescued the beautiful maiden, there is usually nothing left for him to do but write his memoirs and dream of a time when the world was young.

What most distinguishes the generation who have approached maturity since the debacle of idealism at the end of the War is not their rebellion against the religion and the moral code of their parents, but their disillusionment with their own rebellion. It is common for young men and women to rebel, but that they should rebel sadly and without faith in their own rebellion, that they should distrust the new freedom no less than the old certainties—that is something of a novelty. As Mr. Canby[1] once said, at the age of seven they saw through their parents and characterized them in a phrase. At fourteen they saw through education and dodged it. At eighteen they saw through morality and stepped over it. At twenty they lost respect for their home towns, and at twenty-one they discovered that our social system is ridiculous. At twenty-three the autobiography ends because the author has run through society to date and does not know what to do next. For, as Mr. Canby might have added, the idea of reforming that society makes no appeal to them. They have seen through all that. They cannot adopt any of the synthetic religions of the Nineteenth Century. They have seen through all of them.

---

1   Henry Seidel Canby (1878–1961), critic and professor, founding editor of the *Saturday Review of Literature*. The work that Lippmann references is unidentified.

Appendix E: Race, Immigration, and the National Culture, 1920–25

[There is now a substantial body of criticism that attends to ways in which *The Great Gatsby* evokes debates about American racial and cultural identity that were shaping reactionary public policy and informing the nation's popular and esoteric art and its vernacular culture in general. The novel alludes to the reactionary position early when Tom Buchanan spouts the thesis of a recent "scientific" book about the imminent doom of "the white race," and the novel here and there casually notes the presence of darker immigrants or migrants as constituents of the modern American scene. Insofar as the novel is about what we now commonly think of as an "American dream" of economic opportunity and self-making, that dream spoke more to the millions of immigrants pouring into the country since the turn of the century than to established Americans like Nick Carraway, whose "clan" goes back three generations. Insofar as *The Great Gatsby* is a novel of "the Jazz Age" (see Appendix D), we might ask how the defining cultural presence of a Black American art form, even as appropriated and popularized by notable Jewish American composers among others, informs and inflects Gatsby's doomed romantic quest. Can the novel be disentangled from its anti-immigrant, anti-Semitic, and Jim Crow context?

Below, first, are two excerpts from the book on which Tom's "Rise of the Colored Empires" was modeled: Lothrop Stoddard's *The Rising Tide of Color against White World-Supremacy*. The passages represent the "Nordicist" or Anglo-Saxonist narrative of American history as a potentially tragic process by which a pure founding stock gets displaced by "alien hordes." Fitzgerald was certainly familiar with this idea and the racism it legitimized. (Indeed, Stoddard's book and the Madison Grant book Stoddard cites enjoyed the respectable, conservative imprint of Fitzgerald's publisher, Charles Scribner's Sons.) He did not need to read the popular anti-Semitic tracts of automobile magnate Henry Ford (1863–1947) to be aware of them. The disturbing selections below bear an uncanny relation to the novel, though, most notably in the attention given to Arnold Rothstein (1882–1928), the main model for Gatsby's "maker" Meyer Wolfshiem, and in the identification of the "jazz" issuing mainly from New York City's Tin Pan Alley and Broadway with Jewish-American cultural domination.

Fitzgerald was probably equally familiar with counter-arguments to the effect that the immigrant experience virtually defines what it is to be an American, such as that reprinted here of former New York Commissioner of Immigration Frederick Howe (1867–1940) in his contribution to a landmark 1922 collection of dissident essays, *Civilization in the United States*. There is no evidence that he was familiar with the relatively popular Jewish immigrant novelist and story writer Anzia Yezierska (1880–1970), whose literary career took off at roughly the same time as Fitzgerald's, though she was several years older. The excerpt below from her 1925 novel *Bread Givers* suggests, however, that she had probably read Fitzgerald. Sara Smolinsky, its heroine from "the lower East Side of New York" (from which Gatsby could have come, in Nick's view), embarks on the same project of self-making as Gatsby, with the same consequent rift from her father's home, but with independence rather than romantic possession her ultimate object. Her journey takes her out of New York City westward, the opposite direction from that of Fitzgerald's characters, and to a Waspish, middle-class college town that seems strikingly Fitzgeraldian. The selections from the chapter "College," below, invite readers to consider the world of Fitzgerald's stories from a real outsider's perspective, someone really from "the lower East Side."

The Great Gatsby also appeared in the same year as the landmark anthology *The New Negro*, the central text of what came to be called the Harlem Renaissance, and which conveys and celebrates the rise of people of color both worldwide and in the United States. Its "New Negro" is another American dreamer of sorts, migrating from the South rather than the Midwest to New York City, leaving behind systematic oppression and humiliation rather than dull, provincial conventionality. "New Negroes" make cursory but memorable appearances in *The Great Gatsby*, most notoriously in the caricatured form of those "three modish negroes" being driven by a white chauffeur on the Queensboro Bridge, who make Nick laugh as well as acknowledge the "anything can happen" ethos of jazz-age America—epitomized by Gatsby. Who are these "modish negroes" in the novel, including the nameless "pale well-dressed negro" who alone witnessed the lethal car accident in Chapter VII? Jazz musicians? Cast members of the popular show *Shuffle Along* or its offshoots? Intellectuals or writers? The selections from Alain Locke's "The New Negro" and J.A. Rogers's "Jazz at Home" offer both context for the presence of these figures in a novel about, among other things, the cultural possibilities of postwar New York City and, in Rogers's essay especially, a relatively well-informed account of the nature and national cultural significance of jazz, which names its leading artists as Fitzgerald's novel does not.

This section closes with a contemporary *Vanity Fair* caricature of "the New Negro" as a Black dandy, created by two other contributors to *The New Negro*, the Mexican artist Miguel Covarrubias (1904–57) and the Afro-Caribbean writer Eric Walrond (1898–1966). A willingness to play half-ironically with stereotypes was characteristic of some Harlem Renaissance art, particularly that of its younger generation. Its presence here might further underscore an underlying kinship between those "modish negroes" and Gatsby, with his pink suit and "circus wagon" of a car. Tom's mockery of these accoutrements ensures that Gatsby can never transcend a certain clownishness in his bid for class; and Tom more pointedly attaches a racial threat to Gatsby's adultery with Daisy when he imagines such promiscuity across class lines as leading naturally to "intermarriage between black and white."]

1. From Lothrop Stoddard, *The Rising Tide of Color against White World-Supremacy* (Charles Scribner's Sons, 1920), 261–62, 303–04

[The racial trajectory of modern America]

Probably few persons fully appreciate what magnificent racial treasures America possessed at the beginning of the nineteenth century. The colonial stock was perhaps the finest that nature had evolved since the classic Greeks. It was the pick of the Nordics of the British Isles at a time when those countries were more Nordic than now, since the industrial revolution had not yet begun and the consequent resurgence of the Mediterranean and Alpine elements had not taken place.[1]

---

1 Pseudo-scientific categories for different branches of the white "race" established in the late nineteenth century. "Nordics" (also commonly known as "Teutons") were of predominantly Germanic and Anglo-Saxon descent; "Mediterraneans" were predominantly southern European and noteworthy for their dark complexion; "Alpines" were predominant in central and eastern Europe, derived from the peasantry that made up the vast core of the European peoples, and were credited with establishing agriculture in Europe.

The immigrants of colonial times were largely exiles for conscience's sake, while the very process of migration was so difficult and hazardous that only persons of courage, initiative, and strong will-power would voluntarily face the long voyage overseas to a life of struggle in an untamed wilderness haunted by ferocious savages. Thus the entire process of colonial settlement was one continuous, drastic cycle of eugenic selection. Only the racially fit ordinarily came, while the few unfit who did come were mostly weeded out by the exacting requirements of early American life.

The eugenic results were magnificent. As Madison Grant[1] well says, "Nature had vouchsafed to the Americans of a century ago the greatest opportunity in recorded history to produce in the isolation of a continent a powerful and racially homogeneous people, and had provided for the experiment a pure race of one of the most gifted and vigorous stocks on earth, a stock free from the diseases, physical and moral, which have again and again sapped the vigor of the older lands. Our grandfathers threw away this opportunity in the blissful ignorance of national childhood and inexperience." The number of great names which America produced at the beginning of its national life shows the high level of ability possessed by this relatively small people (only about 3,000,000 whites in 1790). With our hundred-odd millions we have no such output of genius today.

The opening decades of the nineteenth century seemed to portend for America the most glorious of futures. For nearly seventy years after the Revolution, immigration was small, and during that long period of ethnic isolation the colonial stock, unperturbed by alien influences, adjusted its cultural differences and began to display the traits of a genuine new type, harmonious in basic homogeneity and incalculably rich in racial promise. The general level of ability continued high and the output of talent remained extraordinarily large. Perhaps the best feature of the nascent "native American" race was its strong idealism. Despite the materialistic blight which was then creeping over the white world, the native American displayed characteristics more reminiscent of his Elizabethan forebears than of the materialistic Hanoverian Englishman. It was a wonderful time—and it was only the dawn!

---

1 Madison Grant (1865–1937), leading eugenicist, advocate of restrictive immigration laws, and author of *The Passing of the Great Race* (1916), from which the following quotation is taken.

But the full day of that wondrous dawning never came. In the late forties of the nineteenth century the first waves of the modern immigrant tide began breaking on our shores, and the tide swelled to a veritable deluge which never slackened till temporarily restrained by the late war. This immigration, to be sure, first came mainly from northern Europe, was thus largely composed of kindred stocks, and contributed many valuable elements. Only during the last thirty years have we been deluged by the truly alien hordes of the European east and south. But, even at its best, the immigrant tide could not measure up to the colonial stock *which it displaced*, not reinforced, while latterly it became a menace to the very existence of our race, ideals, and institutions. All our slowly acquired balance—physical, mental, and spiritual—has been upset, and we today flounder in a veritable Serbonian bog,[1] painfully trying to regain the solid ground on which our grandsires confidently stood.

["The Crisis of the Ages"]

"Finally perish!" That is the exact alternative which confronts the white race. For white civilization is to-day coterminous with the white race. The civilizations of the past were local. They were confined to a particular people or group of peoples. If they failed, there were always some unspoiled, well-endowed barbarians to step forward and "carry on." But to-day *there are no more white barbarians*. The earth has grown small, and men are everywhere in close touch. If white civilization goes down, the white race is irretrievably ruined. It will be swamped by the triumphant colored races, who will obliterate the white man by elimination or absorption. What has taken place in Central Asia, once a white and now a brown or yellow land, will take place in Australasia, Europe, and America. Not to-day, nor yet to-morrow; perhaps not for generations; but surely in the end. If the present drift be not changed, we whites are all ultimately doomed. Unless we set our house in order, the doom will sooner or later overtake us all.

And that would mean that the race obviously endowed with the greatest creative ability, the race which had achieved most in the past and which gave the richer promise for the future, had passed away, carrying with it to the grave those potencies upon

---

1 After English poet John Milton's name for Lake Serbonis in Egypt, a marshy tract covered with shifting sand (see *Paradise Lost* II.592).

which the realization of man's highest hopes depends. A million years of human evolution might go uncrowned, and earth's supreme life-product, man, might never fulfil his potential destiny. This is why we to-day face "The Crisis of the Ages."

2. From Henry Ford, *Jewish Influences in American Life*, vol. 3 of *The International Jew: The World's Foremost Problem* (Dearborn Publishing Co., 1921), 37, 39–43, 64–65, 67, 69–70, 72–74

"Jewish Gamblers Corrupt American Baseball"

There are men in the United States who say that baseball has received its death wound and is slowly dying out of the list of respectable sports. There are other men who say that American baseball can be saved if a clean sweep is made of the Jewish influence which has just dragged it through a period of bitter shame and demoralization.

Whether baseball as a first-class sport is killed and will survive only as a cheap-jacket entertainment; or whether baseball possesses sufficient intrinsic character to rise in righteous wrath and cast out the danger that menaces it, will remain a matter of various opinion. But there is one certainty, namely, that the last and most dangerous blow dealt baseball was curiously notable for its Jewish character.

[...]

The storm began to be heard as far back as 1919. The Cincinnati Nationals [Reds] had defeated the Chicago Americans [White Sox] in the World Series of that year, and immediately thereafter the country became a whispering gallery wherein were heard mysterious rumors of crooked dealing. The names of Jews were heard then, but it meant nothing to the average man. The rumors dealt with the shady financial gains for a number of Jew gamblers of decidedly shady reputation.

But "they got away with it," in the parlance of the field. There was not enough public indignation to force a show-down, and too many interests were involved to prevent baseball being given a black eye in full view of an adoring public.

[...]

Then came the big scandal. A Cook County grand jury was called into session at Chicago and asked to investigate. When this grand jury had completed its labors, eight members of the Chicago American League team were under indictment for throwing the World Series of 1919, the previous year, to the Cincinnati Reds. And all along the line of the investigation the names of Jews were plentifully sprinkled.

[...]

It becomes necessary at this point in the narrative to give a brief "Who's Who" of the baseball scandal, omitting from the list the names of the baseball players, who are sufficiently known to the public. The list will comprise only those who have been in the background of baseball and whom it is necessary to know in order to understand what has been happening behind the scenes in recent years.

[...]

[...] [T]here is Arnold Rothstein, a Jew, who describes himself as being in the real estate business but who is known to be a wealthy gambler, owner of a notorious gambling house in Saratoga,[1] a race track owner, and is reputed to be financially interested in the New York National League Club.

Rothstein was usually referred to during the baseball scandal as "the man higher up." It is stated that in some manner unknown he received the secret testimony given before the grand jury and offered it to a New York newspaper. However, the fact is this: the grand jury testimony disappeared from the prosecuting attorney's safe-keeping. It is stated that, when Rothstein found out it did not incriminate him, he then offered it for publicity purposes.

[...]

Rothstein is known on Broadway as "a slick Jew." That he is powerful with the authorities has been often demonstrated. His operations on the turf have led to suggestions that he be ruled off.

---

1   Also known as Saratoga Springs, a city in upstate New York.

"Jewish Jazz Becomes Our National Music"

Many people have wondered whence come the waves upon waves of musical slush that invade decent parlors and set the young people of this generation imitating the drivel of morons. A clue to the answer is in the above clipping.[1] *Popular music is a Jewish monopoly. Jazz is a Jewish creation.* The mush, the slush, the sly suggestion, the abandoned sensuousness of sliding notes, are of Jewish origin.

Monkey talk, jungle squeals, grunts and squeaks and gasps suggestive of cave love are camouflaged by a few feverish notes and admitted to homes where the thing itself, unaided by the piano, would be stamped out in horror. Girls and boys a little while ago were inquiring who paid Mrs. Rip Van Winkle's rent while Mr. Rip Van Winkle was away.[2] In decent parlors the fluttering music sheets disclosed expressions taken directly from the cesspools of modern capitals, to be made the daily slang, the thoughtlessly hummed remarks of high school boys and girls.

[...]

It is the purpose of this [...] article to put Americans in full possession of the truth concerning the moron music which they habitually hum and sing and shout day by day, and if possible to help them to see the invisible Jewish baton which is waved above them for financial and propaganda purposes.

Just as the American stage and the American motion picture have fallen under the influence and control of the Jews and their art-destroying commercialism, so the business of handling "popular songs" has become a Yiddish industry.

Its leaders are for the most part Russian-born Jews, some of whom have personal pasts which are just as unsavory as *The Dearborn Independent* has shown the pasts of certain Jewish theatrical and movie leaders to be.

The country does not sing what it likes, but what the vaudeville "song pluggers" popularize by repeated renditions on the stage,

---

1 Refers to an excerpt of a *New York Times* article of 1920 which Ford provides. It recounts federal charges leveled against seven music publishing corporations (including Irving Berlin's) for violating anti-trust laws.
2 Allusion to the popular 1914 song "I'm the Guy That Paid the Rent for Mrs. Rip Van Winkle," by George Fairman (1881–1962).

until the flabby mind of the "ten-twent'-thirt'" audiences begin to repeat it on the streets. These "song pluggers" are the paid agents of the Yiddish song agencies. Money, and not merit, dominates the spread of the moron music which is styled "Jewish Jazz."

[...]

Tin Pan Alley is the name given to the region in Twenty-eighth street, between Broadway and Sixth avenue, where the first Yiddish song manufacturers began business. Flocks of young girls who thought they could sing, and others who thought they could write song poems, came to the neighborhood allured by dishonest advertisements that promised more than the budding Yiddish exploiters were able to fulfill. Needless to say, scandal became rampant, as it always does where so-called "Gentile" girls are reduced to the necessity of seeking favors from the eastern type of Jew. It was the constant shouting of voices, the hilarity of "parties," the banging of pianos and the blattering of trombones that gave the district the name of Tin Pan Alley.

The first attempt to popularize and commercialize the so-called "popular" type of music was made by Julius Witmark, who had been a ballad singer on the minstrel stage.[1] He ceased performing to become a publisher, and was soon followed by East Side Jews, many of whom have become wealthy through their success in pandering to a public taste which they first debased.

Irving Berlin, whose real name is Ignatz or Isadore Baline, is one of the most successful of these Jewish song controllers.[2] He was born in Russia and early became a singer and entertainer. With the rise of "rag-time," which was the predecessor of "jazz," he found a new field for his nimble talents, and his first big success was "Alexander's Rag-Time Band"[3]—a popular piece which by comparison with what has followed it, is a blushing, modest thing.

---

1 Julius Witmark (1870–1929), songwriter, performer and, most successfully, partner with his two brothers in the music printing business M.
   Witmark & Sons (bought by Warner Brothers in 1929).
2 Irving Berlin (1888–1989), born Israel Isadore Baline, one of the most
   popular and beloved American songwriters; he wrote what is widely regarded as America's unofficial national anthem, "God Bless America," in 1918.
3 More precisely, "Alexander's Ragtime Band," a popular Irving Berlin
   song published in 1911.

It is worth noting, in view of the organized eagerness of the Jew to make an alliance with the Negro, that it was Jewish "jazz" that rode in upon the wave of Negro "rag-time" popularity, and eventually displaced the "rag-time."

Berlin has steadily gone the road from mere interestingness to unashamed erotic suggestion. He is the "headliner" in homes as well as in the not-too-particular music halls, but his stuff without its music sometimes savors of vile suggestion.

The motif of this business can be clearly seen in the "Berlin Big Hits." There are the so-called "vamp" songs, such as "Harem Life," and "You Cannot Make Your Shimmy Shake on Tea."[1]

Among the "successes" is the song entitled, "I Like It."[2] It is a "vamp" song which has been sung everywhere, even by myriads of children who could not appreciate the full suggestion of the words, but were hypnotized by the atmosphere which the words created when sung; and by older folks who would not under any circumstances *speak* the words of the song, but who are victims of the modern delusion that a little flashy music covers a multitude of sins.

[...]

Ministers, educators, reformers, parents, citizens who are amazed at the growth of looseness among the people, rail at the evil results. They see the evil product and they attack the product. They rail at the young people who go in for all this eroticism and suggestiveness.

But all this has a source! Why not attack the source? When a population is bathed in sights, sounds and ideas of a certain character, drenched in them and drowned in them, by systematic, deliberate, organized intent, the point of attack should be the cause, not the effect. Yet, that is precisely where the point of attack has not been made, presumably because of lack of knowledge.

It is of little use blaming the people. The people are what they are made. Give the liquor business full sway and you have a population that drinks and carouses. After preaching abstinence to the victims for a century, the country turned its attention to the victimizers and the abuse was greatly curtailed. The traffic is still

---

1 Berlin songs performed in the *Ziegfeld Follies of 1919*.
2 Mildly bawdy song of 1921 by Berlin.

illicitly carried on, but even so, the best way to abolish the illicit traffic is to identify the groups that carry it on.

The entire population of the United States could be turned into narcotic addicts if the same freedom was given the illicit narcotic ring as is now given the Yiddish popular song manufacturers. But in such a condition it would be stupid to attack the addicts; common sense would urge the exposure of the panderers.

A dreadful narcotizing or moral modesty and the application of powerful aphrodisiacs have been involved in the present craze for popular songs—a stimulated craze. The victims are everywhere. But ministers, educators, reformers, parents, and public-spirited citizens are beginning to see the futility of scolding the young people thus diseased. Common sense dictates a cleaning out of the source of disease. The source is in the Yiddish group of song manufacturers who control the whole output and who are responsible for the whole matter from poetry to profits.

Next to the moral indictment against the so-called "popular" song is the indictment that *it is not popular*. Everybody hears it, perhaps the majority sing it; it makes its way from coast to coast; it is flung into the people's minds at every movie and from every stage; it is advertised in flaring posters; phonograph records shriek it forth day and night, dance orchestras seem enamored of it, player pianos roll it out by the yard. And by sheer dint of repetition and suggestion the song catches on—as a burr thistle catches on; until it is displaced by another. There is no spontaneous popularity.

It is a mere mechanical drumming on the minds of the public. There is often not a single atom of sentiment or spiritual appeal in the whole loudly trumpeted "success"; men and women, boys and girls have simply taken to humming words and tunes which they cannot escape, night or day.

The deadly anxiety of "keeping up with the times" drives the army of piano-owners to the music stores to see what is "going" now, and of course it is the Yiddish moron music that is going, and so another home and eventually another neighborhood is inoculated.

But there is no *popularity*. Take any moron music addict you know and ask him what was the "popular" song three weeks ago, and he will not be able to tell. These songs are so lacking in all that the term "popular" means as regards their acceptableness, that they died overnight, unregretted. Directly the Yiddish manufacturers have another "hit" to make (it is always the public that is "hit") a new song is crammed down the public gullet, and because it is the "latest," and because the Yiddish advertisements say that it is a "hit," and because the hired "pluggers" say that everybody is singing it, that song too becomes "popular" for its brief period, and so on through the year. It is the old game of "changing the styles" to speed up business and make the people buy. Nothing lasts in the Yiddish game—styles of clothing, movies nor songs; it is always something new, to stimulate the flow of money from the popular pocket into the moron music makers' coffers.

There hasn't been a real "popular" song of Yiddish origin since the Jewish whistlers and back-alley songsters of New York's East Side undertook to handle musical America—not one, unless we except in genuine gratitude George Cohan's "Over There,"[1] a song which came out of a period of strain and went straight to the people's heart.

Two facts about the "popular song" are known to all: first, that for the most part it is indecent and the most active agent of moral miasma in the country, or if not the most active, then neck and neck with the "movies"; second, that the "popular song" industry is an exclusively Jewish industry.

3. From Frederick C. Howe, "The Alien," in *Civilization in the United States: An Inquiry by Thirty Americans*, edited by Harold E. Stearns (Harcourt, Brace, 1922), 337–42, 346, 350

The immigrant alien has been discussed by the Anglo-Saxon as though he were an Anglo-Saxon "problem." He has been discussed by labour as though he were a labour "problem"; by interpreters of American institutions as though man existed for institutions and for institutions which the class interpreting them found advantageous to its class. Occasionally the alien has been discussed from the point of view of the alien and but rarely from the point of view of democracy. The "problem" of the alien is largely a problem of setting our own house in order. It is the "problem" of Americanizing America. The outstanding fact of three centuries of immigration is that the immigrant alien ceases to be an alien when economic conditions are such as properly to assimilate him.

---

1   George M. Cohan's (1878–1942) popular patriotic song of 1917, the year of America's entry into World War I.

There is something rather humorous about the way America discusses "the alien." For we are all aliens. And what is less to our liking we are almost all descended from the peasant classes of Europe. We are here because our forebears were poor. They did not rule over there. They were oppressed; they were often owned. And with but few exceptions they came because of their poverty. For the rich rarely emigrate. And in the 17th and 18th centuries there was probably a smaller percentage of immigrants who could pass the literacy test than there are to-day. Moreover, in the early days only suffering could drive the poor of Europe from their poverty. For the conditions of travel were hazardous. The death toll from disease was very high. It required more fortitude to cross the Atlantic and pass by the ring of settlers out onto the unbroken frontier than it does to pass Ellis Island[1] and the exploiters round about it to-day.

The immigration question has arisen because America, too, has created a master class, a class which owns and employs and rules. And the alien in America is faced by a class opinion, born of the change which has come over America rather than any change in the alien himself. America has changed. The alien remains much the same. And the most significant phase of the immigration problem is the way we treat the alien and the hypocrisy of our discussion of the subject.

Sociologists have given us a classification of the immigrant alien. They speak of the "old immigration" and the "new immigration." The former is the immigration of the 17th and 18th and the first three-quarters of the 19th centuries. It was English, Scotch, Irish, German, Scandinavian with a sprinkling of French, Swiss, and other nationalities. From the beginning, the preponderance was British. During the 18th century there was a heavy Scotch inflow and during the first half of the 19th a heavy Irish and German immigration. The Irish came because of the famine of 1848, the Scotch in large part because of the enclosure acts and the driving of the people from the land to make way for deer preserves and grazing lands for the British aristocracy. Most of the British immigration was the result of oppressive land laws of one kind or another. The population of Ireland was reduced from eight million to slightly over four million in three-quarters of a

---

1 Federal immigration center and the point of entry for 70 per cent of American immigrants between 1892 and 1924, located in Upper New York Bay near the Statue of Liberty.

century. The British immigrant of the 17th century, like the recent Russian immigration, was driven from home by economic oppression. Only a handful came to escape religious oppression or to secure political liberty. The cause of immigration has remained the same from the beginning until now.

The "old immigration" was from the North of Europe. It was of Germanic stock. It was predominantly Protestant. But the most important fact of all and the fact most usually ignored is an economic fact. The early immigrant found a broad continent awaiting him, peopled only by Indians. He became a free man. He took up a homestead. He ceased to belong to anyone else. He built for himself. He paid no rent, he took no orders, he kept what he produced, and was inspired by hope and ambition to develop his powers. It was economic, not political, freedom that distinguishes the "old immigration" from the "new."

The "new immigration" is from Southern and Central Europe. It is Latin and Slavic. It is largely Catholic. It, too, is poor. It, too, is driven out by oppression, mostly economic and for the most part landed. Almost every wave of immigration has been in some way related to changes for the worse in the landed systems of Europe. Wherever the poverty has been the most distressing, there the impulse to move has been the strongest. It has been the poverty of Europe that has determined our immigration from the 17th century until now.

The ethnic difference is secondary. So is the religious. The fundamental fact that distinguishes the "old immigration" from the "new" is economic. The "new immigration" works for the "old." It found the free land all taken up. The public domain had passed into the hand of the Pacific railroads, into great manorial estates. Land thieves had repeated the acts of the British Parliament of the 18th century. The Westward movement of peoples that had been going on from the beginning of time came to an end when the pioneer of the 80's and 90's found only the bad lands left for settlement. That ended an era. It closed the land to settlement and sent the immigrant to the city. The peasant of Europe has become the miner and the mill worker. He left one kind of serfdom to take up another. It is this that distinguishes the "old immigrant" from the "new." It is this that distinguishes the old America from the America of to-day. And the problem of immigration, like the problem of America, is the re-establishment of economic democracy. [...]

The "new immigration" from Southern and Central Europe began to increase in volume about 1890. It came from Southern rather than Northern Italy, from Poland, Hungary, Bohemia, Russia, the Balkans, and the Levant. There was a sprinkling of Spanish and Portuguese immigrants. In 1914 South and Central European immigration amounted to 683,000, while the North European immigration was but 220,000. Of the former 296,000 came from Italy, 123,000 from Poland, 45,000 from Russia, and 45,000 from Hungary. These figures do not include Jewish immigrants, who numbered 138,000. Of the North European immigrants 105,000 came from the British Isles, 80,000 came from Germany, and 36,000 from the Scandinavian countries.

Of the 14,000,000 persons of foreign birth now in the country, a very large percentage is of South and Central European stock.

We are accustomed to think of the old immigration and the new immigration in terms of races and religions. And much of the present-day hostility to immigration comes from the inexplicable prejudice which has recently sprung up against persons of differing races and religions. It is assumed that the new immigration is poor and ignorant because it is ethnically unfitted for anything different and that it prefers the tenement and the mining camp to American standards of living and culture. [...]

The "immigration problem," so called, has always been and always will be an economic problem. There are many people who feel that there is an inherent superiority in the Anglo-Saxon race; that it has a better mind, greater virtue, and a better reason for existence and expansion than any other race. They insist there are eugenic reasons for excluding immigration from South and Central Europe; they would preserve America for people of Anglo-Saxon stock. As an immigration official I presided over Ellis Island for five years. During this time probably a million immigrants arrived at the port of New York. They were for the most part poor. They had that in common with the early immigrant. They had other qualities in common. They were ambitious and filled with hope. They were for the most part kindly and moved by the same human and domestic virtues as other peoples. And it is to me an open question whether the "new immigration," if given a virgin continent, and the hope and stimulus which springs from such opportunity, would not develop the same qualities of mind and of character that we assume to be the more or less exclusive characteristics of the Anglo-Saxon race. There is also reason for believing that the warmer temperament, the emotional qualities, and the love of the arts that characterize the South and Central European would produce a race blend, under proper economic conditions, that would result in a better race than one of pure Northern extraction. For it is to be remembered that it was not political liberty, religious liberty, or personal liberty that changed the early immigrant of Northern Europe into the American of to-day. His qualities were born of economic conditions, of a free continent, of land to be had for the asking, of equal opportunity with his fellows to make his life what he would have it to be. The old immigrant recognized no master but himself. He was the equal of his neighbours in every respect. He knew no inferiority complex born of a servile relationship. It was this rather than our constitutions and laws that made the American of the first three centuries what he was. It was this alchemy that changed the serf of Northern Europe into the self-reliant freeman of America.

The immigration problem was born when this early economic opportunity came to an end.

[...]

America is a marvellous demonstration of the economic foundations of all life. It is a demonstration of what happens to men when economic opportunities call forth their resourcefulness and latent ability on one hand and when the State, on the other, keeps its hands off them in their personal relationships. For the alien quickly adopts a higher standard of culture as he rises in the industrial scale, while his morals, whatever they may have been, quickly take on the colour of his new environment, whatever that may be. And if all of the elements which should enter into a consideration of the subject were included, I am of the opinion it would be found that the morals, the prevalence of vice and crime among the alien population is substantially that of the economic class in which he is found rather than the race from which he springs. In other words, the alleged prevalence of crime among the alien population is traceable to poverty and bad conditions of living rather than to ethnic causes, and in so far as it exists it tends [to] disappear as the conditions which breed it pass away.

[...]

The alien of to-day is not very different from the alien of yesterday. He has the same instincts and desires as did those who came in the *Mayflower*. Only those who came in the *Mayflower* made their own laws and their own fortunes. Those who come today have their laws made for them by the class that employs them and they make their own fortunes only as those aliens who came first permit them to do so.

4. From Anzia Yezierska, *Bread Givers* (Doubleday & Co., 1925), 209–15, 217–20

From Chapter XVI, "College"

That burning day when I got ready to leave New York and start out on my journey to college! I felt like Columbus starting out for the other end of the earth. I felt like the pilgrim fathers who had left their homeland and all their kin behind them and trailed out in search of the New World.

I had stayed up night after night, washing and ironing, patching and darning my things. At last, I put them in a bundle, wrapped them up with newspapers, and tied them securely with the thick clothes line that I had in my room on which to hang out my wash. I made another bundle of my books. In another newspaper I wrapped up food for the journey: a loaf of bread, a herring, and a pickle. In my purse was the money I had been saving from my food, from my clothes, a penny to penny, a dollar to a dollar, for so many years. It was not much but I counted out that it would be enough for my train ticket and a few weeks start till I got work out there.

It was only when I got to the train that I realized I had hardly eaten all day. Starving hungry, I tore the paper open. Ach! Crazy-head! In my haste I had forgotten even to cut up the bread. I bent over on the side of my seat, and half covering myself with a newspaper, I pinched pieces out of the loaf and ripped ravenously at the herring. With each bite, I cast side glances like a guilty thing; nobody should see the way I ate.

After a while, as the lights were turned low, the other passengers began to nod their heads, each outsnoring the other in their thick sleep. I was the only one on the train too excited to close my eyes.

Like a dream was the whole night's journey. And like a dream mounting on a dream was this college town, this New America of culture and education.

Before this, New York was all of America to me. But now I came to a town of quiet streets, shaded with green trees. No crowds, no tenements. No hurrying noise to beat the race of the hours. Only a leisured quietness whispered in the air: Peace. Be still. Eternal time is all before you.

Each house had its own green grass in front, its own free space all around, and it faced the street with the calm security of being owned for generations, and not rented by the month from a landlord. In the early twilight, it was like a picture out of fairyland to see people sitting on their porches, lazily swinging in their hammocks, or watering their own growing flowers.

So these are the real Americans, I thought, thrilled by the lean, straight bearing of the passers-by. They had none of that terrible fight for bread and rent that I always saw in New York people's eyes. Their faces were not worn with the hunger for things they never could have in their lives. There was in them that sure, settled look of those who belong to the world in which they were born.

The college buildings were like beautiful palaces. The campus stretched out like fields of a big park. Air—air. Free space and sunshine. The river at dusk. Glimmering lights on passing boats, the floating voices of young people. And when night came, there were the sky and the stars.

This was the beauty for which I had always longed. For the first few days I could only walk about and drink it in thirstily, more and more. Beauty of houses, beauty of streets, beauty shining out of the calm faces and cool eyes of the people! Oh—too cool....

How could I most quickly become friends with them? How could I come into their homes, exchange with them my thoughts, break with them bread at their tables? If I could only lose myself body and soul in the serenity of this new world, the hunger and the turmoil of my ghetto years would drop away from me, and I, too, would know the beauty of stillness and peace.

What light-hearted laughing youth met my eyes! All the young people I had ever seen were shut up in factories. But here were young girls and young men enjoying life, free from the worry for a living. College to them was being out for a good time, like to us in the shop a Sunday picnic. But in our gayest Sunday picnics there was always the under-feeling that Monday meant back to the shop again. To these born lucky ones joy seemed to stretch out for ever.

What a sight I was in my gray pushcart clothes against the beautiful gay colours and the fine things those young girls wore. I had seen cheap, fancy style, Five-and-Ten-Cent Store finery. But never had I seen such plain beautifulness. The simple skirts and sweaters, the stockings and shoes to match. The neat finished quietness of their tailored suits. There was no show-off in their clothes, and yet how much more pulling to the eyes and all the senses than the Grand Street[1] richness I knew.

And the spick-and-span cleanliness of these people! It smelled from them, the soap and the bathing. Their fingernails so white and pink. Their hands and necks white like milk. I wondered how did those girls get their hair so soft, so shiny, and so smooth about their heads. Even their black shoes had a clear look.

Never had I seen men so all shaved up with pink, clean skins. The richest store-keepers in Grand Street shined themselves up with diamonds like walking jewellery stores, but they weren't so hollering clean as these men. And they all had their hair clipped so short; they all had a shape to their heads. So ironed out smooth and even they looked in their spotless, creaseless clothes, as if the dirty battle of life had never yet been on them.

I looked at these children of joy with a million eyes. I looked at them with my hands, my feet, with the thinnest nerves of my hair. By all their differences from me, their youth, their shiny freshness, their carefreeness, they pulled me out of my senses to them. And they didn't even know I was there.

I thought once I got into the classes with them, they'd see me and we'd get to know one another. What a sharp awakening came with my first hour!

As I entered the classroom, I saw young men and girls laughing and talking to one another without introductions. I looked for my seat. Then I noticed, up in front, a very earnest-faced young man with thick glasses over his sad eyes. He made me think of Morris Lipkin, so I chose my seat next to him.

"What's the name of the professor?" I asked.

"Smith," came from his tight lips. He did not even look at me. He pulled himself together and began busily writing, to show me he didn't want to be interrupted.

I turned to the girl on my other side. What a clean, fresh beauty! A creature of sunshine. And clothes that matched her radiant youth.

"Is this the freshman class in geometry?" I asked her.

She nodded politely and smiled. But how quickly her eyes sized me up! It was not an unkind glance. And yet, it said more plainly than words, "From where do you come? How did you get in here?"

---

1 East–west thoroughfare running through the lower east side of Manhattan.

Sitting side by side with them through the whole hour, I felt stranger to them than if I had passed them in Hester Street.[1] Wasn't there some secret something that would open us toward one another?

In one class after another, I kept asking myself, "What's the matter with me? Why do they look at me so when I talk with them?"

Maybe I'd have to change myself inside and out to be one of them. But how?

The lectures were over at four o'clock. With a sigh, I turned from the college building, away from the pleasant streets, down to the shabby back alley near the post office, and entered the George Martin Hand Laundry.

Mr. Martin was a fat, easy-going, good-natured man. I no sooner told him of my experience in New York than he took me on at once as an ironer at fifty cents an hour, and he told me he had work for as many hours a day as I could put in.

I felt if I could only look a little bit like other girls on the outside, maybe I could get in with them. And that meant money! And money meant work, work, work!

Till eleven o'clock that night, I ironed fancy white shirtwaists.

"You're some busy little worker, even if I do say so," said Mr. Martin, good-naturedly. "But I must lock up. You can't live here."

I went home, aching in every bone. And in the quiet and good air, I so overslept that I was late for my first class.

[...]

In spite of the hard work in the laundry, I managed to get along in my classes. More and more interesting became the life of the college as I watched it from the outside.

What a feast of happenings each day of the college was to those other students. Societies, dances, letters from home, packages of food, midnight spreads and even birthday parties. I never knew that there were people glad enough of life to celebrate the day they were born. I watched the gay goings-on around me like one coming to a feast, but always standing back and only looking on.

One day, the ache for people broke down my feelings of difference from them. I felt I must tear myself out of my aloneness.

---

1 Street in the lower east side of Manhattan populated mainly by Jewish immigrants from Eastern Europe.

Nothing had ever come to me without my going out after it. I had to fight for my living, fight for every bit of my education. Why should I expect friendship and love to come to me out of the air while I sat there, dreaming about it?

The freshman class gave a dance that very evening. Something in the back of my head told me that an evening dress and slippers were part of going to a dance. I had no such things. But should that stop me? If I had waited till I could afford the right clothes for college, I should never have been able to go at all.

I put a fresh collar over my old serge dress. And with a dollar stolen from my eating money, I bought a ticket to the dance. As I peeped into the glittering gymnasium, blaring with jazz, my timid fears stopped the breath in me. How the whole big place sang with their light-hearted happiness! Young eyes drinking joy from young eyes. Girls, like gay-coloured butterflies, whirling in the arms of young men.

Floating ribbons and sashes shimmered against men's black coats. I took the nearest chair, blinded by the dazzle of the happy couples. Why did I come here? A terrible sense of age weighed upon me; yet I watched and waited for someone to come and ask me to dance. But not one man came near me. Some of my class-mates nodded distantly in passing, but most of them were too filled with their own happiness even to see me.

The whirling of joy went on and on, and still I sat there watching, cold, lifeless, like a lost ghost. I was nothing and nobody. It was worse than being ignored. Worse than being an outcast. I simply didn't belong. I had no existence in their young eyes. I wanted to run and hide myself, but fear and pride nailed me against the wall.

A chaperon must have noticed my face, and she brought over one of those clumsy, backward youths who was lost in a corner by himself. How unwilling were his feet as she dragged him over! In a dull voice, he asked, "May I have the next dance?" his eyes fixed in the distance as he spoke.

"Thank you. I don't want to dance." And I fled from the place.

I found myself walking in the darkness of the campus. In the thick shadows of the trees I hid myself and poured out my shamed and injured soul to the night. So, it wasn't character or brains that counted. Only youth and beauty and clothes—things I never had and never could have. Joy and love were not for such as me. Why not? Why not? ...

I flung myself on the ground, beating with my fists against the endless sorrows of my life. Even in college I had not escaped from the ghetto. Here loneliness hounded me even worse than in Hester Street. Was there no escape? Will I never lift myself to be a person among people?

I pressed my face against the earth. All that was left of me reached out in prayer. God! I've gone too far, help me to go on. God! I don't know how, but I must go on. Help me not to want their little happiness. I have wanted their love more than my life. Help me be bigger than this hunger in me. Give me the life that I can live without love....

Darkness and stillness washed over me. Slowly I stumbled to my feet and looked up at the sky. The stars in their infinite peace seemed to pour their healing light into me. I thought of the captives in prison, the sick and the suffering from the beginning of time who had looked to these stars for strength. What was my little sorrow to the centuries of pain which those stars had watched? So near they seemed, so compassionate. My bitter hurt seemed to grow small and drop away. If I must go on alone, I should still have silence and the high stars to walk with me.

5. Alain Locke, from "The New Negro," in *The New Negro: An Interpretation*, edited by Alain Locke (Albert and Charles Boni, 1925), 3, 5–16

In the last decade something beyond the watch and guard of statistics has happened in the life of the American Negro and the three norns[1] who have traditionally presided over the Negro problem have a changeling in their laps. The Sociologist, the Philanthropist, the Race-leader are not unaware of the New Negro, but they are at a loss to account for him. He simply cannot be swathed in their formulae. [...]

Could such a metamorphosis have taken place as suddenly as it has appeared to? The answer is no; not because the New Negro is not here, but because the Old Negro has long become more of a myth than a man. The Old Negro, we must remember, was a creature of moral debate and historical controversy. His has been a stock figure perpetuated as an historical fiction partly in innocent sentimentalism, partly in deliberate reactionism.

---

1 From Norse mythology, female deities responsible for weaving human destiny.

[...]

The day of "aunties," "uncles" and "mammies" is equally gone. Uncle Tom and Sambo[1] have passed on [...]. The popular melodrama has about played itself out, and it is time to scrap the fictions, garret the bogeys and settle down to a realistic facing of facts.

First we must observe some of the changes which since the traditional lines of opinion were drawn have rendered these quite obsolete. A main change has been, of course, that shifting of the Negro population which has made the Negro problem no longer exclusively or even predominantly Southern. Why should our minds remain sectionalized, when the problem itself no longer is? Then the trend of migration has not only been toward the North and the Central Midwest, but city-ward and to the great centers of industry—the problems of adjustment are new, practical, local and not peculiarly racial. Rather they are an integral part of the large industrial and social problems of our present-day democracy. And finally, with the Negro rapidly in process of class differentiation, if it ever was warrantable to regard and treat the Negro *en masse* it is becoming with every day less possible, more unjust and more ridiculous.

In the very process of being transplanted, the Negro is becoming transformed.

The tide of Negro migration, northward and city-ward, is not to be fully explained as a blind flood started by the demands of the war industry coupled with the shutting off of foreign migration, or by the pressure of poor crops coupled with increased social terrorism in certain sections of the South and Southwest. Neither labor demand, the boll weevil[2] nor the Ku

---

1 Originally characters in Harriet Beecher Stowe's (1811–96) abolitionist novel *Uncle Tom's Cabin* (1852), the names came to signify demeaning stereotypes of deferential, ingratiating, or harmlessly clownish Black American men. The common meaning derives more from "the popular melodrama" Locke refers to—and particularly the pervasive minstrel versions of Stowe's novel known as "Tom shows"—than from the novel itself. The term "Sambo" may also owe something to Helen Bannerman's popular children's book *The Story of Little Black Sambo* (1899), though the titular character is South Asian.

2 An insect that devastated cotton crops in the American South between the 1890s and 1920s.

Klux Klan[1] is a basic factor, however contributory any or all of them may have been. The wash and rush of this human tide on the beach line of the northern city centers is to be explained primarily in terms of a new vision of opportunity, of social and economic freedom, of a spirit to seize, even in the face of an extortionate and heavy toll, a chance for the improvement of his conditions. With each successive wave of it, the movement of the Negro becomes more and more a mass movement toward the larger and the more democratic chance—in the Negro's case a deliberate flight not only from countryside to city, but from medieval America to modern.

Take Harlem as an instance of this. Here in Manhattan is not merely the largest Negro community in the world, but the first concentration in history of so many diverse elements of Negro life. It has attracted the African, the West Indian, the Negro American; has brought together the Negro of the North and the Negro of the South; the man from the city and the man from the town and village; the peasant, the student, the business man, the professional man, artist, poet, musician, adventurer and worker, preacher and criminal, exploiter and social outcast. Each group has come with its own separate motives and for its own special ends, but their greatest experience has been the finding of one another. Proscription and prejudice have thrown these dissimilar elements into a common area of contact and interaction. Within this area, race sympathy and unity have determined a further fusing of sentiment and experience. So what began in terms of segregation becomes more and more, as its elements mix and react, the laboratory of a great race-welding. Hitherto, it must be admitted that American Negroes have been a race more in name than in fact, or to be exact, more in sentiment than in experience. The chief bond between them has been that of a common condition rather than that of a common consciousness; a problem in

---

1 A white supremacist terrorist organization originating in the American South after the Civil War in reaction to Reconstruction and the granting of citizenship to freed Black Americans. Having virtually disappeared by the mid-1870s, it was reborn after 1915 partly in response to D.W. Griffith's landmark racist film *The Birth of a Nation* (1915), which portrayed the earlier Klan's reaction against the mythic threat of Black domination in epic, heroic terms. The Klan had a more national membership from the mid-1910s to the mid-1920s, composed largely of provincial white Protestants: it anathematized not only Black Americans but also Jews, Catholics, and immigrants more broadly.

common rather than a life in common. In Harlem, Negro life is seizing upon its first chances for group expression and self-determination. It is—or promises at least to be—a race capital. That is why our comparison is taken with those nascent centers of folk-expression and self-determination which are playing a creative part in the world to-day. Without pretense to their political significance, Harlem has the same rôle to play for the New Negro as Dublin has had for the New Ireland or Prague for the New Czechoslovakia.[1] [...]

When the racial leaders of twenty years ago spoke of developing race-pride and stimulating race-consciousness, and of the desirability of race solidarity, they could not in any accurate degree have anticipated the abrupt feeling that has surged up and now pervades the awakened centers. Some of the recognized Negro leaders and a powerful section of white opinion identified with "race work" of the older order have indeed attempted to discount this feeling as a "passing phase," an attack of "race nerves" so to speak, an "aftermath of war," and the like. It has not abated, however, if we are to gauge by the present tone and temper of the Negro press, or by the shift in popular support from the officially recognized and orthodox spokesmen to those of the independent, popular, and often radical type who are unmistakable symptoms of a new order. It is a social disservice to blunt the fact that the Negro of the Northern centers has reached a stage where tutelage, even of the most interested and well-intentioned sort, must give place to new relationships, where positive self-direction must be reckoned with in ever increasing measure. The American mind must reckon with a fundamentally changed Negro.

[...]

In the intellectual realm a renewed and keen curiosity is replacing the recent apathy; the Negro is being carefully studied, not just talked about and discussed. In art and letters, instead of being wholly caricatured, he is being seriously portrayed and painted.

---

1 Locke's analogy associates the New Negro renaissance with other roughly contemporary movements on the part of colonized "races"—the Irish vis-à-vis the British, the Czechs vis-à-vis the Austro-Hungarian Empire—to create modern, national cultures.

To all of this the New Negro is keenly responsive as an augury of a new democracy in American culture. He is contributing his share to the new social understanding. But the desire to be understood would never in itself have been sufficient to have opened so completely the protectively closed portals of the thinking Negro's mind. There is still too much possibility of being snubbed or patronized for that. It was rather the necessity for fuller, truer self-expression, the realization of the unwisdom of allowing social discrimination to segregate him mentally, and a counter-attitude to cramp and fetter his own living—and so the "spite-wall" that the intellectuals build over the "color-line" has happily been taken down. Much of this reopening of intellectual contacts has centered in New York and has been richly fruitful not merely in the enlarging of personal experience, but in the definite enrichment of American art and letters and in clarifying of our common vision of the social tasks ahead.

[...]

The Negro mind reaches out as yet to nothing but American wants, American ideas. But this forced attempt to build his Americanism on race values is a unique social experiment, and its ultimate success is impossible except through the fullest sharing of American culture and institutions. There should be no delusion about this. American nerves in sections unstrung with race hysteria are often fed the opiate that the trend of Negro advance is wholly separatist, and that the effect of its operation will be to encyst the Negro as a benign foreign body in the body politic. This cannot be—even if it were desirable. The racialism of the Negro is no limitation or reservation with respect to American life; it is only a constructive effort to build the obstructions in the stream of his progress into an efficient dam of social energy and power. Democracy itself is obstructed and stagnated to the extent that any of its channels are closed. Indeed they cannot be selectively closed. So the choice is not between one way for the Negro and another way for the rest, but between American institutions frustrated on the one hand and American ideals progressively fulfilled and realized on the other.

There is, of course, a warrantable comfortable feeling in being on the right side of the country's professed ideals. We realize that we cannot be undone without America's undoing. It is within the gamut of this attitude that the thinking Negro faces America, but with variations of mood that are if anything more significant than the attitude itself. [...]

More and more, however, an intelligent realization of the great discrepancy between the American social creed and the American social practice forces upon the Negro the taking of the moral advantage that is his. Only the steadying and sobering effect of a truly characteristic gentleness of spirit prevents the rapid rise of a definite cynicism and counter-hate and a defiant superiority feeling. Human as this reaction would be, the majority still deprecate its advent, and would gladly see it forestalled by the speedy amelioration of its causes. We wish our race pride to be a healthier, more positive achievement than a feeling based upon a realization of the shortcomings of others. But all paths toward the attainment of a sound social attitude have been difficult; only a relatively few enlightened minds have been able as the phrase puts it "to rise above" prejudice. The ordinary man has had until recently only a hard choice between the alternatives of supine and humiliating submission and stimulating but hurtful counter-prejudice. Fortunately from some inner, desperate resourcefulness has recently sprung up the simple expedient of fighting prejudice by mental passive resistance, in other words by trying to ignore it. For the few, this manna may perhaps be effective, but the masses cannot thrive upon it.

Fortunately there are constructive channels opening out into which the balked social feelings of the American Negro can flow freely.

Without them there would be much more pressure and danger than there is. These compensating interests are racial but in a new and enlarged way. One is the consciousness of acting as the advance-guard of the African peoples in their contact with Twentieth Century civilization; the other, the sense of a mission of rehabilitating the race in world esteem from that loss of prestige for which the fate and conditions of slavery have so largely been responsible. Harlem, as we shall see, is the center of both these movements; she is the home of the Negro's "Zionism."[1] The pulse of the Negro world has begun to beat in Harlem. A Negro

---

1 A movement originating among European Jews in the late nineteenth century to establish a national home for Jewry in Palestine, a Black "Zionism" by analogy defines "African peoples" worldwide as diasporic or dispersed and in quest of a common, racially based national home.

newspaper[1] carrying news material in English, French and Spanish, gathered from all quarters of America, the West Indies and Africa has maintained itself in Harlem for over five years. Two important magazines, both edited from New York, maintain their news and circulation consistently on a cosmopolitan scale. Under American auspices and backing, three pan-African congresses have been held abroad for the discussion of common interests, colonial questions and the future co-operative development of Africa. In terms of the race question as a world problem, the Negro mind has leapt, so to speak, upon the parapets of prejudice and extended its cramped horizons. In so doing it has linked up with the growing group consciousness of the dark-peoples and is gradually learning their common interests. As one of our writers has recently put it: "It is imperative that we understand the white world in its relation to the non-white world." As with the Jew, persecution is making the Negro international.

As a world phenomenon this wider race consciousness is a different thing from the much asserted rising tide of color. Its inevitable causes are not of our making. The consequences are not necessarily damaging to the best interests of civilization. Whether it actually brings into being new Armadas of conflict or argosies of cultural exchange and enlightenment can only be decided by the attitude of the dominant races in an era of critical change. With the American Negro, his new internationalism is primarily an effort to recapture contact with the scattered peoples of African derivation. Garveyism[2] may be a transient, if spectacular, phenomenon, but the possible rôle of the American Negro in the future development of Africa is one of the most constructive and universally helpful missions that any modern people can lay claim to.

Constructive participation in such causes cannot help giving the Negro valuable group incentives, as well as increased prestigé [sic] at home and abroad. Our greatest rehabilitation may possibly come through such channels, but for the present, more immediate hope rests in the revaluation by white and black alike of the Negro in terms of his artistic endowments and cultural contributions, past and prospective. It must be increasingly rec-

---

1 *Negro World*, founded by Marcus Garvey (1887–1940) and Amy Ashwood Garvey (1897–1969) in 1918.
2 Black nationalist ideology of Marcus Garvey, founder of the Universal Negro Improvement Association.

ognized that the Negro has already made very substantial contributions, past and prospective, not only in his folk-art, music especially, which has always found appreciation, but in larger, though humbler and less acknowledged ways. For generations the Negro has been the peasant matrix of that section of America which has most undervalued him, and here he has contributed not only materially in labor and social patience, but spiritually as well. The South has unconsciously absorbed the gift of his folk-temperament. In less than half a generation it will be easier to recognize this, but the fact remains that a leaven of humor, sentiment, imagination and tropic nonchalance has gone into the making of the South from a humble, unacknowledged source. A second crop of the Negro's gifts promises still more largely. He now becomes a conscious contributor and lays aside the status of a beneficiary and ward for that of a collaborator and participant in American civilization. The great social gain in this is the releasing of our talented group from the arid fields of controversy and debate to the productive fields of creative expression. The especially cultural recognition they win should in turn prove the key to that revaluation of the Negro which must precede or accompany any considerable further betterment of race relationships. But whatever the general effect, the present generation will have added the motives of self-expression and spiritual development to the old and still unfinished task of making material headway and progress. No one who understandingly faces the situation with its substantial accomplishment or views the new scene with its still more abundant promise can be entirely without hope. And certainly, if in our lifetime the Negro should not be able to celebrate his full initiation into American democracy, he can at least, on the warrant of these things, celebrate the attainment of a significant and satisfying new phase of group development, and with it a spiritual Coming of Age.

6. From J.A. Rogers, "Jazz at Home," in *The New Negro: An Interpretation*, edited by Alain Locke (Albert and Charles Boni, 1925), 216–24

Jazz is a marvel of paradox: too fundamentally human, at least as modern humanity goes, to be typically racial, too international to be characteristically national, too much abroad in the world to have a special home. And yet jazz in spite of it all is one part American and three parts American Negro, and was originally the nobody's child of the levee[1] and the city slum. Transplanted exotic—a rather hardy one, we admit—of the mundane world capitals, sport of the sophisticated, it is really at home in its humble native soil, wherever the modern unsophisticated Negro feels happy and sings and dances to his mood. It follows that jazz is more at home in Harlem than in Paris, though from the look and sound of certain quarters of Paris one would hardly think so. It is just the epidemic contagiousness of jazz that makes it, like the measles, sweep the block. But somebody had to have it first: that was the Negro.

What after all is this taking new thing, that, condemned in certain quarters, enthusiastically welcomed in others, has nonchalantly gone on until it ranks with the movie and the dollar as foremost exponent of modern Americanism? Jazz isn't music merely, it is a spirit that can express itself in almost anything. The true spirit of jazz is a joyous revolt from convention, custom, authority, boredom, even sorrow—from everything that would confine the soul of man and hinder its riding free on the air. The Negroes who invented it called their songs the "Blues," and they weren't capable of satire or deception. Jazz was their explosive attempt to cast off the blues and be happy, carefree happy, even in the midst of sordidness and sorrow. And that is why it has become such a balm for modern ennui, and has become a safety valve for modern machine-ridden and convention-bound society. It is the revolt of the emotions against repression.

[...]

The origin of the present jazz craze is interesting. More cities claim its birthplace than claimed Homer dead.[2] New Orleans, San Francisco, Memphis, Chicago, all assert the honor is theirs. Jazz, as it is to-day, seems to have come into being this way, however: W.C. Handy, a Negro, having digested the airs of the itinerant musicians referred to, evolved the first classic, *Memphis Blues*.[3] Then came

---

1 Natural or artificial riverside embankment, a prominent feature of New Orleans.
2 That is, more than the seven Greek cities that named themselves as Homer's birthplace, recognizing the greatness of the ancient epic poet after his death.
3 "Memphis Blues" (1912) was the third blues song published (as sheet music) in history; Handy (1873–1958) also wrote the "Beale Street Blues" (1919), alluded to in Chapter VIII.

Jasbo Brown,[1] a reckless musician of a Negro cabaret in Chicago, who played this and other blues, blowing his own extravagant moods and risqué interpretations into them, while hilarious with gin. To give further meanings to his veiled allusions he would make the trombones "talk" by putting a derby hat and later a tin can at its mouth. The delighted patrons would shout, "More, Jasbo. More, Jas, more." And so the name originated.

As to jazz itself: at this time Shelton Brooks, a Negro comedian,[2] invented a new "strut," called "Walkin' the Dog." Jasbo's anarchic airs found in this strut a soul mate. Then as a result of their union came "The Texas Tommy," the highest point of brilliant, acrobatic execution and nifty foot-work so far evolved in jazz dancing. The latest of these dances is the "Charleston," which has brought something really new to the dance step.[3] The "Charleston" calls for activity of the whole body. One characteristic is a fantastic fling of the legs from the hip downward. The dance ends in what is known as the "camel-walk"—in reality a gorilla-like shamble—and finishes with a peculiar hop like that of the Indian war dance. Imagine one suffering from a fit of rhythmic ague and you have the effect precisely.

The cleverest "Charleston" dancers perhaps are urchins of five and six who may be seen any time on the streets of Harlem, keeping time with their hands, and surrounded by admiring crowds. But put it on a well-set stage, danced by a bobbed-headed chorus, and you have an effect that reminds you of the abandon of the Furies.[4] And so Broadway studies Harlem. Not all of the visitors of the twenty or more well-attended cabarets of Harlem are idle pleasure seekers or underworld devotees. Many are serious artists, actors and producers seeking something new, some suggestion to be taken, too often in pallid imitation, to Broadway's lights and stars.

---

1 A semi-legendary figure.
2 Popular vaudeville entertainer (1886–1975).
3 The exact origin of some of these vernacular dances is indeterminate. The "Texas Tommy" migrated to Harlem from the San Francisco area and was featured in the 1913 revue *Darktown Follies*. The more famous Charleston became popular after the 1923 musical revue *Runnin' Wild*—notably after the action of *The Great Gatsby* takes place. The musical featured a number called "The Charleston," music by James P. Johnson (1894–1955), lyrics by Cecil Mack (1873–1944).
4 Goddesses of vengeance in Greek mythology.

This makes it difficult to say whether jazz is more characteristic of the Negro or of contemporary America. As was shown, it is of Negro origin plus the influence of the American environment. It is Negro-American. Jazz proper, however, is in idiom—rhythmic, musical and pantomimic—thoroughly American Negro; it is his spiritual picture on that lighter comedy side, just as the spirituals are the picture on the tragedy side. The two are poles apart, but the former is by no means to be despised and it is just as characteristically the product of the peculiar and unique experience of the Negro in this country. The African Negro hasn't it, and the Caucasian never could have invented it. Once achieved, it is common property, and jazz has absorbed the national spirit, that tremendous spirit of go, the nervousness, lack of conventionality and boisterous good-nature characteristic of the American, white or black, as compared with the more rigid formal natures of the Englishman or German.

But there still remains something elusive about jazz that few, if any of the white artists, have been able to capture. The Negro is admittedly its best expositor. That elusive something, for lack of a better name, I'll call Negro rhythm. [...]

In its playing technique, jazz is similarly original and spontaneous. The performance of the Negro musicians is much imitated, but seldom equaled. Lieutenant Europe, leader of the famous band of the "Fifteenth New York Regiment," said the bandmaster of the Garde Republicaine, amazed at his jazz effects, could not believe without demonstration that his band had not used special instruments.[1] Jazz has a virtuoso technique all its own: its best performers, singers and players, lift it far above the level of mere "trick" or mechanical effects. Abbie Mitchell, Ethel Waters, and Florence Mills; the Blues singers, Clara, Mamie, and Bessie Smith; Eubie Blake, the pianist; "Buddy" Gilmore, the drummer, and "Bill" Robinson, the pantomimic dancer—to mention merely an illustrative few—are inimitable artists, with an inventive, improvising skill that defies imitation.[2] And those who

---

1 James Reese Europe (1880–1919), jazz composer and bandleader who served as a lieutenant in the all-Black 369th US Infantry Division; the Garde Republicaine was a branch of the French Armed Forces.
2 Abbie Mitchell (1884–1960), singer and actress; Ethel Waters (1896–1977), singer and stage and film star; Florence Mills (1896–1927), charismatic entertainer who rose to stardom in the 1921 hit musical revue *Shuffle Along*; Clara Smith (1894–1935), Mamie Smith (1883–1946), and Bessie Smith (1894–1937), unrelated, pioneering

know their work most intimately trace its uniqueness without exception to the folk-roots of their artistry.

Musically jazz has a great future. It is rapidly being sublimated. In the more famous jazz orchestras like those of Will Marion Cook, Paul Whiteman, Sissle and Blake, Sam Stewart, Fletcher Henderson, Vincent Lopez and the Clef Club units, there are none of the vulgarities and crudities of the lowly origin or the only too prevalent cheap imitations.[1] The pioneer work in the artistic development of jazz was done by Negro artists; it was the lead of the so-called "syncopated orchestras" of Tyers[2] and Will Marion Cook, the former playing for the Castles of dancing fame,[3] and the latter touring as a concertizing orchestra in the great American centers and abroad. Because of the difficulties of financial backing, these expert combinations had had to yield ground to white orchestras of the type of the Paul Whiteman and Vincent Lopez, organizations that are now demonstrating the finer possibilities of jazz music. "Jazz," says Serge Koussevitzky,[4] the new conductor of the Boston Symphony, "is an important contribution to modern musical literature. It has an epochal significance—it is not superficial, it is fundamental. Jazz comes from the soil, where all music has its beginning." And Leopold Stokowski[5] says more extendedly of it:

blues singers (the latter nicknamed "Empress of the blues"); Eubie Blake (1887–1983), composer and pianist, co-wrote the music for *Shuffle Along*; Buddy Gilmore (1880–?), pioneering jazz drummer; Bill "Bojangles" Robinson (1878–1949), tap dancing legend, singer and film star.

1 Will Marion Cook (1869–1944), pioneering musical theater composer and bandleader; Paul Whiteman (1890–1967), white bandleader, dubbed "King of Jazz" by mainstream press in the 1920s, whose February 1924 Aeolian Hall concert "An Experiment in Modern Music" may be anachronistically alluded to in Chapter III; Noble Sissle (1889–1975), composer and bandleader, co-wrote the music for *Shuffle Along* with partner Eubie Blake; Sammy Stewart (1891–1960), pianist and bandleader; Fletcher Henderson (1897–1952), pioneering jazz bandleader; Vincent Lopez (1895–1975), pianist and bandleader.

2 William H. Tyers (1876–1924), pioneering composer and bandleader.

3 Vernon Castle (1887–1918) and Irene Castle (1893–1969), popular ballroom dancing couple and early film stars credited with modernizing ballroom dancing in the 1910s.

4 Serge Alexandrovich Koussevitzky (1874–1951), Russian-born composer and conductor.

5 Leopold Anthony Stokowski (1882–1977), British-born composer and conductor of the Philadelphia Orchestra.

"Jazz has come to stay because it is an expression of the times, of the breathless, energetic, superactive times in which we are living, it is useless to fight against it. Already its new vigor, its new vitality is beginning to manifest itself…. America's contribution to the music of the past will have the same revivifying effect as the injection of new, and in the larger sense, vulgar blood into dying aristocracy. Music will then be vulgarized in the best sense of the word, and enter more and more into the daily lives of people…. The Negro musicians of America are playing a great part in this change. They have an open mind, and unbiassed outlook. They are not hampered by conventions or traditions, and with their new ideas, their constant experiment, they are causing new blood to flow in the veins of music. The jazz players make their instruments do entirely new things, things finished musicians are taught to avoid. They are pathfinders into new realms."

And thus it has come about that serious modernistic music and musicians, most notably and avowedly in the work of French modernists Auric, Satie and Darius Milhaud,[1] have become the confessed debtors of American Negro jazz. With the same nonchalance and impudence with which it left the levee and the dive to stride like an upstart conqueror, almost overnight, into the grand salon, jazz now begins its conquest of musical Parnassus.[2]

Whatever the ultimate result of the attempt to raise jazz from the mob-level upon which it originated, its true home is still its original cradle, the none too respectable cabaret. And here we have the seamy side to the story. Here we have some of the charm of Bohemia, but much more of the demoralization of vice. Its rash spirit is in Grey's popular song, *Runnin' Wild*:

> Runnin' wild; lost control
> Runnin' wild; mighty bold,
> Feelin' gay and reckless too
> Carefree all the time; never blue

---

1   Georges Auric (1889–1983), Erik Satie (1866–1925), and Darius Milhaud (1892–1974), French "modernistic" composers within a classical music tradition. Auric and Milhaud belonged to a group known as "Les Six." Milhaud's "La création du monde" has been considered a model for the "Jazz History of the World" played at Gatsby's party in Chapter III.

2   Mount Parnassus, home of the Muses in Greek mythology.

Always goin' I don't know where
Always showin' that I don't care
Don' love nobody, it ain't worth while
All alone; runnin' wild.[1]

Jazz reached the heights of its vogue at a time when minds were reacting from the horrors and strains of war. Humanity welcomed it because in its fresh joyousness men found a temporary forgetfulness, infinitely less harmful than drugs or alcohol. It is partly for some such reasons that it dominates the amusement life of America to-day. No one can sensibly condone its excesses or minimize its social danger if uncontrolled; all culture is built upon inhibitions and control. But it is doubtful whether the "jazz-hounds" of high and low estate would use their time to better advantage. In all probability their tastes would find some equally morbid, mischievous vent. Jazz, it is needless to say, will remain a recreation for the industrious and a dissipater of energy for the frivolous, a tonic for the strong and a poison for the weak.

For the Negro himself, jazz is both more and less dangerous than for the white—less in that, he is nervously more in tune with it; more, in that at his average level of economic development his amusement life is more open to the forces of social vice. The cabaret of better type provides a certain Bohemianism for the Negro intellectual, the artist and the well-to-do. But the average thing is too much the substitute for the saloon and the wayside inn. The tired longshoreman, the porter, the housemaid and the poor elevator boy in search of recreation, seeking in jazz the tonic for weary nerves and muscles, are only too apt to find the bootlegger, the gambler and the demi-monde who have come there for victims and to escape the eyes of the police.

Yet in spite of its present vices and vulgarizations, its sex informalities, its morally anarchic spirit, jazz has a popular mission to perform. Joy, after all, has a physical basis. Those who laugh and dance and sing are better off even in their vices than those who do not. Moreover, jazz with its mocking disregard for formality is a leveller and makes for democracy. The jazz spirit, being primitive, demands more frankness and sincerity. Just as it already has done in art and music, so eventually in human relations and social manners, it will no doubt have the effect of putting more

---

1 From the 1923 musical revue *Runnin' Wild*, music by James P. Johnson, lyrics by Cecil Mack, sung by Gilda Grey.

reality in life by taking some of the needless artificiality out. [...] Naturalness finds the artificial in conduct ridiculous. "Cervantes smiled Spain's chivalry away," said Byron.[1] And so this new spirit of joy and spontaneity may itself play the rôle of reformer. Where at present it vulgarizes, with more wholesome growth in the future, it may on the contrary truly democratize. At all events, jazz is rejuvenation, a recharging of the batteries of civilization with primitive new vigor. It has come to stay, and they are wise, who instead of protesting against it, try to lift and divert it into nobler channels.

---

1 George Gordon, Lord Byron in *Don Juan* (1819–24); the allusion is to Miguel de Cervantes's *Don Quixote* (1605).

7. Miguel Covarrubias, "The Sheik of Dahomey," in
Miguel Covarrubias and Eric D. Walrond, "Enter, the
New Negro, a Distinctive Type Recently Created by the
Coloured Cabaret Belt in New York," *Vanity Fair*
(December 1924), 60

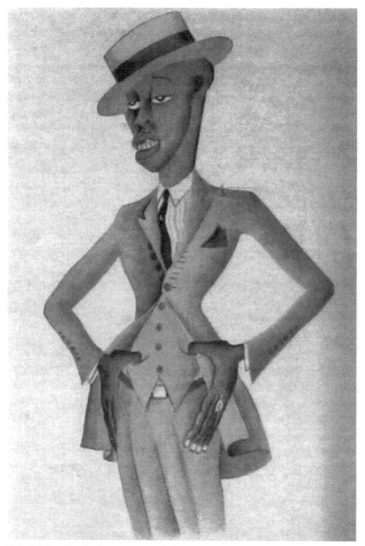

"Nothin'—Ah don't care whut it is—can get mah boy recited.
Nothin! And talk about havin' a way with wimmin, ain't nobody can
tell him nuthin' ... He's a dressin' up fool, dat boy is, an' he sure's got
luck with de high yalla ladies."

Works Cited and Select Bibliography

Textual Resources

Atkinson, Jennifer E. "Fitzgerald's Marked Copy of *The Great Gatsby.*" *Fitzgerald/Hemingway Annual,* vol. 2, 1970, pp. 28–33.

Bruccoli, Matthew J. *Apparatus for F. Scott Fitzgerald's "The Great Gatsby.*" U of South Carolina P, 1974.

Fitzgerald, F. Scott. *The Great Gatsby: An Edition of the Manuscript.* Edited by James L.W. West III and Don C. Skemer, Cambridge UP, 2018.

——. *Trimalchio: An Early Version of "The Great Gatsby.*" Edited by James L.W. West III, Cambridge UP, 2000.

Biography and Letters

Brown, David S. *Paradise Lost: A Life of F. Scott Fitzgerald.* Belknap Press of Harvard UP, 2017.

Bruccoli, Matthew J., editor. *F. Scott Fitzgerald: A Life in Letters.* Simon & Schuster, 1994.

——. *Some Sort of Epic Grandeur: The Life of F. Scott Fitzgerald.* 2nd. revised ed. U of South Carolina P, 2002.

Bruccoli, Matthew J., and Judith S. Baughman, editors. *F. Scott Fitzgerald on Authorship.* U of South Carolina P, 1996.

Bruccoli, Matthew J., and Margaret M. Duggan, editors. *The Correspondence of F. Scott Fitzgerald.* Random House, 1980.

Bryer, Jackson R., and Cathy W. Barks, editors. *Dear Scott, Dearest Zelda: The Love Letters of F. Scott and Zelda Fitzgerald.* St. Martin's, 2002.

Kuehl, John, and Jackson R. Bryer, editors. *Dear Scott/Dear Max: The Fitzgerald-Perkins Correspondence.* Charles Scribner's Sons, 1971.

Mizener, Arthur. *The Far Side of Paradise: A Biography of F. Scott Fitzgerald.* Houghton Mifflin, 1951.

Taylor, Kendall. *The Gatsby Affair: Scott, Zelda, and the Betrayal that Shaped an American Classic.* Rowman and Littlefield, 2018.

Turnbull, Andrew, editor. *The Letters of F. Scott Fitzgerald.* Charles Scribner's Sons, 1963.

West, James L.W., III. *The Perfect Hour: The Romance of F. Scott Fitzgerald and Ginevra King, His First Love.* Random House, 2005.

Bibliographies and Reference Guides

Bruccoli, Matthew J. *F. Scott Fitzgerald: A Descriptive Bibliography*. U of Pittsburgh P, 1987.

——, editor. *F. Scott Fitzgerald's "The Great Gatsby": A Literary Reference*. Carroll & Graf, 2000.

Gross, Dalton, and Maryjean Gross. *Understanding "The Great Gatsby": A Student Casebook to Issues, Sources, and Historical Documents*. Greenwood Press, 1998.

Criticism

Barnhart, Bruce. "Forms of Repetition and Jazz Sociality in *The Great Gatsby*." *Jazz in the Time of the Novel: The Temporal Politics of American Race and Culture*, U of Alabama P, 2013, pp. 97–132.

Berman, Ronald. *"The Great Gatsby" and Fitzgerald's World of Ideas*. U of Alabama P, 1997.

——. *"The Great Gatsby" and Modern Times*. U of Illinois P, 1994.

Beuka, Robert. *American Icon: Fitzgerald's "The Great Gatsby" in Critical and Cultural Contexts*. Camden House, 2011.

Breitwieser, Mitchell. "*The Great Gatsby*: Grief, Jazz, and the Eye-Witness." *Arizona Quarterly*, vol. 47, no. 3, 1991, pp. 17–70.

——. "Jazz Fractures: F. Scott Fitzgerald and Epochal Representation." *National Melancholy: Mourning and Opportunity in Classic American Literature*, Stanford UP, 2007, pp. 263–80.

Bruccoli, Matthew J., editor. *New Essays on "The Great Gatsby."* Cambridge UP, 1985.

Churchwell, Sarah. "'The Balzacs of America': F. Scott Fitzgerald, Burton Rascoe, and the Lost Review of *The Great Gatsby*." *F. Scott Fitzgerald Review*, vol. 14, 2016, pp. 6–30.

——. *Careless People: Murder, Mayhem, and the Invention of "The Great Gatsby."* Penguin, 2014.

Clymer, Jeffory A. "'Mr. Nobody from Nowhere': Rudolph Valentino, Jay Gatsby, and the End of the American Race." *Genre*, vol. 29, no. 1–2, 1996, pp. 161–92.

Corrigan, Maureen. *So We Read On: How "The Great Gatsby" Came to Be and Why It Endures*. Little, Brown, 2014.

Curnutt, Kirk. "Fitzgerald's Consumer World." *A Historical Guide to F. Scott Fitzgerald*, edited by Kirk Curnutt, Oxford UP, pp. 85–128.

———, editor. *A Historical Guide to F. Scott Fitzgerald.* Oxford UP, 2004.

Dubose, Michael D. "From 'Absolution' through *Trimalchio* to *The Great Gatsby*: A Study in Reconception." *F. Scott Fitzgerald Review*, vol. 10, 2012, pp. 73–92.

Garrett, George. "Fire and Freshness: A Matter of Style in *The Great Gatsby*." *New Essays on "The Great Gatsby,"* edited by Matthew J. Bruccoli, Cambridge UP, 1985, pp. 101–16.

Gidley, M. "Notes on F. Scott Fitzgerald and the Passing of the Great Race." *Journal of American Studies*, vol. 7, no. 2, 1973, pp. 171–81.

Hitchens, Christopher. "The Road to West Egg." *Vanity Fair*, May 2000, pp. 76, 80, 84, 86.

Irwin, John T. *F. Scott Fitzgerald's Fiction: "An Almost Theatrical Innocence."* Johns Hopkins UP, 2014.

Kenner, Hugh. "The Promised Land." *A Homemade World: The American Modernist Writers*, Johns Hopkins UP, 1975, pp. 20–49.

Kruse, Horst. *F. Scott Fitzgerald at Work: The Making of "The Great Gatsby."* U of Alabama P, 2014.

Lehan, Richard. *"The Great Gatsby": The Limits of Wonder.* Twayne, 1990.

Mangum, Bryant, editor. *F. Scott Fitzgerald in Context.* Cambridge UP, 2013.

Marcus, Greil. *Under the Red, White, and Blue: Patriotism, Disenchantment and the Stubborn Myth of "The Great Gatsby."* Yale UP, 2020.

Miller, James E., Jr. *F. Scott Fitzgerald: His Art and His Technique.* New York UP, 1964.

North, Michael. "F. Scott Fitzgerald's Spectroscopic Fiction." *Camera Works: Photography and the Twentieth-Century Word*, Oxford UP, 2005, pp. 109–39.

Nowlin, Michael. *F. Scott Fitzgerald's Racial Angles and the Business of Literary Greatness.* Palgrave, 2007.

Pekarofski, Michael. "The Passing of Jay Gatsby: Class and Anti-Semitism in Fitzgerald's 1920s America." *F. Scott Fitzgerald Review*, vol. 10, 2012, pp. 52–72.

Piper, Henry Dan. *F. Scott Fitzgerald: A Critical Portrait.* Southern Illinois UP, 1965.

Prigozy, Ruth, editor. *The Cambridge Companion to F. Scott Fitzgerald.* Cambridge UP, 2002.

———. "Introduction: Scott, Zelda, and the Culture of

Celebrity." *The Cambridge Companion to F. Scott Fitzgerald*, edited by Ruth Prigozy, Cambridge UP, pp. 3–27.

———. "'Poor Butterfly': F. Scott Fitzgerald and Popular Music." *Prospects*, vol. 2, 1976, pp. 41–67.

Railton, Ben. "Considering History: *The Great Gatsby*, Multicultural New York, and America in 1925." *Saturday Evening Post*, vol. 10, April 2018, saturdayeveningpost.com/2018/04/considering-history-great-gatsby-multicultural-new-york-america-1925.

Roulston, Robert, and Helen Roulston. *The Winding Road to West Egg: The Artistic Development of F. Scott Fitzgerald.* Associated University Presses, 1995.

Sanderson, Rena. "Women in Fitzgerald's Fiction." *The Cambridge Companion to F. Scott Fitzgerald*, edited by Ruth Prigozy, Cambridge UP, pp. 143–63.

Sklar, Robert. *F. Scott Fitzgerald: The Last Laocoön.* Oxford UP, 1967.

Stern, Milton R. *The Golden Moment: The Novels of F. Scott Fitzgerald.* U of Illinois P, 1970.

Way, Brian. *F. Scott Fitzgerald and the Art of Social Fiction.* Arnold, 1980.

Collections Including Previously Published Criticism

Bryer, Jackson R., editor. *F. Scott Fitzgerald: The Critical Reception.* Burt Franklin & Co., 1978.

Dickstein, Morris, editor. *Critical Insights: "The Great Gatsby."* Salem Press, 2010.

Donaldson, Scott, editor. *Critical Essays on F. Scott Fitzgerald's "The Great Gatsby."* G.K. Hall, 1984.

Kazin, Alfred, editor. *F. Scott Fitzgerald: The Man and His Work.* World Publishing, 1951.

Lockridge, Ernest, editor. *Twentieth Century Interpretations of "The Great Gatsby."* Prentice-Hall, 1968.

Mizener, Arthur, editor. *F. Scott Fitzgerald: A Collection of Critical Essays.* Prentice-Hall, 1963.

Other Works Cited

Crunden, Robert. *Body and Soul: The Making of American Modernism.* Basic Books, 2000.

Fitzgerald, F. Scott. *The Crack-Up.* Edited by Edmund Wilson, New Directions, 1945.

—. *This Side of Paradise.* Edited by James L.W. West III, Cambridge UP, 1995.

———. *This Side of Paradise.* Edited by James L.W. West III, Cambridge UP, 1995.

Frank, Joseph. *The Widening Gyre: Crisis and Mastery in Modern Literature.* Rutgers UP, 1963.

Mencken, H.L. "The National Letters." *Prejudices: Second Series,* Knopf, 1920.

Noah, Timothy. *The Great Divergence: America's Growing Inequality Crisis and What We Can Do About It.* Bloomsbury, 2012.

Perrett, Geoffrey. *America in the Twenties: A History.* Simon & Schuster, 1982.

Wilson, Edmund. *Classics and Commercials: A Literary Chronicle of the Forties.* Farrar, Straus, 1951.

———. Review of *Ulysses,* by James Joyce. *New Republic,* vol. 26, 5 July 1922, p. 164.

From the Publisher

A name never says it all, but the word "Broadview" expresses a good deal of the philosophy behind our company. We are open to a broad range of academic approaches and political viewpoints. We pay attention to the broad impact book publishing and book printing has in the wider world; for some years now we have used 100% recycled paper for most titles. Our publishing program is internationally oriented and broad-ranging. Our individual titles often appeal to a broad readership too; many are of interest as much to general readers as to academics and students.

Founded in 1985, Broadview remains a fully independent company owned by its shareholders—not an imprint or subsidiary of a larger multinational.

For the most accurate information on our books (including information on pricing, editions, and formats) please visit our website at www.broadviewpress.com. Our print books and ebooks are also available for sale on our site.

broadview press
www.broadviewpress.com